The Dragon's Head

BOOKS BY
DORIS LESLIE

Novels

FULL FLAVOUR
FAIR COMPANY
CONCORD IN JEOPARDY
ANOTHER CYNTHIA
HOUSE IN THE DUST
FOLLY'S END
THE PEVERILLS
PERIDOT FLIGHT
AS THE TREE FALLS
PARAGON STREET
THE MARRIAGE OF MARTHA TODD
A YOUNG WIVES' TALE
THE DRAGON'S HEAD

Biographical Studies

ROYAL WILLIAM : *Life of William IV*
POLONAISE : *A Romance of Chopin*
WREATH FOR ARABELLA : *Life of Lady Arabella Stuart*
THAT ENCHANTRESS : *Life of Abigail Hill, Lady Masham*
THE GREAT CORINTHIAN : *Portrait of the Prince Regent*
A TOAST TO LADY MARY : *Life of Lady Mary Wortley Montagu*
THE PERFECT WIFE : *Life of Mary Anne Disraeli, Viscountess Beaconsfield*
I RETURN : *The Story of François Villon*
THIS FOR CAROLINE : *Life of Lady Caroline Lamb*
THE SCEPTRE AND THE ROSE : *Marriage of Charles II and Catherine of Braganza*
THE REBEL PRINCESS : *The Life of Sophia Dorothea, Princess of Celle*
THE DESERT QUEEN : *The Life and Travels of Lady Hester Stanhope*

DORIS LESLIE

The
Dragon's Head

HEINEMANN: LONDON

William Heinemann Ltd
15 Queen Street, Mayfair, London W1X 8BE

LONDON MELBOURNE TORONTO
JOHANNESBURG AUCKLAND

01718547 First published 1973
© Doris Leslie 1973

25414273 7

Printed in Great Britain by Cox & Wyman Ltd
London, Fakenham and Reading

PROLOGUE

November 11th 1918

To: Sir Lucian Halstead, K.C.V.O., M.D., F.R.C.P.
Private and Confidential

Dear Old Luke,

So this is it! The war to end all wars. And here am I with *my* end in sight since you have never stuffed me up with platitudinous bedside cheer of recovery which you know would cut no ice with me. I've outlived my three score years and ten and I don't care how soon I may be done with this too, too, *un*solid flesh. I lie here under my window, propped up on cushions by that starchily bright and breezy female you have brought to nurse and dose me when the bloody Thing wakes up to gnaw at my vitals which I tell you is nothing so bad as the bullet you yanked out of me in that Abyssinian skirmish under Napier of Magdala in '68, half a century ago!... *Tempus fugit*. It doesn't. It crawls when one has nothing left to live on more than memories.

Do you remember, but of course you do, how when we came back to H.Q. you sent in your resignation as a Lieutenant from the A.M.C. because you told the Colonel you couldn't get enough medicine as an Army surgeon and the C.O. said that if you left he'd be losing the best doctor they had and you said that was why you were leaving! But I stuck it out until the Boer War that lost me a leg at Spion Kop and landed me in the Intelligence at Whitehall with a Brass Hat ... How I ramble on, but I've nothing else to do so you must bear with me while I unburden.

As I lie here I can see over the roof tops of my eyrie in St James's the darkening sky ablaze with red from the bonfires lighted on suburban commons and on Hampstead Heath, and I can hear the shouting and yelling and hullabaloo in celebration of the Armistice. Yes, and a few more hundred young lives gone west today until the last bang went off. God alone knows how many millions of German and Allied youth have been slaughtered in this four years' holocaust, among them my two sons, the one killed at Mons and the other at Gallipoli. It is my regret that I was too crippled and too old to be in it.

But while you have reached the height of your career, I have nothing much to show for what life has done to me more than that I have a son who sits in the House of Lords, and a grandson who got a Blighty one and was sent home with it before the end and a granddaughter, too. Aha! That makes you sit up if you haven't skipped all this tedious palaver while I get down to telling you what no other living soul has known since she, who is part of it, is gone. But she sent for me – how many years later! – whom I had not seen since before the birth of our son and long after my marriage to Hilda who died a year before the war ... Yes, she sent for me, she was a widow then, knowing she had as short a time to live as I have now. And she told me for the first time her name and that of the son she bore to me while in wedlock to her husband. Then I had to tell her that I knew her and our son's name, for in the Intelligence it is our job to know much that one is not supposed to know.

It is an incredible story and you don't have to believe it, but on my dying oath it is the Gospel truth.

I must take you back to the beginning, to a morning in the seventies. I was home on leave and strolling in the Park with an eye to the women, and what women they were in those days! Very different from the hipless, breastless young things who have done their bit in the W.A.A.C.s and the Women's Emergency Corps and as

2

V.A.D.s, God bless 'em! And now they'll get the vote they've been screaming for and good luck to them ... Well, there was I sauntering along, home on short leave to blew what little I'd got from the death of my great-uncle Rodney, little enough it was too, bar an impoverished baronetcy which my father did not live to inherit and nothing worth having of the entail, when a carriage and pair stopped at the barrier. It contained a woman. A parasol shaded her face but I could see she was worth looking at twice.

A footman got down from the box and approaching me said: 'Excuse me, sir, but her ladyship presents her compliments and invites you to drive with her.'

I was flabbergasted. I couldn't think of any ladyship of my acquaintance who would want to pick me up if 'ladyship' she were and not a well-established professional who had taken a fancy to me at sight. I, as a youngster, was much favoured by the women, who would fall for my six feet two and my red hair which I so heartily abhorred and had a bellyful of being called 'carrot-nob' at school, that I had all to do to hold them off who would have held me on (especially the C.O's wife with a face like the back of a cab!). But I was nothing loth to take advantage of her offer which had in it a spice of adventure.

I got into the carriage and was graciously received.

'Pray excuse this somewhat unconventional invitation, Sir Richard' (So she knew my name!) 'but do you not recollect that we met at the late Sir Rodney Harrington's golden wedding reception? How sad that your uncle died so soon afterward. Yet he lived to a good old age.'

I had no recollection of having met her at my great-uncle's golden wedding or anywhere else. All I remembered of it was an awful crush although I may have been introduced to her among a host of other women with names mumbled and polite exchange of nothings. The old chap died a few weeks after that. I was his sole heir and he my guardian until I attained my majority. I only saw him when home on holidays from school or on leave. Nor did I know much of my mother's family she being an only child as was I. But I readily agreed that I remembered her well with the usual fatuous compliments as to how I could have forgotten one so beautiful, etc.... She was beautiful, not young, or rather not young to me in my early twenties and she in her thirties as I guessed her; and I, of an age that is drawn to women older than myself, was immediately attracted.

We drove round the Park talking generalities, touching on the Franco-Prussian war which was in everybody's mouth with the flight of Napoleon the Third and his wife Eugenie to Britain, to be received in the welcoming arms of the Queen. And from there to my mother's people, the Griersons, and back again to me and the Harringtons of whom she seemed to know as much or more than I myself knew of them. She knew my father had been Member for Northampton in the second Derby–Disraeli Ministry and that he, heir to his uncle's baronetcy, died of typhoid when I was about ten, and that my mother had died three years later. I had few if any relatives other than old Rodney. The Crimean war wiped out my father's two brothers, neither married. This meant that I became heir to the baronetcy which had been bought by an ancestor for a thousand pounds when James the First was creating 'little barons' to pay his debts. But though she knew all about me I knew nothing of her, not her name nor where she lived and who she was or could have been.

As we drove round the Park she asked me where I was lunching. I told her at my club; she gave the order to drop me there, nor did it surprise me since she knew so much about me that she should have known my club in Pall Mall where I was deposited with these parting words.

'May I call for you here tomorrow at this time that you may take luncheon with me?'

4

So that was how it began but how could I have known how it would end?

After that we met on three, no – four occasions; never at her London house but at a Queen Anne cottage, scarcely a house, in the village of Hampstead. She told me she rented this 'small retreat' she called it, as a refuge from the superficialities of London social life, although they had a place in . . . She hesitated to say where and substituted vaguely 'in the country'. All precautions were taken to preserve her and her husband's anonymity. We drove to Hampstead each time in a hired hackney, not in her carriage. I guessed she wished to keep our meetings secret from her servants. There were seemingly no resident domestics at the cottage. The luncheon was brought in a hamper, all cold, with champagne; none to serve it. A picnic lunch each time.

It was on the fourth day of my visit to that little village house that she unfolded her incredible story. An older man might not have been gulled by what could have appeared to him as an implausible fabrication as excuse for an *affaire* with a personable youth on the part of a woman sexually frustrated in her marriage. Or, more likely still, as at her first approach to me I was inclined to think, she was the mistress of an elderly and wealthy protector who bored her stiff that she sought fresher younger satisfaction. But I, who had so slight an experience of women more than the garrison hacks at home and abroad or the bought experiments of the alcove (which I believe I had only visited twice for my initiation) or occasional flirtatious interludes with well-chaperoned young girls whose mothers would have encouraged me, impoverished heir to old Rodney that I was, I swallowed all she had to tell me, an infatuated credulous youngster, as if she voiced the word of God.

As a girl of eighteen she was married to a cousin, several years older than herself. They had been married sixteen years and were childless. His only brother, a middle-aged bachelor, had died suddenly some years before. And now her husband's sole heir was a cousin once removed. He had a most unsavoury reputation. An habitual drunkard, he had been court-martialled from his regiment for cheating at cards, had run through what little money had been left him by his father. He had also been found guilty of forging a brother officer's name on cheques and had done a term of imprisonment as result of it. The disgrace of all this had gone far to cause his father's death from an apoplexy.

Her husband must have been sterile and, after the death of his only brother, it had preyed on his mind to the verge of a mental breakdown that his sole heir should be this ex-jailbird, a profligate, to inherit his name, peerage and estates. It was at his suggestion, not hers (although her maiden name was the same as his, she being his cousin on the paternal side) that they should seek a father for his son who, if born in wedlock and acknowledged his, would be legally if not morally his heir. He it was who first inaugurated inquiries about me with whose people in the past he had been acquainted.

'That you were eminently suitable both physically and socially to be the father of his heir,' she said, 'was his choice, not mine.'

By this time I believed I was in love with her although I had never betrayed myself till then; a youthful mad infatuation that caused me, inexcusably, to burst forth with:

'His choice! As if I were a stallion to be used for a brood mare!'

I was beside myself and, goaded by her calm judicious way of presenting me with this preposterous suggestion, I hardly knew what I was saying for I was red-hot at the insult her husband had heaped on her to justify his cause and retrieve his name from ruin and disgrace should his rightful heir come into possession. And even should he predecease his heritage, he had married, so she told me, and had begot himself a son.

I saw her face, drained of all colour at my outburst. She was years older than I, but so lovely. . . . I can see her now, her eyes like great dark pools in that whiteness.

'I deserve this,' she whispered. 'I cannot blame you. I, who am of his blood, am equally determined to save our name from dishonour. Our mutual ancestor was one of the Sealed Knot, as they were known, who were instrumental in restoring the King, the second Charles, to his Throne. The peerage was bestowed on him for services rendered.'

A younger generation than hers and mine – and yours, my friend – would doubtless ridicule this ancestor-worshipful stuff that savours of Chinese veneration, but we, the Victorians, for she, I and you, advanced and modern medico though you are, can still remember our King George's grandmother and her Jubilee, we who fought in her wars.

And I, hanging on my *incognita*'s every word, applauded this traditional loyalty.

I heard her say: 'Forget what I have told you. I had no right to be a party to so outrageous a request. Forget it,' she said, 'and forget me.'

I saw her tears.

That broke me. Lost of all control, inexperienced and callow as I was, I became in that instant a man with a man's knowledge that she cared for me, not just for that to which I, with her husband's cognizance, must be used but as her lover and . . . her mate.

I caught her in my arms. I prayed her not to send me from her. The stammering phrases were wrung from me in words I cannot write. I implored her pardon for my presumption in daring to tell her that I loved her with all my heart and soul, with all of me, now and for ever. I believed it at the time. . . . I believe it still.

I felt the tremble of her body. Her eyes, shamed, tear-drowned were raised to mine. What troubled her? Fear. Yes, fear. Love made me bold to know she feared I feigned too ardent an avowal to save her the humiliation of this 'outrageous request'.

'I love you,' I repeated it. 'All that I am, all I ever shall be, my whole life, my whole self'. . . I can't go on. I recall each word as if just spoken engraved upon my memory and resurrected as I lie here . . . waiting to be called to her again if she – who knows? – should call to me wherever she is or wherever I may be. One gets fanciful, or senile, doped and jabbed as I am to quiet the Thing.

She took my face between her hands. She was not tall but just tall enough to reach my shoulder where she laid her head to tell me in so low a voice I could scarcely hear her say:

'If love were all, and if you will take what I am pledged to give, I could not send you from me. But the honour of his name – and mine – is more than love.'

Nauseating sentiment you, the man of science, will call this bathos – bathos to you and, as I write it after all these years, bathos to me, the hard boiled Brass Hat that I was, and yet – am still a boy in love with the only love of his life.

She said in that same little voice, almost a child's voice:

'But love is not all. . . . If you will take me and if our union should bear us a son you will not hear from nor see me ever again. If no son is born, or a daughter, then we will be together again in the hope we may . . .'

'You mean,' I cried, red as my hair (we Harringtons are all red, not known as the 'Red Harringtons' for nothing), 'that if I, as my young unmated setter, am not "proved" when served – ' I was too crazed with passion to speak save in words fit only for the kennel – 'that I am to be *used* until proved again?'

She bowed her head on my chest. My heart was thumping like a madman's. (It's thumping now!) She touched where it raced under my waistcoat.

'Is this hurry all for me?' And then: 'My darling!' Yes,

8

she called me that which I had never called a woman. 'If love were all – ' how she harped on it – 'I would go with you and be with you to sing the swansong of my womanhood.' As I recall it she said those very words. I thought them poetical and believed them. I think she believed them too. Rank sentiment. That's all been wiped out since the world exploded four years ago. Those boys who have survived and seen and suffered hell let loose, and those girls too, those bravely dedicated young creatures homing from their hospitals out there, or from the W.A.A.C.s or those young mothers even now bearing the sons who will never see their fathers dead or dying in mud and blood in the dawn of today's final gun and bomb blast, sentiment is not for them who have known life and death in the raw.

'You are so young,' she said, 'so much too young for me who am thirteen years older than you and have never known love or a lover until now.'

And I felt her mouth cling to mine.

When at last I could speak:

'What is age?' I managed to articulate. 'Age is timeless. A thousand years are but as yesterday. And there are all ... our tomorrows.'

I stayed with her in that Hampstead cottage two days and nights. She dismissed the old village woman who came in to clean the place, saying the cottage would be closed for a while. She also sent a message to her husband to tell him she would be away for those two nights. It irked me to know it was with his approval and knowledge that I was given to her in their mutual conniving to save their 'name'.

Those two nights we were undivided. I think, I dare to think that all I felt for her was to some small extent reciprocated, untried and wanting though I was.

I do not know how I went from her in the early morning of the third day while she slept. Beside her on the pillow I put the letter I had written with the signet

9

ring from my finger which I implored her to wear – for me.

I never saw or heard from her again until she sent for me almost half a century later, and then she told me her name (which I already knew) and the name of our son. I have seen him in the Lords. I have heard him debate. His hair is as red as a fox or mine, as it was. . . .

So I have told you all this, my friend and executor of my Will. I ask you to read it, seal it and place it in your bank to be buried with me. No one other than yourself must ever read or know of that which I have told you. I will give it you when you visit me again.

I think there is not long for me to wait before this goes with all that is left of my hulk. Goodbye and God bless you, dear old Luke.

Yours ever till death and afterwards, if there *is* an afterwards.

Dick

*   *   *

Obituary

Extract from The Times, *17th January 1919*

Colonel Sir Richard Harrington, 9th Baronet, created 1616, late of the Coldstream Guards, D.S.O. has died on 16th January aged seventy-two. . . . Served under Lord Napier of Magdala in the Abyssinian War of 1868 and in the Boer War. . . . He married in 1891 Hilda, daughter of the Rev. Paul Ardingley. She died in 1913. His two sons were killed in the war. With his death the baronetcy becomes extinct.

ONE

'Nurse!'

Sister, her hatchet face beneath the white starched floating headgear, expressed resigned disapproval of these incompetent V.A.D.s, necessary though they were in this epidemical crisis. Advancing like a ship in full sail she repeated in a series of staccato barks:

'Nurse! Did – you – not *hear* me?'

'Yes, Sister.'

'Blanket bath Number Seven – at – once! Have you charted him?'

'Yes, Sister.'

With a sound between a snort and a sniff, Sister took the chart from above the bed of Number Seven, examined it, folded her lips till she looked to have no mouth, and said:

'A hundred and four point two. Fetch a basin of tepid water – and – bathe him – down. Don't stand there staring, nurse. Fetch it!'

'It' was fetched. Sister rustled off, and nurse, having stripped the tossing, muttering, highly flushed Number Seven, proceeded to bathe him down and dry him. This done she covered him, raised his pillows, as another nurse in striped cotton and somewhat less starched than the blue-belted, blue uniformed Sister, accosted her, holding out a strip of sterilized gauze.

'Here, Ross-Sutton, you've to put this on. We've all got to wear them. Matron's orders.'

'Why?'

'Ours not to reason why. You've left Number Four on the bed-pan. I was just in time to prevent him from falling off on to the floor to crack his skull. Good thing Sister didn't see or you'd have been for it. And there's another half dozen come from Southampton and no room for more than two of them. So they've been sent off to Millbank, who won't want them there. They are all 'flu cases dumped on us!'

She too went. Number Seven's mutterings had temporarily ceased; and under the bandage that swathed his forehead and one eye, she discerned in the other eye a gleam of inquiry.

'Your name . . . Sut'n. Ross-Sut'n, is it?'

'Yes.'

'My name too . . . 'Fore was born. Thirsty. Wanna' drink.'

Barley water poured from a jug on the bedside locker was held to the dry cracked lips; a mouthful swallowed and as quickly ejected.

'Wha's this? Cat's piss? . . . Want scotch.'

'You mustn't have whisky, er, scotch. Drink this up. It's good for you.' And she thought: So he's a Yankee. They all call whisky scotch. 'Come along, drink it up.'

'My name . . . Russ'tn . . . Canada 'fore I was born. . . . Three months in hospital ship. Blighty one. North Africa . . . Allenby. . . . Say,' he struggled up. 'I'm bloody hot. This heat's wors'n desert. Tell you . . . gotta get out of here . . . late for parade.'

He was wandering again.

She lowered him on to his pillows, felt his pulse, checking its rapid beat with the watch pinned to her apron. A small crease appeared between her eyebrows, while from beneath her cap a stray wisp of red-gold hair escaped.

'Ross-Sutton!'

The same nurse had come back.

'You're to go to Number Four. I'll take this one. Doctor's on his way with Sister. Put on your mask for goodness' sake. Here, I'll tie it for you.'

12

The mask tied and adjusted, hiding her nose and mouth, nurse went to Number Four who was in the hiccups.

'Why you – *hic* –,' he asked, 'wearing – that – *hic*?'

'He's not stopped,' Number Three announced from the next bed, 'since five ack emma.'

'Yes, I know.'

Smoothing the rumpled pillows of Number Four whose latest most violent hiccup had hoisted him up: What, she wondered as she laid him down, *did* she know of this ghastly thing that was killing them off who'd come through four years in the trenches, the Somme, Gallipoli, the R.F.C., and – everywhere and now, dying like flies of this whatever it was. Not 'flu as it used to be. A sort of plague. And this one . . . She wiped beads of clammy sweat from his face, and remembered Sister had said they'd have his bed tomorrow. Oh, no! Not this one, too! So young. Nineteen. Younger than I. The young and the old ones go first. There's Daddy with it now and he . . . and if I got it . . . But I mustn't get it. I won't get it because who'd look after Ronnie? Only him left. And Nannie. Oh please God don't let anything happen to Daddy or me or Nannie or . . . Don't let Ronnie have it. Or else let us all go. . . . I'm getting nervy. Dog tired.

She glanced at the clock above the entrance to the ward. Six o'clock and my half day. Better go off now. . . . And to a flustered V.A.D. who came hurrying in: 'I say, Holden, I'm off now. Should have been off at fourteen hours. Had two stiffs on me today.'

'I had three,' said Holden.

'And there'll be this one here tonight. Are you on night duty?'

'No, but I offered, as Jenkins and Drummond and Lambton are down with it. Isn't it awful?'

'Where's your mask?'

'Somewhere – I've lost it.'

She was rummaging in her apron pocket.

'Better take mine.'

She untied it and handed it to Holden who took it and covered her nose and mouth.

'Doctor', said Ross-Sutton, 'will be here any minute. I'm going before I'm caught. So long, young Holden.'

'So long,' mournfully answered 'young Holden', who was at least three years older than the twenty-year-old Ross-Sutton.

Outside the house in Grosvenor Square, her father's house that he had lent as a military hospital, she stood in the corpse-cold fog which obscured the naked trees in the Square, hugging herself in her coat for warmth while she waited for a taxi. After an interminable ten minutes she succeeded in halting a leisurely taxi-cab at the kerb.

'Where to?'

'St John's Wood.'

'Nothin' doin', Missy,' was the guttural reply. 'Too far in this fog.'

'Please. Not very far. Just beyond Lord's.'

'Right y'are. 'Op in.'

She hopped in, was driven at a crawl through the deepening fog, and deposited at a door in the wall of a house in Avenue Road. By the hazy light of a street lamp she saw the driver was an old fellow, sixtyish. No young ones left. As she handed him his fare he sneezed and, shivering, told her:

'I've got it, I think.'

'Let me feel your pulse.'

Oh, Lord, yes, she thought and said: 'Go straight home and to bed. Tell your wife or someone to get a doctor to you.'

'Ain't got no wife. Killed in the last Zepp raid. Lost both me sons in the war. No daughter. Nobody.'

She gave him ten shillings.

'Keep warm. You'll be all right. Where do you live?'

'Stepney, Miss.'

'What address?' She scribbled it down as he told her.

'I'll try and get to see you. If not I'll send someone to look after you.'

Not a hope, she reflected as, evading his wheezy thanks, she pushed upon the door in the wall of the garden. No private nurses available. Perhaps I could go over to him tomorrow sometime. Poor old thing . . .

She walked up the path to the house her father had taken furnished for the duration with an option of a year's renewal of the lease. Letting herself in at the front door with her latchkey, she was met in the hall by a pippin-faced old person in grey.

'Why so late? You look perished. Go and have your bath and I'll bring you up your supper.'

'How's Daddy?'

'Better, thank God. Temperature down to ninety-nine, but Ronnie's got it now.'

'Oh, no!'

'Only mild, doctor says. Not the bad kind − more like the old 'flu. Go along to your bath, darling. I'll put some carbolic in the water and you can soak yourself.'

'And you, Nannie, are you all right?'

'Right as rain. Haven't I nursed your father and Ronnie and you through scarlet and measles and mumps and never caught anything? One never catches anything from one's own babies. Go along now. I'll be up to you presently.'

'I must see Daddy first.'

'Just for a few minutes, then. Don't keep him talking.'

She took the stairs two at a time. Her father was sitting up in bed reading the evening paper. A man of the middle forties, his red hair grizzled at the temples, his chin showing a stubble of copper-coloured beard. Removing his spectacles as she bent to kiss him, he waved her aside.

'Not too near. I'm still full of germs.'

'So am I, which makes me immune. How do you feel, ducky?'

'Pretty awful. One always feels worse when the temperature's down. Ronnie's got it now.'

'So Nannie says, but only mildly according to the doctor. Not the real thing – I mean this they call 'flu isn't. I heard doctor telling Sister yesterday that it's an acute toxaemia.'

'I won't have you at that hospital any longer,' her father said, 'taking up his spectacles again to resume his perusal of the day's stock markets.

'Exchequer Bonds up a half. . . . You only joined for the duration and you put a year on your age regardless of what I could say, as usual.'

'I can't send in my resignation yet. None of us expected *this* and we're terribly short staffed. You're not to get up till you've been normal for forty-eight hours. We never let them up till then. I'm going to have a bath. See you later.'

Nannie bustled in.

'You'll do nothing of the sort. You'll have your bath and go straight to bed. There's chicken broth for you, my lord. And could you do with a bit of broiled chicken?'

'I could do with a pint of mild and bitter,' she was told with a grin that recalled the schoolboy of thirty years ago.

'A glass of wine for your lordship, the doctor said. Not that nasty beer.'

'Good enough! Tell Wilson to open the Lafite.'

A white-haired butler appeared at the door.

'The Lafite, Wilson.'

'Yes, my lord. God be praised.'

A widening grin spread across the slightly freckled cheeks.

'God will have all to do acknowledging praise of thankfulness from half His kingdom here on earth!' And pointing a finger at his daughter: 'Do as Nannie tells you. Go to bed.'

'A funny thing happened in my ward today,' she said,

ignoring this. 'I have a fellow down with it who was trying to say he has the same name as mine. He has a bad go of this 'flu. Frightfully confused. Couldn't make out half he was mumbling about. A Canadian I think.'

'Come along, Felicity,' from Nannie, 'mustn't keep your father talking.'

'It's I who've done the talking.' She blew her father a kiss and turned down a corridor to her brother's room.

A Great Dane lying at the foot of the bed got up to greet her.

She knelt to hug him.

'Hope he won't get it,' Ronnie said.

'Dogs don't get our sort of thing.'

'How's the Guv'nor?'

'Better. Let's have a look at you.' She took out her thermometer. 'Under the tongue. Don't bite it.'

Having felt his pulse, she removed the thermometer and:

'Have I bust the mercury?' her brother inquired with his father's grin.

'You'll do. Only a hundred and one. You're to stay put – not to get up till the doctor says you may. And I'll bring you a bed pan. You mustn't go to the lav.'

'My lord,' Wilson had entered with a glass of wine on a salver. 'His lordship sends you this.'

'No, Wilson, he mustn't. Not till his temperature's down. Hot lemon water and aspirin.'

'But, my lady – '

'Don't listen to Daddy. I know what he ought to have and what not to have.'

'Be damned to that!' Ronnie made as if to get out of bed.

Felicity held him back. 'Don't be a silly ass. Do you want to have pneumonia? That's what they get as complications and that's what kills them.'

'Poor blighters, yes. To have come through all of it and then to go off with this!'

'How's your arm?'

'Sir Henry says I'm lucky not to have lost it.'

'If anyone but Sir Henry had operated you probably would have. Gangrene is the devil.' And to the old butler, still hovering: 'He can have some chicken broth, Wilson. No solids yet.'

'Very good, my lady.'

'So long, Ronnie. I'll be back when I've had my bath.'

Nannie was waiting for her in her room with a hot water bottle.

'I'll put this in your bed and you'll go straight there after your bath.'

She had her bath, soaked luxuriously for half an hour and went to say goodnight to Ronnie. He was not in his room, nor was the dog.

'Ronnie! Where are you?...Nannie!' she called over the bannisters. 'Where's Ronnie?'

Wilson from the hall answered her.

'His lordship's in the garden with the dog, my lady.'

'No! You shouldn't have let him.'

'He was gone before anyone saw him, my lady. He is coming back now.'

Ronnie in an overcoat, followed by the Dane, was on the stairs.

'Ronnie, you damn fool!' Felicity met him on the landing. 'Are you mad? Going out – and in this fog!'

'It's lifted now. Roger wanted to go. He hasn't been all day.'

'Why couldn't you have rung for Wilson or someone to take him – or me?'

'You were in your bath, and anyway you know he won't go with anyone else when I'm laid up. You remember how he was when I came back from hospital and had to lie up with this damned arm.'

'You're more trouble than a ward full of Blighties. Get a hot water bottle for him, Wilson, and don't you' (to her brother) 'go assing about like that again.'

Nannie brought her supper, chicken broth, sausages and mash. When she came to fetch the tray:

'Ronnie'll be all right,' she said. 'It's not the 'flu. Just one of those feverish colds he always gets. Going out with the dog is nothing to what he had to do, stuck in the mud in the trenches.'

'The R.F.C. don't stick in the mud in the trenches unless they're shot down – '

'Which, thank God, he wasn't.'

'Only a bullet in his arm that got him gangrened . . . A-h-h,' Felicity yawned widely. 'I'm all in. Good night, Nannie.'

'Good night, lovey. Sleep well.'

Nannie went out with the tray, and Felicity, after switching off her bedside lamp, snuggled down into her warmed bed and did sleep well until her alarm clock woke her at seven in the morning.

Annie, the housemaid, brought her breakfast of porridge, two sausages, toast and a large pat of butter.

'I'm fed up with sausages, Annie, and this is more than my butter ration, surely?'

'It's Lord Ronulshere's butter, m'lady. He's not havin' no breakfast. The doctor's with him.'

'The doctor? So early?'

'Nannie sent for him, m'lady. His temperature's up.'

Felicity rushed to the window, saw the doctor's car outside and was out of the room like a rocket to find the doctor in the hall at the telephone.

'Yes, Matron . . . Yes, I quite understand, but I must have a night nurse as well as a . . . No, I do not wish him to be moved . . . I have tried Montagu Square, also Weymouth Street . . . No, nothing possible yet, not until next week . . . Yes, I'm sure you will . . . Yes, 101 Avenue Road.'

'Doctor!' Felicity had paled while she listened, 'Are you trying to get a nurse for Ronnie?'

'Yes, I am. He has given himself pleurisy. Your nurse tells me he went out in the garden with the dog last night.'

'Oh!' She caught a tooth beneath her underlip. 'I knew that would happen! I warned him. He is already run down through that arm. Doctor, if you can't get a nurse you must let me nurse him until you can get one.'

'I want two, a day and night nurse. You can't do both, day *and* night.'

'I can! I've had to before at the hospital when we're overcrowded, not only with 'flu cases but Blighty ones. I suppose you don't think I'm capable – just another of those V.A.D.s that Sister thinks are nothing much above a ward maid, only fit to scrub floors and empty bed-pans!'

'I don't think that at all. As a matter of fact I've heard very good reports of you from the house physician at Grosvenor Square. He took over from his son who joined the R.A.M.C. at the outbreak.'

'Did you – did he really?' She flushed with pleasure. 'I didn't think Doctor had even seen me or if he had that I was just another – ' she treated him to a tolerable mimicry of Sister's staccato bark – 'of these – tiresome – society – girls who can't even – give a catheter without – spilling it?'. . . And as she saw him smile, she told him, 'I've been nursing for two and a half years now. I'm not just a first year trainee. You can't *not* let me nurse Ronnie . . . Please!'

'My dear child, it isn't that I doubt your capability, but – ' he gave her a keen glance, noting the eager light in eyes just not green under long dark lashes that with red hair ought to have been white. . . . An old wives' tale, this, that long lashes and transparent, shell-like skin might betoken T.B. The boy, he recollected, had a patch on the lung when he was at Eton and he had advised a winter at Davos. 'But I'm not going to allow you to risk unnecessary infection, especially if you are debilitated with overwork.'

'I'm not debilitated and, Doctor, I'm going to nurse him whether you like it or not, until you get someone else or someone better. And Nannie can share it with me – she'll love that. I can easily get leave of absence from Matron –

compassionate leave. After all I'm only voluntary for the duration and I could have packed up after the Armistice except that this beastly 'flu was starting then and now it's epidemical. I shan't get it any more than you will get it. We're immune, being with it all the time.'

He had taken out his prescription pad and was scribbling on it.

'This is for your brother and this – ' he made another hieroglyphic scrawl – 'is for you. Take it every four hours. And since you're determined, and I, having brought you into the world,' his kindly old eyes scanned the charming uplifted face with its provocative blunt-cornered mouth and a sprinkling of freckles on the impudent tip-tilted nose – 'I am aware you have a will of your own that beat us all when we gave you up for gone with bronchitis at five weeks old.' He handed her the prescriptions. 'Get these to the chemist at once. I'll look in again at noon.'

Wilson, standing at the ready, offered the doctor his hat, helped him into his coat, and opened the door for him.

'I will take it to the chemist, sir.'

Felicity flew to Ronnie, who was sitting up in bed reading the *Daily Mail* with Roger, the Great Dane, lying on the floor at his bedside. The dog lifted his head at her entrance but did not move.

'He's been there all night,' Ronnie said. 'He won't leave me.'

'I'll take him out presently. What you've to do is stay where you are. Don't you dare get up.'

His face was flushed; his eyes very bright.

'Why all this fuss? I'm all right. I feel perfectly all right.'

'The higher the temperature, the better you feel.'

She arranged his pillows and covered him with the blankets.

He made an impatient movement.

'Leave me alone, can't you? I'm a hundred per cent

better than I was yesterday. Take Roger if he'll go, and for God's sake leave me *alone* – all this fussing!'

He was not left alone. She and Nannie shared the nursing all that night and the next day. The doctor came twice. The second time he brought Sir Lucian Halstead.

The father left his bed to see the consultant and was hustled back by Felicity.

'I don't want a relapse from you. Sir Lucian says,' she mendaciously reported, "that there's nothing to worry about. Doctor Cree wanted another opinion. You know how careful he is.'

'I insist on seeing Halstead.'

'You can't. He's gone.'

He had not gone. He was telephoning his hospital for a nurse to be sent as soon as possible.

Later in the evening oxygen cylinders were brought from the chemist, but no nurse.

'I can administer it,' she told the doctor who had come for the third time. 'I've had to give oxygen when we're short staffed.'

'You will not. You'll go to bed,' he told her, 'or I'll have you on my hands as well.'

'She won't go, Doctor,' Nannie said.

'She will.'

He half led, half dragged her, to her room.

She removed her cap and apron, unfastened the collar, lay down on her bed and was instantly asleep to be wakened by a sound of sobbing in the room next to hers: Ronnie's room . . . Who? . . . What?

Force of habit and training made her put on her cap and apron, and with trembling fingers to fasten her collar, telling herself: 'It's Nannie. She's dead beat. Too old for this . . . all night. If only that nurse . . . '

In Ronnie's room the oxygen cylinders had been laid aside; a fire blazed fiercely on the hearth casting a distorted shadow of Nannie on the walls where incredible blue roses entwined within a green trellis appeared to

22

sway as if in a breeze. Nannie's sobs had ceased. She was breathing heavily and slightly rocking back and forth where she stood.

Felicity saw her father seated in an armchair, his shoulders bowed, his head sunk in his hands. No sound came from him.

She tore away the sheet that covered the motionless figure on the bed where, stretched across the feet of it, the Great Dane lay on guard.

Her brother's face, no longer fever flushed, was waxen; the lips, just parted as if about to speak with the glint of teeth between them.

'Ronnie, no . . . *no*!' And again in a whisper, 'No!'

She leaned over him taking that lifeless, still warm hand in hers, and heard her father's strangled voice:

'My son . . . my son, and I . . . am spared. Why? Why?'

She knelt beside him drawing his head into her arms.

Nannie silently went out, leaving them together.

Extract from The Times

On 12th February 1919, Flight Lieutenant Viscount Ronulshere, Royal Flying Corps, only son of the Earl of Rodborough. Funeral on 16th February at Rodborough Abbey, Calloden, Norfolk.

TWO

The war had been over for more than two years and the crippled world raised its battered head from the blood-stained poppy fields of Flanders where the young unburied dead had lain rotting until commemorated by a forest of white crosses.

On 11 November 1920 King George V had released the flag that veiled the Cenotaph in the first of the three minutes' silence. . . . Lest we forget.

But those who had survived, who were not incapacitated for life with loss of limb or sight; or languishing in military hospitals undergoing interminable treatment for shell shock; those others who, on their triumphant homecoming, had been hailed as heroes by a grateful nation, what of them? . . . *Lest we forget*. And they already were forgotten.

Through London's streets and the streets of the great industrial cities, those lost survivors of Armageddon marched in hopeless out-of-work processions, wearing frayed war ribbons on their ragged coats. Or on the pavements at the kerbs of London's vast department stores they stood in dreary groups, playing instruments, blowing trumpets, strumming banjos; or occasionally they would break into croaking choruses of bygone marching songs : *Pack up your troubles in your old kit bag*. . . . But they had no kit bags now.

In shop windows waxen images were temptingly displayed in garish colours, no longer any mourning black or widows' weeds, while the Bright Young Things, too young to have done their 'bit' in the war as did their older sisters, and heedless of the outstretched caps offered by those lost ones in hope of a sixpence from indifferent passers by, would dash into the nearest perfumery department to buy Coty or Houbigant, or Chanel's *Numéro Cinq* with which to spray themselves in readiness for the *thé dansant*.

On an afternoon in mid-summer this, the latest post-war craze, was in full swing at the house of Mrs Thistlewaite in Avenue Road. That house which Lord Rodborough had leased during the war, had now reverted to its owner, Mrs Thistlewaite or, more correctly, to her husband, Albert. He, an insignificant, self-effacing cypher in his wife's domain, seemed to exude a perpetual apology not only as it were for his existence completely over-shadowed by his much better half, but for the wealth he had inherited from his father and for which it is not unremarkable to suppose he had been wed.

His wife, Ethel, chose to be known as Ellen since, she lamented to those of her fellow 'bomb-dodgers' who had taken refuge from the Zeppelin raids on London in the safety of the home counties: 'How could I possibly have called myself Ethel Thistlewaite? Too dreadfully tongue-twisting, like those oral exercises that are given to cure stutterers!' A somewhat tactless remark if overheard by Albert who also suffered from a slight impediment of speech, rather a hesitancy than a stutter, but none the less an irritant to Ethel (*alias* Ellen). Yet the worst irritant of all, worse even than Albert's unexpectedly vexatious re-fusal to leave London during the raids, except on short visits to the house she had taken in Haslemere – 'Not for *my* convenience,' she assured him, 'but for yours. And now people will think I am afraid of the bombs when I am only considering *you* and *your* safety.'... More than all such tiresome annoyances and her usually acquiescent husband's mild objection to her command, was the source of Albert's wealth.

Albert's grandfather, a plumber's apprentice born in

Liverpool some eighty years before, had migrated to London at the age of twenty-one with barely as many pounds in his pocket and in his head an accumulated knowledge, as of a squirrel's hoardings, of all to do with sanitary arrangements that, in the 'sixties, compared with twentieth-century requirements, were of the most primitive sort. One may excuse and forbear with Mrs Thistlewaite's shuddering recoil when confronted in ladies' retiring rooms of London's fashionable restaurants with Waite's Lavatory Pans, those luxuriously modern installations seen throughout the length and breadth of Britain and in every bathroom and W.C. of the mammoth hotels that were springing up, a mushroom growth risen on the sites of war-deserted mansions in Mayfair.

In the St John's Wood house with its late Regency façade and gardens back and front Mrs Thistlewaite had recently installed two more luxury bathrooms *en suite* with bedrooms, and in each one the abhorrent name had been omitted from the unmentionable article that had brought to her Albert a large five-figure income and the chairmanship, at his father's demise, of 'Waites'.

Not that Albert had much to do with the business thereof, in fact it is doubtful if he did more than give his consent to the proposals of the Board upon which had been suggested as director the name of the Earl of Rodborough that, in conjunction with two barons, a baronet, and an air marshal, would impress likely shareholders in Waites.

If Albert had any interest other than his London garden, in which he took much pride, he may have been seen nostalgically wandering in the precincts of Whitehall; for time was when after leaving Cambridge where he, surprisingly, had managed to take an honours degree in modern languages, as result of which he obtained a minor appointment in the Foreign Office. . . . 'And how', his wife privately conjectured, 'he got there at all with that background, is a miracle . . . or money.' Which before their

26

marriage had even taken him to Russia on a tour of the European capitals.

He was not 'there' now, however, for apart from the nominal chairmanship of Waites, he seems to have done nothing.

Let us now return to Mrs Thistlewaite's third *thé dansant* which took place on a Saturday of Ascot week on an afternoon in 1923. Albert, having had nothing to eat since his breakfast, arrived back from wherever he had been that morning to find luncheon long finished, and the dining-room invaded by their war-depleted male staff now consisting of a butler and one footman plus several hirelings, arranging a buffet; and Ethel – he begged her pardon, *Ellen* – in a taking.

'Really, Albert! To expect to be served with luncheon at half past two when I *told* you it was only an omelette at twelve thirty! And the cook who has all to do with only one kitchenmaid, the second as you know is down with German measles and we shall probably *all* get it – so tiresome! That comes of employing one of these ex-land girls entirely untrained and the only kitchenmaid cutting sandwiches for fifty and heaven knows how many more will come gate-crashing or if Fortnum's will send the order for ices in time and the refrigerator not working although they *promised* to send at once so we shall have melting ices and warm champagne cocktails – and now you expect to be given luncheon!'

'No, n . . . not at all,' apologized Albert. 'A sandwich is all I need.'

'Then you must wait', snapped his wife, 'until they are cut, or make do with bread and cheese.'

Having made do with bread and cheese, Albert was inconspicuously acting host to those of the younger generation for whom the party was held with a few of Mrs Thistlewaite's particular cronies.

From the drawing-room where the dancers were jazzing to the strains of a ukulele orchestra composed of four perspiring *café-au-lait*-skinned Hawaians in red satin coats, white ducks, and open-throated shirts displaying a glimpse of bronzed chests, Albert emerged toward the buffet to thread his apologetic way through a milling crowd of youngsters.

Having asked for and been supplied with a cup of tea, Albert secured what he thought to be a sardine sandwich and was caviare, which he greatly disliked. A second attempt proved almost as unsatisfactory when found to be anchovy.

'Try one of these, Mr Thistlewaite. They are quite innocuously egg.'

Turning, he was confronted by a girl in one of the new full-skirted calf-length *thé dansant* dresses, her copper-red bobbed curls bound with a tinsel fillet.

The face of Albert, a chubby face surmounted by a crop of tow-coloured hair sprouting greyish wings either side of a rounded forehead, gave that face oddly the effect of an elderly cherub which brightened in pleased recognition.

'Lady Felicity, de . . . lighted you are here. I . . . understood you were at Rodborough.'

'Unfortunately, no. I mean,' she hastily corrected, 'not that I'm unfortunate in being here instead of what was my home until a month ago, but it isn't my home any more, if you get me?'

He got her, sympathetically.

'I did hear that Lord Rodborough had . . . contemplated selling the Abbey but I did not realize it was actually a . . . *fait accompli*. Yes?'

'Yes. It is to be a health centre – sort of hydro hotel where people go to be rid of too much fat or *vice versa*, and to be generally rested and tranquillized after coming to from belated war damage to their nerves and their finances. Daddy, poor lamb, is one of those who have been stung by pre-war speculating in Russian and German stock and every other possible sinking ship of his capital, and now that Ronnie . . . ' her voice faltered, 'now that he has no son to carry on, and the Abbey wasn't entailed and anyway it's a great barrack of a place to keep going with inadequate staff and nothing to pay them with, and so . . . there you are.'

'As most of us are in . . . deed,' was the reply to this from one whose many ships were well afloat. 'A health centre, I think you said?'

'Yes, and I thought I could have been of some use there being of no use anywhere else now, and when this chance came I made Daddy take it. He will be paid enough with the land on which they intend building a golf course on some of it, to keep the more ravening wolves from our doors.'

'A very commendable attitude on your part, but,' with a gallant little bow, 'if I may say so you under . . . estimate your admirable . . . qualities in describing yourself as of no use save in a health centre attending upon persons suffering from ob . . . esity or attenuation or neuroses when,' another little bow, 'your presence anywhere is a solace for war-weary eyes.'

'Eyes haven't been war-weary these five years,' said Felicity. 'Just look at them now – those who never had anything to do with the war. Their eyes are full of pep – the effect of cocktails, or in there,' she jerked her head in the direction of the drawing-room, 'where they are doing this latest import from America, the Charleston. We have all gone American since the Yankees insist they won the war for us!'

'May I dare present myself as a hopeful aspirant to induce you to honour me with the latest transatlantic import, Lady Felicity?'

This somewhat laboured address, apparently emanating from the air, caused her to swing round to meet the appraising glance of a tall man with hair sleek and dark as a seal's, and a moustache like an eyebrow above a small thin-lipped mouth.

'You have the advantage over me,' she told him coolly, 'as you know my name and I don't know yours.'

'If I may enlighten your . . . ladyship,' Albert hesitatingly interposed, 'and if I am not mistaken, allow me to introduce Prince . . . Riabovitch.'

'And you have the advantage over me, sir,' said the other with a smile that revealed remarkably fine teeth as he echoed, 'in that you know my name and I don't know yours.'

'Then you ought to,' Felicity took him up sharp on the faint mockery his repetition of her previous remark implied, 'since he happens to be your host unless, of course,' she wrinkled her impertinent tip-tilted nose, 'you gate-crashed here.'

'*Touché!*' he laughed, a whispering laugh, 'but with all due respect to Mr − ?'

'Thistlewaite,' was apologetically prompted from that gentleman.

He bowed acknowledgement.

'I did not gate-crash, as you,' to Felicity, 'put it, but I might have done had I realized . . . ' he sunk his chin in the wings of his collar looking down at her from under hooded lids, "that you were to be among the guests!'

He is just a bit too polished, she thought, but Russian − what can you expect? He sounds like something out of Chekhov even to the name.

He was now addressing Albert. 'Sir, I must ask your pardon for not having known to whom I am beholden for this happy − ' he spread his hands in a slightly foreign gesture − 'encounter with the much admired and photographed in the *Tatler*, the *Sketch* and − ' he shrugged immaculate shoulders − 'all the gossip columns who delight to extol the Lady Felicity Ross-Sutton. But', as Albert made as if to speak, 'I have still to know where you have met or seen me that you are acquainted with my name.'

Albert put his head a trifle on one side while he strove

to recollect, and achieved with an effort: 'Was it . . . were you at the Hotel Berchielli in Florence . . . last year?'

'Ah, so that's it! Of course. My cousin who so much resembles me we might be twins– he was concierge at an hotel in Florence last year, I remember. As he speaks five languages including English he is in demand in continental hotels for tourists. We, who are, unhappily, refugees from Czarist Russia have found a haven either here in Britain or in other compassionate countries.' And again returning to Felicity: 'May I have the honour of the Charleston or whatever it is they are performing in there?'

A slight lift of his hand indicated the doorway through which several young people who had finished with the buffet were intent on regaining the floor.

'If Mr Thistlewaite will excuse me?'

Albert bowed and beamed assent to Felicity's murmur: 'But of course . . . Pray do. Were I a . . . several years younger I might dare to ask for the honour my . . . self.'

'Quite a die-hard pre-war *politesse*,' the prince commented with that same rather attractive whisper of a laugh. 'One seldom comes across it in England these days, but then he is presumably Victorian. He may well have been in his thirties when the old Queen died.'

They had now gained the drawing-room. Wide long french windows opened on to a lawn edged with flowering shrubs and azaleas. Paved paths fringed a colourful herbaceous border. The westering sun shining on young heads, on the flushed faces of girls, and on the walls painted in pale pastel blue as if a piece of the sky had strayed, lighted to a golden radiance the opulent room with its heavy crystal chandeliers, and on gilt-framed pictures by Alma-Tadema and John Collier, these Ethel's pride as the garden was her husband's. And, unobtrusively hung in a corner as if apologetic as their owner, were a couple of small Dutch paintings described by Ethel as 'hideous and vulgar'; one depicting a fish stall, its vendor selling his wares to a stout peasant woman in a white coif and voluminous skirt, every detail meticulously observed; the other of two men playing dice. Neither picture was more than eighteen inches square.

The prince halted before these and adjusting a monocle that dangled from a cord against his waistcoat he peered closely saying:

'Unless I am much mistaken these are by Gerard Dow.'

'Gerard Dow? Quite possible. We took this house furnished during the war but only these two and a few of this lot were there then.' Felicity gave a disparaging glance at 'this lot'.

'I would rather like to suggest to Mr Thistlewaite,' said he, still engaged on his examination of the pair, 'if he were prepared to sell these quite possible Dows.'

'Are you,' she asked, 'interested in the seventeenth-century Dutch school?'

'Not so much as in the Tuscan primitives and the Italian Renaissance. I have acquired a small art gallery in Duke Street where I strive to earn an inadequate but absorbing livelihood, and also to recuperate something of my youth in collecting such of the world's treasures that may chance my way once in a while and before *my* world crashed', he thinly smiled, 'to disaster.'

She endeavoured to offer a sympathetic rejoinder to this allusion to the tragedy of White Russia, but unable to produce more than a commiserating sound, she hastened to tell him:

'You speak perfect English. Did you live in England before the – ' she hesitated to say it – 'revolution?'

The monocle dropped from his eye.

'No, I never was in England until after 1918, but from my birth I had English nurses, and as a child I had English and French governesses. We spoke French and English as fluently as our own language. We were tri-lingual. In fact at my home in St Petersburg we spoke English more than we spoke French or Russian. Shall we join in these convolutions?'

32

It was a song rendered in waltz time from a late Victorian drawing-room repertoire and crooned by the majority of the younger ones. And as the prince held her, his body rhythmically attuned to hers, he hummed low-voiced the words of it:

' "Because God made thee mine I'll cherish thee-ee." Sentiment is not entirely dead in this new age,' his arm slid lower to her waist, 'but I fear we shall soon lose all that is left of it, thanks to Freudian psychology which is accountable for more than our dreams and, or, pre-natal influences. I seem to remember that one of England's up-and-coming brilliant young satirists of this post-war generation has given a reason for certain of our exhibitionists' perversions as due to our childhood's infatuation for a rocking-horse.'

She rippled into laughter, thinking: He has a . . . something. Then, as the music came to a long drawn out finale accompanied by a clapping of hands, he said:

'Shall we go into the garden? Do you not find it rather hot in here?'

He offered her his arm and as she took it he pressed it to his side. . . . H'm, she thought, not slow in coming forward. A bit *too* continental. And, a little distrustful of him and her own slight thrill of response to this not very subtle overture, she disengaged and walked an arm's length beside him to the garden.

On the lawn tables had been placed attended by hireling waiters offering refreshment, soft drinks and champagne cocktails to those others who had come to cool themselves in the shade of an ancient apple tree and, surprisingly, a Wellingtonia.

'This must have been here when St John's Wood *was* a wood and part of a private estate – the Eyre estate. I wonder how long ago when all here was open country. I believe', she said, 'there is an Eyre Arms still.'

'In an age when the internal-combustion engine had not been thought of even by Leonardo who made his first experimental efforts with a flying machine. Your island in the middle of the North Sea, divided by a narrow strip of channel between you and France will, in another forty years or so, cease to be an island when aeroplanes make a girdle round about the earth, as Puck has put it, in forty minutes.'

'Wasn't it Graham White,' Felicity accepted an iced drink from one of the hired waiters, 'who called for three cheers for the Frenchman who – I forget his name?'

'Paulhan,' supplied the prince.

'Yes, and who made an exciting flight in a high wind and landed safely in Manchester?'

'In 1909 when you were still in pigtails.'

'I never wore pigtails.'

'At school then.'

'Nor did I ever go to school. I had a series of English and French governesses like you had, and have suffered ever since from abysmal ignorance of my own country's history, beyond Victoria. I expect you know a good deal more about England and English history than I do.'

'It was part of my school years' curriculum to learn of our Czar's maternal connections with the great Empire of his august relative Queen Victoria.'

'And I never even realized that he was connected with our royalty. You see what an ignoramus I am.'

They were now almost alone in the garden. The other occupants of the tables were leaving, although the young dancers in the drawing-room were hard at it with a fox-trot. From behind the garden wall could be heard the impatient hoot of cars as chauffeurs lined up in a queue.

The prince, declining a cocktail offered by another of the waiters, said:

'Shall we join the dance or have you had enough of it?'

'Quite enough of it.' She rose. 'I must go back. My father will be home by now and I have to see to his dinner.' And to the waiter who stood before her with a tray of drinks, 'No, thank you.'

34

His face was vaguely familiar. He had a deep scar over one eye half hidden by a lock of blond hair that appeared to have been carefully placed to conceal it.

A war casualty, she supposed, and looked again. Their eyes met. She was thinking: I've seen him somewhere. In hospital or where? The prince was asking: 'Have you a car, or if not may I drive you wherever you wish to go?'

'Our flat is in Ashley Gardens, but please don't trouble. I can get a taxi.'

'No trouble. It will be my pleasure if I may.'

His car, a small chocolate-coloured Daimler coupé, was parked behind a line of others, and as they drove off she side-glanced him.

Etched against the window his profile with its high-bridged nose and the firm articulation of chin and jaw, the seal-dark hair sleeked back from a high-domed fore-head, were reminiscent of a portrait by Raphael. He may have cultivated the resemblance, since his interest lay in the masters of the Renaissance which, she thought, may be based on his self-imposed image. . . . He is full of affec-tations but that might be in self defence against what he and others of his kind have escaped to become exiles in a foreign land. What happened, she wondered, to those who didn't escape after the Bolsheviks murdered the Czar and all the Romanovs? She noticed his hands on the wheel, long-fingered hands with polished, almond-shaped nails. On the fourth finger of the left hand nearest to her was a heavy gold crested ring. She found him disturbingly provocative and frowned at herself for her attraction to one whom she instinctively mistrusted. Which, she argued, is unfair, just because he is a foreigner. One mustn't be so insular. Our insularity will be our downfall in the end. He was saying:

'I heard you mention to our host, this, er, Mr Thistle-waite – that your father has sold Rodborough Abbey, which is to be a health centre. I know Rodborough, or rather that part of Norfolk. One of my compatriots – '

without turning his head his hooded eyes slid round to hers – 'is a receptionist at an hotel in Cromer. It was used as headquarters for your army during the war, I believe, and reopened about two years ago.'

'So was Rodborough, which was H.Q. for the R.H.A. in training. And as fast as one lot went out more new ones came in. They made a ghastly mess of it. So you know Rodborough?'

'Only exteriorly. I had not the opportunity to see it with visitors on a tour of inspection.'

'You wouldn't have in any case. Tourists who came to see it before the war – chiefly for the picture gallery – weren't allowed in when the army was there. It is rather awful exteriorly since one of my great-greats added a mock-Tudor wing to what Vanbrugh made of it built on the site of a Carthusian monastery, destroyed under Henry VIII, which is why it is called an Abbey. Vanbrugh followed Blenheim with it. There is still some Anneish loveliness left in the panelling and the snail-and-shell carving which hasn't all suffered from the army's vandalism and a Zepp bomb. There was an aerodrome near there and Jerry was after it.'

'It is still an airfield, is it not? What is the name of it – something St Mary?'

'Pulham St Mary. It's quite a good way from Rodborough but the one at Fordington is nearer. There's talk of building a giant airship on the lines of a Zepp, only much better and more modern, at Fordington which will, I suppose, be a huge munition factory to ruin the countryside. Fortunately no longer *our* countryside.'

'When,' he asked with that slide of his eyes, 'does this health centre open?'

'Some time early next year they hope. There's a lot to be done to it yet. Trained nurses to engage and dietitians and masseuses. I had thought of taking up massage to help out.'

'In which case,' he said, and this time he looked at her

36

straightly with a show of his fine white teeth, 'I would apply to be the first of your patients.'

Receiving no responsive encouragement to this somewhat obvious attempt to engage her, he went on: 'You had some famous pictures at Rodborough, I understand.'

'Hardly any now. We have taken away everything that is saleable including the Adam fireplace in the Adam wing built on after Vanbrugh had finished with it and when the Regent – he wasn't the Regent then – had more or less discovered the Adam brothers for Carlton House. There is a Lely and a Kneller left and a supposed-to-be Rembrandt and a couple of Leightons which the Victorians loved and I loathed, so they wouldn't have mattered when Jerry did his stuff but what *did* matter was a Constable, a Corot, a Morland, and an almost certain Lorenzo Monaco bombed to bits. Another of my great-greats bought it in Florence about two hundred years ago. He probably paid about twenty pounds for it. We are hoping to sell the Kneller and the Lely, one of Charles the Second's girls, and also the Rembrandt which Daddy thinks is a Rembrandt and I don't. They are at Christie's at present and the Rembrandt is undergoing controversial argument among their experts who are X-raying it and doing lord knows what to it before they pass it to be bought by the Americans, the only people who can afford to buy it!'

'Although I cannot afford to buy it would I be allowed to see this supposed-to-be Rembrandt?'

'I shouldn't think so while Christies are sitting on it.'

They were now passing Hyde Park Corner and as the traffic along Grosvenor Place was increasing on the way to Victoria Station, conversation flagged while the prince negotiated the avoidance of hurrying taxis and cars. Within a few minutes they had come to the quiet of Ashley Gardens. Having ascertained the number of her flat, the prince drew up opposite Westminster Cathedral.

'I would ask you to come in for a drink,' she said, 'only it is the cook's night off and I have to get my father's dinner. He has been in the Lords all day, goodness knows why considering he has only opened his mouth in the Upper House six times in these twenty years since he first took his seat when my grandfather died.'

'So among your many accomplishments you undertake the duties of a cook?'

'If you can call the burnt offering of a grilled chop or raw mutton an accomplishment. There are only two chops or I would invite you to join us.'

'I would like it of all things, but,' as he helped her out, 'may I ask you to join *me* to dinner? What about to-morrow evening?'

'No, I am sorry. I have to go to Rodborough tomorrow and I won't be back until Tuesday.'

'In that case would Wednesday next suit you? And if you would care to see my modest gallery perhaps you would come after closing time, which is at five-thirty? I could then show you those of my exhibits which might interest you.'

'Well. . . .' She hesitated, thinking: He's not lost much time. If he thinks to start something, am I on or off? . . . One needn't be on if one wants to be off and he makes a change from these half-baked, left-over temporaries who were never sent out. The best of them who *were* sent out have gone West. . . . All this went through her mind while she paused before her answer:

'Thanks, yes, I'd like to see your gallery and dine with you. Would it be black tie? I haven't any decent clothes for anywhere smart.'

'Would you prefer a quiet dinner which is not in the least smart, no jazz, no dancing, and I can promise you something better than a burnt offering or raw mutton.'

'If I am not back until after Wednesday,' she allowed herself a loophole to call it off if she decided not to call it on, 'can I have your telephone number so that I can ring you if I can't make it?'

'I trust you will not need to ring me except to say you

will meet me at this address.' He produced a card. 'And it will not, if you prefer it, be black tie.'

'If I don't phone you, then you'll know I'm coming. About sixish?'

'Splendid. The light is still good in these long evenings.'

He watched her mount the steps to the entrance of the mansion block of her father's flat. She turned to wave him a goodbye.

He bowed profusely, almost to the knees.

'*Au revoir.*'

'I thought those young people would never go,' said Mrs Thistlewaite when the last of them had departed, and she and Albert were having supper – 'Not dinner tonight,' had been the mandate. 'Mrs Pembury has had enough to do with only one kitchenmaid. I have given her the evening off.' Albert would prefer but did not say he would rather have had cold beef and pickles than the remains of the *pâté de fois gras* and a tournedos, the kitchenmaid's effort, followed by a somewhat dilapidated *pêche Melba* left over from the buffet.

'That Russian Prince What's-his-name brought by Mrs Pickering-Smythe,' said Ethel spooning *pêche Melba*, 'is a very distinguished-looking man. I had no chance of speaking to him more than a few words, he was so taken up with Lady Felicity. Mrs Pickering-Smythe is a relative of his. She is, of course, Russian, and married Pickering-Smythe long before the revolution. She must be seventy if a day. He was one of the Leicestershire Pickerings, or he may have been Smythe and added a Pickering on to it from the distaff side. Anyway she is connected with this Prince Thingummybob who, she says, is a Romanov, if she's to be believed. Pickering-Smythe met her – again we only have *her* word for it – when he went to St Petersburg on a holiday and knew some of our Embassy men. He couldn't have been very young when he married her for even if he was younger than she, he must have been about forty when they married. She's far too fat. I wonder she doesn't diet.'

'Pickering-Smythe', vouchsafed Albert, 'made his money in . . . munitions.'

'Which', snapped Ethel as the butler and footman retired, 'is better than lavatory pans.'

'And more luc . . . rative possibly.'

'You needn't complain since the odious things have made you almost a millionaire.'

'I don't complain,' Albert negatived mildly. 'Waites has its uses of a less haz . . . ardous source of danger than the making of bombs and other weapons of destruction.'

'One has to have munitions in case of another war.'

'Which we hope,' Albert devoutly uttered, 'will never be in our . . . time.' And to the footman who had entered with coffee: 'Is there any cheese?'

Stilton and biscuits were supplied, and while Ethel took her coffee black and Albert took his white: 'The prince seemed to be very attentive to Lady Felicity,' remarked Mrs Thistlewaite. 'She's a pretty girl and must have had a good many offers for her title if for nothing else, but she isn't every man's taste – too forthright and abrupt and of course Lord Rodborough hasn't a bean. They sold or they let the Grosvenor Square house. They were always hard up and with that great Rodborough place to run he is probably hoping she will marry money – one of these war profiteers who are all getting knighted for their contributions to whatever party is in. Let's hope it won't be Labour next time. People seem to think it will, if so – help us all. Have you finished?' She rose from the table not waiting to know if Albert had finished or not.

'I shall go to bed as soon as I have listened to the news,' said his wife. 'I want to hear what they say about that dreadful man, Ramsay MacDonald.'

Albert obediently followed her to the boudoir where, placing the ear-phones of the crystal set behind such of her elaborately curled and not entirely authentic hair as encroached upon her rather large ears, she sat expectantly agog.

Albert opened the evening paper, read the headlines, yawned, and said:

'I think I'll take a turn in the garden.'

He did not take a turn in the garden; he went instead to his study and made a call on a secrecy switch. If anyone had cared to listen at the door, he or she might have noted that he spoke with no hesitancy, but his wife had often remarked on this when she would ask him to speak for her on the telephone.

'Room 52 . . . 101 here. I would like an appointment with . . . ' his voice dropped to an almost indistinguishable murmur, 'tomorrow . . . Yes. 10.30? . . . No, nothing of much significance but there might be . . . radiations, shall we say? . . . No . . . Yes. Possibly. Has double 20 sent in a report? Not yet? Tomorrow then. Ten-thirty. Right.'

He hung up the receiver on its hook, sat staring at it with a frown between his negligible eyebrows and a pout of his lips that made him look more than ever like a cherub, but one that was suffering from an anxiety complex. Then presently, he unlocked a cupboard, took out a bottle and poured liberal whisky into a glass, returned the bottle to the cupboard and re-locked it.

Having thus refreshed himself he made another telephone call. 'Double 20? I have an appointment with X at ten-thirty tomorrow. Can you come to my club at twelve? Good . . . No, not at all. You did very well. I'll see you then. Goodbye.'

* * *

On the following Wednesday Felicity, who had decided not to take advantage of the loophole, arrived at the gallery in Duke Street on Wednesday shortly after six o'clock. Having paid the taxi and before she went into what appeared to be a picture shop and nothing so grandiose as the prince's 'modest gallery', she paused before the window to see displayed one solitary exhibit depicting the Grand Canal at Venice and inscribed on a small brass plate 'Canaletto'.

How, she wondered, does he get his money to buy these masters which I'll bet this one isn't? Or if it is, it's after Canaletto and a good time after ... So here we go.

And there we went to be effusively greeted by Prince Riabovitch.

'I hardly dared to hope! I have been on tenterhooks waiting for your phone call, fearing to hear you could not come.'

Releasing her hand which he held rather unnecessarily long, he said, leading her into the first room about fifteen feet square, 'These are all moderns. A few show promise. They are mostly by young artists, among them two of my compatriots whom I consider should be encouraged.'

Felicity politely examined each of these and of which she had no great opinion. The majority were of the ultra-modern school and not particularly interesting or arresting. She made approbatory if unconvincing remarks to which the prince, with his thin-lipped smile, replied:

'I see you have a perceptive intuition that can discern or depreciate the mediocre and which is lacking in many of our foremost experts. Their knowledge is acquired, rather than innate, from close association with the buying and selling of masterpieces.'

'I don't know,' she said, 'that I have any knowledge or perception, but at Rodborough I was brought up with some of the best before the Zepp bombed them. That Canaletto – we had a Canaletto which my father sold and it *was* a Canaletto. May I be forgiven if I don't believe that one in the window is the real thing?'

'Your unerring instinct is correct. I too have my doubts of it nor was it my desire to label it Canaletto, only the lady who has asked me to sell it for her has tried to convince me it is genuine and insists I keep it named as such. If a buyer should bid for it, I would, of course, give him my opinion as to its authenticity. The lady who owns it was she to whom I am beholden for the felicitous meeting with the Lady Felicity – ' he showed his teeth – 'no unpardonable pun intended. She it was who brought me to that *thé dansant*. She is Mrs Pickering-Smythe, a relative of mine who married one of your compatriots long before you or even I were born. Now in this room,' he conducted her under an arch into an inner compartment rather smaller than the first, 'are those of my own collection which are, alas, for sale since I needs must in order to exist, having no other means.'

She saw he had managed to procure a fine selection of three or four which she thought to be genuine examples of the Tuscan school, and was enthralled by a Bartolommeo depicting a Madonna and Child.

'Not of his best,' the prince said. 'His earlier and most delicate work, after he became a friar, is at Lucca where his Madonna with St Stephen and St John the Baptist hangs in the Duomo. And here we see this, attributed to Perugino, one of the greatest and most personal artists of the fifteenth century, although' (he moved on to the next picture) 'I do not love him as I love the simple mystical beauty of Angelico.'

Imbibing with an almost sensuous enjoyment the visionary loveliness expressing the very spirit of Christianity in a Fra Angelico's marvellously sweet virgin, 'How', she asked, 'did you come by it?'

'Angelico has left us his legacies through the length and breadth of Italy and these – ' he gestured – 'the Bartolommeo and these other two, were in my father's house at St Petersburg which by a miracle I managed to smuggle with me when I and those few of us escaped. I am loth to offer them for sale to some avid American as I think I never can bring myself to part with them, but I have no permanent home yet in which to cherish them.'

So to the remainder of his exhibits, having passed from the three Italians to the French School that included a Lancret and a Boucher. 'Both,' he said, 'equally doubtful,

43

although an American buyer or an English war profiteer will dispute my attempt to disillusion them for it is against my principles to pass off a fake as genuine, and there is always the chance I may be mistaken. I shall probably lose my sense of honesty when I have been in this business long enough, for it is, though I shudder to admit it, a business.'. . . Then on to the Dutch, a Cuyp.

'I can almost hear the munching of those cows,' said Felicity, who recognized the Cuyp as the real thing; and also a possible Pieter de Hooch. . . .

He can't, she thought, be so hard up as he makes out to have acquired a collection that even if half of them *are* fakes could be worth about twenty thousand.

'And now,' said he, 'if you are not bored with what you have graciously endured with appropriate appreciation, may I offer you a drink?'

He led her into his office furnished with a wide mahogany mid-Victorian desk and two file cabinets ranged against one wall of it. Opening a cupboard he asked what she would have and supplied her with a dry martini. She watched him mix and shake a cocktail, telling her: 'This is my own concoction, basically vodka laced with curaçao and brandy. I would not suggest you try it as it is not every one's taste.'

'I am sure it isn't mine. I should have no head for it.' She raised her glass to him. 'Cheers. I can't drink. I never could. If I have more than two cocktails I become insensible.'

Just then the telephone rang on his desk.

'Excuse me.' He took up the receiver.

'Yes? . . . Oh, Natasha . . . No, nothing certain yet as far as I understand. Have you seen Sir Lucian? . . . What does he think? . . . Well it might be some time before . . . To-morrow? Just a minute, I'll look in my diary.'

And to Felicity nibbling an olive from a dish he had placed before her, and while he covered the receiver: 'Do forgive me, this is Mrs Pickering-Smythe. She will talk for an hour unless I cut her short . . . ' And without looking at his diary which Felicity saw was on the table next to the telephone, he said: 'I am so sorry, Natasha, tomorrow evening is impossible . . . No, nor Friday, I shall be away. I have to go to a sale in, er, Sussex. . . . No, not Lord Pulborough's sale. . . . May I ring you? . . . Monday or Tuesday? . . . Yes, I'll let you know,' his eyes rolled resignedly ceilingward. . . . 'Do forgive me, my dear, there's the bell, I am expecting a client. . . . Yes, it is a wonder you got me here, I am not usually so late. . . . Goodbye.'

He hung up with a sigh of relief. 'She is non-stop once she starts, but a dear soul. She was asking me about the Rodborough health centre.'

Felicity's eyes widened. 'How can she know about it? It hasn't been advertised yet.'

'She says she heard of it from Sir Lucian Halstead, her doctor, who has advised her to undergo treatment to reduce her avoirdupois. She is sadly overweight. I expect the company engaged on launching Rodborough Hydro are acquainting all Harley Street with the project.'

She nodded. 'I suppose so, but it will be some months before it opens.' And she refused a second drink.

'Shall we', said the prince, 'be making a move?' He glanced at his wrist watch. 'I ordered a table for seven forty-five. I thought you would prefer not to arrive at a time when others are hurrying in to gourmandize. It is a quiet restaurant, conspicuous only for its cuisine, and many of its clients do not come until after eight thirty.'

His little Daimler was at the kerb; he drove, avoiding the worst of the theatre traffic by a circuitous route into a narrow lane behind Covent Garden. Nothing conspicuous indeed was the sign of the Chanticleer above a striped awning under which stood two bay trees in tubs either side the door.

A bowing host received Riabovitch in a strong French accent.

'I am 'appy to see m'sieu le prince after too long a time, and Madame – ?'

The Lady Felicity Ross-Sutton was presented.

'I 'ave ze honneur, miladi.'

After more bows and hand washings he ushered them to a secluded table facing the room; a long room, its walls decorated with frescoes depicting near caricatures but recognizable of well-known persons who were, presumably, habitués, among them Riabovitch.

'Who did these?' she inquired as she sat. 'That one has got you exactly.'

'They are done by various artists. It is the haunt of many in the world of art, literature and the doyens of the theatre who prefer to meet here rather than at the more popular Café Royal and where I hope you will find the food to your liking.'

'I don't know much about food,' she admitted. 'If I ever had a palate I lost it during the war for I was just out of the schoolroom and rice puddings when I joined up as a V.A.D. and in hospital our meals were pretty awful even for rations.'

He handed her one of the two menus offered by a waiter.

'Perhaps your choice of these will restore your lost palate.'

She shook her head.

'Too much *embarras de richesse*. Won't you choose for me?'

'Would you prefer to start with caviare or smoked salmon?'

'May I have caviare? I am trying to acquire a taste for it.'

'A better choice than the smoked salmon because I suggest it is followed by lobster *à l'amoricaine*, and then,' he scanned the printed page, 'a *filet mignon*?'

A wine waiter approached; the prince consulted him in

an undertone, and to her: 'Will you have a cocktail or sherry?'

'I've had one cocktail and if wine is to come I think I would like, if it doesn't shock you, just a tonic water.'

He gave his whispering laugh which, she thought, is just not a snigger; it comes through his nose. Wonder if he's adenoidal. . . . He was saying: 'You are so charmingly naïve and unaffected, so different from these precocious hectically Bright Young People who seem to be spawned from the aftermath of post-war degeneration.'

'Except', she said, 'that there is always a reaction after wars. I believe the same was the case after the Napoleonic wars. Of course it has to be a great war devastating the whole of Europe like Napoleon did and as the Kaiser tried to do, not just a localized war in South Africa like the Boer War. You can't blame the young for trying to get some enjoyment out of a life that broke up their homes by taking their fathers and . . . and brothers for there's bound to be a rehabilitation when a new world is built upon the ruins of what the war did to this planet and all of us on it. As for those you call the Bright Young People I'm a bit too old to be one of them, being in my mid-twenties now, and I've seen what those in their later teens have not, these debs and the boys who were still at school when we were in the war. I learned a lot about war, the hard and grim way, nursing those who fought for us and I saw what war had done to them, so many boys in their teens too, who went out just before the armistice and came back blinded, armless, legless. . . . If war came again and if I were a man I'd be a conchie!'

'I think you would not,' he smiled down at her. 'You would always fight for justice and for right.'

'Did your revolutionaries who murdered your Czar and all his family, and exiled all of you who were loyal to him, were *they* fighting for right and justice?'

He looked with clouded eyes into the glass of sherry he held before he replied:

'Let us judge not lest we be judged. They fought and they killed for their beliefs. They had suffered injustice, they had borne with monstrous hardships, taxed beyond their strength or will, even as the French before them who revolted after long endurance while the nobles lived on the sweat and toil of their labour.'

Caviare was brought and created a halt in the discussion, resumed by Felicity as she gingerly sampled the succulent sturgeon's roes.

'You,' she said, 'are more tolerant than I would be and than we, my forbears, were when Cromwell's rebels murdered our King. We had a murdered king, too, you know, in our civil war. Your war' (slowly she masticated toast) 'was anything but civil. We were a house divided. Half of us fought against the Stuart, the other half fought with him. Some of my ancestors were fighting against him, brother against brother, father against son, but another of us helped restore his son to the Throne.'

'We in Russia made every effort to restore our Imperial monarchy,' said he. 'We of the White forces were fighting a losing game against the Reds until the Reign of Terror wiped us out. The Bolsheviks had become absolutely ruthless. I had already made my escape, but news filtered through to us of the appalling conditions and the massacres of people who were martyred for their Czarist sympathies. Then came the murder of the Imperial Family which occurred during anti-communist rioting at Ekaterinburg.'

'Do you think that the murder of a reigning monarch and his innocent children is a justifiable protest against a government's injustice to the rank and file, the peasants, the workers, they who starve that their overlords may feed on the fat of their lands?'

'There were some who did think so, and whose sympathies were with the rebels.'

'Then they were traitors to their Czar. I hope that none of them who escaped have come to stir up trouble with the Bolsheviks here – the so-called Communists who are for ever agitating to be represented in Parliament. But if any of these Socialist-*cum*-Communists should get together and find a leader to incite them against our King and monarchy we should soon put them down. They would never stand a chance with us.'

'Yet you too had your revolution in the last century, your industrial revolution which – '

'A bloodless revolution,' she interrupted.

'Yes, but they were within their rights to rebel against the insufferable conditions which your landed gentry imposed upon them, and they did win in the end with your Reform Bill and received a modicum of relief under your Lord Grey.'

'You know a lot about our history's politics. One would think you were in favour of your Bolsheviks or our Socialists, you who have seen or heard of horrors done to your people. Even if you escaped in time not to become a victim of your Reign of Terror, how can you condone them?'

'I do not condone them but I see both sides of the catastrophe that brought about the end of Imperial Russia. It is a question of revolt against capitalism.'

'Yet surely there must always be capitalists where men make money? These war profiteers and industrial millionaires, many of whom began with nothing – they have the brains to make fortunes. And why shouldn't they?'

'Why indeed; but not every man, only a very small minority is born with the brains to become a capitalist . . . Ah, here is our lobster.'

She watched the waiter who had been hovering to serve them, noting his hands, long sensitive hands, and then his face, and she recognized him as the waiter she had seen attending her at the Thistlewaites' *thé dansant* . . . Where, she asked herself, had she seen him before? That blond hair, a lock of it straying over a deep scar on his forehead. Of course! The Canadian, down with the 'flu, said his name was the same as ours. Very confused. High temperature. She would have liked to have asked him if he were ever in the Grosvenor Square Hospital but decided better not to, and in any case Riabovitch gave her no chance to speak to him. Having tasted and approved the bottle offered by the wine waiter he was asking her: 'I trust this hock will be to your liking?'

'I know it will be – a delicious dinner.'

Then as the waiters left them, she with appreciative negotiation of lobster *à l'amoricaine*, said: 'You hold a very broadminded and Christian attitude to what your revolutionaries have done to you and yours.'

And he, passing her a rack of toast Melba, 'Has it not been said that the Son of Man was a socialist?'

'That's what the socialists say in self-excuse or self-defence for their slogans of equal rights, fraternity and brotherhood and all the rest of it churned out to them by the Sidney Webb-idealism and Bernard Shaw, they who were so hot on it in the nineties. But would He have approved of murder to gain their ends? He threw out the merchants – the capitalists – who had turned the Temple into the equivalent of a stock market and made it a den of thieves, but He only thrashed them, He didn't kill them. I'm loving this lobster.'

He gave her a whimsical look from his low-lidded eyes.

'You are full of surprises. Although you are so delightfully naïve and seemingly unsophisticated in direct contrast to these young ultra-moderns, yet you express yourself in terms that one might expect to hear from Lady Astor, your first woman Member of Parliament. I shouldn't wonder if, in a few years' time, we shall see Lady Felicity Ross-Sutton elected member for Rodborough in Norfolk.'

'What! Me?' she laughed derisively. 'I can't even make a speech. I know you will say I can talk nineteen to the dozen and so I can in ordinary conversation with one person only. But to stand up before an audience – no! I

50

had to once when I was inveigled into opening a bazaar and I stood there like a fool with nothing to say except "Thank you very much for asking me to come here and now it is open" or words to that effect. The old lady who got me there was furious. Anyhow it'll be almost six years before I'll be allowed to vote. We have to be thirty for that. Oh, yes, and here's another thing I wanted to ask – or to tell you. When we met at the Thistlewaites' – what a name to have to say quickly! – you said I was much photographed and admired by the gossip scavengers or something of that sort which is how you knew who I was. Well, I am not the columnists' hot news. I have only been photographed twice in the *Tatler* and that was at a rather boring house party and at that bazaar, and once in the *Sketch* at one of the debs' weddings. I've never been a deb, I missed all that, thank goodness, being a V.A.D. and afterwards Daddy hadn't any money to launch me out nor did I want to be launched. I thought you ought to know that I am not a socialite. I am, in fact, inclined to be anti-social. You see?'

'I see, and you tell me nothing that I did not already know. But I had to give some reason for forcing myself upon you without an introduction. I had seen you before somewhere or other, and seeing you again I inquired your name of our hostess and dared to intrude on your talk with our host.'

'And you didn't even know he was your host. Oh, look! Isn't that Diana Cooper, just coming in?'

The restaurant was rapidly filling with late arrivals while Riabovitch entertained her in identifying those he knew by sight or personally.

'He who came in just after Lady Diana is Augustus John, and that leonine-headed fellow with the heavy jowl is the greatest sculptor of this century.'

'Oh, is that Epstein?' Felicity stared, all eyes. 'I can't say I admire his work very much – what I've seen of it – although I know some people compare him with

Michelangelo. I thought his sculptures rather coarse and ugly.'

'Have you not seen his delicate modelling of his little daughter, Peggy Jean, and the head of a very charming lady now in the Tate Gallery who might be the model for an Egyptian princess?' Then while Epstein waited at a nearby table, he was joined by his companion, a beautiful Indian girl. 'She,' said the prince, 'is his latest model; and here, just arriving, is Karsavina.'

Felicity gave a little gasp.

'I have seen her in the Ballet. She is wonderful. I adore the Ballet. We can never be grateful enough to Russia for giving us that which the Bolsheviks haven't destroyed.'

'On the contrary they encourage the Imperial Ballet. The Bolsheviks are not entirely without appreciation of beauty, and some of our foremost dancers are of the new régime.'

The wine waiter appeared with another bottle.

'You really must', said the prince, 'have this with the *filet mignon*.'

'I'll not be responsible for anything I may say or do if I have anything more to drink.'

'In which case I await the result of your irresponsibility with pleasurable anticipation. As for the Ballet, would you care to see the new Stravinsky ballet which is to be presented next week, or earlier than that? Lopokova will be delighting us again in *la Boutique Fantasque*.'

He is going rather too fast, she thought, but I can't resist *la Boutique*. And she temporized: 'I am getting rather booked up now because I am going to take a course of massage – not that I'll be any good at it. The Rodborough health place is very choosy, only engaging the most experienced of nurses and masseuses, but if they won't take me on for that – it will be ages before I am qualified, if ever – I might be shoved in to do night work, sitting up with nerve cases who are afraid to sleep alone.'

So she left his invitation with another loophole and,

having finished all there was of the excellent dinner and more than half the bottle of Beaujolais which he insisted she should share with him, she decided it was time to leave.

Feeling a trifle dizzy from unaccustomed wine, and inclined to sudden laughter for no apparent reason, she was driven back to Ashley Gardens.

'I have enjoyed myself im-*mensely*,' she told him with careful emphasis, 'and I think I am just a little tight. But it has been a lovely evening. Thanks aw-fully.'

'May I hope that such an evening may be repeated for your enjoyment?' He helped her out of the car, walked with her up the steps of the block to her flat, and lifting her hand to his lips he bade her, '*Au revoir*, Félise. Do you know your sentimental Swinburne's poem, "I loved you for that name of yours long ere we met, Félise"?...*Bon soir*, Félise.'

Her father was in his study when she let herself in with her latchkey. He sat in a deep armchair, his head drooping and faint sounds coming from his half-open mouth. As she entered the room he moved his head, jerking it up, to say:

'Where have you been? They never told me you were out and I had dinner alone.'

'I told Nannie to tell you but she's getting forgetful and, poor darling, deaf. I've had dinner with a Bolshie.'

'With a what?'

Rodborough's head jerked up again as if pulled by a wire.

'A Bolshie or near to one. He's an émigré prince and seems to be a sort of socialist idealist, like the Sidney Webbs, championing the underdog – his own underdogs – and taking the revolution and the murder of his Czar as all part of a Utopia where all men are equal. He didn't put it into those actual words but that's what he meant. . . .' She held a hand to her head. 'I'm a bit squiffy. He gave me a lot to drink.'

'The devil he did.' Her father sat upright. 'I'll not have

you going out with bogus princes – Bolshies or whatever – and coming home half seas over.'

'Don't be Edwardian, darling. You'll be ordering me a chaperone next. I like getting squiffed. It's a change from Nannie's bedtime malted milk. Oh,' as she made for the door she turned, 'he has a picture gallery and wants to see the Rembrandt if Christies haven't passed it. You might do a deal with him. He has some good pictures but nothing very particular. The Rembrandt might be possible. I told him it wasn't a certain thing, but he'd not think twice about selling it to an American for a . . . anyhow he'd give you a good price for it. We need it, don't we?' She dropped a kiss on his forehead where the red grizzled hair receded. 'Good night.'

THREE

From the Commonplace Book of me, Felicity Ross-Sutton

I have been reading a lot of the diaries Commonplace Books they called them of the girls ('young ladies' in those days) of the 18th and early 19th centuries to say nothing of Fanny Burney who has become immortalized. And as I seem to be a hopeless failure at anything I try to do – I'm no damn good at massage was turned down and the matron at Rodborough told me that her staff *must* be qualified nurses even for night duty. I suggested I might sit up with nerve cases but she'd have none of it. I could she said be a receptionist if I really wanted to be of some use in – (snobbishly) 'Your ladyship's old home. I would be very agreeable to oblige your ladyship in that respect to receive applicants . . .' No thank you. So that's it. I might have a shot at journalism with a view to becoming a writer. I remember when I met Arnold Bennett I forget where – ages ago just after the war – and he said if you want to be a writer (I must have told him I had thoughts about that. Very silly of me because I expect heaps of people women especially tell famous authors they want to be writers) and he said 'To be a writer you ought to start by keeping a diary.' So here it is and not a proper diary and I don't suppose I'll keep it up.

Well, I've been haunted by Riabovitch, Alex-eei short for Alexandrovitch, I suppose, as he asks me to call him and he *will* call me Fèlise which is rather sick-making. I can't shake him off. I wonder do I want to. I'm not really attracted more curious I think. He puzzles me. I can't make him out. If he's a White Russian why does he stick up for the Bolshies? Anyway he is useful to take me to the Ballet and I was thrilled to go behind at Covent Garden and be introduced to Karsavina and Lopokova. Both a bit disappointing close to and covered in grease paint. As for this other one (Russton as he now says is his name). More mystery! I'll write it down exactly as it happened.

I was walking home from Bond Street yesterday having called in at Sotheby's with that 18th century gold snuff box I found in a drawer in Daddy's desk while I was hunting for notepaper. We've run out as usual. Daddy wastes such a lot trying to type, which is even worse than my own two finger efforts. (Memo I must go to a typing bureau and learn to type since we can't afford a secretary.) And there was this lovely little snuff box. I asked Daddy about it and he said it had belonged to his father who took snuff and that it was probably left over from one of the great-greats. So I told him I'd take it to Sotheby's and have it judged. It might fetch a good price. We need it to pay Foster's wages and in any case if I learn to drive which I intend to do we shan't need a chauffeur and he can get rid of the Rolls which is vintage and buy a mass production one in part exchange. So off I went with the snuff box and a nice young man looked it over and said it was circa 1730 and a very pretty piece. They always call pieces pretty even if they are large and heavy like the Queen Anne tallboy which one of them came to see and we sent it to them but it only fetched half they thought it would Anne being out of date just now they vary according to what the dealers want for the Americans who are buying all our stuff. Anyway I left the snuff box there and walked back through St. James's Park and stayed by the lake watching the waterfowl and thinking that Charles II must have stood here to watch his waterfowl. He stocked the lake as I recall one of his biographers said. And while I stood there watching and loving the goldy sort of blue-ish day with a feeling of spring in the air and a scent strangely of primroses considering there are no primroses out yet but I saw a few crocuses in the grass behind the railings and had a nostalgic longing for Rodborough. Not for the Abbey which is such a muddley built-on mess of a place but for the woods and the wild part of the grounds and the spinney where the first spikes of the daffodils will be coming up if they haven't run the nine hole golf course there. Yes they're going to have a nine-hole golf course for the patients (I shall never be a writer if I go in for non-stop unpunctuated sentences) and then suddenly a voice behind me said Lady Felicity Ross-Sutton almost in my ear. I swung round and there was that waiter! He didn't look in the least like a waiter then being dressed like a stockbroker (without the topper which I believe stockbrokers wear) or a Civil servant in a bowler hat and well-tailored overcoat that looked like Savile Row. I am putting all this down because it is part of my impressions of him and increased the sense of mystery surrounding him who is hired out as a waiter and I was now certain I nursed him through the flu in 1919.

'So you know my name' I said eyeing him over. 'But I don't know yours although the first time I saw you or it may have been the second time you told me you had the same name as mine, Sutton you said it was but your temperature was right up so you weren't talking sense.'

'I am talking sense now,' he said, 'when I tell you my name may once have been the same as yours but it isn't now. It's Russton. Names get changed you know, particularly since the war if they sound at all German.'

'But neither Ross nor Sutton is German sounding' I told him 'and how did you know who I am? I know who you are because besides having had to bath you –'

'Yes, pity I wasn't more alive to that!'

– 'to get your temperature down,' I said coolly, 'I saw you at the Thistlewaites' handing me a cocktail or something and again at the Chanticleer and now you turn up looking like something out of Throgmorton Street –'

'Without the topper,' he put in.

'Just what I was thinking. Are you a thought reader like those people in the music halls who tell us all about ourselves with a confederate in the audience?' I said it jokingly but half believed it because I couldn't really place him as a waiter.

'Nothing like that,' he said, 'yet I sometimes get a sort of thought transference with people to whom I feel an affinity.'

c

I had nothing to say to this being more mystified than ever. His voice had hardly a trace of the accent which I associated with him as being slightly American when he was delirious. We were still standing by the lake and a duck with her ducklings came floating by. He took a packet of something from the brief case he carried I noticed then that he carried a brief case and from a paper packet he fumbled for some bits of cake and threw it to the duck. She and her brood fell on it.

'Do you come here often distributing largesse to birds?'

'Quite often when I have time off.'

'From waiting?'

'Yes.' He had finished the last of what he had brought and we both turned to walk together away from there. It seemed quite a natural thing to do. For my part I was interested. For his part was he trying to get fresh I wondered?

'What,' I asked him, 'did you do when you left the army? Were you non-commissioned?'

'Yes. I could have had a commission but preferred to be a ranker.'

'Are you Canadian?'

'No. I went to Canada when I was two years old. Later I was sent to England to school. First to a prep school and then to Winchester where my father went and then to Toronto University where I stayed just long enough to take my degrees before war broke out and I went back to England and joined up. But although I lived some of my life in Canada I was born in England of English parents so I am English.'

'But why if you took degrees – what in by the way?'

'In maths and languages. A first in maths and a second in languages.'

'Then if you have a first and second why do you take jobs as a waiter? Couldn't you have been a schoolmaster?' I suppose it was cheek of me to keep on at him in this way but I was determined to find out who and what he was. He didn't seem to mind. He answered quite readily.

'I could have been a schoolmaster in a prep school or even maths master at Winchester if I'd applied for it but I wasn't keen on teaching junior schoolboys algebra and geometry, besides I see more of life in the job I've undertaken. I can come and go places. I can always get a job at hotels in the South of France where the new rich sprawl on the beaches sun-bathing and are lavish with their tips. I was at Monte Carlo last year,' he chuckled, 'when they rounded up the gang who got an American millionaire's jewels. His wife's jewels, if you remember, worth a quarter of a million.'

'I don't. So you didn't go back to Canada after the war?' I kept on at him. I can't think why. Just something about him I couldn't get at.

'I had nothing to go back for – or rather to stay there for,' he said after some hesitation. 'My father died during the war. He and my mother had separated as a matter of fact. She went off with another man. An American, rolling in money. It rather broke up my father. There was a divorce and my father had the custody of me.'

'You have no brothers or sisters?'

'No. So as there was only myself left and no home anywhere I stayed on in England when I was demobbed.'

We walked on awhile in silence. I glanced at him sideways. He was smiling to himself. He had taken off his bowler and the thin wintry sun shone on his hair gilding it. I saw the scar under a lock that had fallen over his forehead. I asked him, 'That wound over your eye which half sliced your head – I remember I had to change the dressings when you were sent to us with the flu. How and where did you get it?'

He told me how.

'In Palestine when a Turkish sniper got me. That's how I got my Blighty one. I came home in a hospital ship just in time for the flu!'

So he came back to the flu being so debilitated it's a wonder he didn't die of it as did Ronnie . . . (Oh, Ronnie to have come through all that hell and then . . .) I think something rolled out of my eye as I thought of Ronnie dying when his arm was only just healed and he had all his life before him at twenty-three and he not the only one out of millions and Russton said – I am calling him Russton as he says that's his name a sort of combination of Ross-Sutton – 'You mustn't take other people's troubles too much to heart.

You did a splendid selfless work looking after all of us who did come back and I have to thank you for the fact that I'm here walking in a London park with you on an almost spring day.'

I told him 'You don't have to thank me. I didn't pull you through that plague which was striking down so many thousands. I only did what I was told to do by Sister who had her orders from the doctor. They were wonderful those doctors fighting day and night not only in hospitals but all over the country regardless of infection.'

'As so were you.'

'To tell you the truth,' I said, 'I was in a blue funk lest I'd get it because Daddy already had it and I was terrified in case my brother should get it as he was a Blighty one too having all but lost his arm when he crashed coming back from Flanders. He was in the R.F.C. And he did get it and he – died.'

He said: 'I know he died.'

I stared at him.

'How did you know?'

'It was in all the papers.'

'But you were too ill to read the papers.'

'No I wasn't. You were on leave when I was able to sit up and take notice. I read about your brother's death and that you had been nursing at your father's house in Grosvenor Square turned into a hospital and so I was interested to see you with my whole eye at the Thistlewaites'.'

'Are you hired – do you let yourself out,' I corrected in a hurry – 'to parties and things?'

'Sometimes. The Thistlewaites borrowed me from the Chanticleer that day!'

By this time we had come to the gates of the park.

'I've got a car here,' he said, 'can I drive you wherever you want to go?'

A car! And he a waiter and dressed up like that. I wondered if he was some man's valet and in his time off had pinched his boss's clothes so I said 'No thanks. I live only a short way from here. Ashley Gardens. Goodbye. Nice to have seen you and looking so well,' putting on my V.A.D. voice.

He said, 'Must it be goodbye? Am I not to see you again for a walk through the park? What about Richmond next Sunday? Sundays are my days off.'

Me, a bit flustered. 'I don't think I can manage Sundays. My father expects me to be with him.'

'Doesn't he play golf on Sundays or do you have to play with him?'

'No, I don't play. I can't get the ball off the tee and he's a four handicap . . .' I was beginning to want to walk with him again in a park. Even if he was a waiter he had taken a first in maths and what did it matter if he *were* a waiter – a real one. I quite liked him. Not exactly good looking. He had a comic mouth that turns up at the corners when he smiles which gives him rather an endearing little boy look, and the good eye the one that hadn't got the slice over it is a very good eye a sheer periwinkle blue. Mine are green being a redhead. How I hate my hair. If only I'd been a blonde like he is but if so he might not have wanted to walk in a park with me. They don't always like their own colour . . .

The walk in Richmond Park which did eventually take place is briefly recorded in the 'Commonplace Book' under February 26th.

Russton (he said his Christian name was Ronald) fetched me from the flat. I only told him Ashley Gardens and gave him no telephone number so he must have driven round the blocks looking for our names or asked the porters. Anyway he found me and sent the porter up to say he was there. Richmond Park was looking lovely such a wonderfully early spring I expect we shall have snow in April. He asked if I would like to ride there if he could bring horses. I said I would so he arranged it for next Monday. . . .

Further extracts from the 'Book' formulate the gist of that ride which may have gone something like this.

On another 'wonderfully early spring' day she met him as arranged outside the entrance to her flat. Having seen her father off to golf, she told Nannie, who saw her in her habit, that she was going to ride in Richmond Park with one of the men she had nursed in hospital and whom she had met again at the Thistlewaites'. Avoiding more questions she made a hurried exit and disappeared down the lift calling to Nannie at the door: 'I may not be back to lunch'. And to the lift boy, 'Tell her in case she didn't hear. She's rather deaf.'

Russton was waiting for her in a red Aston Martin. He drove expertly through the traffic taking short cuts behind Hammersmith and so to Barnes Common and the gates of Richmond Park. There a man on a fine grey horse and leading another dismounted as the car approached. He was a short, stocky fellow with the look of a jockey but not young, middle-aged, and wearing well-worn breeches and a shabby tweed coat. Russton got out of the car, had a few words with him and came back to Felicity.

'This', he said, 'is a friend of mine,' introducing him as: 'Frank Hobson, who runs a livery stable here in Richmond and looks after my two for me – that's mine, the grey, and also the mare. I've recently bought her. She's just two years old and looks to be a winner.'

If Felicity were mildly surprised that Russton, whether a waiter or not, could afford to keep a couple of horses one of which looked to be a winner, she made no comment. She was at the mare's head, a handsome chestnut with a white star on her forehead and a restless white to her eye.

She said: 'She's a beauty. Do you race her?'

'I hope to later on. I'll ride her today and you can ride Egmont. He is quieter than the mare. She might be a bit too much for you.'

'I have ridden almost as soon as I could walk,' she retorted, nettled, 'and I have yet to find a horse that's too much for me.' And then she flushed as she saw him smile and hated herself because he might have thought her bragging. 'As of course,' she records it, 'I was – a little.'

'Next time,' he said, 'you can try her but she's too fresh today. This is her first good outing for two days, isn't it,

Frank?' To Hobson who nodded and: 'Take the car,' he was told, 'and bring it back in about – ' he looked at his wrist watch – 'two hours or, if later, I'll ring you.'

'Right, sir.' He touched his cap, which again somewhat surprised Felicity as did also the 'sir'. Then handing over the mare to Russton he led the other horse forward and made as if to give Felicity a leg up, but she had swung herself into the saddle and was leaning over to shorten the stirrup leathers. 'I like to ride short for a gallop,' she said. 'I remember a good grassy stretch uphill here where I used to ride sometimes when we were in London before the war.' She stroked the grey's neck. 'He's lovely too but much older than the mare, isn't he?'

'Yes, he's ten and ripe for another ten, I'm hoping.'

'Have you had him long?'

'Since he was foaled. I went to fetch him back from Toronto when I was demobbed. Now, shall we?'

They broke into a canter and she, who had not ridden for several weeks, not since they had finally sold Rodborough, was elated with the joy of it. 'What a beautiful action he has!' she cried. 'It's like sitting in an easy chair.'

It was a crystal bright morning, the sun high in the blue where feathery transparent clouds drifted breeze-blown, light as swansdown. Oak trees spread their shadows across the grass and springing fern fronds as they passed, to merge with their own tall shapes astride their mounts, while bird song welcomed the sun and this early breath of spring. She was hard behind Russton although at full gallop; the mare was certainly fresh and well ahead until he slowed to allow her to come up with him.

'I'll admit she may be rather too much for me today,' she said, panting, 'but not,' she added quickly, 'on another day.'

'And let's hope there will be another day,' he said with that lift of the mouth she had described as his 'little boy look'.

63

They rode quietly on now to give the horses a breather, until, 'Oh, see!' she pointed with her riding crop, 'the deer.'

A tall stag with his doe had come silently through the greenery to stand quite still and close to them as they halted their horses. 'How tame they are,' she whispered, 'and there's another one, look – so pale a fawn she might be white.'

' "The lily white doe Lord Ronald had brought leapt up from where she lay, dropped her head in the maiden's hand and followed her all the way". . . . And then it goes on later with "He turned and kissed her where she stood" I think I've gone wrong here – and tumpty tumpty tumpty tum, "if you are not the Lady Clare we two will wed to-morrow's morn and you will still be Lady Clare. . . ." I see in Debrett that your second name is Clare.'

She tapped her heel against the horse's side and rode ahead; he caught up with her at once.

'I didn't think', she told him, 'there was anyone under thirty today who read and could quote Tennyson, or if he did it was to scoff at him. We of the post-war generation profess to despise sentiment, and Tennyson is surely the arch-sentimentalist.'

'That may be, but I am not under thirty. I am a year over it as a matter of fact. Today.'

'Is it your birthday?'

'Yes, it is; and I could not have had a nicer birthday present than this ride with you. Can I hope to have a birthday lunch to follow? We can find a hotel. The Star and Garter in my young days in London – '

'I thought', she interrupted quickly, 'you were in Canada in your young days.'

'Not all of them. Some of the time I was at prep school and Winchester and there was an uncle – he got killed in the war – I used to stay with him in the holidays. He had a house near here at Coombe Hill. I was about to say that the Star and Garter used to be the place to come for a decent meal – quite the thing to do twenty or so years ago – to drive out here in the evening and dine on the terrace, but since the war it is a hospital for war casualties. You can see those who can walk walking or being wheeled about in their hospital blue. So what about my phoning Frank to pick us up? I'll tell him where. There's a place on the Hill.'

'But I can't go to lunch in a hotel like this,' she objected.

'Why not?' he eyed the slim figure and the jodhpured leg in its shortened stirrups nearest to him, gripping the grey's satin side. 'You look stunning.'. . .

'So that, she ends up her account of the day's outing, was definitely that.'

When she arrived home Nannie greeted her with: 'Three phone calls for you, two from that Russian prince and one from Lady Caversham who wants to know why you've not been to see her lately. You had better ring her up and tell her you'll be going. Who's this young man you've been out with all day?'

'Not all day. It is not yet four o'clock, and didn't I tell you he is one of the patients I nursed in the hospital.'

'Five years ago that was, and to turn up again now!'

Felicity made no comment to that which she knew was intended to lead up to more about this nameless young man who had 'turned up again' now. She went to her room and changed from her habit, took a bath and telephoned her great-aunt – her mother's only aunt – Lady Caversham, leaving a message that she would come to see her ladyship tomorrow afternoon if convenient.

No sooner had she replaced the receiver than Riabovitch came through to her.

'Félise! I've been trying to get you. I have tickets for *Les Sylphides* tonight from a client who is ill and unable to use them, and has handed them over to me. Will you come to the Ballet and have supper at the Embassy afterwards?'

'Oh, well . . . I don't know. I've only just come in from riding at Richmond and I'm a bit tired.'

'At your age riding at Richmond shouldn't tire you and you have a good three hours to rest before we meet. Please. I haven't seen you for more than a week.'

'*Les Sylphides*, you said?'

'Yes, and the Embassy afterwards, unless you don't want to?'

She thought: Do I want to? And have I anything to wear for the Embassy? My old Lucille . . . 'Thanks. I'd like to. . . . Can't miss Sylphides.'

'Good. I'll call for you at seven-forty-five.'

She hung up the receiver and stood looking at it.

In the old days, she reflected, all this could only mean one thing. He'd be asking my father for my 'hand'. Do I want him to have it? I don't know. I just don't *know*. . . . There had been at least three before him who had wanted her 'hand' but had not asked her father for it, merely casually suggested, 'Shall we? Honestly I'm mad about you.' Or, 'I'm not keen on marriage but I can't get you any other way – ' Or, simply, 'Let's get married.' Not any one of them would she have even considered marrying. Did she want to be married or was she a confirmed spinster as some men are confirmed bachelors? As a woman she could not have any trial trips. Bachelors could have a dozen, but spinsters must be virgins all the days of their lives. Of course many of them were not, especially now they have the vote. . . . I wouldn't shy at a trial trip myself if I liked anyone enough.

The Ballet as usual enthralled her. She had taken pains with her face, deplored her hair and noticed a sprinkling of more freckles than ever on her nose from the effects of the sun which, although not yet quite spring, had brought them out. Russton had remarked on them while they sat at luncheon in the hotel on the Hill eating cold beef and pickles, her choice in preference to roast pork. He had said, 'You're as freckled as a cowslip.'

66

'Do you mind them?' she asked him, thinking: that's the nicest thing that's ever been said about freckles!

'Mind? I adore them – and your hair.'

'I hate my hair. Carrots.'

'Chestnut, like my mare.'

And now as she sat with Riabovitch in the stalls at Covent Garden, she was conscious of and a little resented her involuntary response to his proximity, his arm just touching hers; but no word other than their mutual enthusiasm for Karsavina and Massine, encroached upon more intimate discussion when, during the interval, he brought her a gin and tonic and gave himself a brandy. Then later to the Embassy Club. There were several celebrities of stage and society present and among them, somewhat to Felicity's surprise, a party of four over which presided, very much in evidence as hostess, Mrs Thistlewaite, with her husband and a portly gentleman whom Riabovitch recognized as Sir Malcolm Barlow, K.C., accompanied by a faded little woman in puce, presumably his wife.

'He has recently taken silk,' said the prince, 'and is one of the foremost criminologists of our day.'

Other notabilities were pointed out to her by Riabovitch, who seemed to be acquainted with a great many of them although they did not appear to know him. 'That is Mrs Hwfa Williams,' he indicated a resplendent lady at a nearby table, 'one of your famous society hostesses; and there, just coming in, the well-known American star of revue, Tallulah Bankhead. Ah, yes, and a compatriot of mine, Rakovsky, the Russian *Chargé d'Affaires* over here who has been busy establishing himself as the latest lion of London drawing-rooms. And that lovely lady with him is the Countess of Warwick, who professes to champion the revolutionaries.'

'Yes,' said Felicity, 'we know all about her. She is her own best publicity agent.'

And now, greatly more to her surprise, she saw Russton

attending on the table of the *Chargé d'Affaires*, Rakovsky, and Lady Warwick.

I can't believe it! was her first reaction to this. What is he? *Who* is he? A waiter on his 'on' days or something else on his 'off' days? As today in Richmond Park and other days, and a thoroughbred and a half-bred fetched over from Canada. He didn't get him over here on his wages as a waiter, and how can he afford to keep the pair of them with his 'friend' who calls him 'sir'. 'I give it up.' She concluded this aloud and blushed to her eyebrows to hear herself say it, and saw the prince's inquiring look at her: 'You give up what?'

'Only some speculation,' she fabricated hastily, 'as to why so eminent a, er, criminologist as Sir Malcolm, um, Bartlett did you say – ?'

'Barlow,' corrected Riabovitch.

– 'should come to disport himself in the midst of these frivolities when he has probably – ' She was rather gabbling now, for Russton's sound eye had met hers between a second and a second, and she saw that uplift, briefly, of the corners of his mouth – 'I mean he may just have come from the Old Bailey after having committed someone to death by hanging.'

'He is rigidly opposed to capital punishment, I understand, but as the law will have it so must he; yet I gather he has said that had he defended Mrs Thompson in the Bywaters-Thompson case he would have got her off, although Sir Henry Curtis-Bennett made a wonderfully good effort. Shall we dance?'

It was a fox-trot crooned by the younger ones: '*You made me love you, I didn't want to do it . . .*' Her cool hair, shingled in the nape, the latest fashion, was against his lips, his cheek a quarter of an inch from hers, but over his shoulder she saw Russton standing by the Thistle-waites' table taking an order. No further sign of recognition passed from him to her. Then, as they followed the dancers on the narrow floor, she saw directly in front of them, partnering one of last year's much-publicized debs, a short, fair-haired young man with a prettyish pink face and boils on his neck above his collar.

'You see who he is?' whispered the prince in her ear.

'Not – ?'

'I've seen him before,' she whispered back, 'but never so near as this. His photographs flatter him as Prince Charming. Am I guilty of *lèse majesté* if I say he is almost the double of the boy who delivers our groceries?'

Riabovitch uttered a muted laugh. 'Our own young Czarevitch might easily have passed as an errand boy. Blood doesn't always out.'

'Unless', she retorted, '*let* out – in murder!'

He made no immediate reply to that until, as the dance ended and they returned to their table: 'There is some doubt', he said, 'that the Czarevitch suffered the same fate as did his father and the rest of his family. In fact there is a belief that not only he but one of his sisters is alive. Revolutionaries are not all intentional murderers, you know.'

A waiter was hovering. 'Ah yes! I did order. *Escalopes de veau*, they do it rather well here.'

The waiter – not Russton, she was relieved to see – bowed and hurried off while Riabovitch resumed: 'I hope you like *escalopes de veau*. It was remiss of me not to ask.'

'I like anything. I don't care what I eat in this sort of place. I like watching people.'

'Quite so.' He obviously wasn't listening to that, intent on the subject which he now continued.

'I was saying that not all revolutionaries are murderers. I did not go to a university. I was taught by tutors at my home in St Petersburg, but I had a good many friends at the university, students who were idealists rather than revolutionaries. They would argue and debate endlessly about the future of the world and the Rights of Man, professing heartily, and I think sincerely, against the accumulation of wealth by individuals, that is to say the capitalists. They demanded equality for all, defiant of authoritative bureaucracy. They were infected with the bacteria of revolution and that resulted, as with the French, in a nation-wide epidemic which, contrary to belief, did not – at least not in Russia – entirely germinate among the down-trodden working classes and peasants but also among the intelligentzia that draws its beliefs from those Marxist others whom they regard as demi-gods. From the scattered seeds sown by such as these were the Bolshevik revolutionaries born.'

You have a bee in your bonnet about Bolshevism, she wanted to say but didn't. He got on to this the first time I dined with him. . . . Instead she said:

'Some of our own varsity boys hold similar beliefs as do your students. There is a club somewhere in Soho founded in 1917. I was taken to it once by one of them. They were all, or professed to be, Socialists, demanding equality and down with capitalism for the betterment of man, and red hot for Labour. It's an infection that attacks the young like measles and chicken-pox. Most of them get over it. Some don't and then they hope to stand for Parliament. Some do – with aspirations to become Prime Minister! There was a member to whom I was introduced whose name is Attlee. A rather insignificant little man who works in the East End among the poor. He hadn't much to say but I gathered he was very earnest – another of your idealists.'

They ate in silence for a few minutes while he sampled the wine, and she sipped from the glass filled by the waiter. The band was playing a seductive waltz.

'Shall we?' suggested Riabovitch.

They got up and joined the dancers. As they passed the Thistlewaites' table they were delightedly hailed by Ethel calling:

'Won't you join us, Prince, and – Lady Felicity?'

Riabovitch halted, his arm reluctantly sliding from Felicity's back.

70

'Madame,' he bowed effusively; and Ethel introduced them with some aplomb as: 'His Highness, Prince Riabovitch, and Lady Felicity Ross-Sutton.' The two men stood, and Albert offered her his chair: 'What a p . . . leasant encounter, Lady Felicity and, er, Prince . . . Pray join us.'

A waiter, at a gesture from Mrs Thistlewaite, supplied two more chairs.

Without seeming ungracious, Riabovitch was persuaded to accept the invitation with which Felicity, *faute de mieux*, unwillingly complied.

Sir Malcolm, whose somewhat goggly eyes were fixed admiringly upon her, said:

'I know your father, Lord Rodborough. We are both members of the Athenaeum.'

And Felicity thinking: What a waste of those escalopes, smiled up at him saying: 'Yes, my father is a member but he doesn't often go there.'

'Too busy in the Upper House,' boomed Sir Malcolm, 'I presume?'

'He has only to my knowledge spoken six times in about twenty years,' was her reply to that.

And he, greedily goggling, 'You could scarcely have been born twenty years ago so you can hardly have known.'

She thought, he may be a leading light of the Bar but I'd say he's a lecherous old rip and his wife, poor little thing, looks like a plucked hen. . . .

Coffee was brought, served by Russton. She smothered a giggle as again for the briefest second, their eyes met. Then he moved to the next table occupied by Lady Warwick and the Russian *Chargé d'Affaires*.

The conversation at the Thistlewaites' table now became general. . . . 'Which,' so Felicity records it, 'was all about nothing. Mrs T. taken with the flushes – her time of life, I suppose – was full of the P. of W. dancing again with that deb and saying, "I wonder if she will be his

Royal Highness's chosen. She is, after all, the daughter of a duke, so it isn't the law any more that they must marry royalty. He ought to be married soon." '

And so, thought Felicity, should I, but I won't. . . .

In her Commonplace Book she adds an N.B. to her account of that night's entertainment.

> Russton was waiting almost exclusively on the Russian *Chargé dAffaires* and Lady W. but I did see Mr T. signal to him in that timid way of his to give him an order in his mumbly voice that brought him a glass of iced water. With the glass was a note and after reading it Mr T. asked permission to be excused for a moment. 'One of my co-directors on the Board has asked for a word with me. He is over there –' he indicated vaguely to somewhere that couldn't possibly be seen among the dancers. He got up and shambled off and Mrs T. barked to him as he went: "Surely you don't have to discuss business with your Board *here?*'
>
> Poor little man. I imagine Lady Barlow and he are equally brow-beaten by their respective mates. I suppose Mr T. is also a capitalist when you think of the millions of Waites W.C.s there are all over Britain and perhaps all over Europe. I hope he gives some of it to charity but she probably wouldn't let him. . . .

Riabovitch drove her home in a taxi and having seen her to the entrance of the flat after telling the driver to wait, he asked:

'May I come in? I have something to say to you that could not be said there.'

The light of the street lamp fell full on his face. His eyes, very dark, seemed to smoulder as he gazed down at her.

'What – must you now?' she said. 'It is past two o'clock.'

'Yes, please. Now. I must.'

She felt an apprehensive stir of her heart. She could guess what that something he had to say would be.

Without another word she went before him into the hall. A sleepy night porter got up from his seat and ushered them into the lift. It stopped on the third floor. She took a latch key from her bag and opened the door.

'I never let my old nurse wait up for me,' she told him and led the way into the drawing-room. The fire in the grate had almost burnt itself out. She switched on the lights. There was a Thermos and a covered dish of sandwiches on a side table.

'This,' she said pointing to the Thermos, 'is my nightcap. Malted milk that Nannie always makes me have. I often throw it down the sink.' She was trying to speak lightly, fending him off. 'But I could do with these sandwiches, having been done out of most of the good supper you ordered.' She lifted the dish cover and took a sandwich. 'Will you have one? They are very good. Potted meat made from Nannie's own recipe.'

He shook his head and came to her, taking her hand as she raised the sandwich to her lips.

'Félise! You must have seen – have known how I feel about you.'

His almost black eyebrows were drawn together over his eyes which, seen in the lights of the red-shaded wall brackets, seemed to reflect a red spark as if, she thought, he had a fire inside him. His hand closed over hers.

'No, don't!' she made a laughing thing of it. 'You are squashing my sandwich and I'm hungry.'

'So am I!' He released her hand; the crumpled sandwich fell to the ground as he gathered her into his arms. 'Hungry for you, Félise. I want you – I need you. Marry me. Will you? Can you?' He bent his head and fastened his mouth on hers. In that long stormy kiss she burned in response to his passion. So it had come as she had known and feared and . . . hoped?

From out of far-off vacancy as she wrenched away from him she heard herself say:

'I . . . didn't know . . . I can't be sure. You must give me time.'

73

'You did know,' he said. 'You must have known, but I'll give you all the time in the world.'

And with that abruptly he turned and left her.

She waited until she could hear the slow closing of the front door and the rise of the lift for which he had rung. Then she went over to the table and finished the sandwiches.

All the time in the world . . . for him?

FOUR

Lady Caversham, the childless septuagenarian widow of General Sir Jeremy Caversham, K.C.V.O., and aunt of the late Lady Rodborough, Felicity's mother, lived with her companion, Miss Bates, five servants, a parrot and a Pekinese in a house in Green Street.

Felicity, having lain awake from two-thirty until five on the morning after Riabovitch's declaration and his sudden departure while she debated as to whether or not she wished to be given all the time in the world for her answer and if it should be in the affirmative or negative, presented herself to her Great Aunt Harriet on the afternoon of that same day.

She was received in a drawing-room lavishly furnished with Louis Quinze gilt chairs, mostly reproduction; a ceiling painted, after Leighton, exhibiting semi-nudes in flowing garments surrounded by Cupids bearing flowery wreaths, a quantity of bric-à-brac and occasional tables; also a grey parrot in an immense cage between the two tall windows and, at the feet of Lady Caversham, a dog basket with no dog in it.

Great-Aunt Harriet's husband had left her in her seventieth year a considerable income derived from an annuity that disappointingly lost Lord Rodborough his expectations of a substantial legacy to his daughter, who could not have cared less about it either way.

'So you are here at last,' was the greeting offered by Aunt Harriet with a much berouged cheek to be dutifully kissed. 'Your father has not been near me for three months and you not for three weeks. A new hat?'

'No, Aunt, two years old.'

'You look pale. Ring for tea.'

Tea was brought on a trolley laden with a silver tea service, an iced cake decorated with sugared violets, dishes of *petits fours* and wafer-thin sandwiches.

'You don't have to,' said Aunt Harriet as the butler made as if to pour out. 'She will. You can go.'

He went.

'No sugar, no milk. Lemon. I'm banting,' her ladyship informed her great-niece who was wielding the heavy Georgian teapot. 'Put on three pounds. Must take 'em off. You're too thin. Skinny. No busts. No bottoms. Girls of today. No hair. Do you like mine?'

Hers was a palpably black wig entwined with some not very real pearls. Without waiting for a reply to that, Lady Caversham reached for a sandwich, saying while she masticated: 'What's this I hear of you and a Russian prince gallivanting all over the place and a picture gallery?'

Again no answer to that question while Felicity uncomfortably wondered, not for the first time, if Aunt Harriet were quite so deaf as she professed to be. She wore, on this occasion, a gown of sapphire-blue velvet, a dog collar of some more pearls, these real ones, and a hearing aid concealed on her chest by a fall of rose-point lace, yet she often used an ear trumpet.

'I may be hard of hearing,' said Aunt Harriet, 'but none so deaf as those who won't hear or only hear what they want to hear. And what *I* want to hear is – has he any money? Most of these Russian émigrés have nothing. Quite a few of them Bolshies. Have a slice of the cake. The cook made it specially for you. Why violets? Mixing you up with Jeremy's sister Violet. My age. Came for two nights a week ago. She's seventy-five. The cook too. No teeth. I have. All but four. Molars.'

Felicity, whom long custom had inured to Aunt Harriet's inconsequential speech in which, if she asked a question, she seldom waited for or indeed expected an answer, cut a slice of the cake and asked herself who could have been talking to Aunt Harriet about her and Riabovitch. Someone who had seen her with him must have retailed it to the old lady's hearing aid or trumpet.

'It's a delicious cake,' she said.

'These Bolshies,' Lady Caversham pursued. 'He encourages them.'

'Who encourages whom, Aunt?' ventured Felicity now out of her depth.

'Eh?' Her ladyship inclined an ear. 'MacDonald of course. Ramsay. If he were not so good looking he wouldn't have stood a chance. The Londonderry all over him. But it's time we had a change. The Conservatives in too long. The Liberals are done for. Lloyd George did for them. The dole. I have a good recipe for freckles. Found in an old book. Belonged to my grandmother. Distilled from water of pineapples and crushed strawberries. I'll give it you. Bates will make it up.'

Felicity thanked her and asked: 'Do you think Labour will stay in, Auntie?'

'Certain. He has charm. The women. If you've finished. Ring.'

Felicity rang and the butler appeared.

'Tell Bates to come. Have you done your doodies, darling?' This not to the butler, to the Peke that had followed him into the room and whose age as dogs' ages go, equalled Lady Caversham's. He was lifted on to her lap, his black protruding eyes fixed on the trolley. 'Cream, Simpson. In a saucer. Only a drip. There then, angel,' as the saucer with the drip was placed under his button of a nose. He lapped, sighed, and jumped down to ensconce himself in his basket.

The trolley was wheeled out and Miss Bates came in; an emaciated hen-faced virgin of fifty whose forehead was corrugated in perpetually inquiring and anxious lines.

'Recipe for freckles, Bates. Book calls vices of the skin. Crushed strawberries and pineapple water.'

'Yes, Lady Caversham, but there are no strawberries at this time of the year.'

'Nonsense. What about bottled? Or strawberry jam? Why vices? If no strawberries. Lemon. Just as good. Put it in a flask and bring it here. Or if not ready before Lady Felicity goes have it sent round to her.'

'Yes, Lady Caversham. How nice to see you, Lady Felicity, and looking so well.'

'Did you say – ' Aunt Harriet raised her hearing aid from under its cascade of lace – 'looking so well? A stock phrase. She doesn't. Too pale. Too thin. So are you.' Her ladyship cackled. 'Both on the shelf and need to be taken off it. Too late for you, Bates, and if Felicity don't take care, too late for her. Girls are marrying at eighteen now. Few men left. Have to grab what they can get. Not so sure about this prince. Probably bogus. Most of them are.'

Felicity got up.

'I'm afraid I must go, Aunt. I have to see a man about a – '

'Dog?' put in Aunt Harriet with a grin that showed all her yellow top teeth. 'Men used to say that in the nineties. Meaning a bitch. Couldn't get one of their own kind unless they married 'em. Hanging round the stage door of the Gaiety in my time. Half the peerage of the future will be the sons of chorus girls. Why not? Good honest stock. We're too closely inbred. Mongrels more intelligent than sons of champions. He's one,' pointing a finger at the somnolent Peke. 'Has a dozen champions behind him but his father was a fool. Always had doubts of his granddam. Had a mongrel once. More intelligent than the whole House of Commons and that's not saying much. Who wants to be the wife of a Russian whether Red, White or Pink? Ever heard of Zinoviev?'

'No, Aunt.' Felicity was pulling on her gloves. 'Who is he?'

'One of 'em. Not here. Over there. I have a nephew out of Jeremy's sister's lot. In the F.O. Been over to Russia. Known a mouthful. Didn't tell me but I keep my ears open – without this!' she rearranged the fall of lace. From beneath it was emitted a series of squeaks. 'Will have my aurist see to it. Beastly thing. Can't beat an ear trumpet but so obtrusive. Like a gramophone stuck on you. If not about a dog about what?'

'A car, Auntie. I'm learning to drive. Daddy will sell the Rolls and we'll have a cheaper one.'

'Rodborough has no money. Used to have. I knew your grandmother. Pretty woman. Also a Ross-Sutton. Your father born after sixteen years. Pity there's no heir. There should be one knocking about somewhere. Your father ought to know but don't expect he'd want to.' She nodded closing her lips on that as if she never meant to open them again.

The parrot, a grey, gave a loud squawk, swinging back and forth on its perch, preceding the words 'Silly old bastard damyereyes.'

'Naughty Polly.' Lady Caversham shook an admonishing finger. 'Your Uncle Jeremy bought him from a sailor in a pub. Years ago. Before we were married. He's eighty. Live for ever. Picked up bad language. So amusing. Greys talk. Greens don't. Not like these. I knew a woman had a grey. Talked. Not so much as this one. She thought it was a he and it laid an egg. Polly horrified the Vicar. Not that I go to church. He visits me in hope. Will never come again. Last time Polly,' Lady Caversham cackled again, 'called him a silly old – something worse. Thought I'd taught it him.'

''Bye Auntie,' squawked Polly echoing Felicity's farewell.

'Scratch a poll Auntie silly old bugger.'

Miss Bates came to see her out.

'That dreadful bird,' she whispered. 'Lady Caversham doesn't seem to mind. I think she encourages him.'

Leaving Green Street Felicity hailed a taxi and was driven to the Euston Road. There, in a garage flanked by a large window in which were ranged cars of various sizes and makes, she was met by a smiling young man in over-alls.

'I have just been over her, miss – m'lady. She's all right. There's not another the likes of her at the price in a month o' Sundays. She's given away to you for a hundred and fifty.'

'You said a hundred.'

'Not this one, miss – she's the latest model. What you saw was two years old.'

'I don't like the colour.' Felicity walked round to inspect the latest model, a Standard. 'Green does something to me. Unlucky. I had a green coat and my dog – I adored him – he was a Great Dane, my brother's dog, died of eating rat poison that some swine had laid down to get rid of the rats in our stables. And before that I had a green dress and my brother died. I know it's silly.'

'We all has our fancies, miss. I've mine. I sat down thirteen to a table once and was the first to get up and my mother died.'

'She would probably have died in any case, but I can understand how you feel. Have you one of the same year as this in another colour?'

'Sorry, miss, no. But I can spray her for you. What colour would you like?'

'Dark blue, if it isn't cheating because it is green underneath.'

'Dark blue it shall be and no extra charge if cash down.'

'All right.'

She did some rapid thinking. Daddy doesn't know of this. He'll have a fit when I tell him he must sell the Rolls and get rid of Foster. We just can't pay all these wages. I've got a hundred saved up from my dress allowance, have bought no clothes for ages and if Sothebys sell the snuff box – it should fetch at least fifty, maybe more, and if Riabovitch takes the Rembrandt which isn't one . . .

'Right,' she said. 'But you must wait until I've had four more lessons and then I'll buy it. You'll keep it for me?'

80

'Sure, m'lady. I'm sending the same chap to take you tomorrow. At what time would suit you?'

'About eleven at the flat.'

Out again in the Euston Road she got on a bus bound for Victoria Station. From there she walked to Ashley Gardens. At the entrance to her block of flats she saw the chocolate Daimler and glimpsed the head of Riabovitch at the wheel, waiting for her to come back, of course, having been told she was not at home.

She darted behind the car, crossed the road and went into the Cathedral. Mass was being sung and the great church half filled with devotees. She would often go in there; it gave her peace and a feeling of reverence and uplift. She had never received much religious instruction. At Rodborough, before her mother died and afterwards when she and her father were in residence on the few occasions during the war, she would go to Callodon church with him, less from devotion than because he felt he ought to set an example to the villagers of whom he was still the 'Squire', although almost all the cottages and the home farm had been sold to the purchasers of the Abbey. She seldom spoke to her father of his beliefs. She guessed him to be an agnostic. Was she?

Kneeling there in that vast place, with the light of candles on the altar and the officiating priests in their colourful vestments, hearing the chanting of the glorious Latin she found herself saying inwardly, O, God, if You are here and everywhere – give me faith. Let me believe. Is Ronnie with You? Is there a heaven? If You are *not*, then what is the use of living for us to become dust and ashes? Nothing. Why all this if You are nothing? Why these astronomical millions of worlds – the stars are worlds, millions of light years away – some we can see, some too far ever to see even by the most powerful astronomers' telescopes. Why, if You, the First Cause, didn't make them are they there? *Make* them as if you were a mechanic. But aren't You a mechanic or a master scientist of Divine Intelligence who has made everything from an earthworm to a mountain, You who can move mountains? Suppose the story of Genesis is only folklore handed down through the ages to those nomadic tribes of Arabs, the Jews. Six days shall you labour and on the seventh – very good for them to have a day of rest. What then? Why should half the human race and so many of them with highly intelligent first-class brains, those eminent theologians, believe? And why should some of us be given immortality here on earth – Shakespeare, Beethoven, and all those marvellous inspired painters of the Italian Renaissance, if we, when dead, are only to moulder away into nothingness? 'Men have died and worms have eaten them but not for love.' But You died for love, so the Gospels tell us. You came here on earth as a man – an ordinary working man that we should believe in You and be saved. Be saved from what? The beastliness and sinfulness of living? The horrors of wars? But You didn't save us from wars. Why *not*? This world has always had wars. The Jews, your chosen people, were continually at war one with another. Why? Why do You allow it? Why did You let all these millions of boys and men, Germans, British, French, why let them all be slaughtered? Is that love? O, God, she covered her face, help me to believe. Help me to know what to say to Riabovitch. . . . Yes, and why do You allow these revolutions and murders if You are a God of Love? But you don't allow it. It is not *Your* will, it is the will of man, of us who are blind and greedy and grasping, mistaken, misguided. Perhaps that is what is meant by the devil. The devil in man. Yet Lucifer was an angel once. There must be good, a part of You in all of us. Even in murders. Thou shalt not kill yet we go on killing ourselves. . . .

The organ swelled to its magnificent finale. In the hush that followed the amplified voice of the officiating priest resounded through those splendid halls: '*Dominus vobiscum*', and the fresh young voices of the choir boys: '*Et cum spiritu tuo . . .'* '*Ite missa est*', and the sweetly sung response: '*Deo gratias.*'

The congregation was filing out. The perfume of incense filled her nostrils, the same, she thought, as was used in the Temple or the synagogue that Jesus would have attended when He was a Jew here on earth. This Church is only what the Jews believed in even to the sacrifice, of an animal but not of a man. . . . And they killed Him.

She still knelt there after the last of them had gone. She was alone in that great vaulted place; and a feeling of peace, of serenity such as she had never known, held her spellbound until a step behind her caused her to uncover her face and look up. Alexei, softly treading, stood beside her.

'I saw you come in,' he said, low-toned. 'I came in after you. I, too, have heard His voice. This is the only living Church.'

She rose from her knees.

'You believe that? But then you would. The Russian Orthodox Church is almost the same as the Catholic – the only living Church. I can believe that too.' She spoke as did he in hushed undertones. 'It has endured since He died for the Church. He told Peter didn't He? "On you I will build this rock," or something like that. I'm not up in theology or the Gospels or anything much. But if I *were* anything I'd be a Catholic.'

They walked to the entrance and, as they passed out, Riabovitch turned and genuflected to the high altar at the head of the long aisle.

Dusk had fallen; the sky was a steely grey pricked with faint stars. Holding her elbow to guide her across the road between the cars and taxis lining up at the Cathedral's doors: 'Am I to come in,' he asked, 'or am I to go away from you? It must be now or never.'

Her heart gave an upward leap and sank, while she strove to speak lightly.

'You said all the time in the world and it is only twenty-four hours since you . . . since I asked for time to think about it. . . about us.'

'I had hoped you were thinking, or had thought, when I found you kneeling in prayer.'

His low-lidded eyes seemed to burn into hers; his face in the light of the street lamp looked creased and thin, his mouth close-lipped.

'I don't know if I was in prayer,' she still spoke in a light tone to cover the hurry of her heart that had leapt again at his words and that hot, dark, penetrating gaze of his. 'I was thinking about life and its beginnings and . . . its ends. Not yours or mine,' she added, 'not *our* ends, but all . . .' she faltered, thinking of Ronnie, 'all our ends.'

He came a step closer to her.

'I want our lives joined for ever now and hereafter, never to end.'

'No!' she moved sharply away from him. 'Please. I . . . You haven't given me time . . . yet.'

And she left him without another word or look.

* * *

Lord Halstead of Wigmore, K.C.V.O., M.D., F.R.C.P., who, as Sir Lucian Halstead, had received a peerage in the Dissolution Honours for his medical attention to Royalty and two prime ministers, was taking his after luncheon coffee in the lounge of the Athenaeum.

Lord Rodborough, having become a personal friend of Sir Lucian, and had been one of his sponsors to his peerage in the Lords, saw him in the dining-room, failed to catch his eye at a distant table and followed him into the lounge.

'So here you are,' he said unnecessarily. 'I watched you devouring the steak-and-kidney pudding. Best thing they do here. Have you seen the midday paper?'

'No, I haven't time. I read it at night.'

Lord Rodborough lowered himself into the large leather armchair beside the old physician. White-haired, rubicund, rosy-gilled, he carried his seventy-odd years with an upright military air.

Pouring himself a second cup of coffee, Lord Halstead remarked,

'I don't often come here for luncheon but my cook has died and I'm hoping for another. Difficult to find a good one these days. Servants aren't as they were before the war. Won't go into service – not the young ones. Since I lost my wife I don't seem to be able to cope with this new young lot. Of course I have my butler and my secretary – they're getting old. As aren't we all. Not you,' he added cheerily, 'you've another thirty years before you.'

'I don't know that I want another thirty years of this post-war world and a Labour Government in, and all these Communists. By the way, I see that Snowden has fulfilled the party's fears that he whom Beatrice Webb – that Socialist crank – called chicken-hearted, will be cutting down expenditure.'

'He hasn't made much of an effort so far with three ha'pence off sugar.'

'I give them a year – eighteen months at most, before the next election,' pursued Rodborough. 'There's too much hob-nobbing with the Soviet Union for the country to stomach them. Negotiations broken off in 1918 and now restored haven't helped Britain's relations with France and Germany. You know what the King is supposed to have said or written in his diary, which somebody must have seen – or not, just guessed, or overheard him say it – that he wondered what his "dear Grandmamma would have thought of a Labour Government".'

Lord Halstead drained his cup.

'You can't come to terms with a man-eating tiger.'

'Ah, so you think Russia is out for blood again?'

'Capitalist blood, yes.' He got up. 'I must be off. I have an appointment at Buck House.'

'Anyone ill there?'

'No, just a routine visit.'

'The Queen likes your bedside manner,' grinned Rodborough.

'I'm walking there,' said Lord Halstead. 'I like to walk off a full luncheon which I do not usually eat. One good meal a day is enough at my age, and yours too or at any age from thirty. A midday snack after a light breakfast is ample.'

'If you are walking I'd like to go with you. It's all on my way home.'

'Right. The exercise will do you good if you've also had that steak-and-kidney pudding.'

As they passed St James's Palace and along into the Mall, Lord Halstead remarked:

'Your health centre is pulling in a good many patients anxious to be rid of their various complaints, either genuine or imaginary. You should be doing well out of it.'

'How? I get nothing out of it. I sold it to this company lock, stock and barrel, the land too, most of which had already been sold after I . . .' His voice shook a little . . . 'lost my son. I've no heir, at least none apparent. There was, I believe, a blood relative, a cousin of my father's, dead now – and he would have been his heir if I hadn't appeared late in his life. He, this cousin, was a wrong'un. He's dead too, so my wife's father told me. He was a High Court Judge and knew more about the family than I did. There might have been sons or grandsons of this cousin. If so I never heard of them and the peerage looks to end with me. Pity Felicity isn't a boy. Not that it matters. Inherited peerages will be done for if we have a Labour Government in for any length of time.'

'None the less Labour will hand out peerages right and left to augment their party in the Upper House. You say you appeared late in your father's life. How late?'

'They had been married fifteen or sixteen years. My

grandmother was his cousin too and several years younger than he. My wife's aunt, Lady Caversham, always makes out there was some reason why I was born so late.'

'It is not uncommon for a child to be born after several years of marriage. I have a patient whose first child was born after twenty years of marriage. The latest child-bearing age is legally fifty-one. Well' (the doctor halted as they neared the Palace gates), 'I see my car has arrived to drive me back to Harley Street. By the way, there's a Mrs Pickering-Smythe who came to consult me and is anxious to enter the Rodborough Clinic to reduce her weight – if she thinks it will have any effect. To reassure I told her to try it by all means. Half of them go there to try it out if they've nothing better to do. But careful diet-ing and expert massage can't do any harm if they want to spend their money *pour passer le temps*. You should have insisted on being given shares in it or have become a director.' He held out his hand. Rodborough took it.

'Come and dine with us some time. I can't give you so good a dinner as you would get at the club but we can have a game of chess.'

Lord Halstead, having been received and welcomed by an august lady on his usual routine visit, returned to his car and was driven back to Harley Street.

Reflecting on his conversation with Rodborough: So, he thought, I am the only living soul who knows how he came to be born. If there is an heir ought one to investi-gate, make inquiries on behalf of a possible successor if, as I suspect, he knows nothing about it? After all, Rod-borough was born in wedlock and accepted as his father's only son if Dick Harrington was to be believed, and how should I doubt? He was in full command of his faculties and straight as a die. No romancing of a dying man whose mind was wandering from the effect of drugs. I ordered far too small a quantity to have any such effect. As for Rodborough being Dick's son, no possible doubt of that.

He's a 'Red Harrington' all right and has the same bone structure, but not so good-looking as Dick.... Well, I've kept his trust in me so why should I go raking it up to find a missing heir? Although if there is one he has only to go to Somerset House and look up the birth dates of any Ross-Sutton of some fifty years ago and of more recent years, and the deaths of same. And if any son or grandson of the 'wrong 'un' were killed in the war the W.O. would know of it. However, it's none of my affair or is it? I kept a copy of his confession, no one but I could ever see it – it's locked in my safe, sealed and to be destroyed unopened at my death. But while I live I have the evidence should any claimant arise. In any case should a possible heir put in a claim he could be proved the heir without my evidence....

His car drew up at his house where his next patient, Prince Riabovitch, had already arrived.

He had come to consult him, he told the physician, not for himself but on behalf of his relative Mrs Pickering-Smythe, who he understood had asked Lord Halstead if she could be admitted to the Rodborough Health Centre. Would the rules or regulations permit her to take drives in her car and to receive visitors – himself, for instance, as her only blood relative here in England? As Lord Halstead was doubtless aware, the lady is Russian, the widow of a British subject. He hoped that her condition was not of any serious or permanent nature, more than – a thin-lipped smile accompanied the words – 'excess of avoir-dupois'?

'No, nothing serious at all,' he was assured, 'but rest and dieting is advisable, and by all means she would be allowed visitors within reason and at the discretion of the house physician in charge.'

Riabovitch thanked him, paid his fee to the doctor's secretary as he went out, took a passing taxi and was driven to the flat of Rakovsky, the *Chargé d'Affaires* of the Soviet Union.

At the same time as the meeting between these two was taking place Lord Rodborough strolled leisurely homeward after having called at a tobacconist's in Victoria Street to buy two hundred cigarettes of his favourite Turkish brand. When he came to his block of flats he saw a car outside, his daughter at the wheel and a young man on the kerb in earnest conversation with her.

Unseen by Felicity her father heard:

'So now, Miss – m'lady – you can say you've passed with honours s'far's I'm concerned. You'll get your licence and the car will be delivered to you tomorrow.' As he opened the door for her, Rodborough advanced.

'What's all this? You've been taking driving lessons?'

'Yes, why shouldn't I?'

'You didn't tell me.'

'There's a lot I don't tell you, ducky, until it's time for you to know. This is my father, Lord Rodborough.' She introduced the young man as 'my instructor,' who said: 'Pleased to meet you, m'lord, and if I may say so you can be proud of her ladyship, havin' picked it up so quick after a dozen lessons. Some takes four dozen.'

'Have you bought a car?' demanded her father. 'Not that thing I hope?'

'No, m'lord,' the young man answered for her; 'this is only what we use for learnin'. 'Er ladyship's car is a beaut.'

'What's a Bute?' Rodborough wished to know. 'I've never heard of that make.'

'He means she's a good car,' giggled Felicity taking his arm, 'and yes, I have bought her – given away to me for a hundred and fifty.'

'Given away for –' exploded his lordship. 'Who's paying for it?'

'I am, darling. Tell your boss,' she called over her shoulder, 'that I'll pay for it tomorrow. And thanks awfully for teaching me so well.'

'My pleasure, Miss. I don't often get so good a pupil.'

D

'Daddy,' she had sighted a parcel under his arm and recognized the wrapping. 'Are those your gaspers?'

'Not gaspers – not the muck you smoke.'

She took the parcel from him.

'Please, I'll buy you some more,' and she handed the parcel to her instructor. 'Take these from me in gratitude. No, Dad, you won't go short. . . . You'll run me round to the shop, won't you? It's only in Victoria Street.'

He would have run her to Land's End had she wished it, as would he and others who had come under her spell, of which she was unconscious. And perhaps that was the secret of her charm for the few who sensed it.

When after purchasing two hundred cigarettes of her father's favourite brand in replacement of those she had filched from him, she returned to find him having tea and reading the latest edition of the evening paper.

'I'll have a cup too,' she said; 'and here are your cigs.'

'Did you put them on my account?' he asked suspiciously.

'No, I paid for them myself. You can owe me for them if you like. Two pounds ten for two hundred. Mine are only threepence for ten.'

'If you want tea,' her father told her, 'ring for a cup.'

She rang. The cup was brought; she poured and filled it, took a sandwich, munched and with her mouth full said:

'I believe I'm engaged, Dad.'

'Engaged?' He looked up from the headlines of a report in the Commons debating the formidable rise in unemployment attributed to the Labour Party by the Opposition. 'Tonight? Where are you going? Aren't you in for dinner?'

'Oh dear!' she swallowed a crumb, choked on it in laughter. 'I mean engaged as a possible end to marriage.'

'Engaged?' he repeated it as it slowly dawned. 'Who to? Not that instructor fellow and you buying a car from him or his "boss" as you call him? And on whose money? Not mine, I can tell you that.'

'Now listen. Put away that rag and pull yourself together. I've bought the car on my savings from my dress allowance and what Sothebys will give me for the snuff box.'

'Snuff box? What snuff box?'

'You'll hear about that later. You can sell the Rolls and you can pay me back for a new cheaper car on what you'll get in exchange for the Rolls, and you'll save on Foster's wages. You can't afford a Rolls *and* Foster. I'll be your chauffeur. . . . Now don't fuss. As for being engaged I'm not sure that I am. I said I *believed* I am.'

'Who to, for heaven's sake?' exclaimed her flustered father.

'To whom,' she corrected. 'I hope you'll be more careful of your grammar if you ever speak again in the Lords. But as most of them went to Eton or Harrow they won't know if you slip up. Winchester turns out the best of the lot and quite a few of them are Labour.' (Or, remembering Russton, waiters!) But this she did not say. Instead: 'To *whom*, you wish to know? I wish I knew myself. It seems at present as if it were Riabovitch.'

'Good God!' Her father set down his cup with a clatter in its saucer. 'Not that Russian ape?'

'He is a Russian certainly, but not an ape any more than you and I and all *homo sapiens* are if we allow ourselves our origin of species as per Darwin. He doesn't in the least – ' she took another sandwich – 'resemble an ape physically, although he is as good a mimic as any in the Zoo in that he has acquired a perfect English accent, having only been over here since the revolution. He has some quite good pictures. He runs a gallery in Duke Street and seems to know a fake from the real thing. He specializes in the Tuscan Primitives and knows all about them, unless that is mimicry acquired too. He hasn't any money – probably more than we have, but is likely to make a fortune selling to the Americans who fall for his persuasive salesmanship.'

'Has it,' Rodborough asked drily, 'persuaded you?'

'You mean to sell himself to me? Don't be daft. Nothing doing there. He has nothing to sell to *me*. Not his title. They are two a penny in his country.'

'And will soon be two a penny here with Labour in.' Her father opened the parcel of cigarettes she had bought for him, extracted a carton of twenty, filled a gold cigarette case and offered it to her.

'No, thanks. I don't like yours.' She took from her bag a yellow packet. 'It is time,' she said thoughtfully, inhaling, 'that I was thinking about marriage. I'm rising twenty-five. But the thing is – I can't fall in love.'

'Then don't have him or any man until you do,' her father said decisively.

'But, Daddy, suppose I can't – ever? I just don't seem able to find any man – at least any man whom I can love and live with until death us do part, or whatever it is they say at weddings. And if there is a man who appeals to me, one whom I think I could sleep with in the same bed and share my life and have my children without being *in* love with him or to love him as one ought to love one's husband – '

'Then I tell you – don't.' He rose and was searching for an ash tray. Felicity passed him one. And again he repeated: 'Don't. There's no hurry. Twenty-five is no age. Your grandmother was thirty-six when I was born. And – ' he stood over her, laying a hand on her shingled head – 'I can't lose you yet. You're all I have.'

'Darling,' she too was on her feet. 'You'll make me cry. If I ever do get married I'll not leave you. We'll all three live together and perhaps I could find you a wife and then you could have a son and heir again.'

From the Commonplace Book of me, Felicity Ross-Sutton
May 6th 1924

I have told Daddy about R. and also that I don't know whether to or not. It gave him a shock, poor lamb, but I do see his point besides not wanting to lose me he doesn't want a Russian for a son-in-law maybe a Bolshie or at least he has Bolshie sympathies but so have some of those boys I have met at that club where they get together and talk of the betterment of man and equality and all that sort of Socialist jargon. I am attracted I'll admit but against my will and inclination. He has a mesmeric quality the way his eyes look into you as if he can see right down to your bones and that isn't just the kind of lecher look that some of the older ones have when they stare like the K.C. at the Embassy that night with the Thistlewaites. Mrs T is always pestering us to dine. She collects titles like some people collect butterflies and stamps and as Daddy is the only earl on the board of directors of Waites she takes them in order of precedence ending up with the Air Marshal. The last time we dined there she had at least thirty at the table loaded with silver and Riabovitch! She addresses him as Your Highness if she isn't calling him Prince for the benefit of her equally snobbish friends whom she is out to impress. And imagine! Russton was there as one of the two hired footmen. I can't believe he does this just for the money unless he is really trying to write a book about post-war conditions and life before the war that led up to it and all this infiltration of Communism since the Soviet upheaval. He did say something to that effect when we rode last time at Richmond. Said he was studying a cross section of society and had done some articles on it for the new highbrow Conservative quarterly The Messenger.

He did tell me his nom de plume. It sounded like Bickerstaff but that was Richard Steele I think who wrote for the Tatler not our Tatler the eighteenth century one under Anne. He may have cribbed it. He's quite knowledgeable for a waiter if he is one doing it for a living which I can't believe as he keeps two horses in a stable of that friend who calls him sir and has been a jockey. He, Russton, is going to race the mare at Cheltenham as a try out eventually for the Oaks.

The friend Frank has a son eighteen who is a jockey too. Its all very odd. I don't like mysteries. As for Riabovitch he told me – he rang this morning – to say he is going to Rodborough for a few days he is taking a relative of his as a patient the Russian-born widow of an Englishman. She must be that Mrs Pickering-Smythe who brought him to the Thistlewaites' thé dansant where we first met. He has been hanging round me ever since. Hasn't once mentioned the word 'love' always 'want'. There's a difference. Anyway since he made that proposal if it was a proposal I don't let him get very far when he rings me. I hang up with excuses – Daddy is calling me or I must rush I have an appointment. Russton also rang up today. I don't know how he got my number. It's ex-directory. Asks to ride at Richmond to-morrow (Sunday) his day off. That will be the third time we've gone. I'm puzzled about him too. Am I between the devil and the deep blue sea. Or rather the Red Sea! The last time Alexee-i, or however it's spelt, and I met before he made his 'proposal' can't now remember when that was. I think we'd lunched at that place which sells such good oysters somewhere in Soho not far from the Club he said he was interested in the airfield at Fordington said he was thinking of learning to fly. I told him I thought Fordington wasn't a training centre for flying as they were building air ships on it and that he'd have a better chance of training at Poulton St Mary which was a training airfield during the war for the R.F.C. or there is Hendon where Graham White has his training school and there's also a country club there where they have thé dansants and a golf course too. Said he would try both.

It was a glorious green and golden day when Felicity and Russton came to the gates of Richmond Park, where Frank awaited them with the horses. Felicity had asked Russton if he would let her ride the mare.

'Please. I really can ride, you know.'

After some persuasion and a word from Frank: 'The mare's been well exercised these last few days. I've taken the stuffing out of her. The lady could well manage her now.'

'Your blood be on your head if you do,' said Russton.

'We'll hope her blood isn't on *my* head if she lets me and herself down,' retorted Felicity.

Frank grinned as he held the mare for her to mount.

'Will you shorten the stirrups, Frank?'

'No, m'lady. Best ride her long as she's used to it. You'll find her easier.'

So off they went at a slow canter. A little breeze loosened the few isolated hawthorn bushes shedding their shell-like petals, white and pink among the yellow gorse. Bird song was riotous as they breasted the rising greensward where Felicity let the mare have her head, calling to Russton several paces behind: 'She's lovely! I could ride her to the moon. I'll race you!'

Up and over the hill crest she went, the mare responding to the light weight of her rider and her gentle hands when suddenly from a gorse clump a solitary stag ran out, startled by the galloping hooves, and stood straight in their path. The mare swerved, bucked, kicked up her heels, and Felicity, unprepared, was shot over her head into the gorse. The stag fled and so did the mare.

Russton shouting: 'Stay, Jess! Stand!' called her to a halt. He came up to Felicity, dismounted, knelt. She lay on her side, one leg bent under her.

'God!' he breathed as he turned her face upward and saw a trickle of blood beneath her eye where she must have struck a stone. Her eyes were closed; the long lashes, darker than her hair, lay like crescent moons on her cheeks. Her eyes fluttered open. Some colour that had left her face returned in a quick flush. 'I'm all right,' she said in a little voice that held the ghost of a laugh. 'And don't say I told you so.' She struggled to sit up. 'Where's the mare?'

'She's here.' He jerked his head in the direction where Jess was nuzzling the long grass at the side of the track. 'Are you hurt?'

'I think I've done something to my leg. It's the first time – ' her voice gained strength to say – 'that I've ever come off. Not since I was a kid. It was that stag. He scared her ... Ooh!' she gave a small yelp of pain as she made to get on to her feet and sank down again. 'I think I've done something to my knee.'

'Let's see. Can you undo your jodhpurs?'

'I can, but – '

'I'll undo them for you.'

'No – turn your back!'

'If I must. I'm not interested in your drawers or whatever you wear underneath them.'

'You can look if you like – there's nothing to see. Oh hell!' A slight whimper accompanied that. 'I wonder if I've slipped a cartilage.' She had unfastened her jodhpurs and let them slide down. There were a tight fit and it took some painful time working them over the injured knee joint. Russton removed her boot.

A stockinged leg was presented for his inspection.

'Let's have this off too,' he told her.

She rolled down her stocking. The knee was swollen and blood oozed from a cut.

'This would have been a proper gash,' said he, 'if you weren't wearing your kit. It might well be a slipped cartilage. The thing is – how am I going to get you back?'

'I'll ride, of course.'

'You won't and you can't.' She made another effort to stand and sank back muttering: 'Damn!'

'You see?' He got up from where he knelt and fetched his horse which was standing quietly where he had left him a few yards behind. He then went to the mare, slid an arm through her reins and led her forward. 'Now I'll walk her, and ride mine with you – like this.' He lifted Felicity and placed her on his horse, her legs dangling over the side of the saddle, ' – so here we go.'

'It's three miles from the gate,' she said; her forehead in a frown of pain. 'And what sort of sight does this look if people see us riding pillion, me with a boot and my jodhpurs off!'

'I hope someone does see you. If we come to the road I'll get them to telephone Frank to bring the car to us here. The thing I like most – or one of the things I like most about you,' he said, 'is the way you take what comes and no argument.'

'What's the use of argument? I've come off your mare – so shaming. I've been too cocksure and it might have been worse. I might have broken her knee instead of mine and then you could have said what you're dying to say.'

'If I told you what I'm dying to say,' he answered with his 'little boy's' grin, 'you might not want to hear it. Wait a minute.' He took out a clean folded handkerchief while his horse stood patiently, and with his arm still through the mare's reins and telling her: 'Lean down,' he staunched the small flow of blood from under her eye. 'A good thing it is under your eye and not in it. We'll have some plaster on that when we get you home.'

From Felicity's journal or 'Commonplace Book' as she calls it we gather that when eventually she did get home she records:

> . . . So here I am with a slipped cartilage a plaster on my face Nannie in a fuss and the doctor saying I must lie here for at least a week. May be longer if I know anything about it. I had a fellow with a slipped cartilage when I was V.A.D-ing but it may have been worse than this. He was incapacitated for three weeks. I'm not lying up for three weeks. No fear. Daddy bombarding me with questions Nannie having told him I have been riding at Richmond on a day when he is at golf. . . .

Which from her brief account of her father's bombardment we may assume he too was in 'a fuss'.

'Who have you been riding with at Richmond? Riabovitch?'

'No, it isn't.'

'Who then?' demanded Rodborough. 'Nannie tells me you are always going to Richmond with someone or other. Who is he? And what sort of mount have you been riding to get you in this state?'

'Not always – only three times. And the mare I rode is a race horse.'

'Then what do you mean by riding a race horse? You are not a jockey.'

'No, but I could be.'

Her father rumpled his thinning hair.

'What have you been up to? Buying a car, pinching my snuff box to offer it to Sothebys, learning to drive – all without my knowledge and careering off with some Tom, Dick and Harry and getting yourself engaged to a Bolshie Russian! I tell you,' said the vexed peer, 'I've had enough of it. Good thing you can't get up to any more wild goose chases for a week at least.'

'I'm not going on any wild goose chases and I'm not engaged – yet – to Riabovitch, and he with whom I ride is not Tom, Dick or Harry; he is an ex-patient of mine. I nursed him when he was down with the 'flu at Grosvenor Square. I've come across him once or twice lately. He's a waiter.'

'A waiter?' came the inevitably shocked echo.

'Among other things.'

'What other things?'

'That's what I have to find out. He is by way of being a sort of free-lance journalist as well, a writer of political articles in *The Messenger*, that new Conservative quarterly. His name if you want to know, is Russton.'

'I don't care what his name is. I won't have you picking up any Tom, Dick or Harry.'

'Darling, how you do repeat yourself. And I don't pick up anyone. They,' she giggled, 'pick up me.'

'You go too far,' said her father with conviction. 'I am not amused.'

'Nor am I to have put out my knee, but better than that I should have put out a prospective Oaks winner's knee.'

'Race horses?' Rodborough expressed increased interest. 'Does this – ah – waiter own a stable?'

'He probably will if the mare wins at Cheltenham and later in the Cambridgeshire.'

There was an eloquent pause.

'Well, at least,' said Lord Rodborough, 'I presume he is an Englishman and', he added conciliatorily, 'a man of various parts.'

'Those parts I have seen', replied the irrepressible Felicity, 'are quite adequate.'

'Now, lovey,' Nannie came bustling in, 'Doctor says I must dress that cut on your knee again and put another plaster on your face. We don't want any festering.'

And from Felicity's record of events to date, we have:

Today the day after I put out my knee Wilson brought me a huge bunch of roses and carnations done up with ribbon and bought at that place in Bond Street where they charge the earth. I sent some to Aunt Harriet for her birthday as from me (but Daddy paid) five guineas and nothing so many or so good as these. Does he do it on the tips he gets for waiting? The envelope was addressed to me but a card enclosed said for Lady Clare from Ronald and a P.T.O. says Hope your knee which has gone out has gone in. R. . . . He knows my second name is Clare, Mummy's name. He got it from Debrett.

So that was it and Daddy none the wiser. Nor to tell the truth am I.

FIVE

Mrs Pickering-Smythe, with Riabovitch in cousinly attendance, arrived in due course at Rodborough Health Centre and was graciously received by Matron; buxom, well-bosomed, upholstered in blue with flowing headgear and an imposing row of ribbons on her ample chest, as the insignia of her status. Having nursed in India before the war and having been Assistant Matron in a Red Cross hospital in Flanders, she had become the leading light and lodestar of the Rodborough Health Centre, at least in her own estimation, which placed her as high as a Major General, the most recent patient of the V.I.P. class.

Her welcome to Mrs Pickering-Smythe was only less gracious than that accorded to Riabovitch, to whom she felt uncertain whether she should curtsy or not and compromised, since she decided he was not of Our Royalty (nor perhaps of any Royalty unless connected with the late Czar), by bowing low over his proffered hand and addressing him as 'Your Highness'.

So 'Your Highness' it was and had to be, especially as the Rodborough Health Centre had not seen the last of the prince after depositing Mrs Pickering-Smythe with Matron. For he, too, wished to take a course of treatment, being interested in learning to fly at the airfield near Fordington, and he wanted a check on his health to be sure his heart was fit enough for heights.

'But Fordington hasn't an airfield for training pilots,' was the reminder of Sister, second in command to Matron. 'It is surely a Government research station for building airships.'

'I expect His Highness knows what he is about. He will

be given a thorough check up. He looks well enough. A very pleasant gentleman. You would hardly take him for a foreigner.'

Had Matron overheard the conversation between 'His Highness' and Natasha Pickering-Smythe, she would certainly have taken him for a foreigner, since they spoke Russian; and Natasha expressed herself astonished that Alexei Alexandrovitch should wish to take lessons in flying.

'I had a pilot's licence in Russia,' she was told. 'You wouldn't know of this as you were in England at the time, but I will have to take an English pilot's tests if I fly here. There is a future in civilian flying. More and more aircraft are being built here and in Russia, who is determined to compete with Britain in the air or –' he paused a moment – 'in aerial warfare.'

'Oh no, my dear,' said she comfortably, 'there will be no more wars in our time.'

'Not in yours, Natasha, perhaps, but I think, if I stay the course, in mine.'

'I don't believe it. Has not the League of Nations arranged by treaty that all enemy nations will live in peace together since the war that they said will end all wars?'

'Let us hope,' Alexei took out a cigarette case, 'May I? Or is it taboo in this charming room?'

'My treatment does not start until tomorrow when the house physician will check me and prescribe a diet and massage and –' she shuddered '– some horrible mud baths I have no doubt. Yes, it is a charming room, one of the best in the house with a communicating bathroom but –' she raised bejewelled, plump hands '– what a price! Do you intend also to become a patient here? If so you must make a great deal out of your picture gallery if that – ' she hesitated a moment and added '– if that is your sole means of support?'

He smiled thinly.

'My sole means suffice my modest wants.'

'Not so modest, *dushka*, if —' playfully she shook a be-diamonded forefinger '— what I hear is true: that you are frequently seen at expensive places and restaurants with Lady Felicity Ross-Sutton. Your name is so much coupled with hers that one cannot help asking — '

'Do not ask,' he deftly interposed, 'and you will hear no lies.' He blew a smoke ring, watched it waft to the ornamented ceiling and said: 'I have been somewhat per-turbed of late, having had news concerning Anna.'

'Anna?' Mrs Pickering-Smythe's full, red-salved lips fell apart, forming an incredulous O. 'Your *wife*? But', she cried, 'she is *dead*!'

'As I have always understood. We know she was in attendance on the Czarina, and that she too had been an ardent adherent of Rasputin. So,' he shrugged his shoulders, 'Anna, the poor misguided little fool,' he got up to stub his cigarette in an ash tray, 'but enchantingly pretty — Rakovsky, who can only have heard this at third hand, intimated to me the last time I saw him that Anna, or someone very like her, had been seen a few weeks ago in Moscow with Chicherin, who was Trotsky's right hand in 1918. He has since become in charge of the Foreign Office in Moscow.'

'Our — England's Foreign Office?' again in wonder asked Natasha.

'England has no Foreign Office in Bolshevik Russia.' He took another cigarette. 'Chicherin is a man of some in-fluence in the highest circles, and,' he repeated his shrug and a thin-lipped smile, 'Anna would know which side to butter her bread.'

'But, Alexei Alexandrovitch,' accusingly the forefinger was pointed, 'you did not scruple to leave Anna to her fate when the earthquake blew up the whole Czarist régime. You disgracefully threw in your lot with the Reds. You were infected with the Karamazov type of intellectual. They are the same in this country and in-

102

credibly dangerous. My poor George,' she manufactured tears and wiped both eyes with care for their mascara, 'he saw what was coming to Russia long before the Terror. Poor George,' she sighed gustily, 'how I miss him.'

'I can understand that,' with veiled sarcasm Alexandrovitch sympathetically concurred. 'He has left you well provided, your poor George.' Who, he added inly, was her rich George and had made a fortune in munitions before and after Armageddon, from which she reaps the benefit. . . .

The next morning when Natasha had been thoroughly examined by one of the two house physicians, she began her treatment, starting with a foam bath followed by massage and, after having suffered considerable sweating, she was permitted to rest, then served with her midday meal. This consisted of dry toast, unsweetened lemon water, a hard-boiled egg and a peach.

'You may have a peach twice a week,' the nurse who brought the tray conceded, 'it is one of the only fruits allowed to diabetics.'

'I am not a diabetic, am I?' was the startled response to this.

'No, dear, no, but your diet is almost the same as what we give to diabetics. You won't know yourself after three weeks of your treatment. You will have lost most of this superfluous weight and will look years younger.'

To look years younger and to lose most of her superfluous weight of fourteen stone and have it brought down to eleven or even ten might, Natasha considered, be worth three weeks' starvation and all that pummelling and rubbing and those horrible hot sweat baths, not at present mud baths. They were to come.

On this doubtfully cheerful prognosis, Natasha resigned herself to her boiled egg, sour lemon water, and a dry and rather spongy peach.

Riabovitch underwent a similar if less drastic treatment; that is to say he was not ordered baths or massage, only a diet – 'To lower the hypertension,' the young doctor, fresh from Guy's, advised him. 'No beef or mutton, no alcohol, very moderate smoking if you must,' with a glance at the packet of unopened Turkish cigarettes on his bedside table, 'only two or three a day and no drastic exercise. A drive in your car, a little walking and as much rest as possible.'

'I would like to take drives in my car, but it is not with me here. I suppose I can hire one from a garage or somewhere?'

He had been brought in Natasha's Rolls which served its purpose as far as taking him to Rodborough to save his petrol but it had been sent back to London until wanted.

There was a car hire garage at Calloden, he was informed.

The room allotted to the prince, somewhat to Matron's dismay, was one of the least expensive at Rodborough as it overlooked a courtyard and several garages. These had once been the stables and the incessant coming and going of cars, either those of the patients who had brought their own, or taxis from the station at Dereham, the nearest town, kept up a continuous disturbance.

Having disposed of the luncheon brought to him, hardly more palatable than that with which Natasha had begun her diet, its main course of sustenance being the boiled leg of a fowl that had been alive for some few years, and a glutinous tablespoonful of tapioca pudding. If Rodborough had any sense, conjectured the prince, he would have insisted on taking shares in this company. They are making a fortune on the food alone or the lack of it.

He then consulted a telephone directory beside his bed and called the number of the local garage, ordering a car to be sent to Rodborough Abbey within the next half hour. After which he made a trunk call to London and left a message that Mr Rakovsky would ring him at – he gave the number of the Abbey – and the extension number of his room.

When the car arrived Riabovitch was driven to Fordington Research Station where he told the driver to wait. The great gates were closed but a uniformed official came from them suspiciously to ask him his business.

'I wish to see the manager,' Riabovitch told him loftily.

'The manager,' he was truculently informed, 'can see no one without an appointment. And I must know if you' – he stressed the 'you' as indicative of one who looked, if he did not speak, like a foreigner – 'were expected.'

Riabovitch handed him his card.

It had the desired effect.

'I will telephone Major – ' the name evaded Riabovitch, 'to know if he will see you, Sir,' capitalizing the S as if to royalty.

He backed into a telephone booth beside the gates. The thin smile of the prince narrowed as he watched him speak, replace the receiver and return.

'Major Armstrong will see you, Sir. I cannot leave my post but if you will walk to the main entrance – cars except those of the staff are not allowed through the gates – you will be met and taken to the Major's office.'

The interview that took place in the office of Major Armstrong at Fordington was almost but not quite to the satisfaction of Riabovitch. He found this Major Armstrong, whom he likened to a bulldog, to be a square-jawed, square-faced individual with deep-in eyes and a voice so deep-toned to match that it might have been a growl.

Unimpressed by the name on the card: 'Take a pew, won't you?' was offered. 'What can I do for you?'

Taking the 'pew', a chair facing the Major seated behind a desk on which were two telephones, a file containing papers and a silver cigarette box, Riabovitch made known what could be done for him and inwardly hoped it would not lead to doing *for* him. He did not feel altogether at ease with this square-headed, dog-faced fellow typical, he judged, of a sprung-up ex-army governmental bureaucracy.

'I understand that pilots can be trained here. I have my wings – my pilot's certificate obtained before the revolution in Russia from which I escaped to your hospitable country. I am anxious to purchase, if possible, an aircraft for my personal use in the hope, when granted naturalization' (which until that moment he had not contemplated but thought it to be an added means to his ends) 'if I', he continued, 'a White Russian, would be permitted to hold a pilot's certificate for commercial or passenger flights in Imperial Airways.' This being a moiety of his 'ends'. 'One has to live.' He gave a deprecating shrug. 'I have opened a picture gallery that does not pay its way and will have to close down unless I can subsidize its losses. I, and others of my compatriots, are finding the struggle for existence hard going.'

Unaffected by the struggle for existence of immigrant Russians whether White or Red, the Major said:

'With regard to the purchase of a plane for your private use I can put you in touch with the Handley Page Transport Company – they manufacture aircraft – that is if you could afford the price of it, which I think would scarcely subsidize your losses in pictures. As for the chance of you being given a pilot's certificate for Imperial Airways you had better cut it out. Our regular services to and from London to the continent are already well enough staffed with post-war survivors of the R.F.C. and newly qualified recruits from what is now the R.A.F. But if you wish to fly your own plane I can give you an introduction to the chap who can advise you about that better than I.'

He helped himself to a cigarette and passed the box on his desk to Riabovitch who, politely declining, replied:

'I would be most grateful if you can do so because, even if I would never be allowed to hold an Imperial Airways certificate here, the fact that I have flown my own aircraft in Russia might obtain me a, er, a European certificate?'

Not a snowball's chance in hell, was Armstrong's un-uttered remark.

He said: 'You could try for it if you had your own kite. But you'll find it costly.'

'I am prepared to sell one or more of my treasured works of art that I saved from the wreckage of my home in St Petersburg, to buy a plane if it were possible. And may I,' he went on, circumventing Armstrong's evident desire to be rid of him, 'ask of you one more favour?' Adjusting his monocle which he seldom used save when he felt it necessary, not for his outer but for his inner vision 'If I might inspect your factory here – it is a factory, is it not?'

'No.' Short and decisive was the answer to that; and after a pause: 'It is a Government research station where we endeavour to perfect the lighter-than-air machine on the lines of a Zeppelin, but more satisfactory.'

'There have been some unfortunate experimental disasters, have there not?'

The Major refused to be drawn. 'The R 38 exploded at Hull,' he said guardedly, 'though in 1919 the R 34 crossed the Atlantic, but if you would care to – ' Armstrong got up '– I'll show you round.'

How much of the immense interior of Imperial Airways research station was 'shown round' to Riabovitch and left to Armstrong's discretion, is debatable. The prince, imbibing every detail, was offered little more than he already knew; yet he was thankful even for this small concession which decided him that the new generation of airships which had followed the almost obsolete Zeppelin of the Germans, would prove economically hazardous to maintain and to moor. It would be the aeroplane that must serve in any aerial warfare of the future in preference to the giant airships now under construction in this and other capitalist countries.

He left with profusive thanks and an invitation for the Major to visit his gallery in Duke Street next week at the private view of an exhibition of contemporary art.

'One of the exhibitors gives his impression of an airfield and hangars with an aeroplane in flight, a Handley Page, which I believe was one of the first starting from Hounslow on the London–Paris passenger service. Another gives a cubist's idea of the interior of the aeroplane – its anatomy, so to speak. He is enthusiastically air-minded – ' he smiled thinly '– and a compatriot of mine.'

Armstrong said he would be interested to see the exhibition if he could find the time, which he had not at present. However . . .

Hands were shaken. Riabovitch was conducted back the way he had come, and arriving at the gate, where his hired car awaited him was driven off; nor did he observe a fair-haired young man in a shabby old Ford, wearing shabbier tweeds and a cap pulled well down over his eyes who was at the gates and reading the *Sporting Times*. When beckoned by the uniformed official, he left the Ford and went into the telephone booth. After speaking into the mouthpiece he replaced the receiver, nodded to the gate-keeper, started his car and followed Riabovitch at a careful distance. On arriving at Rodborough he halted at one of the lodges where a man with an ex-serviceman's ribbon on the lapel of his coat came out to him.

A few words were exchanged and:

'Tap all calls from room 34,' were his directions to the ex-serviceman, who asked him:

'Any luck, sir?'

'What do you think?' was the answer with a grin.

'He'd get nothing out of the Major, sir, if that's what he's after. I have the kettle on, if you would like a cup o' tea. I can get it in two ticks.'

The cup o' tea, augmented by hot buttered toast, lengthened the two ticks to twenty minutes before the young man, leaving the Ford in the lodge-keeper's yard, drove back at top speed to London in a red Aston Martin.

*   *   *

It was nearing the end of the season, an uneventful season compared with that of the year before which had seen the marriage of the Duke of York to the Lady Elizabeth Bowes-Lyon. It had also seen the launching of the submarine X$_1$, one of the twenty-four similar-type vessels that had been built at Chatham, but this was the largest and costliest of them all. At Wimbledon, the preceding year of 1923 had seen Mlle Lenglen win her fifth championship, and Lord Derby his first Derby winner with his colt Sansovino, the first time the Derby had been won by a member of the family who founded it more than a century before. And now in that ending summer of 1924, with Cowes over, the Royal Family at Sandringham, and later bound for Balmoral, while on the Scottish moors the guns were preparing for the twelfth, Felicity paid her bi-monthly visit to Lady Caversham.

'So you and your father are still in London. So am I,' remarked her ladyship. 'Cannes full of new rich. I am too old and fat to sprawl half naked on French sands. Don't strip well. Used to. You would. Why don't your father take you?' And, without waiting for an answer to that: 'How's your Russian? He in Town too?'

'Yes, Aunt. But he's not *my* Russian.' (Yet, was inwardly added.) 'He's learning to fly, or rather he can fly but has to pass his flying test here. He flew in Russia before the war.'

Aunt Harriet made a sound between a snort and a cough, took a pastille from a shagreen box on the occasional table beside the doubtful Louis Quinze sofa, rubbed her chest above the hidden hearing aid, and, sucking the pastille, said:

'London more tolerable in August than anywhere else.

Half empty. All flocking to the Continent or Blackpool. For the masses. Brighton for the Jews. I like Jews. Not the Poles or Russian Jews. Tartars most of 'em. Or Bolshies. Lenin. Say their prayers to him. And Karl Marx who started it. But the others. Moiseiwitch. Music. Art. Not Epstein. Don't think much of him. Here's tea.'

The trolley was wheeled in laden as usual with silver, sandwiches and the inevitable iced cake.

'Rose-leaves today,' said Lady Caversham, 'in honour of you. Thinks your name's Rose. Mixed you up with Jeremy's sister. Had her eightieth birthday last week. Came to tea. Getting gaga. The cook I mean. Rose been dotty for years.' Removing with a finger tip an adhesive remains of the pastille from her gums, Aunt Harriet swallowed it and said: 'About that Russian. You going to marry him?'

Felicity who had come prepared for cross-examination hedged: 'I might. On the other hand I might not.'

'No catch in tacking princess on to your name with no money behind it. Besides . . . ' Aunt Harriet took a sandwich, bit into it, made a face and said: 'Fish paste. Told her never fish paste unless she makes it herself. Besides there's too much hobnobbing with MacDonald's lot. Holding hands with Communist Russia. Come to better terms. Pah! Fatheads.'

'Fatheads,' screeched the parrot, 'you bastard.'

'Cut yourself a slice of the cake,' said Lady Caversham. 'If you don't like it give it to Polly. She's losing her touch. All icing and no taste. Picked that up in the pub. Must you go?'

Her rouged old cheek was offered to receive Felicity's kiss. 'Mind Chin-chu.' The Peke curled in his basket stretched himself, yawned and with Chinese dignity stepped on to the carpet almost under Felicity's feet. She stooped to stroke his satiny head. 'Don't mind me,' he seemed to say, fixing her with his baleful prominent treacle-black eyes, 'I am only ten thousand years older and more civilized than you.'

'Shall I give you a bit of the cake?' asked Felicity, 'instead of Polly?'

'He won't look at it,' said Aunt Harriet. 'Despises sweet things. Likes savoury rice. Wants to go out.'

Chin-chu, avoiding Felicity's overture, had walked sedately to the door, tail furled.

'Ring for Bates,' said Lady Faversham, 'she'll take him.'

Bates, rung for, appeared with a collar and lead and, attached to Chin-chu, she conducted Felicity down the stairs and into the hall, saying worriedly:

'Do you not think her ladyship's conversation is becoming more difficult to follow? She goes from one topic to the other so quickly and it is so disconnected.'

Felicity nodded.

'Her thoughts outrace her words, that's why, but she looks very well.'

'She is very well, thank God,' agreed Miss Bates with modified fervour, 'considering her age. Goodbye, Lady Felicity, it is always a pleasure to see you.'

Felicity walked home through St James's Park. The westering sun gilded the spinach green of late summer's trees and the grass, yellowed here and there from August's fervent heat, seemed to reflect the glow from above as if the earth had smouldered.

As she mused on Aunt Harriet's probing of her intentions regarding Riabovitch. . . . *My* intentions! she asked herself. Why mine? What about his? In the old days of Victoria and Edward, intentions were man's prerogative. Not now. We are men's equals, or we should be now we have the vote and can be M.Ps. I am sitting on the fence but he is making no move to take me off it either by force or persuasion. I think I'd prefer force. . . . Love! How could one define as love what he professed to feel for her, or she for him? Never once had he mentioned love, always 'want'. Does he think he can just take what he *wants* – in marriage? 'No! definitely, no!' She spoke this aloud and started at the sound of her own voice echoed by a voice behind her.

' "Definitely no" – what?'

She swung round.

There he was in his Throgmorton Street or civil servant's get up as he had accosted her months ago almost in this very place in this same park.

'Are you trailing me – or is it "tailing me" as the detective thrillers call being shadowed by the police?'

He ranged himself beside her as she resumed her walk.

'If I am "tailing" you it is just my luck to have caught up with you here where first we met – or *not* where first we met, for our meeting dates back to five years ago. I often take this way to, um, to my room where I can be contacted by phone for,' again the slightest hesitation, 'for a job.'

'Waiting?' She glanced askance at him.

'They also serve who only stand – and wait. But you haven't told me why so "definitely no" as applicable to what?'

'You haven't given me a chance to tell you anything. I was merely speaking my thoughts. I do sometimes talk to myself for want of a better audience.'

'You should have no difficulty in finding an audience.'

'Perhaps, had I something to say, which I haven't. Where, if I may ask, is your room? Where do you live? You have never told me.'

'Not far from where you live as the crow, or the plane, flies but poles away from Ashley Gardens in, or near, um, Pimlico.'

'I haven't seen you lately to ask how the mare did in the Cambridgeshire. I looked through the entries but I didn't know the name by which she was registered. What is it?'

'She is Lady Clare by Lord Ronald out of Felicity.'

'I don't believe you.'

'You don't have to. When are we to ride again at Richmond?'

'When you are not waiting to stand and serve.' They had come to the gates of the park. 'Here is the parting of our ways.'

'Why should our ways part?' He looked down at her with that in his eyes from which she found it difficult to disengage. 'I can go your way or my way to – Pimlico. What about Richmond on Sunday?'

'I am not too keen on riding until I am sure my knee won't play me up.'

'May I phone you?'

'No. Goodbye.'

He raised his bowler. 'Definitely not goodbye.'

She walked swiftly away, her cheeks hot and then came back to ask: 'Did she – did you win with your Lady Clare?'

'She came second, but I'll win with her next time.'

'You are very sure.'

'One has to be.'

She left him standing there bare-headed with the last of the sun on his hair.

While, after leaving Felicity, Russton walked to his 'um-room' in Pimlico, Mrs Thistlewaite, who had recently persuaded, or commanded, Albert to buy a 'place' in the country – 'Not too far from Town where I can entertain for week ends', was now busily engaged with the re-decoration of the 'place' Albert had acquired. She made some demur at first that he should have considered a derelict old manor house in Norfolk.

'Why Norfolk?' she wished to know. 'Why not Surrey or Sussex? Norfolk is so flat and uninteresting.'

'Surrey, Sussex or the nearer home counties,' he explained, 'will soon be built over. Now that motor cars are the businessman's means of trans . . . port in pref . . . erence to trains when he can get to his office by road in under the hour you will not have the privacy you . . . '

'Privacy enough,' she cut in with, 'if you could bestir yourself to buy something with twenty odd acres like – ' she mentioned the name of a sugar king – 'has bought at Sunningdale.'

'There is nothing to be had at Sunningdale that you would care for,' she was told, 'and you would find it sub . . . urban around there.'

'Not with Ascot next door. Why not Ascot?'

But Ascot had proved to be as difficult as Sunningdale to find anything that Ethel would care for, so Norfolk it must be.

And now at the end of September Ethel (Ellen) was immersed in re-decoration. The house required extra bathrooms en suite with the four best guest rooms, with, of course, the objectionable name of Waites obliterated from all necessary equipment.

'No need,' she said, 'to advertise the things in our own house.' And a very fine house it was when all had been completed to Ethel's satisfaction.

Originally Tudor restored in the reign of Anne with an Adam dining-room added under George III, it had turned out to be far better than Ethel had expected. 'One can only hope,' she said, 'that we shan't be disturbed by the noise of aeroplanes from that aerodrome at Fordington.'

Albert hoped so too, but he did not think there would be aeroplanes from there as he understood it was an Imperial Airways station for building airships.

'Airships! Not,' Ethel almost screamed it, 'not Zeppelins! Good heavens – making Zeppelins so near to us! Why didn't you tell me before you bought the place costing thousands? You must sell it. I won't stay here where they are making Zeppelins!'

'No, my dear, n . . . no,' Albert hurriedly assured her. 'Zeppelins are German. These are different. Much better as I am told.'

'Who told you? And why didn't the solicitor who drew up the deeds of the house make proper inquiries?'

'He did, and that's how I know it is Imp...erial Airways sub...sidized by our Government.'

'Waste of money,' declared Ethel. '*Our* money. We'll have to pay for Government airships or whatever they are. That's what comes of Labour and MacDonald. We're taxed to the hilt as it is. All these unemployment benefits. *Pay*ing them to be unemployed!'

'Fifteen sh...illings a week isn't very much for men to live on, even now it is raised to eighteen,' ventured Albert, 'especially in the dis...tressed areas. The coal mines and...'

'Do stop nattering!' cried Ethel. 'You get on my nerves. Anyone would think you approved of Labour, a lot of Socialists – Communists if we but knew. I am glad you are within easy distance of the Rodborough Health Centre. It is where *you* ought to be. You potter about doing nothing and your stammer is getting worse. You need a course of treatment at that place and so do I. All this worry of getting settled here in the Manor and the cost of it has worn me out. I need a rest and once I've engaged staff for Hollywell I mean to have it.'

Albert agreed that most certainly she needed rest. But for himself there was no need...

'I am putting on too much weight,' his wife complained. 'She *will* use pints of cream in her sauces and sweets and she won't be told. I shall have a chef at Hollywell, men cooks are better than women. Rodborough, they say, is wonderful for reducing. Mrs Pickering-Smythe lost almost one stone in three weeks when she was there, and Prince Riabovitch was there too. Not to reduce, just for a check up on his heart, so Mrs Pickering-Smythe told me, because he wants to fly. And that reminds me – '

She went to her desk in the window that overlooked the garden in the St John's Wood house. 'The Prince phoned me – ' She consulted her diary – 'last Tuesday when I came back from Dereham. There is no bedroom ready yet at Hollywell and the inn at Dereham is awful. Just as well you didn't come. They have no twin beds and I couldn't bear to sleep with – Oh, yes, he asked – the Prince asked about the Gerard Dows.' She laid aside the red-morocco-bound diary. 'What he wanted to know was, would you sell them?'

'Would I...? Albert's negligible eyebrows almost touched his negligible hair that grew low on his pinkening forehead. 'Does he want to buy them?'

'Obviously. He has a picture gallery and a valuable collection, some for sale and some he keeps for sentiment. They came from his home in St Petersburg. Very sad,' said Ethel briskly, 'that he should have lost so much, and all his relatives except Mrs Pickering-Smythe, who being married here is, I suppose, British as the widow of an Englishman. I think she helps him out – if not she ought to since her husband must have left her well provided for with his munitions.'

'Wh ... what,' said Albert patiently, 'did you tell Riabovitch?'

'I told him he could have them as a gift. That I couldn't bear the things and would be glad for him to take them away.'

'They are worth a lot of ... money,' said Albert, turning even pinker.

'I can't help that. You know perfectly well I have always hated them.'

'We could perhaps,' he suggested, 'have had them at ... Hollywell?'

'Where at Hollywell? Not in the drawing-room which is entirely French – Louis Quinze. Nor in the dining-room which is Adam. I will not have them *any*where unless you want them in your study at the manor. I am putting all the rubbish in there.'

'I would like to have them in my st ... udy,' appealed

116

Albert, 'if,' with unwonted temerity, 'I am not permitted to have my own pictures anywhere else.'

'You can have the things in your bedroom if you wish, or in the stables or the attics or the cellar for all I care, but you are not having those hideous Dutch things in any of *my* rooms.'

The most expensive and exclusive interior decorator in London had been engaged to furnish, curtain, carpet and make all necessary alterations regardless of expense at Ethel's orders for, since the war, Waites had boomed to increase Albert's income by half as much again, and the Norfolk manor house that had been bought for her by Albert, was now an excellent replica of a Hollywood movie star's home.

All this had emboldened Albert to say: 'Why not change the name to Hol . . . lywood Manor?'

To that remark, taken by Ethel in no good part, she had turned on him saying: 'Do you imply that my taste and Mr Brewster's taste is like a movie star's? Do you not know – but of course you wouldn't – that he, Brewster, has managed to buy me a genuine Adam fireplace for the dining-room and you compare his *wonde*rful taste with that of a common movie star?'

'Only because,' nattered Albert, 'it ra . . . ther reminds me of that pre . . . mier we saw last week of a film with . . . I forget her name . . . Glory Something was it?'

'So I will tell the Prince,' said Ethel, 'that he can have those hideous Dutch things if he wants them but that you would rather keep them for yourself.'

'Thank you, my dear. I would if . . . you don't mind.'

Ethel took up the telephone on her desk, called a number, and:

'Is that you, Prince? . . . Ellen Thistlewaite here. I am so very sorry but my husband wants to keep those Gerard Dows . . . Oh, how good of you. Are you sure? . . . I would have *given* them to you but as they're not mine to give . . . No, he won't sell them . . . Oh, really? I would *love* to see your private view ... My husband?... He doesn't know anything about art but I am sure he would like to come ... Oh, how interesting. Cubist impressions of aeroplanes. Perhaps you will dine with us afterwards?... Well, some other time?'

The private view of modern art at the Riabovitch gallery in Duke Street was well attended by those who wished less to see the exhibits than to meet and mingle with their fellow socialites. Among the celebrities whom the Prince had invited was, prominently, the Prime Minister, Ramsay MacDonald, a handsome presence with his mane of greying hair, his warm Scots accent, his easy charm and aristocratic bearing that belied his acknowledged and prideful birth as the son of a Scottish farm labourer. His Chancellor of the Exchequer, Philip Snowden, was there, and the ubiquitous Lady Warwick, also Lady Londonderry, her rival for the favour of 'Gentleman Mac', as his friends and enemies dubbed him. There were a few famous authors and others well on the way to be, the lions and the lion cubs. Of those lions whose names had resounded through the literary pre-war world and were still the leading lights of their professions, could be seen Arnold Bennett, superciliously eyeing the cubist aeroplane and giving his stuttering opinion of the same ... 'It is an ab-absolute tr-travesty. Per-perpuerile'. . . . H. G. Wells looked in with Rebecca West and went out again. A sprinkling of Bright Young People, three of whom at least had gate-crashed, took no notice of the exhibits, imbibed the cocktails offered by two hireling waiters, and chatted *haute voix* of the latest craze, psycho-analysis:

'My dear, have you read *Married Love* by Marie Stopes?... Oh, but you must. You don't have to be married to ... 'Of course you can ... ' 'Trial trips. I'm all for it.' ... 'How *can* you know until you've tried!' ... 'the Eton crop, and you know what *that* is supposed to signify ... ' 'Yes, we'll all be bi-sexual ... ' 'My dear, she invited me down for the weekend – there was a thunder-storm . . . Yes, we had drunk a lot of champagne, she got it from the Guards' mess, and she came to my room, said she was scared of thunderstorms and' . . . 'Oh, *much* more exciting than men' . . . 'But of course *she*'s one' . . . 'Have you read *Ulysses*, James Joyce? So amusing and mar-vellously uninhibited. . . .'

Mrs Thistlewaite with Albert in tow had just arrived. She made a good entrance carefully got up in one of the newest three-piece suits of pastel blue georgette, waistless and belted round the hips, the *tout ensemble* capped by a cloche hat that hid all of her hair.

After being effusively greeted by Riabovitch and sight-ing Lady Warwick, she asked: 'I should so *love* to meet her, Prince . . . May I?'

She was introduced, but her ladyship having seen a new arrival, Ivor Novello, the darling of the theatre-going public with his musicals, who had immortalized his wartime marching song: '*Keep the home fires burning*', to him, with one accord, she and Lady Londonderry gravi-tated; the Brighter Younger ones encircling him in hope of a word or a look from those beautiful dark eyes, chorused ecstatically: 'Isn't he too *divine*!' . . . I'd never miss a first night of . . .' 'Heard he doesn't like women . . .' 'Sick of them I should think!'

Felicity Ross-Sutton was the last to arrive, by which time the crowd had thinned.

Riabovitch, forsaking Mrs Thistlewaite, who had attached herself to him after Lady Warwick had barely acknowledged the introduction, being engrossed with Chancellor Snowden, was waylaid *en route* to Felicity by Rakovsky. The Soviet *Chargé d'Affaires* had become one of London's fashionables since he had held a party to celebrate the opening of Chesham House which had been the Imperial Russian Embassy and was now the Bolshevik domain. Half London had been there and everyone thought it 'too terribly amusing', to see those advanced young 'moderns' who declared for Labour sporting red carnations in their buttonholes and red ties in defiance of abundant white ties.

Halting Riabovitch on his way to greet Felicity, Rakovsky, who held a filled cocktail glass, spoke low-voiced in Russian to his host, turning in the middle of a sentence with a splenetic exclamation at the sound of an apologetic 'I . . . I beg your par . . . don, sir' from Mr Thistlewaite who had inadvertently jogged his arm and spilled some of the drink on Rakovsky's sleeve. 'M . . . ost careless of me.'

'Not at all. Please,' Rakovsky, unconvincingly assured him, 'it is not'ing.'

'It will not . . . stain, I hope, sir,' murmured Albert, flustered.

'No, sairtainly not,' politically polite. 'The goot English cloth it will not spoil.'

One of the hired waiters approached with a napkin.

'Allow me, sir.' Deftly he applied the damask to Rakovsky's 'goot English cloth'.

'Bring another drink,' ordered the Prince.

'*Mais, non, mon cher.*' This time Rakovsky spoke in French. 'One makes depart at the instant.'

Riabovitch detained him with:

'But first let me present Mr Thistlewaite, who owns a pair of excellent Gerard Dows.'

'*Enchanté, monsieur.*' Rakovsky bowed and Albert, flattered at that 'excellent' attributed to his precious Dows, returned Rakovsky's bow full measure.

Rakovsky having made his departure, Riabovitch was now free to find Felicity, and having sighted her accepting a drink from the waiter who had attended to Rakovsky's sleeve, he approached her, and waving aside the waiter, said: 'You are dining with me tonight, yes?'

'Am I?' She raised to her lips the glass the waiter had offered, tasted it, and set it down on a nearby small table. 'This is vodka, isn't it?'

'Yes, madam,' the waiter said. Her eyes, in a look of recognition, met his. She flushed and told Riabovitch, 'I daren't take vodka if I am to dine – and drink – with you. And where are we to dine?'

'Did I not ask you if you would honour my humble flat, which is just above the gallery?'

'Is it? I didn't know. I have never visited your flat, nor did I know where it is.'

'You know now. A recent acquisition. . . .'

The last of the guests had gone. Riabovitch and she were alone in the gallery after the waiters had cleared away the glasses and the remnants of the cocktail party.

'We dine à *deux*,' he told her, and opened a door into his office that led through another door up a staircase into the three-roomed flat above, where he relieved her of her hat and coat.

'What a charming room!' she exclaimed as she entered where a small centre table was laid with silver and red Venetian glass. The walls were hung with the Italian masters that had adorned the gallery. An Aubusson carpet was laid upon the parquet floor; the window curtains were of tapestry threaded with gold.

Dinner, promptly served by a silent-footed fellow with a high-cheek-boned Slavonic face, consisted of bortsch soup as a first course followed by caviare and a brace of partridge. A *crêpe Suzette* which Alexei manoeuvred over a flame at a side table brought the dinner to its finale with a dish of fruit, peaches, grapes, a sliced pineapple, port – refused by Felicity – and coffee.

'A Lucullan feast,' she said. 'You have a wonderful cook.'

'I thank you, my dear,' he raised his glass to her. 'I am the cook. The birds were prepared earlier today and all my man had to do was to obey my instructions.'

The table cleared, the candles lighted in red glass holders, and the man silently withdrawn, Alexei said:

'Am I never to have my answer?' He offered her a

cigarette box. She shook her head and produced from her handbag a yellow packet.

'Do you object to gaspers? I don't like Russians.'

'So.' Mock dolefully he sighed, 'I hoped in vain. I am sorry since both I and the cigarettes I smoke are Russian.'

They left the table and sat together on a divan heaped with coloured cushions opposite the empty fireplace. The ormolu clock on the mantelpiece was flanked either side by two small Chinese figurines on gilded stands; the one rotund and genially smiling, a hand outstretched above his naked belly; his neighbour on the left of the clock wore on his head a kind of cocked hat and on his face a slanting grin.

'A sly fellow that one,' said Alexei watching the direction of her eyes as he lit her cigarette from a lighter. 'He nods if you tap him on his head. He is a jester, hence his cap. See how he grins at a secret he shares with himself. He is a few hundred years younger than the fat old man who is always smiling and telling you to rub his navel and he will grant you your wish. He is the god of plenty. The Chinese worshipped him as the Catholics worship their saints.'

'Does he grant your wish or wishes?'

'I have not asked him yet but he will as I await your answer. If he fails me I – ' he drew in the smoke of his cigarette '–I will smash him.'

'Oh, no, you can't do that – such a kind old man! Besides he must be valuable if he is hundreds of years old.'

'About eight hundred to be exact, but,' he shrugged, 'what is valuable or of value? Is there not something in the Bible that says a good woman is priced above rubies? I have yet to know a woman who is so priced unless,' he leaned toward her, 'it were you.'

She moved away from him.

'Can I have an ash tray?'

He passed one to her.

'How you – what is the word – *déjouer* in French –

frustrate me. You return my regard for you as no more than – I have no words to express in English all I feel so deeply here.' He laid a hand on his chest. 'I could say in French more easily what I would say, for in English it would sound to you ridiculous, sentimental. The English are so restrained. It is your insularity that makes you avoid all that is in your hearts. In Russia we give of ourselves without restraint.'

'Which accounts,' she said drily, 'for your revolution?'

'What came to Russia had to be. It was like a volcano that lies inactive in the bowels of the earth waiting to rise to the surface and pour its molten lava on a village at its foot. Or an earthquake as in San Francsico. Or the war that was to the Kaiser what the doctors call a "grumbling appendix", which the doctor in St Petersburg called mine before the war, and performed the operation before it perforated. Your King Edward the Seventh made appendicitis fashionable, and then everyone was having appendicitis here in England.'

She shook with inward laughter.

'Félise! You are amused. You make fun of me. You think I am your fool?'

'No, neither mine nor anyone else's fool. I was only thinking that you, who seem to despise sentimentality – and so do I, or I think I do – but you go to the other extreme to be anatomical for fear of sentiment.'

'I was speaking of the cause of revolution,' he said offendedly. 'Not the love of men for women.'

'I did not hear you mention love if that's what you were trying to tell me in French which you couldn't say in English.'

'My God!' He seized her roughly by the shoulders. 'How you are pleased to torment me. I want to marry you. For the third time of asking, will you marry me?'

His eyes, burning into hers, seemed to reflect in each a red spark from the red shaded lights of a chandelier above the table. 'I need you, I want you!' His mouth fastened on her parted lips. She did not resist. Half hypnotized she responded to the attraction he roused in her against her will as, with an effort, she released herself and rose to her feet, saying:

'Marriage is a bond for life. I can't bind myself to any man for life unless – '

'Unless? On what conditions? The Church that ordains until death do us part?'

'Yes. Those are the only conditions on which I will marry, and it must be a certainty.'

'I,' he said, still seated, 'I *am* certain. If you come to me and are my wife, it will be for ever while we live and though we die.'

She had moved over to the mantelpiece and was examining the god of plenty. His shining white belly was temptingly offered. She rubbed her forefinger across his navel and whispered below breath a wish: 'Give me a man I can love and know that it will be for ever until death – and afterwards.'

He, watching her, said :

'You have told him your wish. He won't fail you.'

She left the little fat god to examine an embroidered banner that stood on a Sheraton stand. It was worked in petit point with the heraldic colours and bearing the crest of a dragon's head.

'Is this your family crest?' she asked.

'It is. And our motto as you see under the coat of arms is *Metuenda corolla draconis*.'

'What does it mean?'

'It means "The Dragon's Head" or, more literally, "crest, is to be feared".'

'It is beautifully worked. Who did it?'

There was a moment's pause while he came to her saying quietly:

'My wife.'

She turned on him; her face paled as she repeated:

'Your wife? You are, or – were married?'

'I *was* married. Félise, do you suppose I would have asked for you had I a wife living?'

'No, I suppose. . . . Are you divorced?'

'She is dead.'

'How? When? Tell me about it.'

'Come here, then.'

He took her hand and led her to a writing desk under the window. On it was a photograph of two women, one much younger than the other; a beautiful face with hair bobbed under like that of a mediaeval page.

Felicity looked closer.

'Who are they? Is the young one – how pretty she is – was she your – ?

'That is Anna, my wife whom I married as a boy of nineteen and she a girl of twenty. *Un mariage de convenance*, arranged by our parents when we were children. This photograph was taken just before the revolution. She was a lady-in-waiting to the Czarina. When the revolution began those who could escape did. I tried to make her leave the threatened Court and come with me to England, but she, like the Czarina who is with her in this photograph and whom she adored, had fallen under the influence of Rasputin. As you know, or may not know, the Imperial Family were murdered in July 1918. There were appalling tales of Bolshevik butchery, much of which as is often the case when the press get hold of anything, was grossly exaggerated. But we do know of the horrors done by the extremists to the royalists and to the Imperial Family, none of whom, so far as we can tell, escaped. Nor did my poor little Anna, faithful to her love for the Empress. It was after the cataclysm that I knew Anna had suffered the extreme penalty. I was in Moscow at the time – I and one or two friends whose relatives also had been victimized. Had we then been at the Court we too would have suffered the same end. As it was we were forced to go disguised for had we been recognized as Whites and royalists, the Bolsheviks would have killed us.

Although some of the churches remained still open hundreds of priests were murdered. I will not give you the horrors that were done in the name of Communism promoted by anti-religious propaganda. Life for us of the *ancien régime* was simply a question of saving our skins. The houses and estates of those who, like myself, had possessions, the capitalists – it was a Marxist sin to have capital – all privately owned property was confiscated. My parents, fortunately for them, died before the war and I had no brothers. My sister Maia whose husband was of the White Army, he was killed at Yalta by the Bolsheviks. She managed to escape to New York and is now married to an American.'

While he recounted this in his quiet, slightly foreign accent she who listened with ever-increasing compassion, was drawn to him as never before as it came home to her that he harboured no disruptive bitterness against the hideous fate that had overtaken him and others whose only crime was that of birth, born of a capitalist society.

As if taking that thought from her, he said:

'You see it *was* like a volcano. There had been minor eruptions as far back as 1905, but the unrest, chiefly of the peasantry as in your industrial revolution, was spasmodic. Can one hold it against them who were ground under the heel of their overlords, starving as did your own people – the Havenots did they call them? – while the nobles, their landlords and employers batted – no, I have that wrong, I mean – '

'You mean battened?' She smiled with him.

'Yes, battened, a word not translatable in Russian – the employers who battened on their labour – paid them a miserable pittance to keep body and soul alive.' He had been chain-smoking while he talked and every so often as he stubbed out his cigarette and took another she noticed a convulsive movement of his jaw, the only sign of emotion in his dispassionate account of the Revolution which she guessed was but the briefest outline of the upheaval that had sent him, a fugitive, from his native land.

'You said you went about disguised. How did you manage to get away?'

'If', he told her, 'I could write a book on it none would believe me. I was torn between my hope to save Russia – the Russia I had known and to which my family for generations had belonged, and the alternative to – to throw in my lot with the revolutionaries. Not,' he emphasized it, 'not to save my skin as so many others did, but because I believed Russia could only be restored to sanity by accepting a compromise, to amalgamate the Whites with the Reds, to give both sides their ells – as you say – as they demanded, and not their bare inches. You see the Bolsheviks were taking everything from us. They closed down all private banking accounts. I tried to see clearly why – because the capitalist banks and those who ran enormous accounts had allowed millions of people to die in dire poverty. Starvation. Private ownership of property should be abolished with fair shares for all, yet it should be discriminate according to their way of life.'

'Yes, that is the Socialist slogan of today. But what of your escape? And how did you bring these – ' she pointed to the Italian masters on the walls '– how did you get these away from Russia if all your possessions were confiscated?'

'My house in St Petersburg was seized but I had salvaged a key to the back entrance. Unluckily it was bolted on the inside. I had reconnoitred in my disguise of dark glasses and I grew a beard and took a job – or rather several jobs for I was unskilled and no good at anything manual or in a factory except' – he laughed that whispering laugh of his – 'except I was not too bad at painting. Not pictures, interior decoration, that is to say for workmen's houses. I and Feodore, Count Mikailovitch, with whom I shared an attic, was my accomplice. Together we broke into my old house that had become a shambles.

127

Most of the art treasures had been removed, but these few of the Italians had been left. They obviously didn't care for them. They took the Cézannes and a Matisse.'

'Wasn't it a risk? Supposing you had been discovered taking away your pictures?'

'We had to risk it – either that or living hand-to-mouth in an assumed identity for ever. Others had managed to escape so why shouldn't we? But some of those who got away were acting as agents for the Bolsheviks and well paid for it, both here and in America and in other capitalist countries.'

'You mean spying for Bolshevik Russia?'

'As the lesser of two evils. Some of them were working on principle, for their beliefs. Did you not have the same sort of thing in your civil war? Royalists fighting against the – what were they called? – the Roundheads because they cut off their long hair, and many Royalists went over to Cromwell's side and must have spied for him too.'

'You know our English history, it seems.'

'A smattering learned from my English governesses and tutors in my boyhood.'

'So you got into your house? How, if the door was bolted?'

'By breaking a window. It was easy.'

'What happened to your friend? Did he get away with you?'

'Yes, but he went to Switzerland. He had relatives there. And now,' he took her hand and crushed her fingers in his close dry clasp, 'you know all I can tell you of myself – of my other life which is to me a dream or – a nightmare.'

Not looking at him but at the coat of arms embroidered on the banner: 'The Dragon's Head is to be feared,' she said. 'Is that your way of life, to be feared? Or have you learned to fear because of your . . . nightmares?'

He drew her into his arms.

'Not now that I have you to waken me.'

Again his mouth sought hers. She was surrendered to

that timeless kiss. Yet presently, disengaging, a furtive doubt crept in, not of him but of herself.

'This doesn't mean, does it,' she had moved away again, not trusting his propinquity nor her response to it, 'that we are – engaged? I hate the word "engaged". All those announcements. "A marriage has been arranged between..." The social columnists would love to get hold of it. "Prince Riabovitch and Lady Felicity"... Oh, no! I couldn't have that. We are both free to change our minds, aren't we? No one need be told yet. Not even my father.'

'My mind,' he said, 'will never change, but you...' he took another cigarette, his eyes searched hers, piercingly, 'you have changed in this half hour, no, in this half minute. You are like that creature, the chameleon, that changes its colour from its surroundings.'

'Am I? Perhaps I *am* like a chameleon. Perhaps I have taken my colour or the change of it from what you have told me of your nightmares. I was living that awfulness with you. But I think –' she knitted her forehead '– I think it was that I see you now, not as I thought you were, but as...'

She paused. Her voice dwindled.

'As what?' He put the cigarette between his lips and was seeking his lighter. 'And what did you think I was or that I am?'

'It was something you said earlier on about not wanting to live for ever as an assumed identity.'

'Yes? And so?' He lighted the cigarette, his face in the tiny flame looked closed and tense.

'And so,' she turned to look at the dragon's head crest again, 'I wondered if you are still –' she spoke lightly, not to make too much of it to hurt him who, God knew, had been hurt enough – 'were still assuming an identity.'

He took that light tone from her.

'But of course! One does not go hunted in dark glasses and a beard with hounds on your track to tear you to pieces without always having ready an identity to put on and take off when not required. Who can say with any truth "I am"? There are in each one of us a thousand idiot voices all crying "this is I", but only God has the right to say "this is I".'

'Yes,' she murmured. 'He said "I am that I am."'

'And I say,' he took her hand in both of his, 'that you are for *me* – now and for all time.'

'Sir,' the silent-footed man had entered and spoke in broken English. 'A chentleman is komm.' He added a few words in Russian.

And in Russian he was answered. To Felicity Alexei said:

'This is a man who has come about a picture that I asked him to deliver. I did not know he was coming this evening. Please don't go. He must wait.'

She took up her hat and coat.

'No, I must go. I was going in any case.'

'I will run you home.'

'Don't bother. Can your man get me a taxi? . . . Good-bye. It has been a lovely evening.'

He went with her down the stairs. In the gallery a man was seated and rose as they entered. He too spoke in Russian to the prince who answered him in English.

'Just wait a moment. You said you would telephone me when you were coming for the picture.'

More voluble Russian, evidently excusing himself for not having telephoned.

At the door the prince raised Felicity's hand to his lips, saying: 'An unforgettable evening. I will see you to-morrow?'

'Not tomorrow because,' then laughter gleamed, 'to-morrow never comes.'

SIX

When on 9 October 1924 the first Labour Government in British history dissolved to be faced with a third general election in three years after barely ten months in office, 'tomorrow' *did* come in a headline from *The Times*: 'A BANKRUPT PARTY. RED DESIGNS ON BRITAIN.'

This was followed in *Punch* with a cartoon showing a Russian as a scruffy sandwich man carrying a placard in bold letters announcing: 'VOTE FOR MACDONALD AND ME'.

Then, on 25 October, four days before polling the bombshell burst, dropped by the *Daily Mail*:

CIVIL WAR PLOT BY SOCIALIST MASTERS
MOSCOW ORDERS TO OUR REDS
GREAT PLOT DISCLOSED

The Great Plot disclosed was in a letter from Moscow sent to the Central Committee, British Communist Party, dated 15 December 1924 and signed: Zinoviev.

It contained a dramatic and spine-chilling exhortation to incite revolution in Britain.

'*It is indispensable to stir up the masses of the British proletariat to bring into movement the army of unemployed proletarians whose position can only be improved after a loan has been granted to the S.S.S.R. . . . A close observation should be kept on the leaders of the Labour Party because these could easily be found in the leading strings of the bourgeoisie.*' And it stressed that '*in the event of war, it were possible to paralyse all the military operations of the bourgeoisie, and make a start in turning an imperialist war into a class war. . . .* There was much more of it running into twelve hundred words and emphasizing that *armed warfare must be preceded by a struggle against the inclination to compromise, embedded among the English workmen against the idea of peaceful extermination of capitalism. Only then will it be possible to count upon complete success of an insurrection.'*

The effect upon the public of these startling pronouncements was primarily to dismiss them as the usual exaggeration of the Press to seize on any suspicious rumour to do with Communist Russia. But an immediate protest from the Foreign Office to the *Chargé d'Affaires* of the Soviet Government and a prompt denial from Rakovsky, gave reason to doubt the authenticity of the 'Red Letter' as it came to be known, particularly as Rakovsky declared it to be a 'gross forgery'. Yet there were some in highest quarters who believed the Letter to be a genuine attempt to stir up civil war; and MacDonald's hesitation in dealing with the case served to prompt further criticism from the Opposition against the Prime Minister and his Party.

There now began a 'Red Spy' scare promoted by much of the Conservative Press in a vigorous attempt to associate Labour with Communism. Leaflets were distributed stating: 'There are many Communists today in our so-called "Labour Party" and so strong are they that even our Socialist Government must do their bidding.'

It was evident that the Labour Government had been run to earth in a systematic witch-hunt.

Lord Rodborough, lunching with Lord Halstead at their club, prior to a debate in the Upper House concerning these divers explosions in the Press and the serious conclusions to be drawn from them by the Foreign Office, discussed the burning topic of the day.

'The King', said his physician, who probably knew more of the monarch's opinion in the crisis than even the head of his government could know, 'is reluctant to grant a dissolution, partly because there have already been two

132

general elections in – this will be the third in as many years – but also to refuse would be to suggest discrimination.'

'MacDonald's election tour,' said Rodborough, attacking steak-and-kidney pudding, 'has touched him on the raw, yet he is putting up a good fight against a strong offensive. Did you read his speech on his Welsh tour when he asked why the Opposition go about sniffing like mangey dogs on a garbage heap? He has a sound support, particularly among the miners in South Wales, and my guess is it will be touch and go who wins in spite of Zinoviev.'

'Yes, though the letter whether genuine or not has left its mark. The F.O. won't accept it as a forgery and the bulk of the Labour Party support Rakovsky's protest against the publication of the letter in the *Mail*. However, time will show.'

'But time is running out. The race has begun and the winning post is in sight with the Conservatives two lengths ahead.'

They ate in silence for a few minutes, Halstead demolishing *sole meunière*, and Rodborough his steak and kidney.

Stilton followed and coffee; Rodborough ordered a double brandy, offered one to the old doctor who refused it. 'I never take spirits during the day, especially when I am consulting.' Halstead looked at him shrewdly from under his white-shelved eyebrows. 'My secretary tells me you have made an appointment. Anything wrong?'

'Nothing much. I'm not sleeping too well, and I find I'm getting a bit breathless – off my game at golf. I'm worried about Felicity. She's got herself privately engaged – or semi-engaged, a sort of understanding – with that Russian fellow, Riabovitch. An émigré prince or something. Has a picture gallery in Duke Street. Do you know him?'

'Only because he consulted me on behalf of some relative of his, a Mrs Pickering-Smythe who took a cure for weight reducing at your health centre.'

'It's not my health centre. . . . No,' to the waiter, 'black.'

Coffee was served.

'You shouldn't take it black if you aren't sleeping too well,' said the doctor. 'What's wrong with this Russian that you don't approve of Felicity getting herself involved with him?'

'I don't say there is anything *wrong* with him. I've only seen him once. She brought him in for drinks. He seems a knowledgeable sort of chap about pictures, not that I know much about art. Felicity knows more than I do in that line, and he has quite an intelligent approach to the upheaval that brought the Czarist dynasty to its end. He sees both sides of the inevitable cause of it; but for one thing, he hasn't any money, or at least not enough for what I'd like her to have as I can't give her much. Besides I'd rather she married one of us. This Zinoviev affair has made all Russians, White or Red, suspect.'

'You can't tar them all with the same brush, but I see your point. If I had a daughter,' said the childless Halstead, 'I'd steer her clear, if I could, of any Russians these days.' He got up. 'I must be off – can't attend the debate, am chock-a-block with appointments this afternoon. The younger generation will have their own way. No good worrying. They'll do what they want to do. Parental influence is dead as the dodo.'

'Yes,' Rodborough drained his brandy glass, 'but you haven't a daughter, and mine is all that is left to me. If I lose her to the wrong man – '

'That's her look-out, not yours.'

'Brandy. Same again. Double,' said Rodborough to the waiter.

'I wouldn't if I were you.' Halstead gave him another keen glance. 'You've had the best part of a bottle of

Beaune already. Get along to the debate. It should be interesting with a minority of Labour peers upholding their party's defalcation in defence of the Red Letter scare.'

Rodborough shook his head.

'I can't think why any hereditary peer can be Labour, but I'll bet MacDonald will hand out peerages enough at the dissolution or the New Year's honours if he's in again, to get himself a backing in the Upper House.'

'Even without that,' Halstead reminded him, 'there are quite a few of the younger so-called intelligentzia among the hereditaries who are satellites of their 'Gentleman Mac'. I'll be seeing you at Harley Street.'

Despite the hopes of the Labour Party the result of the election was catastrophic for MacDonald. The Conservatives romped home with four hundred and fifteen seats as against a hundred and fifty-two won by Labour; and the Liberals, as also-rans, lost a hundred and sixteen seats, almost all to the Conservatives. Asquith was the most notable of their losses in a straight fight against Labour at Paisley.

The landslide to the Conservatives was generally attributed to the Zinoviev letter that started the 'Red Spy' mania and did nothing to lessen a general mistrust of all Russians and, in the case of Lord Rodborough, his hostility to Riabovitch as a suitor for Felicity.

When the excitement of the election had subsided, although the famous letter and its sinister significance was still being investigated by the Foreign Office and our Secret Intelligence who, with few exceptions, were convinced it could be no forgery, Lord Rodborough tackled his daughter on the subject of her engagement – 'to this Russian fellow, if you *are* engaged?'

'If you like to call it "engaged",' she said. 'I would rather think of it as "walking out". The maids, in what used to be the servants' hall, had a much more sensible way of conducting their courtships than making a thing of an "engagement". I believe that in former times – in the seventeenth and early eighteenth centuries – a "betrothal" was considered to be as binding as a marriage.' She favoured her father with an impudent grin to which he retorted:

'Don't prevaricate. Are you or aren't you going to marry him?'

'Look, Dad, we've had this out before. I've told you – I might or might not. He'll wait till I'm sure. He's in no hurry, nor am I.'

Said Rodborough worriedly: 'He is in no position to marry. What do you think you'll live on? His picture gallery? That won't keep you in hairpins or petrol for this car of yours.'

'We don't use hairpins.' She passed a hand through her bobbed curls, 'and my petrol costs not much more than five packets of Gold Flake. So you needn't worry about *that*.'

'For which,' muttered Rodborough with laboured sarcasm, 'is something to be thankful for. You'll have your gaspers and your car even if you have to live on bread and cheese.'

'Which I'd much prefer to caviare. Don't try to do the heavy father on me, ducky. We're not Edwardians any more, we're Georgians. By the way, what did Lord Halstead say about you? Nannie said you'd consulted him. Why didn't you tell me?'

'There was nothing to tell. He has limited me to six cigarettes a day – have to take it easily, and go slow on golf. He has given me a tonic. Nothing the matter with me. Only you.'

'Me? Why me?'

'I want you to be happily married if you have to marry, and to an Englishman. Not to a pauper prince and a Russian.'

'The Pauper Prince. That's an idea. Sounds like a

musical by Ivor Novello. I might try my hand at writing a libretto and send it to him.'

Her father removed his spectacles – he was reading *The Times* – and eyed her with disfavour.

'I know that whatever are my wishes in the matter, you'll go your own way. You always have and always will so it's no good talking to you.'

'Talk away as much as you like. Not that anything either of us do or don't do, or want or don't want, will make any difference. I'm a fatalist. What is to be will be. . . .'

Extract from Felicity's Commonplace Book

I haven't written anything in this for more than a month. It isn't a proper diary. I'm writing it because if I live to be very old and alone – how awful it must be for old people who are left alone and outlive their friends and everyone who belongs to them especially the very poor. (N.B. The Government must do something for them. Give them enough to live on which they don't give them yet) so if that happens to me I should have some record of when I was young. I feel a hag these days. Did some canvassing for the election. Didn't have time or energy to put it down in here. I got a lot of votes or promise of votes from the Labour districts. I asked to do the doubtful slummy parts and I deliberately called at the houses and tenements that had Labour posters stuck in their windows. Daddy said I'd probably get a black eye from them and didn't like me doing it. I had quite an amusing experience at one of the houses – a dreadful dirty looking slum house inhabited by about a dozen down and outs, and a man in a cap with a red scarf round his neck and his clothes all covered in paint or something came out of the door. I began telling him the jargon and he stopped me and asked in a very belligerent manner 'What do you think you're doing with all that?' Meaning my posters and leaflets and things. I told him 'You can see what I'm doing with them, can't you?'

I had twisted my ankle the day before when I fell dashing after a bus and couldn't get the car as it was in dock having its battery recharged and the water tank leaking, so I had to walk, and what with that and the old cartilege keeps on playing me up I was limping a lot. Anyway it looked very much as if I was going to get the black eye Daddy tried to put me off with. But no! He stuck out his hand – a filthy hand – and said 'Put it there, mate and good luck to you and all of us!'

I began to ask him 'Are you one of us?' But he forestalled me by saying, 'I've been a Conservative ever since I had the vote.'

So I said 'What is your job?' He said he worked for a firm of house painters, so I said, 'Will you convert your mates who need to be converted to vote Conservative and tell them what I would have told you about our aims and purpose?' He said 'No, I'll tell them about you . . .' 'What about me?' And he said 'You doing all this and walking up and down these streets with a game leg for the cause. That'll bring in more votes than all your talk.'

I was quite touched and I got sixty votes for us they told me at the Conservative Association as against six for the Conservatives last time. I'm wandering away from the point from which I meant to write that Daddy has been on at me again about R. I'm just as unsure as ever I was. It's rather like being faced with a high wall and can't make up one's mind to try and climb it without any sign of a foothold to see what's on the other side. Yes and if you did see what's on the other side having managed to get up there and sit on the top of the wall and supposing you saw a lovely house that could be yours how would you know if you would want to live in it even suppose it passed its survey? How can you know until you've tried? R would have a fit if I suggested we should have a trial trip. Being Russian he is a stickler for convention especially about women. But lots of girls do these days – those who have launched out on their own. I'm all for it. Only I don't think I'm keen enough on him for that. There's so much about him that I can't get at. *He* puts up a wall and I can't get on top of it. And then he has had a wife and is a widower. He never told me that until – well, not at first. Why should he as she's dead. He doesn't seem to have been very much in love with her and I don't think he is in love with me. He still has never said so – always 'want'. The snag is that I rather despise myself for the way I feel when he does make love – that is without saying so. He is very hot and then I . . . damn it I wish I were a cabbage or a jellyfish. I don't want to be a sex starved spinster which I shall be if I don't marry him or anyone unless I do as men do and to hell with old Grundy and Victorian hangovers. The Pankhursts have put the kibosh on all that.

One day last week just after the election he asked if I would like to help him in the gallery. I thought it a good idea being at a loose end since I did that job of canvassing and as for Russton I haven't seen him for ages. I expect he's in the South of France or somewhere doing *his* job as a waiter. He must make quite a bit that way in tips. He's a mystery too even more so than Riabovitch who is a product of the Revolution that has brought escapees over here and who likes to think he sees both sides of the cause of revolt being one of the "Intelligentzia" of the Bloomsbury crowd. I know he's in with them and says we mustn't foster inhibitions being all for Freud and Jung and that lot. Then there's Russton. I can't believe he takes those waiter jobs just for money. How can he get enough to make it worth his while to keep those two horses and the mare a possible Oaks runner if not a winner and here I go wandering from the point again. I'm like Aunt Harriet who jumps from one topic to another with no relevant connection. What I wanted to say was that yesterday R told me how I could help him in the gallery. I can two-finger type well enough to do his letters. A lot of them are in Russian and those he does himself in longhand and also I have to tell would-be buyers something about the pictures.

This of course would vary with the subjects. I couldn't tackle the ultra moderns but I now know a little more about the Italian primitives. He wouldn't sell them unless compelled to when he said 'we have a home together where I can keep you as you deserve to be kept' . . . Kept! Like a kept woman I thought but didn't say. Well yesterday while he was putting me wise how to cope with would-be buyers one of those Moderns came in with a picture. He is the Russian who did what R called an anatomical study of the interior of an aeroplane which was on view at his exhibition and there he was with another of them. Not an aeroplane this time – it looked as if it were meant to be the upper part of a woman's naked body. I couldn't see if she had any legs but there was a great eye in one corner and a bright orange and black background and what might have been a tree or a giraffe for all I could tell. R was talking to him in Russian having introduced me to Count Poppycockski it sounded like. He was hideous and cross-eyed which might account for his painting as he obviously can't see straight. Then after more jabbering from both of them R asked me to excuse them as the Count couldn't speak much English and explained that he was saying the picture had a backing to it. Then this Poppycockski or whatever he was took the picture and fumbled with the back of it which opened and showed a kind of panel that he said was where the history of the picture and its meaning was written on the wood the thing being painted on wood and not canvas. There was some writing in red ink on the wood.

When the artist (save the mark!) had gone R said that he – this Poppycockski – was one of the up and coming foremost of the New Art movement which expresses the inner and not the outer thought of Being. (That's how he goes on and which would bore me stiff to live with!) Not photographic vision as with the older and less enlightened school but a regression to the primitives before perspective had imposed itself on vision to produce not what the artist *felt* but what he *saw* as for instance Cézanne who painted trees with pink trunks as he saw them in sunlight . . . And he showed me a reproduction of a Cézanne to prove his point but I couldn't see any resemblance in the thing this one brought to Cézanne's lovely picture of trees even if they were pink.

By the way Mrs Thistlewaite has invited Daddy and me to a house-warming at that place they've bought near Rodborough. It is on the twenty-first of next month. I asked Alex if he had an invitation and he said he had. I don't know if we shall go. It means staying the night. She wrote she would be delighted to put us up.

*   *   *

'All the invitations are out at last,' said Mrs Thistle-waite to Albert, interrupting him at work in his study, his 'work' being a treatise, he told her, on the grafting of white carnations on to blue.

'If it amuses you,' Ethel humoured him, 'get on with it, but I don't want blue carnations in the gardens nor the greenhouse. Nor do I want to lose Macgregor, who resents interference. Even I am not allowed to ask him for grapes until he says they are ripe to cut, so don't offend him for goodness' sake.'

'No, my dear, cer . . . tainly not,' Albert in all humility agreed.

'I have had another request, in writing this time not a phone call, from Prince Riabovitch asking if there is any hope you will sell the Gerard Dows.' She looked to where they hung together on the wall. "They are so ugly. Why do you want them? You don't know anything about pictures or you would buy something really valuable, a Gainsborough or a Romney. Mr Brewster said the Adam dining-room requires eighteenth-century masters and as you haven't any ancestors the least you could do is to provide us with some, even if they are other people's ancestors.'

'Yes,' again was Albert's humble agreement, 'I see your point. A Gainsborough or a . . . Romney or a . . .'

'What I came to say is I have invited all your board of directors and their wives and they've accepted. The Air Marshal answered accepting by return, but I am wondering if I should invite Major Armstrong of the research station. I don't know him or his wife – if he has one.'

'Perhaps,' ventured Albert, 'it would be a . . . neighbourly gesture to invite him.'

'Scarcely a neighbour. He is not of the county and I doubt if he is regular army, probably a temporary who has kept his commission with no right to it as so many do. He is only the manager of the research station, a salaried servant.'

'As the Air Marshal,' again Albert dared to offer an opinion, 'has accepted it might be tact ... ful if Major Armstrong were ...'

Without letting him finish, Ethel said determinedly: 'I shall not put Major and Mrs as I don't know if he is married, but if he is it was *her* place to call on me as everyone else did when we first came here. I shall have to hire extra footmen – our two are not enough to deal with at least a hundred guests if they all come, which I think they will. I am putting Lord Rodborough and his daughter in the best guest rooms, also Prince Riabovitch. Mrs Pickering-Smythe will be staying at that Rodborough health place. She is going to take another course of treatment, she lost so much weight last time.' Ethel was talking to herself more than to him who, his head on one side, listened and nodded approval every now and then. 'Those that can't get back to London,' pursued Ethel, 'though of course half the country will be within driving distance, but the others, if there's no room here, I shall put up at the inn or at Cromer.'

She left Albert to his treatise, and no sooner was she gone than he went to an opposite wall of the oak-panelled room that Ethel had assigned for his study. 'Mr Brewster,' she had said, 'told me I should have to decorate it entirely Tudor or Jacobean which I dislike, so you can have that room for yourself.'

He was much obliged, particularly as his inspection of the walls had discovered a small priest hole dating back to Elizabeth. This was entirely unnoticeable even to the practised eye of Mr Brewster; but Albert (M.A. Cantab.) besides an honours degree in languages, had taken a degree in archaeology which he had never followed up, devoting himself to the pursuit of that he had acquired as a student of languages both ancient and modern. 'And what possible use,' Ethel had said, 'could archaeology be to you or languages as you never speak anything but English?'

They were of evident use to him now, however, when sliding aside a panel in the oak he took from the aperture two facsimiles of the Gerard Dows that hung on the opposite wall. This done he took from the priest hole a telephone. Pressing the secrecy switch he was put through to a private extension line. As usual when he spoke on the telephone, either to make or answer a call, there was no discernible hesitancy in his speech, much to Ethel's annoyance.

'It shows it is just nerves with you,' she had said. 'You don't *have* to speak like a mental deficient.'

Yet there was nothing of the mental deficient in the voice that now addressed: 'Armstrong? ... Urgent. The Borzoi is after the plans of the R Y Z and the Boomerang.' He gave a cherubic chuckle. 'He shall have them ... Yes, both of them. ... Don't know how he guessed but he did. I had copies made of the Dows, you remember? ... Our fellow at the Hague. He got them done by a man who does them for the dealers ... No, I can't let him have the copies, good though they are. He has knowledge enough to spot a fake ... Yes, the A.M. insisted in case of accidents ... I had a report from the Borzoi's man. He's a double but quite useful ... One of theirs brought in a picture with a back slide like mine. They are painted on wood. ... Says no need to report to X until we have something definite to go on. They've got the wind up enough already over this Z business. ... Yes, I think so too. A mare's nest. .. Send an electrician,' another chuckle, 'my study lights have fused. Let me have the photographic copies with diagrams as before but with a difference. And I'll do the translations. No, I don't really mind letting them go. Only sentimental value. I had them in my rooms at King's. ... Very few genuine Dows in this country. The Dutch buy them up. Right. Soon as you can.'

He replaced the telephone and taking the two Gerard Dows that had been in the aperture he extracted a folded flimsy sheet of paper from the wood backing of the picture depicting a fish stall. This he put in a backing behind one of those he took down from the wall and carefully scrutinized the result. He then placed these two in the priest hole, and hung on the wall those he had taken from their hiding place.

No one, he thought, unless he were in the know, which apparently he is, could tell there was anything behind either of them; and he chuckled again. He'll get the plan of the R Y Z and everything else he wants.

About an hour later Ethel returned to find him still engrossed with his botanical treatise.

'Which of your lights has fused?' she demanded.

'All of them,' he told her, 'the ... the wall lights and the desk lamp. Luck ... ily it is daylight still, so I don't need ...'

'An electrical engineer has come from Dereham. He said you phoned for him.' She glanced at the telephone on his desk. 'Why didn't you tell me? Any of our men could have mended a fuse. No necessity to call in an electrician to do it. A waste of money.'

'I didn't think, my dear,' murmured Albert.

'No, you never do. By the way I am going to London tomorrow so I can take those horrid pictures with me and have them delivered to the prince. It is the least we can do for these unfortunate Russian aristocrats who have lost everything in that awful revolution. The prince will sell them and make money out of them. So sad that they are deprived of their estates, their homes, their relatives – murdered with the Czar. Some of them are taking any sort of job. Mrs Pickering-Smythe told me she has a friend, a Russian countess, who goes as cook general employed by some suburban people in Croydon. Of course they don't know who she is. I'll send the electrician up to you but I expect he'll want to test the mains.'

'Yes, thank you,' Albert said. 'I ... expect he will.'

*   *   *

To the Thistlewaites' house-warming eighty-five of the hundred or so invited had accepted and arrived on 21 November. There were several young people among them, and in the great hall that was cleared for them to dance they jazzed to the band brought from London. The older guests distributed themselves either at the bridge tables, which in one of the large reception rooms were prepared to receive those who wished to play, while the rest of them entertained each other with local gossip and criticism of their host and hostess, not always in their favour. The board of directors of Waites and their wives gravitated pleasantly together, but Ethel was somewhat vexed to see that the Air Marshal, whose wife had accepted but did not come because – he apologized for her – their youngest son had mumps, that he, Air Marshal Ironside, engaged in conversation Major Armstrong whose wife had not been invited.

A buffet table was laid the whole length of the Adam dining-room, on the walls of which were hung a sufficiency of ancestors. 'Chiefly mine,' Ethel explained to her guests who paused in their exploration of the rooms to admire the powdered and periwigged staring faces in their heavy gilded frames, 'and those of the Victorians and Regency are Albert's.' There were only three of these among the half dozen of Ethel's.

'We had to store them,' she said, 'until we bought the manor, our St John's Wood house has no room large enough to hang them all.'

How she managed to collect them in less than six weeks had been due to the efficiency of Mr Brewster, whose interior and exterior decorations were greatly admired, and Mrs Thistlewaite's taste received due congratulation.

There was to be a firework display at midnight after supper served at tables for four in the dining-room and hall.

Felicity, seated at a table with her latest partner for the foxtrot who had asked for the supper dance, was joined by Riabovitch and his partner, the daughter of the M.F.H. of the Norfolk and Suffolk hunt. The talk veered from generalities to the 'Red Spy Scare', still of momentous interest, being barely a month old.

'It's these Communists,' said Felicity's young man, who was taking a post-graduate course in economics and was almost certainly, she decided, in with the 'Bloomsbury crowd', for he spoke with iconoclastic vehemence against the Conservatives who 'had ousted the Socialists by a trick – ' the young iconoclast fisted a hand on the table, 'a dastardly trick, to bring MacDonald and his Party down. There's not a word of truth in that Zinoviev letter.'

'I am inclined to agree,' was the prince's contribution to this, 'as so the Soviet *Chargé d'Affaires* has declared. But I cannot think that Mr Baldwin and his Government would countenance or credit what Mr Rakovsky has pledged himself to deny and has lodged his protest against it.'

'Do you know this Soviet *Chargé d'Affaires*?' demanded the young man, whose name had escaped Felicity.

'I am acquainted with him,' replied Riabovitch. 'And despite those he represents and whom I have no reason to uphold, I believe him to be genuinely concerned at the publicity given to this most – ' he paused for a strong enough word – 'most infamous forgery. But', he shrugged, 'there is far too much credence offered to these comparatively minor agitators who follow the aggressive example set by those of my country who were misled in their false idealism based on Karl Marx.'

'Yes, you blame everything on Marx, and they, your revolutionists, say their prayers to Lenin and Trotsky, but' – the iconoclast again fisted a hand on the table – 'how do you know they had not reason on their side?'

'We do not know. That is our tragedy.'

Gladys Hamlyn, the daughter of Sir Charles Hamlyn, M.F.H., is described by Felicity in her account of that house warming at Hollywell, as:

. . . a horse-faced girl with large leathery hands I should think heavy on a mouth and obviously lives for nothing but horses and hounds. Bored with all this talk about the Red Letter as was I the news of it is dying hard. This Hamlyn girl has a whinneying laugh to punctuate anything she said which wasn't much mostly about the meet at Dereham yesterday. . . . And this post-graduate 'Economics' whose name I didn't get was cracking up the Labour Party and making out that this letter of Zinieviv's (can't spell it) was a put-up job of the Conservatives to smash Macdonald. They, or rather the other one got on to the Russian Revolution and R staved him off with his usual seeing both sides of 'our tragedy', as he called it . . . And while this was going on and neither I nor the Hamlyn girl were listening to much of it I suddenly saw Russton! I caught his eye but not a sign of recognition in it. He was serving ice pudding at the next table. Then he came to us and said in my ear: 'Fruit salad or ice pudding, Miss?'

I said I'd have both and while he was helping me I had all to do not to jog his elbow and almost said, Come off it. So he's turned up again doing his waiter's stuff. A footman this time in livery. Hired. Needs the cash I suppose if he wants to keep his two horses and race the mare next year. Wish I knew where he lives. I'd write and ask him who he is and what and why etc. All I know is Pimlico and although I canvassed the slums of Pimlico I saw no sign of him. So I wash him out. . . .

After supper those of the younger guests not playing bridge or the more elderly not fearing the night air, had come on to the terrace to watch the fireworks. The dark river of the November sky was pricked with faint stars and high above a spreading cedar on the lawn a new moon lay on her back upon a silvery drifting cloud.

The first rocket soared skywards and fell in a shower of golden rain followed by a rainbow-coloured downpour to the accompaniment of delighted 'Oh's and 'Ah's from the youngsters grouped together, their voices drowned in a series of bangs that heralded each fiery flight. Footmen brought chairs for the not-so-young to be seated where, wrapped in furs and shawls, they contributed polite if less enthusiastic applause and wondered how long it would go on before they could leave for their neighbouring homes or, if staying the night, for their beds.

Riabovitch had sought and found Felicity among the crowd of young people gazing upward at the ever-changing kaleidoscopic reds, greens, blues and gold interspersed with flaming Catherine wheels and a wondrous gigantic crown studded with rubies, sapphires, emeralds, that disintegrated to descend in gem-like sparks.

'Are you happy?' whispered Alexei, taking Felicity's hand. 'Such a child as you are! You're loving this Guy Fawkes nonsense, yes?'

'Yes,' with a touch of defiance, 'I am. Ronnie and I – ' she faltered – 'we used to have fireworks on Guy Fawkes night – at Rodborough ... Ooh!' as another Catherine wheel flared up, 'that was a beauty.'

'Are you warm enough in that light cloak?' he asked. 'There is a cool breeze rising.'

'Quite warm enough. It is more like a night in late summer than November.'

She released her hand from his and moved away. He went with her, saying: 'I have not had a chance to see or speak with you alone the whole evening. Won't you come in and let us sit somewhere? See, this is the last of it.'

Across the grape-bloom sky golden letters blazed to spell 'GOOD NIGHT'.

'Quite ingenious,' murmured Alexei ... 'Please. Do come in. They are serving hot soup in the dining-room.'

At the buffet Felicity looked for Russton. He was not to be seen among the footmen serving soup from a tureen. She supposed that having finished the job for which he had been hired he had gone home, if he had a home.

But he had not finished his 'job'. He was valeting the rooms of the men who were staying the night. One of the

148

house footmen had taken over the wing where two of the Waites directors and their wives were to sleep; the others, driving back that night, had already left. Having taken the Air Marshal's suit and that of Lord Rodborough to be pressed, Russton went to the room next to Rodborough's which was occupied by Riabovitch. There he spent some time carefully inspecting the pockets of an overcoat and day suit and those of a dressing-gown, an exotic affair of purple orchids on a green and red background threaded with gold; embroidered on the chest was the crest of a dragon's head.

The Dragon's Head is *not* to be feared, he grinned to his inner man. Finding nothing of interest in any of these pockets he examined the toilet accessories on the dressing table. Taking up one of the silver-backed brushes, these also bearing the Riabovitch crest, he ran his finger round the edges of the brush and took up another. He pressed the back of this and it flew open. Swiftly Russton extracted a flimsy folded paper.... Aha! Our Dragon is taking no risks – nor are we! he told himself. He was looking closely at the diagram and the writing in French, German and English. Then producing a notebook from his pocket he made a quick copy of the paper, laughed again softly, replaced it, closed the spring of the brush and went into the communicating bathroom. Russton lifted the lid of the cistern from which the name of Waites was conspicuously absent, satisfied himself there was nothing of interest there, and with the prince's suit over his arm he left the room.

As he passed along the corridor toward the staircase that led through a heavy oaken door to the staff quarters he was met by Mr Thistlewaite coming from his study. With a glance over his shoulder to see that none was in eye or ear shot, Albert spoke in a hurried undertone.

'He has been to Fordington today. Have you got anything?'

'Only this – of yours.' Russton handed him a page torn

149

from his notebook. 'They are taking all precautions. He is carrying copies wherever he goes.'

Albert gave his little chuckle.

'Armstrong said he showed him everything of un . . . importance including the plan of the R 34 that flew the Atlantic in 1919 and is, of course, ob . . . solete. He is not to know that. Wasn't operating then anyway. Armstrong says he took it all in. He is applying to Handley Page for his own aircraft and says he is interested in airships as a possible means of commercial flights which he might eventually pilot. He will prob . . . ably be making notes from memory tonight.'

'Won't get him very far!' grinned Russton. 'I'll be packing his suitcase tomorrow.'

'If he goes back. My wife is inviting Rodborough and his daughter for the week-end.'

'Then,' said Russton with another grin, 'Mrs Thistlewaite will be requiring me to stay for the valeting.'. . .

'Are you staying for the weekend?' Felicity asked her father when she went to say goodnight to him. 'You don't want to, do you?'

'Not if I know it.' He had divested himself of his tail coat and was wrestling with his white tie.

'I'll do it for you.' Doing so, she added: 'I've had Mrs Thistlewaite in a big way. She really is the limit. All these newly painted ancestors! Does she think anyone would fall for them? I'm sorry for poor little Albert.'

'You needn't be.' Lord Rodborough, unfastening his waistcoat and removing its platinum and onyx buttons, was hunting about for the case to put them in.

'Here it is,' she handed it to him from his dressing table.

'You don't have to be sorry for a millionaire as near as dammit,' he told her, stooping to his evening pumps.

'That makes me all the sorrier. I believe millionaires must be the most miserable people on earth. Fancy being able to have everything you want by just buying it! There'd be nothing left for you to wish for and half the fun of life is wishing for something you can't have and if it does turn up how much more exciting than wanting what you think will never happen or can't afford to have, and living on a hope that is at last fulfilled. But millionaires can never know that. Everything they want they can buy.'

'Except,' her father said, 'that which no money can buy as for instance – you.'

'Darling! What a lovely thing to say. But millionaire or not, it isn't everyone who'd want me.'

Rodborough cocked an eyebrow.

'Not even Riabovitch?'

'Oh, he wants me all right, but that isn't the same thing as loving.'

'Are you still keeping him on a string?'

She laughed lightly.

'On a tight rope more like it. I'm telling myself what Asquith told us – wait and see.'

'If,' he said, 'you do see.'

'What,' she asked, 'are you looking for now?'

He was peering round about.

'My stud.'

She went down on all fours groping, found the stud where it had rolled under a chair. 'Here you are . . . Did I tell you – no, I didn't – that Ethel, beg her pardon, Ellen – has given Riabovitch the Gerard Dows?'

Her father jerked up his head.

'She's given them to him?'

'Yes, and they aren't fakes either. He's had them vetted. He'll sell them to the Americans. He needs the cash. The rent of the gallery is overdue and he may have to close down.'

'That will help you a lot, won't it?' said Lord Rodborough acidly, 'while you are waiting to see.'

'I don't rat from a sinking ship. Not that he'll ever

sink. He knows how to weather storms. He has steered clear of the rocks so far and he always will. That's why I like him. He doesn't go whining like some of these émigré Russian *aristos* do about what they've suffered and all they've lost, including their country. He just gets on with making the best of what's left to him.'

'And what is left to him, apart from you?' His lordship was unfastening his braces.

'His determination to get on with the life that he's been thrown into not from choice, from necessity. Have you taken your medicine?'

'Not yet. I will.'

She took a bottle from his bedside table, measured a dose into a glass and added water from the carafe on his wash basin. 'It's your sleeping draught. Lord Halstead has put a tonic into it as well. You are sleeping better, aren't you?' she looked at him anxiously, 'and not so breathless?'

'I went round in seventy-three last Sunday and could have gone round again without a puff. Nothing wrong with me. Halstead is something of an old woman.'

'He has done you good, anyhow. Drink it up.' She held out the glass to him. He took it, made a face. 'Filthy stuff. Ugh!'

'You are a baby, Dad. Do you want a sweet to take the taste out?' She lifted her face for his kiss. 'Good night, ducky.'

'Good night, darling. Don't be in too great a hurry to make up your mind. I'd hate to lose you to – anyone.'

'You won't ever have to lose me. Sleep well.'

She went from him thinking: The trouble with me is I don't believe I shall ever love any man as much as I love him. I expect I'll end up with some old chap of fifty, seeking what the psycho-Freudians call the Father Image.

The next day being Saturday Lord Rodborough wrote a polite note much regretting he could not accept Mrs Thistlewaite's kind invitation for himself and his daughter to stay the weekend, owing to an urgent call that necessitated his immediate return to London. He and Felicity breakfasted in their rooms and left immediately afterwards, avoiding meeting their host and hostess. Felicity driving him back to London stopped at a florist in Ipswich.

'I'm going to send the Thistlewaite flowers from you. It is like sending coals to Newcastle – the place is a hothouse of flowers already – but you have to do something more than just thanking her for inviting us to the party and a weekend. Give me a pound and your card.' He gave her both. 'Now write on it.'

She produced a fountain pen from her bag.

'What shall I write?'

'Surely you know how to thank for that lousy party?... Just put "with many thanks from my daughter and myself for a most delightful entertainment" and sign it.'

As always when Felicity took command he did as he was told.

She went into the shop, bought a spray of orchids for which she paid twenty-five shillings, ordered them to be sent with the card and returned to the car saying: 'You owe me five bob.' Getting into the driver's seat she lowered the window and called to a hooting car behind her:

'Shut that row! It's a lorry in front of me that's holding me up. I'm passing him now – and don't you try to pass me!'

'No need to shout from the car like a street urchin,' reproved her father.

'Street urchins don't drive cars – Blast him! He all but grazed my wing.'

Rodborough blinked ... Their language! This girl of his and all of them have slipped a generation. They manage themselves and she manages me. Do what they like. What should I do without her?... Shouldn't put all my eggs in one basket but where else should I put them?

Ronnie gone. No heir. Father to son without a break for almost three centuries and now . . . dead end.

'I'll drop you home,' Felicity was saying, 'and then I have to go on to the gallery.'

'Is it open on a Saturday?'

'Not to the public in the afternoon but I have to see to something.'

'Why do you get yourself mixed up with that gallery?' grumbled her father. 'Does he pay you for what you do?'

'Of course not. I do his typing. I can type well enough for his letters and filing and I can interview prospective buyers. It saves him having to pay a secretary.' She drew up at a wayside inn. 'I'm hungry. We can get a sandwich if we're not too late for luncheon.'

They were too late for luncheon; but Felicity, leading the way into the private bar, ordered ham sandwiches for two.

'Do you want a drink?' she asked her father.

'I'll have a whisky.'

'One whisky and a tonic water,' she told the barmaid.

'Make it a double for me,' said Lord Rodborough.

'I thought you had been knocked off spirits.'

'I'm on them again as I've always been, in moderation. I don't drink a bottle of this – ' he took the glass from the bar counter where it had been placed – 'in a week.'

He paid the barmaid and moving to a table they ate their sandwiches in silence. Felicity thought, as she glanced at him furtively: I don't like that sort of blue look on his lips. Lord Halstead said he had a slight cardiac murmur, nothing to worry about but those murmurs can lead to something else. Like that fellow in hospital who had a murmur and then I found him . . . Don't! I was on night duty then, but the fool of a house doctor, just qualified, knew damn all about hearts. That 'flu did awful things to hearts, as it did to Ronnie.

She looked at her wrist watch.

'If you've finished we had better get on.'

They got on, and arriving at Ashley Gardens shortly after three o'clock, she left her father there and drove to Duke Street. The prince's Daimler was parked outside the gallery where she left her own car. She went in and through to his office.

He was at his desk, busily writing. As she entered he rose and covering with a paper weight the work on which he had been engaged he went to her.

'What a happy surprise! I did not expect to see you here today. I thought you would have stayed for the week-end at Hollywell.'

'No, Daddy and I had enough of it but I thought you were staying.'

'I too had enough of it. Did you come,' he took her hand and drew her to him, 'expecting *not* to see me?'

'I didn't actually think about it. I knew if the door wasn't open your man would be here to let me in.'

'As a matter of fact he is not here. I give him a day off whenever I can spare him, usually on a Saturday afternoon.'

She released her hand and went to the desk that was scattered with correspondence.

'Is there anything I can do for you now I am here? Anything to be catalogued for the show next week?'

'That is all done, but you should know what you can do for me.'

He had come close to her. She could hear his quickened breath on the words: 'Am I to wait for ever? This uncertainty devastates me.... I want you, Félise. I must have an answer, I must. I cannot endure this ...' he paused, 'this cat and mouse game you play with me ... "I am not sure",... "Give me time" ... "Wait, wait, wait." I cannot wait!'

He pulled her into his arms, forcing his mouth on hers. She responded, weakening against her will to the physical attraction of this man.

At last when she unclosed her eyes to see his face

above hers, white about the lips under the dark streak of his moustache he said:

'If you were any other woman I would not stand for this. I would have taken you and you would not have resisted. No! But because you are what you are, so desirable and so . . . desirous, yet you have in you a sterner quality that may be puritanical or pride, or – '

'I am no puritan,' she broke in with, 'and if I were any other woman I might not have resisted. As for pride, there is no pride between two persons who know themselves to be meant for each other, mentally and physically. There would be no need to wait for the conventional announcement: "A marriage has been arranged", and the ceremonial fuss of it all at St Margaret's or St George's – no!' (as he would have interrupted) 'I mean this. Marriage is too serious an undertaking as far as I am concerned, unless I can be absolutely certain that it would be right for me and for . . . you.'

'For me, yes. For you,' he lifted her hand, turned it palm upward and dropped a light kiss in it, closing her hand upon it, 'as right and as certain as is this, which leaves no memory, no answer that cannot be brushed away. So we go on as we are?'

'Until,' she said not looking at him but down at the hand he had returned to her still closed as if it contained to hold fast the answer to that which he demanded, 'until such time as I can know that I too can . . . want.'

'By God!' he drew in a hissing breath, 'I swear the time will come when I will make you *know* you want me as much as ever I have wanted you!'

SEVEN

Christmas had come and gone, spent quietly at Ashley Gardens by Felicity in bed with what Nannie called a feverish cold and the doctor a dose of 'flu.

'Nothing like the "plague" of 1919,' Felicity told her father when she was up and about again, 'but it's a beast of a bug and very lowering. It is becoming epidemical and I don't want you to get it so we're going away, you and I, for a change of air and scene. Dr Cree says that's what we both should have and so we'll go to – what do you say to Florence?'

Lord Rodborough, who had heard almost none of this, being deep in *The Times* propped before him at the breakfast table in front of his eggs and bacon, said: 'I see that the miners have given a warning notice that the national wages agreement of the previous year is imminent. The miners' federation refuses to discuss the owners' terms. They have handed it over to the General Council of the T.U.C. That will mean ultimate nationalization.'

'Yes, dear.' Felicity reached for the marmalade, 'but what about Florence?'

'Florence?' Her father took toast and buttered it. 'Florence who?'

'Oh, lord!' She turned her eyes ceilingward. 'You weren't listening to a word. I want a holiday and so do you. We haven't been away – not really away out of England since we went to Biarritz three years ago. The doctor says I'm below par and I know I am. I feel so slack – no energy, and he advises both of us, you and me, to go to Bournemouth.'

'Damned if I will!' uttered Lord Rodborough. 'Bourne-mouth! Full of bath chairs and bronchials.'

'Of course not *there*! I said Florence. Italy. Firenze, as Alexei calls it.'

'*He's* not going?' Up went his lordship's head as he halted toast in mid air to his mouth.

'No, but we are. Just you and I.'

'Why on earth do you want to go to Florence?'

'Because I've always wanted to go to Florence, and particularly now that I'm beginning to understand something about the Tuscan Primitives and can see them in the Uffizi and the other galleries.'

'Pah!' his lordship snorted. 'Galleries. You think of nothing else. Tuscan Primitives. Is that how he gets you with *his* gallery and high falutin talk of art? Much he knows about art. Diddling the Americans with a lot of fakes.'

'Some may be fakes but not all, and he wouldn't intentionally sell a fake. Even the greatest experts can be taken in by copies, they are so well done. There are artists, Riabovitch told me, who specialize in that, and sell them for the real thing. Those Gerard Dows Mrs Thistlewaite gave him are worth several hundreds and they *are* the real thing. He says he is keeping them until or unless he *has* to sell them. So what about it?'

'What about *what*?' said her father testily.

'I'm telling you. Florence. It's as much for you as for me that we're going. You are still puffing and blowing and "murmuring". I rang Lord Halstead yesterday and asked him, and he said it is an excellent idea to get away for the rest of the winter out of England. We can be in Florence for the spring, when here it'll probably be snowing. And you can play golf there. Lord Halstead knows Florence well and said there are two courses, one an eighteen hole but too hilly, he said, for you, the other a nine hole. He quite agrees you mustn't be exposed to infection here in

158

London with this 'flu about. Thank goodness you didn't get mine. It's on the increase.'

'And who,' he demanded, 'is going to pay for Florence through the rest of the winter and into the spring? How much will it cost?'

'Less than it would cost us anywhere in England at Bournemouth or Torquay or any of those winter resorts they advertise for bathchair chesty old people. The *lira* is in our favour to something like – I forget exactly what Cook's told me – thousands of *lire* to the pound. It is only the fare that is rather steep but that is made up by the cheaper hotel prices. So I've booked a double *wagon lit* on the Rome express and if by chance we can't go we can cancel it.'

'Well, then,' said his lordship explosively, 'you'll cancel it for we're not going!'

'Yes, we are because I've paid for the tickets.'

'You've paid for – now look here!' Her father thumped a fist on the table to make the crockery jump. 'You go too far. You take too much upon yourself. I won't *have* it. You understand? Paid for the tickets! How? What with?'

'My pearls,' said she calmly. 'I've pawned them for ninety quid and the tickets are ninety-five, so if you write me a cheque for ninety I can get out the pearls. I never wear them.'

'They were your mother's,' he reminded her weakly.

'That's why I didn't sell them, which I might have done.'

'How,' he temporized, 'can I give you a cheque for ninety pounds? I'm overdrawn as it is.'

'No, you're not. I've seen your bank balance. You left your bank book with your balance up to date lying on your desk. You couldn't have looked at it, but anyone else could. And don't forget your half year's director's fees for Waites is due this month and that'll be five hundred, and you've got your dividends coming in any day now, so be an angel, Dad, and let me have that cheque. I'm letting

you off a fiver. I've paid the five out of my dress allowance, although I'll have to buy some new things for
Florence and you can buy me those.'

'Pass the marmalade.... You said there is a golf
course?'

'There are two.' She got up to pass him the marmalade
and to drop a kiss on the top of his head. 'So we'll leave
here in about a month from today and we'll miss the
worst of the winter. Bless you, darling, I'll get your
cheque book and you can pay me back less that fiver,
which is my contribution to our holiday.'

From Felicity's Commonplace Book

I'm writing this in our wagon lit en route for Italy on the
Rome Express and woke to wonderful sunshine pouring
through the windows. We left London in icy cold and fog
and now it looks like spring. We crossed the Alps while we
slept. The train branches off to Florence but we don't have
to change they just transfer us to the Florence line. As we
crossed the frontier early this morning when Daddy was still
asleep with the pill Lord Halstead had given him (Medinal
we used to give that in hospital) two customs officers,
Italians looking rather like our gamekeepers but in slouch
hats stuck with pheasant's feathers asked very politely in
Italian-English if we had anything to declare. I was just out
of bed and had the top of my pyjamas off – was stark to the
waist. They have master keys of course. They murmured
apologies and retired while I covered myself and they came
back and began again as if they had only just arrived. I was
reminded of the plumber who walked into a hotel bathroom
to repair a tap and saw a naked woman getting into the bath
and said, 'Excuse me, *sir*!'

I told them we had nothing to declare and they went off
with a big show of white teeth in sunburnt faces. How
different from our customs officers who only want to catch
us out. I then washed in the W.C. place belonging to our
compartment and Daddy who had slept through it all woke
up. I ordered his breakfast to be brought here, coffee and

rolls. Thought it best for him to have a light breakfast on top of the medinal but I went into the dining car. The steward found a table for me occupied by three men, the only decent place. All the other tables were full.

They were Italians and talking together all the time. They took no notice of me except that one of them got up and offered me his seat near the window as better than being on the outside with the waiters rushing by. They were just finishing their breakfast and went before I had been served. When I came back to our wagon lit quite a long walk and the train tearing along I was jostled and bumped as I went through from one coach to another the whole train full mostly of Americans, Germans and not many English so far as I could tell as I passed them in the corridors. I then found that our beds in our compartment had been made and Daddy dressed but not shaved because of the jolting of the train and that one of the Italians who had given me his seat at the table in the dining car was in our compartment and talking away to Daddy in perfect English. D said this is my daughter let me introduce Mr – no, Marchese Marconi.

I said as he bowed very graciously 'Are you related to the inventor?'

He said, 'I am the inventor.'

Well!

He was charming, oldish, grey haired, blue or grey eyes and one of them a bit fixed and starey. I heard afterwards he had a glass eye. It seemed Daddy had met him in London at some do or other and he had the wagon lit next to ours and was standing in the corridor when he saw D through the window recognized him and came in to talk to him.

We were passing through Santa Margarita (if that's how it's spelt?) and now it seemed like full summer and so hot I took off my coat. Too glorious that glimpse of the Mediterranean and the great mountains rising up from the sea as we rushed past. I was enchanted and dashed back and forth from our window and into the corridor drinking it all in. Much more lovely and exciting than when we went to Biarritz. I had been reading in bed last night a book I had brought with me by Henry James, the Madonna of the Future that describes a young man's first sight of Florence under moonlight and I said how I wished I could see Florence for the first time under moonlight.

Marconi said 'There will be a full moon tonight. I am staying in Florence until tomorrow and then I go to Rome. I would be delighted to show you and Lord Rodborough the Flower City' (as he called it) "under moonlight.'

So it was arranged that he should pick us up at our hotel and take us to dinner and then afterwards show us Florence. But although Daddy accepted M's invitation to dine he said he felt too tired to see sights and hoped to be excused if he went to bed. However he came with us to the restaurant for dinner. It was a marvellous dinner where Marconi took us and the maître d'hotel bowed and scraped to him calling him Excellenzi Senatore Marchese. We drove Daddy back to our hotel and then M and I toured Florence. . . .

And two days later.

I was too tired to write all my impressions when I got back that night so I write them now.

Shall I ever forget my first sight of this beautiful city, so small and yet so great and fraught with history that the very stones conjure up visions of those who trod them. Dante and his Beatrice, Lorenzo the Magnificent, the Borgias and Fra Lippo Lippi sneaking out in his friar's habit to meet a girl. We stood on the Ponte Vecchio and saw the Arno shining in the light of the moon with century-old palaces rising up out of the water where the stars looked to be drowned and where Dante must have passed when he saw and never forgot his Beatrice who was his one and only love. . . . So narrow are the streets it's a wonder how these great palaces could ever have been built to stand on either side of them that almost all are only lanes.

As the moon rose up in the starry sky the streets quietened and the rattle of the vetturi died down. These are the taxis drawn by – oh, the horses, so thin and wretched I can't bear to drive behind them and I make Daddy go everywhere in a hired car.

From the Ponte Vecchio we came on to the Piazza della Signoria. I've learned to spell their lovely names from my

guide book. Breathtakingly beautiful was this Piazza with
the statues shining silver in the moonlight under that lofty
fierce old palace the Palazzo Vecchio the huge fortress
where Marconi told me Savonarola was tried and tortured,
'A mad pathetic creature,' Marconi called him, 'self-con-
demned and self destroyed. Out here,' he said, 'he met his
awful death. He was imbued with every sort of anarchy, a
revolutionist and a fanatical friar who fought against the
Faith that he, a priest, had taught and upheld. . . .' He was
speaking low-voiced about all this in that wonderful place
that seemed full of whispers of the past. We stood in the
shadow of the Perseus of Cellini who held the head of
Medusa to a multitude swarming round the funeral pyre of
Savonarola whilst he burnt and they who had followed his
heretical teachings and who believed in him as in a risen
Christ, rejoiced to see him eaten by the flames where he was
staked until he fell in cinders. . . . I could almost smell the
burning flash and it was as if those statues of marble and
bronze stirred and breathed in that silvery light. . . . I
shivered and Marconi asked if I were cold. 'The nights are
still wintry,' he said, 'but the days are in advance of
summer' . . . No I wasn't cold but I felt fear as if the ghosts
of those long dead were passing by in a shadowy pro-
cession. . . .

And then it did seem as if one of them had stirred from
its marble or stone pedestal and in the dark of that great
towering fortress the Palazzo Vecchio where the moon
could not penetrate or the sun could never shine I saw yes
I saw by a moongleam on his face as he came out of the
shadows who it was had come with us or followed us or . . .
followed me.

Felicity's account of her first sight of Florence under
the guidance of Marconi, and despite her disregard for
punctuation, does give us some idea of the impression
made upon her who, in her deliberate avoidance of what
she deplored as 'sentiment' or in her own vernacular
which could have been 'blah', was a receptively sensitive
young person. And, as Marconi wrote from Rome, he
would 'never forget that memorable night when he was

privileged to show his loved Firenze to one so appreciative of that which was to him the most beautiful city in the world'.

Driven back to her hotel, her escort bade her a fervent goodnight with this at parting, which she has recorded verbatim:

'You may hear some malicious gossip in Florence concerning Marconi's feminine interests, but if any such foolish talk should come to your ears would you please let those who may wish spitefully to discuss me, know that you might have been my own little daughter whom Marconi delighted to offer, even in so limited a time, some of these treasures and their history that have endured and will endure through the ages'.... Then he took her hand and kissed it and went from her. In the light of the hotel's portico she thought she saw a tear in his eye.... He is only half Italian, she remembered as she went in; his mother, he had said, was Irish, but, she told herself, he has all the emotional sensitivity of the Italian as well as that spark of genius which has inspired him to give to civilization the wonders of wireless telegraphy, that same spark which fired Leonardo, Michelangelo and all those immortals whose works are left to us as his will be, only that his great work is not for art or literature, it is for science and the benefit of humanity.

In her bedroom she found a bouquet of flowers and pinned to them an envelope addressed to her containing this:

You told me you were going to Florence and would be here today. I too am visiting relatives. I flew to Milan and arrived before you, and I also saw Firenze under moonlight but not for the first time nor under such auspicious guidance. I have left my friend Count — (the name was illegible, as was much of his writing) whom you have met, in charge of the gallery and my man Serge will attend to essentials. I can only stay here a few days but I thought it a good opportunity to become more intimately acquainted with your father

164

than too brief an introduction at your flat over a drink. I will call for you tomorrow at eleven o'clock unless I hear to the contrary. You can telephone me at my hotel, the Berchielli, if this is not convenient. I would like to take you to Doney's and to luncheon with your father if he will care to meet me again.

Yours ever devotedly
A. A. Riabovitch

At eleven o'clock next morning the page brought up his card. She kept him waiting twenty minutes before she came to him in the hotel lounge. They greeted each other formally under the inquisitive eyes of English and American tourists while she told him:

'My father thanks you for your invitation but as he is playing golf today he is unable to accept and asks you to excuse him.'

'Another time, then,' said Riabovitch; and he added *sotto voce*, 'Praise be! I did so want to show you Florence by daylight and alone, although I am a poor substitute for *il senatore*. So, shall we go?'

Doney's, the fashionable rendezvous in the Via Tornabuoni of Florentine *élite*, was already crowded when Felicity and Riabovitch arrived. He seemed to be well known by Doney, who greeted him with the same effusive welcome as that accorded to Marconi at the restaurant the night before where he had taken her to dinner. A table was at once secured for them in the main room; and from there Felicity was enabled to note, for future record in her 'Book', her impressions of the varied company as they came and went.

The cacophony of voices, predominantly American, intermingled with German, Italian, not many British, rose above the rattle of wheels, the clatter of hooves and cracking of whips as the *vetture* disgorged arrivals amid the hoot of cars. Of the many who could be accommodated in the two small rooms, the officers of the garrison in their light-blue and silver-laced uniforms predominated, to eye American girls, cadge an introduction and aspire to a wealthy wife.

'The Italians,' remarked the prince with a supercilious curl of a nostril, 'or any who lay claim to a title – *marchese, conte,* such as abound here in Florence, many of whom are third, fourth, fifth cousins remotely related to the head of the family, can always find a rich young, or old, American to favour him and marry him and endow him handsomely for life.'

'Why don't you, then,' she asked with an impudent sideways look, 'try *your* luck? You, a prince, would stand a better chance as first in the queue above a *marchese* or even a *duca!*'

She thought he would have taken that in the jesting spirit it was made, and it surprised her to see the lowering of his dark eyebrows over his eyes and his retort with an angry flush:

'So you think I am a fortune hunter and that is why I want you. Yes?'

'No.' She too had flushed, thinking: He has no sense of humour. And she said: 'Don't be ridiculous. What fortune have I or my father? You know, or ought to know, that Daddy had to sell the Abbey because he *had* to, not because he wanted to, being almost broke and having lost so much of his income invested in your country and Germany. And why is it always "want" with you? You "want" everything, including me! But perhaps,' with another glance at his tensed face and tightened mouth, 'it is your way of achievement. Wanting is the desire to possess with you. But some people may want and never get any farther than that.'

'Because,' his face relaxed; he slid a hand under the table to seek and find hers, 'they do not want enough, that is to say, determinedly enough, to gain their desire against all obstacles.'

'But such determination,' she told him, 'all obstacles aside regardless of what the outcome will be for those involved, can lead where your people have led themselves to revolt, assassination, and a complete overthrow of everything that was life as you and your kind had known it.'

He released her hand.

'You should not speak of those that caused the downfall of our *ancien régime* as *my* people. My countrymen, perhaps, born of Russia but not the Russia of today.... And why, in this *dolce far niente* atmosphere of Doney's, are we discussing what all of us have suffered in an overthrow of life as we had known it? Why not enjoy today and allow sufficient of yesterday's evil to be – forgotten. So what will you be wanting now – to drink?'

'A dry martini, please.'

He got up to go to the counter and while she waited his return held up by those before him, she wondered, nibbling an olive from the dish on the table: Why do I let him go on like this indefinitely with no assured end to it? Do I want to marry him or don't I? I just don't know....

He came back with her drink and an officer presented to her as: 'Maggiore Conte – Something-or-other' whose name she could not catch. He wore on his blue and silver laced chest the ribbon of war service, and on his dark-skinned face the appraising look she had already observed in Italians as she passed them in the street or her hotel, as if she were stripped to her bones. He spoke to her in strongly accented English: 'Enchanted, miladi. I am 'appy to welcome you and my friend Riabovitch to Firenze.'

He raised her hand that was on the table to his lips with a click of his heels and an effusive bow.

Alexei invited him to sit; he accepted with alacrity the seat and the drink offered him.

The conversation between them, conducted chiefly by the Major, was to the effect that he would be delighted if Riabovitch and miladi Felice Rosa-Sutone would take luncheon with him and his wife at their villa on the

Piazzale Michelangelo. Riabovitch excused them because he said he was taking Lady Felicity to Fiesole for luncheon.

Having rid themselves of the adhesive Maggiore, Alexei, who had hired a car, drove her up and out of the city between the garden walls of villas, olive groves, and where, in this early spring of Italy, the meadows were blossoming with flowers and the orange trees full of their promise of fruit. Dismissing the driver, who was ordered to return in a couple of hours, they walked past the Villa Palmiera, where he told her Boccaccio's lovely ladies and the gay lords of the *Decamerone* had sheltered from the Black Death that had swept Florence five hundred years ago.

'How beautifully and simply Boccaccio describes the plague-stricken city,' he said as, his hand holding hers, he led her up the hilly way to Fiesole, passing the Dominican Convent on one side and the Villa Medici on the other.

When luncheon was served on the piazza at Fiesole under great striped umbrellas, she found herself drawn to him who spoke with such quiet knowledge and enthusiasm of this country town – 'scarcely a town, just an Etruscan village when once it was a city'.

She ate delicious spaghetti bolognese and drank chianti poured by a smiling waiter into her glass from a flask cased in straw, and watched the childlike chattering townsfolk and the peasant women with bright coloured kerchiefs on their heads driving donkey carts from market laden with fruit, vegetables, flowers and livestock, clucking hens, and here and there a squealing piglet or a tethered kid. She was conscious of a sense of unreality, of detachment, as if in this place of narrow lanes crouched under the nine-hundred-year-old Duomo where the campanile towers high above the vine-clad hills of Vincigliata she had returned to a place of her dreams. She said:

'I have been here before in some other time, some other age. It is familiar to me. There are places I have dreamed and recognize when I dream them again and again. And one of them is this. I felt it in Florence when I saw that glorious city in the moonlight for the first time – was it only last night?'

'Yes,' he caught her mood, 'you *have* been here before, and so have I – with you. As we passed along the way of Boccaccio I showed you the villa that stands on the site of the house where he lived with his father, the Casa di Boccaccio. And you were one of those seven lovely girls who came here with their cavaliers to dance and sing and make love in the sweet country air. And you, with that fiery hair of yours as seen here in Northern Italy too seldom, but was seen by Titian as perhaps he saw you in your reincarnation from those days we both shared here in the hills where a goatherd boy is still singing to his flock as a boy sang to them five hundred years ago. It is the order of things in this circle of recurrent life that you should remember that which through eternity you had forgotten.'

They left the piazza and took a pathway beside a brook bordered by olives and budding orange trees, and so to the waiting car at the foot of the hill.

'I just want to say this,' he took her hand and held it fast, 'that when I go from here to Rome tomorrow –'

'So soon? I thought you were staying for a few days.'

'I have done what I had to do,' he said, 'besides stealing this sight of you, and . . . the joy of you in Tuscany. But I do not wish you to see that Rizzi fellow who will surely make attempt to see you. I beg you not to dine, lunch or drive alone with him or any of these Italians, never without your father. This fellow, Rizzi, to whom I introduced you, is married to a relative of Mussolini.'

'Of whom?'

'Of one of whom you and the whole world will hear a good deal more and will hear of in the future, not far distant maybe. He is the present government of Italy's prime minister. But that is not the main reason I do not wish you to be alone with any Italian. It is because they do not have the same respect for women as we Russians or your Englishmen have.'

'Respect,' she laughed round at him, 'is a word unknown to us of the post-war era in our relations with men. We can take care of ourselves from any man who may try to rape us – if that's what you are getting at.'

'Post-war, indeed,' he murmured. 'And now,' as the car came into the bustling street along Lung' Arno to her hotel, 'if your father is back from golf I would like to see him and let him know that my intentions toward you – as your grandfather would demand – are honourable.'

Extract from Felicity's Book

Daddy was back from golf when we came to our hotel. We have a private sitting-room as the price in lire is so much less expensive than it is in England for an hotel suite. I left them alone together and after about an hour's talk I went in to them and saw that Daddy and he seemed to be on the best of terms! I ordered tea to be brought to us but Alexei said he had not time as he must go back to his relatives with whom he was staying until tomorrow and then he goes on to Rome. I went with him to the entrance lounge to say goodbye and he told me he had offered himself to my father 'for my hand,' he said. I couldn't help saying: 'You have regressed to the Victorians. No man asks for a 'lady's hand' today. What did my father say?'

A said he had told him I must decide for myself.

'Well, I have decided, but must be given a year's grace before we get married and –' he tried to interrupt me '– and before,' I was very firm about this, 'before we make any public announcement.'

He said, 'As you will. You hold me in the hollow of your hand.' 'The hand' I said 'that you have asked my father to give you but no one can give you my hand except me!'

I held it out to him then, my left hand, in front of the concierge and the usual staring women, mostly English residents trying to hear what we were saying. 'But this,' I told him, 'is not the hand you asked my father for, because the left hand doesn't know what the right hand is doing.'

He kissed my hand then as they all do here and so he went his way and I mine. Am not finally committed – yet.

'This Rabbit-o'bitch,' Lord Rodborough, attempting jocularity, achieved while Felicity poured tea, 'appears to have made up his mind for you as much as for himself.'

'Not he nor anyone can make up my mind for me. I have given him a year that we can both be sure, although how can anyone be sure of a life-long relationship until it has been tried?'

'And found wanting?'

'More than likely. Hence the divorce courts.'

Lifting the cover of a silver-plated dish that stood on another filled with hot water, 'Gosh!' she exclaimed, 'muffins. Imagine muffins served with tea in Florence! Have one?'

She passed him the dish.

He shook his head. 'I understand our floor waiter was at the Savoy before the war. He appreciates the appetite of a young English *Signorina*.'

'And not so young either. I'll soon be twenty-six. Quite a hag. About being sure.... Marriage is a binding contract. I think one ought to pay a deposit on it – say a year or two's trial like one pays a deposit before buying a house, and you can have the deposit returned if contracts are not exchanged. You had to pay a deposit on our Ashley Gardens leasehold subject to contract and survey.' She bit into a muffin and said: 'I like the idea of a survey that goes before a contract. If all marriages were surveyed before signing and exchanging contracts – that's to say the signing of the register – what a lot of wife and husband trouble might be saved.'

He handed her his cup to be refilled.

'I see you are becoming something of a cynic in your haggish old age.' He took the cup from her giving her a half quizzical, half anxious look. 'I do try to keep up with

171

you but am left a long way behind. Had I passed my medical for the army on the outbreak I might have seen your viewpoint rather than my own. I'm afraid my standard of what is done or not done is ante-dated. We and my generation are what you and yours so rightly call "die-hards".'

'You aren't anything like the die-hards some of our fathers are. Holden, one of our V.A.D.s at Grosvenor Square, had a trial trip – or if you like it a survey – before she married the man she was engaged to and she was going to have a baby four months before they were married. Her father found out and gave her hell. Refused to let her have a wedding in church – they were married in a registry office where they exchanged *their* contracts and he wouldn't see her or her husband or the baby, his grandson, not for ages; but he has got over it now, she told me, and he has put her back in his Will, having cut her out of it. He is quite pleased about it now because her husband was elected M.P. for – Nottingham, I think it is – at the last election and beat the Labour candidate. But why,' she helped herself to a creamy chocolate-covered cake, 'didn't you pass your medical? I never even knew you had wanted to join up.'

'I thought I might have stood a chance as I got the sword of honour in my cadet corps at Eton. And I hoped to have a shot or two at Jerry.'

'But,' she persisted, 'why didn't you pass? What did they find wrong with you?'

'Age,' he replied ruefully. 'I was over forty.'

'So were a lot of others who joined up.' Her turn to look anxious. 'Anything to do with the murmur?'

'The – ? Oh, that old bee in Halstead's bonnet. No, of course not. My heart has always been sound as a bell. Halstead is getting a bit past it at well over seventy. . . . Not another of those cream buns or whatever they are! You'll be sick.'

'Spaghetti, which I had for luncheon, delicious though

172

it was, isn't very filling. And', she added, swallowing the
last of a second 'cream bun', 'you're not going to play golf
tomorrow, are you? Fancy coming to Firenze to play
golf! I want to go with you to the Uffizi. I've seen nothing
yet, nor have you, of the *inside* of Florence.'

'Not tomorrow. I've fixed up a foursome. It's a good
course.'

'Not the eighteen-hole one? You know it's too hilly for
you. Lord Halstead said – '

'Never mind what Halstead said.' Rising from the table
he went over to a bureau. 'Go along now. I have letters to
write.'

She went along, still wearing an anxious look. . . . So
naughty of him to play on that eighteen-hole course.
Much too hilly. I asked the concierge. No good telling
him. Won't listen. Perhaps it *is* just a bee of old Halstead's.
He was probably a very good doctor thirty years ago. I
never knew Dad had tried to join up. I wonder if it *was*
his age. . . .

When she came to her room she found, as on the day
of her arrival, that it was full of flowers with an envelope
attached, not in the writing of Riabovitch. The florist's
she supposed. Opening it, she read on a card:

I too needed a holiday. And what could be a more delightful surprise than to see in the visitors' book that you
are here in this same hotel. I have not seen you for too long
a time. What about tomorrow? If you are not otherwise
engaged I will be in the lounge at 10.45 and will wait in the
hope you will be there.

R. R.

She buried her nose in a fragrance of roses and carnations, thinking: They are both Rs. Hard to know which is
which. She rang for a maid to bring vases. The flowers
Riabovitch had sent were already wilting. She gave them
to the maid to throw away. . . . So, he's here, she thought
amusedly; two strings, or two Rs, to my bow if I want

173

them, but – a waiter! Of course he's not, unless so hard up he has to be a waiter to keep those two horses. Yet if, as it seems, he is staying here even with the *lira* in our favour, how can he afford to pay for a room in the most expensive hotel in Florence? Unless he *is* a waiter, a lounge waiter, and could then have a look at the visitors' book in the entrance. Perhaps his day off is tomorrow. . . .

The next morning, having kept him waiting half an hour, she came into the lounge. He was seated at a table with a lager in front of him. He rose as she entered and went to meet him with a formal greeting, aware of inquisitive feminine eyes.

'Shall we get out of here?' he asked her, 'where we can talk?'

Along Lung' Arno with its noisy traffic and groups of gesticulating, even noisier Florentine townsfolk whom she believed to be quarrelling but were only indulging in ordinary conversation, and the usual crowds of exclamatory German, English and American tourists, it was impossible to talk below a shout in order to be heard.

'I have a car,' he said. 'We can drive wherever you wish to go, but I suggest the Boboli Gardens where we can sit in comparative quiet.'

A chauffeur-driven Fiat was waiting at the corner of the Via Tornabuoni, and as they drove the short distance to the gardens she said:

'I am glad not to be driven behind one of those poor, half-starved horses. They are the only things I've seen in Florence, so far, that hurts me.'

'Yes, I also. But although some of the good English ladies have appealed to Mussolini on behalf of the R.S.P.C.A., the answer was that it is better that animals should starve than to let children go short of food, because Italy is very broke just now. And they who appealed were reminded that Britain is the only country in the world which has to have a society for the prevention of cruelty to children.'

'Mussolini?' she echoed the name. 'That's the second time I've heard him mentioned. Who is he?'

'Of not much importance yet, more than that he is Italy's prime minister. They still have a king as figure-head. But you, and all of us, will hear of him again, although I believe he barred himself from the League of Nations yet he'll crop up at Locarno in the autumn like a bad penny, or a bad and worthless *lira*.'

She turned to look at him, noting his well-cut Harris tweed suit and the scent of it that reminded her of Ronnie's Harris tweeds, so that she sat silent with moistened eyes that watched the sun on his fair head. Neither spoke for a while, then suddenly:

'Why are you here?' she asked him. 'Are you still waiting – to serve?'

He returned her look with that boyish quick smile of his.

'Yes, I'm waiting and – I'm serving, but I'm on holiday now, just for a day or two. And as I heard you would be here and as I have a job to do in Rome, I thought I might as well be here too. Do you mind?'

'No, why should I? But I do mind that you don't tell me what *is* your job – going to these different places as a waiter or a footman, and I am sure you are neither, unless you *have* to be.'

'I do have to be. It's my job.'

'Not your real job,' she persisted. 'I'll not believe you choose to be a hired waiter or footman as a "job".'

The car stopped at the gates of the Boboli Gardens. Russton told the driver in Italian to come back in an hour.

'You speak Italian, then?'

'I have to know languages, enough to get about in France, Italy and Germany, as a – waiter.'

Passing through the entrance gate of the gardens they strolled along an alley lined with ilex, cypresses and statues, some broken, and found a seat banked by a hedge that would soon be a cascade of roses, now in bud.

'How early spring comes here,' she said. 'It will probably be snowing in England. I wonder – do you remember? – I nursed you at Grosvenor House. You were awfully ill with that ghastly 'flu and you told me you had the same name as mine?'

'Did I?' He looked away from her, intent on watching a small bird alight on a neighbouring bush. 'She's guarding her nest,' he said. 'A little wren. She is bringing her babies food. She has something in her beak.'

'Yes, but you did say your name was the same as mine,' she knitted her forehead. 'So why is it Russton now?'

'If I said so while I was in high fever and delirious, I'd have said anything.'

'Now listen, Russton, if that's your name, I'm not quite a fool. I want to know what you are and what you do. What *is* this "job" of yours? And how can you afford to keep those horses and stay at this hotel even for a night or two, and dress yourself in Savile Row as you obviously do – '

'Hanover Square, as a matter of fact. Why shouldn't I?'

'You were at school in England, Winchester, you said, and at Toronto University. You can't be so hard up as all that.'

'My father paid for my schooling. He did have some money – once. He is dead now, and I was an only son, an only child. I told you that my mother went off with another man. I have never seen her since. And as I want to have horses which I've had all my life, I have to do something to pay for their keep and my pleasure.'

'You were at the Thistlewaites' house-warming and also at the opening of the Riabovitch Gallery's private view, and again at the Embassy Club when I was dining with the prince. I expect you have been there many times since.'

'Only when I am required.'

She was staring straight before her, eyes fixed on an ilex tree.

'How do you know when you are required? How do you get these jobs? Through an agency?'

'Of course. How else could I get them?'

Her eyes came round to his in which she saw a twinkle.

'Not,' she said, 'a *secret* agency – by any chance?'

The twinkle deepened. He gave a little laugh.

'What a one you are for questions! No, it is not a secret agency. Anyone can apply, but they must have certain qualifications.'

'Such as?'

'Knowing how to wait and – serve.'

'I told you, I'm not *quite* a fool.' She got up. 'Shall we walk? I see a fountain and a pond over there. The sun is getting rather hot.'

'And so are you,' he murmured below breath. Then, as they neared the fountain:

'I think,' she said, and surprisingly, before she knew that she had done so, she slipped her hand in his that tightened close on hers, 'I think,' she repeated, 'that I have you taped. But I too can wait – if not to serve!'

EIGHT

The return to London from Florence saw Felicity once again at the gallery in Duke Street during the summer, but the prince was often absent now, 'Seeking,' he told her, 'to replenish the exchequer with more saleable propositions.' He would attend auctions not only in London but in the provinces and also abroad: Rome, Naples, Switzerland, Geneva. From Locarno she received picture postcards of Lake Maggiore.

'What', her father wished to know, 'is he doing in Locarno? He, a Russian, has nothing to do with the Locarno Pact which when finalized will guarantee by Britain and Italy the Franco–German frontier and bring Germany into the League of Nations. Is he buying pictures on Lake Maggiore?'

'How should I know?' was her reply to this. 'I know only what he tells me.'

'Which', said her father looking at her over his spectacles (he was reading his *Times*), 'is about as much as will cover a sixpence if' (glumly) 'he *has* sixpence. I told him when he saw me in Florence that I couldn't settle more than three hundred a year on you. He's not after money, that's one thing in his favour, and not much else.'

Nor was Lady Caversham more favourably inclined to congratulate Felicity on 'This engagement of yours – if you *are* engaged to that Russian. Your father told me he made a formal proposal to him for you. Got a better impression of him this second time he saw him than the first. Says you want it kept quiet. No announcement. Private. No money. Too many of these penniless Russians over here. Woman I know has one of them. Housekeeper.

Says she's Princess Something. They all call themselves Prince. Count. Countess. Sponge on us. What does your father say about this Red Friday business?'

'I didn't know about a Red Friday, Aunt.' Felicity leaned across the tea-trolley to speak in the old lady's inclining ear, 'I only know *Good* Friday and we were in Florence for that. Daddy liked Florence – or rather the golf course there – so much that he stayed a month more than we intended.'

Her ladyship fumbling for her hearing aid under its cascade of lace said: 'Drat the thing! Must have my trumpet. . . . What? Don't mumble.'

Felicity repeated: 'I said I only knew *Good* Friday and not a Red one.'

'Nothing good about a Friday these days. We had a Black Friday four years ago. Those miners and strikes and that. And now it's Red. Everything Red. Red Letters. Red scares. Red spies. Baldwin making a mess of these miners. Another strike if he don't look out. And these Red Russians. Say they're White. Pink. Purple. Don't like it. Different in my day. Russians not all colours of the rainbow. Your Uncle Jeremy used to say "Scratch a Russian and you get a Tartar." Not Tolstoy. Nor the Romanov. Cold-blooded murder. English blood in him. Autocratic. But weak. Like Charles First. Got his head cut off. Stuart blood in your lot. Did you know? Or didn't you? Charles Second. Gay dog.' Aunt Harriet chuckled. 'Had she been a boy he'd have been a duke. Didn't care much about daughters. Very prolific. Can't say that for Rodborough. No heir. Not to speak of. I could make a guess. Don't butt my head against a dead wall.' To which cryptic utterance Aunt Harriet added: 'Little life!' This to the Peke who had come from his basket to scramble up on to his lady's lap. 'He's getting old. Aren't we all? You too. Time you were married to whatever or whoever. Prefer an Englishman. But beggars not choosers. Could double what I'll give you when or if you marry if it's not to a Tartar. . . . Cake?'

Declining cake, Felicity deposited a dutiful kiss on the berouged, wrinkled old cheek offered to receive it, saying: 'I'm sorry, Auntie, I have to go now and I did read about Red Friday in today's *Mail*, but it didn't make much sense to me.'

'Eh? Sense? Nonsense!' So emphatically did Aunt Harriet shake her head that her wig, noticeably more black than when Felicity had last seen her, slipped sideways. Adjusting her wig she said: 'Am white underneath. Easier than dyeing it. Slip it on and off. No need to advertise your age. Can't go by the *Mail*. Northcliffe Press. Sensational. Baldwin rubbing all of them up the wrong way. Miners' Federation! Shouldn't give in to 'em. Granting a subsidy. Why don't your father speak in the Lords? Never opens his mouth. Labour peers have gift o' the gab. Don't give the Tories a chance. What's the hurry? Come and go. Goodbye.'

As she walked back through St James's Park Felicity, watching the play of sunlight and shadow on the grass, remembered, with a start of surprise, that a year had gone by since she had walked this way with Russton. And, although suspicious of his 'job' directed by an 'agency', she had no confirmation of what that job nor the agency by which he was employed could be. Domestic or political, or what? Since that brief meeting in Florence in the spring, she had neither seen nor heard from him until two days ago she had received a note delivered with flowers and the words:

'Wimbledon Common or Richmond on Friday? My day off. R.R.'

And today was Friday and she had heard no more. Of all unaccountable ... Who is he? *What* is he? One had read and heard so much about secret agents during the war, working for us in Germany, yet that was all over. We are at peace or supposed to be. What about Russia? These Bolshies. That Zinoviev letter and everyone, including the Government, believing we were in for a revolution. All died down now. Or has it?... But Russton could have nothing to do with that, unless he is spying for the Bolshies against us?... Of one thing I'm sure. He is not what he says he is, taking odd jobs as a waiter. He must have some money or he couldn't keep those horses and dress as he does off duty, unless he is being paid by – whom? By us or by the Bolshies?

In the burnished blue the westering sky was fiery above the trees and a dark cloud hovering in breathless warmth to presage, she thought, a threatened storm. No wind and not a leaf stirring.

A seat fronting the lake invited her to sit and watch the waterfowl before walking on and into the roaring traffic of Victoria Street. She had intended going into the Stores on her way home to buy a much-needed pair of gloves, but the Stores would be closed before she got there. She looked down at her gloved hands, saw a small hole in the forefinger of one of them, pulled both gloves off and put them in her bag.

A duck and her ducklings sailed by on the glassy water. The same duck that she had seen here with Russton, who had fed her cake unless it were the granddaughter of that one a year or more ago. . . . Yes, and today is Friday and not a word from him.

The thin, elfin voices of children far off, who had come from their foetid slums to play and breathe in London's lungs, were borne to her on the still air. Children of the workless. 'The poor are always with us.' Not these, the children from the mansions of the rich, all taken back to their nurseries to be fed and bathed and put to their luxurious beds. No beds for those others, unless one to be shared by three or four, children of the unemployed, perhaps no food. . . . These awful strikes. The coal miners aren't paid enough to live on. She wished she knew more about the conditions of the miners. She was certain they had right on their side to demand higher wages than – what was it they were getting according to the *Mail* or one of the dailies? About forty-five bob a week? But that must be what they are paid for subsistence, being out of work or refusing to work.

She saw approaching along the pathway, where a few pedestrians had passed, two men, one short the other tall. Distance lent them unfamiliarity until, as they neared, she recognized the taller of the two and thought, if her sight did not deceive her, that she also knew the other except that it could scarcely be he, the little Thistlewaite man walking and talking – if he were talking – nodding his head in answer to, yes, to Russton!

Curiouser and curiouser! Unless Mr Thistlewaite had met him accidentally in the park and was engaging him to wait upon them for a dinner or something. . . . Ah! She had been seen. Spotted by 'R.R.' He said something to the 'little Thistlewaite', who glanced in her direction, gave another quick nod, turned and walked away.

She sat waiting for Russton to come to her. He took his time, not hurrying.

'I telephoned to you this afternoon, having found your number which you refused to give me, but you were out. I wanted to apologize for not having got in touch with you about today, but I was suddenly called to a job.'

'Yes?' She looked at him coolly, noting his hat, not a bowler, too hot for summer, a trilby, a grey flannel suit, and his brief case. 'Called by Mr Thistlewaite, no doubt, to wait at table?'

'Perhaps to wait – with Waites. Forgive inexcusable pun. May I sit?'

'Of course. This seat is supplied by the London County Council for that purpose. Anyone may sit on it.'

Seating himself he gave her a comical look with that schoolboy grin of his.

'You are offended?'

'Why should I be?'

'You have every reason. I should have offered an

explanation why I had not contacted you earlier than this, but my time is not my own.'

'Whose time is it that calls you to – wait with Waites?'

'I will give you chapter and verse for all you wish to know about me when I am able to tell you in my own good time, which is not yet. Enough for this present that I am employed by those who employ me as their servant.'

'Which is as clear as mud,' she said, 'but I have my suspicions and these I will give to you chapter and verse in *my* good time.' She got up. 'I go this way home. Good-bye.'

'Am I permitted to walk with you?'

She said meaningfully: 'Have *you* the time?'

'I am off duty tonight. Will you dine with me?'

This rather staggered her.

'Dine?' she repeated. 'Where? And why?'

'Wherever you wish, and why? Because I have not seen you for too long through no fault of mine, and it gives me pleasure to see you now and ... always. I have been abroad a good deal these last four months.'

They walked on slowly toward the entrance gates. She had nothing to say but thought the more ... Where abroad? Italy, France, Germany or ... Russia? He said he had taken a degree in languages. Did it include Russian? And as if he took that thought from her:

'You are dying to ask me where I have been. My itinerary is varied. I go where I am required for my job.'

'I realize that. Would your job take you to Russia by any chance?'

'If I were ordered to go there but I have not yet been given any chance to serve – and wait in Petrograd. Are you still interested in works of art? I believe you are engaged – '

She interrupted sharply.

'Who told you I am engaged?'

' – in assisting Prince Riabovitch at the Duke Street

gallery I was about to say. You are frequently in attendance there, I understand, helping to sell or arrange exhibitions of pictures.'

'There is very little going on at present,' she answered easily to that, with a sense of relief. 'The prince is also abroad. He has been to Locarno.'

'I wonder I did not come across him. I too have been to Locarno. The tourist season is in full swing there and on Lake Maggiore. So where shall we dine this evening – that is if you will honour me – a waiter.'

Resenting his tone that held more than a hint of mockery: 'I think', she said, 'that I don't wish to dine with you, not because you are, or are not, a waiter but because I don't like mysteries.'

'So you believe I am a mystery? Or in other words – a crook?'

They were nearing the end of Victoria Street, and the noise of motor buses, hoot of taxis, klaxon horns of cars driven to and from the station gave her excuse to stay a reply, for in truth she was half inclined to think him – a crook! Only why, if so, was he walking and talking with the highly respectable, inoffensive Mr Thistlewaite in the park? She could at least ask him that.

'Is Mr Thistlewaite one of your employers?'

'I have been in his employ as you must have seen on various occasions; at the house-warming, and at other times, if you remember.'

'I do remember. Does the Embassy Club also employ you?'

'When I am needed there.'

He stopped at a paper stall. 'Excuse me.' He bought two evening papers. 'One for you.' He handed it to her.

Headlines blazed.

EMERGENCY CABINET MEETING
RED FRIDAY
Prime Minister to see Miners' representatives

'Why are they calling it Red Friday?'

'According to the *Daily Herald*, mouthpiece of the Labour Party, to distinguish it from Black Friday four years ago when there was another immediate threat of a general strike which flopped at the last minute. But', he guided her under her elbow across the road into Ashley Gardens, 'this one won't flop. It is coming.'

All previous doubts and questions unanswered were swept aside in swift alarm.

'Is it really so serious? I know it has been threatened but is it now more than a threat?'

'I believe so. But before we are deprived of food or light, or transport, will you – for the second time of asking – dine with me?'

They had come to the block of her flat opposite the Cathedral.

'Will they hold up food and transport in a general strike?'

'Everything will be held up and we'll all be called to volunteer to drive vehicles, lorries, trains.'

'Trains too? The railway men, will they strike?'

'Railways, shipping, dockers – the whole lot of them, but it may be called off yet or at least staved off for a while. And now for the third time of asking and if it's "no", I'll call *this* off – for ever. Will you dine with me tonight?'

A long pause; she refused to meet his look, half pleading, half amused, while the thought shot through her: If she refused, then would it mean she would never see him again? Why should he be so demanding? What did he want of her?... 'Want'. He had never said *that*, anyhow, but he never said anything else except that it gave him pleasure to see her ... always. She capitulated.

'Very well, on one condition.'

'On any condition to which I can agree.'

'That you will tell me something more about yourself

o

than to give me chapter and verse in your own good time – when it suits you.'

'My time, at present is not entirely my own and there is little enough to tell you about me that you don't already know.'

'You won't commit yourself?'

'I never do. I'm a cautious bloke. So where shall we eat, drink or be merry before I am driving an engine, and you giving first aid to him who has never driven an engine in his life and got himself electrocuted in the tube, or hauling crates from the docks and letting one crash on his head. So shall we go somewhere to dance to a good band or where we can just talk?'

'I think – just talk.'

'Right. What about the Savoy Grill?'

She looked at him straightly.

'Isn't the Savoy rather expensive?'

'No, I'm known there. Besides – it's my night off. I'll be outside here at eight o'clock with a taxi.'

'Won't you come in first and meet my father?'

Their eyes met, hers greyish-green, his blue, one permanently half closed as a result of his war wound.

'I would rather not. I don't think your father would approve of you dining at the Savoy with a waiter.'

'He wouldn't care if you were a waiter, which you aren't. You are British, presumably, and you fought in the war, and that's all which matters to him and I do as I like and dine with whom I like.'

'Do you like me?'

'Yes, as much as I know of you. See you later. Not black tie, is it?'

'No, lounge suit – if it suits you.'

Raising his hat he watched her go up the steps of the block, then hailing a taxi he drove to Whitehall, and there we may leave him.

She changed her dress for one she had bought in

Florence, a summery affair of flowered chiffon, low waisted, belted round the hips with a sash, no hat, her copper-coloured shingled hair almost, but not quite an Eton crop flattened close to her head as much as its natural curl would allow.

A table had been reserved and she was not surprised that he seemed to be well known by the maître d'hôtel, who conducted them to a table by a settee facing the aisle where all who came and went could be seen.

'Have you served here when they are short staffed?' she inquired as she unfolded a napkin.

'Yes, from time to time. Luigi is a friend of mine.'

He too had changed from his grey flannel to a darker suit meticulously tailored.

She smiled to herself. And:

'Have you', she asked, 'come into money that you can afford to dine me here?'

'As a matter of fact I have. I can tell you about that, which is something of me which I haven't told you yet.'

A waiter offered menus to both.

'What will you have? Smoked salmon, caviare or oysters to start with?... No, not oysters. There won't be an R until next month. August is tomorrow and in September when there *is* an R I can take you to a place where we can have the best oysters in the world. Smoked salmon?'

'Yes, please.'

'Smoked salmon for two. And then?'

'Whatever you are having.'

'Point steak. What about you?'

'Just an omelette, thanks.'

Smoked salmon served and appreciatively sampled, 'What is that something,' she inquired, 'that you haven't told me yet about coming into money? Do you mind all these questions?'

'No, I am rather bucked that you take that much interest in me.'

187

'Why shouldn't I when you are such a mass of contradictions? Besides, don't forget I had you all but dying on me once, and nursed you, bathed you, dosed you – '

'And saved my life.'

'Of course I didn't. The doctor did that. Well' (she accepted thinly sliced brown bread from the waiter, squeezed lemon juice on to the smoked salmon) 'go on. You were about to tell me – '

'Yes. How I have now come into what was settled on me by my mother.'

'Your mother?' She poised her fork before placing it between her lips. 'But you said your mother left your father. They were divorced?'

'They were. I told you my father had the custody of me and my mother married an American millionaire. His name –' he hesitated '– I won't tell you his name but he is one of the four multi-millionaires in the States. When my mother married him – I was only nine years old then – her husband settled money on her from which she had the income for life, a life tenancy they call it, and at her death the capital – I understand she insisted on this – should come to me absolutely. So it has come to me. She died eight months ago.'

'Her millionaire husband must have been very amenable. What if she had any children by him?'

'She didn't, but he had three by his first wife – another divorce there. They go in for divorces in America much more than we do here.'

'Eight months ago,' she said thoughtfully. 'So you knew you had come into money, as they call it, when we were in Florence. But you couldn't have known when you bought your horses and one a possible winner that your mother would die while you were still young.'

'I didn't know, and never gave it a thought. I was knocked flat when the lawyers wrote to me from New York to tell me I had inherited quite – something.'

'So you don't have to be a waiter any more?'

'Not for a living, only when I'm wanted.'

'And is that all you have to tell me until I am given the rest of it, chapter and verse? I suppose you are very well off?'

'Passably. About ten thousand a year. Enough to marry on. Will you marry me?'

She laid down her knife and fork. Her face was suffused with a blush of indignation.

'Of all the – do you think I'm to be bought? I wouldn't marry you if you had twenty thousand a year.'

'I see.' He had paled; she saw that the tag end of the scar on his forehead not covered by a lock of fair hair, showed red against his pallor. She felt compunction. She had hurt him, if he could be hurt. But it was really rather much to suppose his money would ...

A waiter came to take away their plates. Russton had left his smoked salmon almost untouched. She said:

'I'm sorry. It was beastly of me, but it is a bit sudden.'

'It's all right. My fault. Very clumsy on my part. I'm not anything of a lady's man.'

'Thank goodness for that. Only you must know you are an enigma and that I can't make you out. I can guess what you are, or what you may be, and am probably all wrong. Have read too many spy thrillers, and there's all this Red Spy scare, dying down now, but it kept us all on tenterhooks while it lasted over the Red Letter and now Red Friday. One can't help wondering which side you are on. Are you *for* us or against us?'

'In other words', his pallor had faded and his face assumed its engaging smile, 'am I operating for the Soviet Union, the Communist Party here or in Russia, or in Europe, come to that, or am I just a con man filling you up with a pack of lies for the fun of it, and being able to take Lady Felicity Ross-Sutton to dine at the Savoy Grill with the best and the worst of them on the tips I've raked in from the South of France and Monte Carlo, and Florence, Rome, Locarno as a waiter in the height of the tourist season, or am I what you would have every right to think I am – a crook?'

'You said it, I didn't, but that' (she was not looking at him now) 'might also be a solution to the enigma you are or seem to be, yet I would prefer to think you're a sort of – special constable.'

'And not far wrong in that. I'll be putting in as a special constable when, or if, we have the General Strike.'

Omelette *aux fines herbes* was served to her, and a point steak to Russton.

He attacked his with appetite and both ate in silence while she let her eyes wander over the people passing their table in the subdued lights of the grill room. Then, suddenly, she stiffened, seeing, or thought she saw, unless it were a chance resemblance, Serge, the Czech manservant and assistant to Riabovitch at the gallery and in his flat. He was with a woman whose face she seemed to remember having seen somewhere, her dark hair clubbed under in page boy fashion, not the prevalent shingle or Eton crop. What, Felicity wondered, was Serge doing here and with her who bore a faint likeness to one of the most recent Hollywood movie stars.

'Excuse me,' leaving his steak Russton got up. 'I've just remembered a phone call I ought to have made. Dinner with you has put it out of my head,' and that smile of his lingered as he added, 'because you have *gone* to my head.'

The wine waiter had come with a bottle of Montrachet; glasses were filled; he left his untouched. 'Do please forgive me. I'll be back in a minute.'

He was back in ten minutes during which time she sat alone, watching Serge where he and his companion were talking, heads close together. Wine was brought, and what looked like caviare. . . . How, she wondered, do they get the money to come here and eat caviare? And how can Russton afford to dine here unless he *has* come into an inheritance or is part of an agency, whether ours or some other, that employs him as a waiter or – a special constable. In other words a secret agent, which her common sense inclined her to reject. I would like to think so, she told herself, because it appealed to her imagination, yet she still adhered to the more feasible solution that he was in actuality an odd-job waiter. . . . But what about his horses? He had those horses before his mother died. If he could afford to keep them and run the mare and fetch Egmont over from Canada . . .

'A penny for them,' Russton said, accepting from a thoughtful waiter a freshly grilled point steak, since the first had been left to grow cold.

'Not worth a penny or ten thousand pennies.'

'You are still suspicious, aren't you? Perhaps you're right. It all sounds rather far-fetched, I admit. But one thing you can be wrong about. If I were in the pay of the Bolshies I would not have named myself Russton. Our Intelligence would have been on to that. Too much like Russia.'

'Oh,' she nodded her head. 'You have me there. So Russton is not your name.'

'I didn't say so.'

'No, but you said you wouldn't have named yourself Russton, which rather suggests that you have taken a name that isn't yours.'

'It is mine. Anyone can call themselves anything. Some Americans tack Lord and Earl on to their names although they profess to despise titles. Will you have another omelette to keep my steak company?'

'No thank you.' He re-filled her glass, then his, raised it and said:

'Here's hoping that I may – hope.'

'Hope of what?'

'That some time or some other time, this year, next year, some time – *ever*, you will marry me with or without ten thousand a year.'

'You can go on hoping. But I think you ought to know I am already booked.'

'I do know that. There isn't much I don't know about you, my Lady Clare.'

'Why do you call me that?'

'Isn't it your name? "And we shall wed tomorrow's morn and you will still be Lady Clare." As for being booked, to the Russian, I presume?... I thought so, bookings like theatre tickets can be cancelled. Will you have an ice?'

'No, thanks.'

The waiter was beckoned.

'Coffee. Black or white?'

To the waiter: 'One black, one white.'

'You have eaten that second steak too quickly,' she said. 'You shouldn't bolt your food. You'll give yourself a duodenal.'

'If so, perhaps you'll nurse me through it. It's a habit with me to bolt my food. We had to in the army.'

'Yes, I forgot. I meant to ask you why you didn't take a commission which you could have done if you were at Winchester. All public school boys could take a commission if they were in their cadet corps.'

'I chose not to be commissioned, preferred to be a ranker. I ended up as a sergeant. As an officer I might never have got above a first lieutenant.'

'I don't remember seeing you charted as sergeant.'

'Don't you? Well, I can't help you there. It was on my chart – but you can check on me at the War Office if you want to.'

'What was your regiment?'

'The R.I.F. Royal Irish Fusiliers.'

'Why Irish? You aren't Irish, are you?'

'No, perhaps you think I should have been?'

'Because you are given to blarney?' She wrinkled her nose, her upper lip drawn against her teeth as a puppy about to bite in fun.

'As you say. No, the reason I chose to enlist in the Irish Fusiliers was because I had an Irish nurse whom I adored and who brought me up, more or less. And she's dead too, now. So you have learned a lot about me while we've dined, haven't you?'

'Yes, a lot, but not enough.'

'There will be plenty more to learn about me some day.'

'You haven't told me if the mare was entered for the Oaks, or where?'

'Not yet. Next year perhaps, if all goes well. Are we going to ride again?'

'I suppose so if you wish to.'

'If *you* wish to.'

Her eyes had wandered to the table where the Czech sat with his guest. Russton also looked in their direction.

'I see your friend the prince's factotum is here.'

'How do you know he's the prince's factotum?'

'I saw him at the private view at the gallery where I was – '

'Viewing?'

'As part of my job at waiting.'

She nodded, smiling to herself.

'I can understand that. Passing drinks to people so you can not only have a good look at them as well as at the pictures, but can overhear what they say. I remember you had to attend to a slight accident with a cocktail on the sleeve of the Soviet *Chargé d'Affaires*.'

'You have studied your spy thrillers and your Edgar Wallace pretty thoroughly, haven't you?'

'I read spy thrillers for relaxation. The modern pseudo-psychological novel is so boring and so badly written.'

She noticed that while they talked he was watching Serge and the woman with him. As they rose to go, after Serge had paid his bill, Russton called for his, and then said:

'How careless of me! I should have offered you a liqueur.'

'I don't want one, thank you, but don't let that stop you if you want one.'

'I don't. And so – ' the waiter brought the bill folded over on a plate. Russton glanced at it and scribbled a signature, put two notes on it as tip, and to Felicity: 'Shall we go.'

It struck her that it should have been herself to suggest that, and he, noting her silence:

'It is not that I want to cut short this too long delayed dinner with you, but when I made my phone call I was reminded of something left undone that I should have done.'

'I was going to suggest that we go in any case,' she told him, with deliberate indifference; 'and I wouldn't wish to keep you from doing what you should have done. Besides, my father will be fidgeting if I stay longer.'

They walked to the entrance.

'Your father disapproves of your dining out with anyone, I mean any man?'

'Not *any* man.'

'With me, for instance?'

'I've no doubt he would rightly disapprove if he knew I was dining at the Savoy with an – enigma.'

And again she drew her upper lip against her teeth in a mischievous, puppy-like grin.

'And when you look at me like that,' he said, a trifle out of breath, 'I – taxi!'

The commissionaire at the entrance had already commandeered one and to him Russton slipped another note and received a salute of thanks.

'I thought you said you were not an officer in the war,' she remarked as they drove off.

'I wasn't.'

'But the commissionaire with ribbons on his chest was in the war, and he saluted you as if you were an officer.'

'That's just his way. He's a friend of mine.'

'Oh yes?'

And no more was said about that; and little else until they came to Ashley Gardens. As he helped her out of the taxi: 'I could get time off tomorrow if you would care to ride?'

'No, I'm sorry. Not tomorrow. I have to be at the gallery quite a good deal of my time while the prince is away. Thank you for the dinner. Goodnight.'

Nannie met her as Wilson let her in.

'Thank God you've come!'

The old woman's usually red-pippin face was grey and drawn.

'Why – ' fear seized her. 'What's the matter?'

'Your father – he's had a heart attack. I called in the doctor – he's ordered him to bed. Only very slight, he said.'

'How,' she managed to articulate out of a dry mouth – 'how and when did it happen?'

'Wilson'll tell you.'

'When?' she turned on the butler.

'I served his lordship's dinner,' she was told. 'He ate it all and drank the best part of a bottle of burgundy and then – '

'And then?'

'He was quite well, m'lady, but presently he rang and I found him in his chair at the desk half fainting like. He said he'd been openin' the window it bein' such a warm night, and then he came over faint. His lordship should have rung for me to open the window. He said he felt sick. I helped his lordship out of the chair and he went with me to the cloak room – and then he vomited and felt better. Nurse phoned for the doctor who said not to let his lordship go upstairs until he'd seen him.'

'Is the doctor with him now?'

'No, m'lady. We got his lordship to bed. Not in his bedroom. The doctor said to have a bed made up down here so he is in the drawin' room.'

She went to the drawing-room at the end of the hall. Her father lay propped on pillows. He greeted her cheerfully and she saw he had some colour in his face, but that did not reassure her. She had seen heart cases in hospital and had learned that colour in a heart attack was not always a good sign.

She felt his pulse.

'Seems all right,' she said. 'You played golf today, didn't you?'

'In the tournament. The last day of it.'

'Better if you'd gone to the House – playing golf in this heat! How many rounds?'

'Two.'

'Oh, *no*! . . . And you had lunch there. What did you eat?'

'Steak and kidney pudding.'

'What a thing to serve on a day like this! It probably had tinned oysters in it. Upset your stomach. And then dinner tonight – what did you have?'

'Salmon, roast lamb, apple pie, and Stilton.'

'You've over eaten, that's what's wrong with you. Now you'll stay in bed until the doctor says you can get up again.'

'He can say what he likes, but I'm going to get up. I won't stay down here in bed – too much to do. Must attend a debate in the Lords tomorrow. All this miners' Federation business.'

'You'll do what you're told for once.'

'Give me the late night final then. It's over on the couch.'

She brought him the evening paper. He reached for his spectacle case on a table beside him and told her: 'You can leave me now. Where have *you* been?'

'Out to dinner.'

'Who with?'

'No one you know.' She kissed his forehead. 'Be good, Dad, and please, *please* do what the doctor says you must do.'

She left him and went to the telephone to ring the doctor.

'Doctor, has Daddy had a heart attack or could it be indigestion? He has had too much to eat today and played two rounds of golf.'

'I didn't know about that, but I suspect a slight coronary thrombosis. I have arranged for Doctor —', he mentioned the name of an eminent heart specialist, 'to see him to-morrow. Can't be too careful. It may be nothing at all except what you say – overeating and two rounds of golf in this heat. But I'm not letting him climb stairs or take any undue exertion until he has had an E.C.G.'

'An electro-cardiogram, is that what it is? We were just beginning to know of them in hospital. Yes, do have a heart specialist to see him. I've always been worried about that murmur.'

'No need to worry. Whatever it is, it's very slight and all he will require is complete rest. So get to bed, Felicity, and don't go worrying yourself.'

She went to bed and did worry herself.

If it were a coronary thrombosis, however slight, it might bring about another. 'O, God,' she prayed, don't let me lose him. What have I left to me if he goes? Nobody. Only Nannie. And she's well on in her seventies. I have only Daddy who matters to me in all the world. . . .'

She slept at last.

The next morning Dr Cree arrived with the heart specialist. Felicity waited in an agony of apprehension while the two physicians consulted together after the specialist had examined the patient.

When she heard them leave her father's study she went into the hall to meet them. At sight of her anxious face the specialist hastened to reassure her.

'Lord Rodborough has had a slight coronary throm-bosis, and if he will obey orders and remain in bed for at least two weeks, when I will examine him again, there is no reason why he should not recover completely from this minor attack and lead a normal life.'

She said:

'I was a V.A.D. in the war and we had three coronaries in my ward, and I do know that they can recur and be fatal a second time. Two of them did have a second and they – died. They were both sergeant majors, over fifty, my father's age.'

'There is, of course, always the chance of a recurrence but I have known cases live long after a second coronary or even a third. You will see that Lord Rodborough keeps to his bed? I am sending in two nurses so that he will not attempt to get up for anything at all.'

'Thank you, doctor. I'll see to it that he obeys orders.'

There now began three weeks of anxiety, nothing lessened by Nannie's hostility to the day and night nurses sent from the National Heart Hospital to attend her father.

'As if I couldn't have done what they do – give him the bed-pan and blanket-bath him. You and I together could have done that. And what they cost too! Eating us out of hearth and home besides their wages.'

'What does it matter so long as they keep him in bed? He wouldn't stay in bed for you or me. The specialist is being ultra careful – not taking any risks. Dr Cree says he is sure Daddy will get well over this and that it's a blessing in disguise to make him go slow on golf and – everything. Lord Halstead said so too.'

Nannie sniffed.

'There'd have been no risk if he'd listened to me which he won't. Not now. Didn't I have him when he was a toddler? Yes, I was under nurse then – only twenty and I got you, my third baby, thirty years later. First your father, then Ronnie and then you. Now listen here. I have to tell you. His lordship is fidgeting himself sick about that Russian prince. I know that. He don't like the idea of you getting engaged to a Russian – prince or nothing. And it might help him if you don't see the prince so often, or better still if you don't see him at all.'

'Oh, Nannie, don't *you* start! I've had it out with Daddy and he knows I'm giving the prince a year before

198

we get properly engaged. Daddy's quite resigned to that and so is Alexei, so don't you fuss.'

For the next three or four weeks, Felicity was seldom at the Duke Street gallery, for despite the two nurses in constant attendance on her father and a good report from the doctors that he had well recovered from his attack, she did not care to be away from him for any length of time.

Riabovitch was back again after his visits to Locarno and elsewhere, on which he was uncommunicative, merely giving her to understand that he had travelled through northern Italy and had not found anything to buy within his means; but he had met and been entertained by Berenson, the famous art critic, in Florence and had learned some useful information concerning the authenticity of a Leonardo bronze bambino in the possession of an American who lived in Florence and had one of the finest private collections of Tuscan primitives in Europe.

They dined twice at the restaurant where he had first taken her in Soho, and once at the Savoy Grill, yet on neither of these occasions did he dwell upon anything personal in their relationship. He did not, as formerly, press her to give him an assurance as to when their engagement could be publicly announced, and indeed he looked to be distrait at their most recent meeting in August.

'You look,' she said, 'as if you were worrying about something.'

He turned to her with his thin smile. 'I have something on my mind which is a perpetual worry to me and all of us, that is to say all who will be affected in Britain with what the leaders of the T.U.C., your Trades Union Congress, are concerned.'

'You mean this bogey of a general strike. But why, if that bothers you, did you go to Locarno? You couldn't have found much to do with pictures there. Or were you interested in this talk of a Locarno Pact, which has been

in all the papers lately as coming in the autumn and supposed to bring peace to Europe?'

He gave a shrug.

'I was there merely *en passant*. Delegates from Britain
and other European countries, including Poland and
Czechoslovakia, are to meet in October, yet I am thankful
to have learned that Russia – not my Russia, Communist
Russia – will be barred from all negotiations of the
Pact.'

'I see,' she said, but didn't. And still wondered why he
should have been to Locarno which was entirely a centre
for political discussion and should have had nothing at all
to do with him, an exile from the Bolshevik Terror in
Russia.

Nor had she seen or heard from Russton since that Red
Friday when they had dined at the Savoy, until later, in
August, she came across him unexpectedly.

It was after having visited Lady Caversham who, more
than ever inconsequent, rambled on, first about her
father's heart attack – 'which mercifully hasn't killed
him. It killed your Uncle Jeremy. Years older than Rodborough. Lucian Halstead – he looks after my old bones.
Arthritis. Says he'll do now. With care.' She looked at
Felicity's hatless head. She had removed her cloche straw
hat; the August day was hot, and her unshingled hair,
growing into a bob, gained her ladyship's attention.

'First Ross-Suttons, you and your father, to be red. But,'
the old lady chuckled 'it's the fashion to be Red. Politically
and socially. The Londonderry won't give up MacDonald.
Not that he's Red, but his party is or was. Dead as mutton
now, but red as your hair. Glad you've done away with
that boy's crop. Yes. I'm thinking of Dick Harrington.'

'Who is he, Auntie?'

'Eh?' Lady Caversham took up an ear trumpet from
beside her on the sofa. Felicity repeated loudly, '*who is
Dick Harrington?*'

'No need to shout. Dead. All of 'em dead. Knew him in

India before your father was born. He'd have been my age. Halstead knew him too and your grandmother. Good looking. Your grandfather wasn't red. None of you's been red till Rodborough. All those years married and then lucky for him. Son and heir. But there *was* an heir. First or second cousin. Bad lot. When your father had that heart attack I began to think. Who's next? There should be a next. Somewhere. Married. Had sons. Dick Harrington red as a fox. Fine handsome young feller. Women all over him. Your father his living spit. Your Uncle Jeremy noticed it.' She nodded her bewigged head. 'Your grandmother and grandfather first cousins. Don't like first cousin marriages. Makes for idiot children. Knew a woman married first cousin. Had a mongol. If so all for the best. Don't want to rake it up if it isn't. How's your Russian? And when do you marry him? If ever. '

'Not settled yet, Aunt . . . I said,' (into the ear trumpet) 'I said *not* settled *yet*.'

'Bolshies. You never know. And these strikes. Even heard the Prince Consort wasn't because Melbourne didn't care for first cousins. There was a Court Chamberlain. Jewish. Albert spit of *him*. Did you read Strachey's Victoria?'

'Yes, Aunt, but what' (striving to pick up disconnected threads) 'has Strachey's Victoria to do with red hair?'

'Eh? Speak up.'

'I said – Never mind.'

'Hope when you do marry he'll have more than a gallery to keep you. Heard of love in a cottage but never in a gallery, unless', she cackled again, 'rogues' gallery. Going?'

'Yes, Auntie, I must. Goodbye.' A dutiful kiss was given. Felicity rose, and was told by the parrot. ''Bye bastard damyereyes.'

'What that bird doesn't know,' Aunt Harriet showed all that remained of her top teeth in a smile stretching to her uttermost wrinkles, 'is more than a cartload of monkeys. I've ordered four dozen candles. You'd better do the same.'

Emerging into Green Street, Felicity was met by Miss Bates leading the Peke.

'Lady Felicity! I am so sorry to have missed you. I've been taking Chin-Chu for his walk in the Park but such crowds! He was quite frightened. I hurried him home. There is a man at Marble Arch on a tub shouting all about the miners and the strike.'

Felicity stooped to the Peke whose tail, unfurled, gave no response to her caress.

'How is he? Looks sorry for himself, doesn't he?'

'He hates crowds. Come along in, Chin-Chu, and have nice boney-boney.'

Miss Bates was favoured with a baleful stare from two goggly, shining black eyes as if to say: 'As you address me in that ridiculous manner may I remind you that I am not an imbecile human child. I am an ancient Chinaman whose ancestors were civilized when yours were savages painted with woad. If you *had* any ancestors, which is unlikely.'

'And how did you find Lady Caversham?' asked Miss Bates.

'Slightly more inconsequent than usual. She was rather taken up with my hair, which is my bane and apparently hers.'

'Oh, no, Lady Felicity. Your hair is lovely!' gushed Miss Bates. 'And I am sure her ladyship thinks so too. But she has been worried lately in case we have a general strike and is making the cook and myself lay in all sorts of things – candles, food for storing, tins of sardines and fruit, pineapples, and even tinned meat for Chin-Chu, but I don't think he ought to have tinned meat. One can never tell what they make it of. Yes, I have observed that her ladyship is given to wandering in her talk more than she used to. She is so very intelligent, really, but her thoughts do run away with her.'

'Why is Aunt Harriet storing candles? You can't eat candles.'

Miss Bates giggled.

'Her ladyship fears if we have a general strike that we shall have no electricity either, so we shall not be able to cook. We have a gas oven and an old-fashioned kitchen range, but if we run out of coal we won't be able to use that, and if the gas workers and electricians go on strike what shall we do?'

'Buy an oil stove, but I don't think we will have the strike.'

'You would have thought so if you could have heard that man – tub-thumping I think they call it. I didn't stay to hear much of it because Chin-Chu was frightened of the crowds, weren't you, buddy-boy?'

'I am never frightened, woman,' Chin-Chu seemed to say with another baleful stare, 'and certainly not of those noisy abominations who call themselves men. Let us go in, it is time for my chicken-breast dinner, which I could not eat midday because you left a box of chocolates within temptation and which I ate.'

'And he was such a g'eedy, g'eedy little boy to eat so many of the chocolates that I had left on a table in my room – such a one for chocolates!' vouchsafed Miss Bates. 'It being my birthday today, Mrs Fremlin, the cook, who remembers it from last year when someone sent me a birthday postcard so everyone could know – she made me some delicious home-made chocolates.'

'Is it your birthday? Many happy returns,' was Felicity's mechanical reply.

'I don't know if', the anxiety lines on Miss Bates' forehead, or all that could be seen of it under her cloche hat, deepened, 'if I *want* many returns; and I can't say', in an unexpected burst of confidence, 'that any of my birthdays have been particularly happy. I have no parents and no one belonging to me now, being an only child. I had a brother who died in infancy, and my few friends whom

I used to know when I was young – younger – are all married. Some of them have gone to live abroad and all have families of their own. . . . Goodbye, Lady Felicity. I – we – do so look forward to your visits.'

Leaving Miss Bates and Chin-Chu to their various occasions, Felicity walked from Green Street to Hyde Park. She was thinking that she wished she had known of Miss Bates' birthday. Too late now to buy her a present, all the shops were closing; but she bethought her of a florist somewhere near and took her way there, ordered a bunch of flowers, attached her card and greetings, and insisted they should be sent at once. Poor Miss Bates who didn't want many returns of her birthday of which few or none had been happy. . . . Just one more of the left-over women, middle-aged or elderly spinsters, with no one belonging to them, forced to be companions to old ladies, a sort of superior servant with nothing to look forward to except a destitute old age unless she could scrape up enough to live on in a miserable bed-sitter from her savings out of the pittance, at most forty pounds a year, doled to her from her employer. . . . Aunt Harriet, who had been her mother's aunt, was no relation to Daddy, so he can't expect anything from her, nor could she if she married Alexei. And if she were left she'd have nobody and possibly no money. What does it matter? What does money matter? It doesn't count if you love a person. That's what bothers me, she thought. . . . Perhaps I can't love any man except Daddy and that's a different sort of love. But how can one know any man until you're married to him? I am too analytical, that's my trouble. All this Freudian stuff. I don't think I'm attractive to men, not the usual kind of hearty man, huntin' shootin' and fishin'. . . .

Her thoughts veering to Russton she surprised herself into believing she could be as attracted to him as he seemed to be to her, but again . . . she was too suspicious and analytical. He could be a 'con' man or a crook or – anything. Not a waiter, of that she was certain, especially as he didn't need the money. Ten thousand a year! Probably all lies.

She had come to the Marble Arch entrance of the Park. Crowds were swarming to where the man described by Miss Bates as 'tub-thumping' stood on a rough-hewn platform attracting a vast audience. This consisted of a heterogeneous collection chiefly, as far as she could see, of the working classes and obviously unemployed. Many she judged to be miners or loafers, down-and-outs come from doss-houses; some in rags and some, a few, well-dressed, who might have been business men or clerks. Here and there a woman who, like herself, had come from curiosity. And among them wives or mothers of those who were there in support of their men's cause.

She edged her way nearer that she could hear what the man was saying or rather shouting above the interjections of applause or occasionally of hecklers.

The speaker was a short, stocky fellow, bearded, grizzle-haired with a high, intelligent forehead. He punctuated his words with gesticulatory emphasis, beating the air with clenched fists. He must have been speaking for some time or he might not have been the same 'tub-thumper' whom Miss Bates had seen. She could hear what seemed to be the middle of a sentence.

...'Yes, you,' he pointed a finger at someone on the fringe of the crowd nearer to the speaker, 'you can put *that* in your capitalists' pipe and smoke it but you won't smoke *us* out! I said next May and I *mean* next May when we'll be faced with the greatest bloodiest crisis this country's ever known in the cause o' justice! We're preparing for it.'

'What with?' was bawled from somewhere in the crowd. 'Bullets? Guns? Poison gas? I fought Jerry in the war an' I got gassed an' I ain't goin' to fight against my King and country for a lot o' bloody buggerin' Bolshies. I'd liefer fight the Germans than – '

'Shut yer mouth!' yelled another. 'We don't want sech

as you fightin' wiv an' for us an' for justice 'cos it's the likes o' you an' your blood-suckin' employers 'oo drains us dry an' don' know what justice is!'

The speaker called in a stentorian voice:

'You – and all of you – shut *your* mouths and let me tell you what you gotta know. And if anyone don't want to listen he can get out!'

There were some who did get out, those of the few that looked to be business men and clerks, but the majority remained, including Felicity, who wanted to hear more of this vociferous 'tub-thumper'.

Raising his voice that all within or without his vicinity could be heard:

'I am goin' to raise a fund – yes, you!' to another who shouted, 'From 'oo you goin' to ryse it? Not me. I'll not give – '

His protest was drowned in a clamour of, 'Let him speak — Blackleg!'

... 'raise a fund,' the speaker continued, undeterred by interruption, 'that'll buy grub distributed to all who may have to go short in the homes of our people. I don't care a damn for any government, army or navy or air force. Let 'em all come!'

'Ay!' from another, 'let 'em all come and try to blast us to hell wiv' their – '

'Right y'are!' yelled the speaker. 'We're ready for 'em. They can come with their bombs and their bayonets – the sods! Bayonets don't cut coal. We'll beat 'em to it. We've already beaten our employers, the strongest government – if you can call it government that – '

'Slave drivers!' was an isolated interjection.

'We're not goin' to starve on what's not enough to feed a cat! You', the speaker continued, 'can lay in stores, buy grub for your children. My old mother has bought a dozen tins of salmon!'

Roars of laughter heralded this pleasantry.

'Let 'em cut our wages,' was the last Felicity heard of this, having heard enough and had her feet trodden on and herself buffeted by the surging mob. 'I said let 'em cut our wages and we'll cut their bloody throats!'

She tried to move away but was held back by the roughs who were pushing and forcing themselves against her and each other to gain closer sight and sound of the speaker. One, a verminous ruffian, his face begrimed with dirt, his clothes half in rags and who stank to heaven, jostled her, laying a filthy hand on her shoulder, and with his face an inch from hers spat into her ear: 'Yah! You in yer fine clo'se wot eats in one dye wot the miners an' their chillearn don't eat in a month. You an' the likes o' you 'ave got it comin' – you'll see!.'

'And you'll see.'

A voice close to her above the din rang out; a voice vaguely familiar followed by a pair of tweed-clad arms that clutched the man round his middle and dragged him away from her, saying:

'The police will have something to say and to do with you – assaulting a lady!'

''Oo's 'salting anyone? An' 'oo the 'ell are you?'

Something, she couldn't tell what, was produced that had a sobering effect.

''Struth! A cop! Lemme go.'

He was released and immediately lost in the crowd.

'As for you,' she looked up into Russton's face, which was one broad grin, 'come out of this. I might have known you'd be butting in where you're not wanted.'

She was too surprised, too shocked, and perhaps too frightened to do anything but allow herself to be led where, with an arm about her shoulders, he managed to find a way through that roaring mob and to the comparative quiet of the entrance to the Park. There and into the Bayswater Road she regained her lost breath.

'*Are* you a – cop? Is that what he called you?'

'It's what he called me and it served its purpose. Come

207

into the hotel here.' A huge modern structure at the corner of the Edgware Road and Oxford Street. 'I guess you'll need a drink or a cup of tea.'

'A drink, please. What's that over there all about?'

'A prelude to what those who partake in it hopefully wish will be a revolution!'

'Oh no!'

'Oh yes. They are going to have the time of their lives – they *think*. It is the product of post-war industrial strife, implemented by Bolshevists in this country.'

'Are there many or any *real* Bolshevists in this country?'

'Enough', he said grimly, 'to ride a tiger, but they don't see the smile on the face of it. What'll you have?'

They had entered the over-ornate lounge of the hotel. A waiter hovered.

'I – I'll have – what I don't have as a rule but under the circumstances, a small whisky and soda.'

'One single Scotch and soda. Bring a syphon and a double.'

'I remember you calling whisky Scotch when you were my patient in hospital.'

'Is that all you remember of me?'

'Almost all.'

'I remember more than almost all of *you* even if I were out of my head with fever. As for you getting yourself mixed up in that racket – '

'I wasn't mixed up in it. I only went there from curiosity.'

'And might have got yourself coshed if I hadn't spotted you.'

'And what were *you* doing there, anyway?'

'Same as you, only more so.'

'What do you mean – more so? More than curiosity?'

'More than, or different from your curiosity. I was reporting. I told you I do articles in my spare time for *The Messenger*.'

208

'But why did he call you a – what was it? – a cop? Are you a sort of policeman?'

'Yes, sort of. Reporters are, you know.'

'I didn't know. Are you being a — a cop when you go to these functions as waiter? Like they have detectives to guard the presents at weddings?'

'Sometimes. All in the day's or night's work.'

'Will you be writing of that racket out there in *The Messenger*?'

'Possibly. Will you have another drink?'

'No, thanks.' She looked at her wrist watch. 'I must go home.' She got up; he too, and went with her to the entrance, ordering a taxi from the commissionaire.

'May I take you to your flat?'

'No need to. I can get a bus.'

'My pleasure.'

A taxi drew up; he helped her in, tipped the commissionaire and gave the address of her flat. They drove off.

'How', he asked, 'is your father?'

'He is much better now.'

'I'm glad of that. I heard he had been ill. Heart, wasn't it?'

'Yes, but how did you know? I've not seen you for ages.'

'Centuries to me. I did hear your father had been ill. I hear quite a lot about you even if I don't see you as much as I would wish to see you which, had I my way, you would never be out of my sight.'

She was silent, thinking: He isn't backward in coming forward, and she said:

'You have been away, haven't you? Where have you been?'

'Here, there, everywhere. I've had a holiday and I'd a fancy to go to Russia.'

'Russia?' She looked at him whose eyes held hers with that in them which caused her an involuntary flutter in the region of her heart. 'Why did you want to go to Russia for a holiday?'

'An interesting holiday. It was time I had a holiday, which I can now afford.'

She nodded, pursing her lips.

'On ten thousand a year, of course. But I shouldn't have thought Russia a particularly happy choice for a holiday. Besides, what of the language?'

'No difficulty there. I made myself understood. I told you I had taken a degree in languages and I'd been swotting up the little Russian I had learned at my varsity with this jaunt in view.'

'And where did your jaunt take you in Russia?'

'To Moscow. There were quite a few Britons there, mostly British Communists. I met Trotsky and Stalin who is the up and coming leader of the Party in Russia. All very well for us to be fobbed off by the poverty of Russia. I stayed in an hotel which has Arnold Bennett's Grand Babylon beaten to a frazzle. There were visitors from all over the world. Intellectual socialists, reporters, like myself, the revolutionary socialists with money. Some of them have money as you probably have known in your 1917 Club.'

'How do you know I've ever been there? And it's not my club.'

'You like to have a finger in current events and to get an inkling of what is going on in and out of the social life to which by right of birth you belong.'

She detected a note of sarcasm in this to which she retorted:

'I don't belong to any social life. But tell me about Moscow.'

'They have their love affairs as we do, only it is freer than with us. Free love is the order of their day. They have their artists, damn good some of them. They have their co-operative stores – what we would call department stores – but you have to produce a pass to get in or out of your hotel if you are staying as a visitor, and everyone is called "comrade" irrespective of his nationality, as the *citoyen* of the French Revolution. Of course it isn't all beer and skittles just now. There are scores of conditions that wouldn't be tolerated here, even though we have our strikes and our own revolutionaries like that gas-bag out there. They have their poverty, their famines and starvation, but they are made to work even on the lowest possible wages; yet they do as they are ordered to do for the good of their cause, mistaken though it is. And I'll hand it to them that after barely ten years they have achieved what we've been striving for and have not yet got anywhere near that which our revolution, our industrial revolution of the last century, was fighting for.'

'To hear you talk,' she said, 'one would think you were on the side of the Bolshies. Alexei – Prince Riabovitch – has similar ideas to yours.'

'Not similar. I hold no brief for grab and greed, nor with the misplaced sympathy for the out-of-works who have no need to be unemployed if they would only take what's given them.'

'The dole that Lloyd George gave them? They can't live on that!'

'Granted, but they could listen to reason and make an effort to avoid party feuds and not to implement these persistent crises in industry. We are still suffering from post-war economic conditions. It is every Briton's responsibility to save his country from what has devastated Russia, and built upon its ruins a savage phoenix to rise and from which they are hoping to create world communism.'

'You are talking as if from your notes for your article in *The Messenger*.'

'I've got it pat. But what I'm concerned with here are the poison seeds scattered to bear fruit from those who are in the pay of, or put their faith in the false idealism of Russia's right to might . . . Here we are at your flat.'

She stood a moment on the pavement hesitating as to whether she should ask him to come in, but lifting his hat he said:

'I hope that we shall have another ride at Richmond in the not too far distant future, if I may ring you up some time. I must away now.'

And she:

'Thank you for coming to my rescue from that awful man!'

Her father, who was now allowed up although not to mount the stairs, was reading the evening paper when she went in to him.

'It's coming,' he said.

'What's coming?'

'The general strike, but there's a temporary lull. It may yet be called off. . . .'

It was called off for six months, yet in the meantime several arrests were made in the autumn of that year. On 12 October the communist leaders were rounded up, their houses ransacked by the police for documents, and all tried at the Old Bailey.

Felicity had not seen much of Riabovitch since he had been abroad for several weeks 'picture hunting' he said. And when she returned to her part-time assistance at the gallery she found herself embroiled in a disturbing occurrence.

She had been attempting to persuade an American to buy one of the 'horrors', as to herself she called the surrealist exhibits brought in by an artist friend of Riabovitch. Having secured for the prince a tidy sum for something which she thought to be the self-expression of a lunatic, she was about to call Serge to begin to lock up when two men came in. The gallery was still open to the public until five-thirty and it was only five and twenty past the hour. They asked if they could see Prince Riabovitch.

'Are you inquiring about pictures?' she asked doubt-fully. They did not look like prospective customers.

They answered abruptly: 'Not pictures,' and when she told them the prince was not available and could she do anything for them, one of them said: 'I have here a search warrant. We are from Scotland Yard.'

Her first thought, when the instantaneous shock of this had subsided, was to summon Serge for she feared they were raiders intent on burglary; but the production of what appeared to be their credentials, while satisfying her as to their intent, did nothing to lessen her alarm.

'Why do you want to search the gallery?' she demanded. 'The pictures and these exhibits are either the property of Prince Riabovitch, or else he is the agent for the artists who wish to sell them.' Then indignation mounting: 'Do you dare to presume these pictures are – are stolen?'

'We presume nothing,' said the other who, until then, had not spoken. 'You are Lady Felicity Ross-Sutton?'

'I am, and what do you want with me or the gallery? And why do you want to search it?'

'Merely a matter of routine,' was the answer to that. And without further parley they walked past her into the office, the door of which stood half open. We can gather from her own account of this intrusion the effect upon herself and what it actually entailed.

From Felicity's Commonplace Book

. . . Am so boiling with fury I can hardly think straight. These two men, policemen in plain clothes which I suppose Russton is in a way – I ought to have guessed that long ago only I don't yet know what it is I am guessing! Well, they barged past me without any apology or permission and went into the office. Riabovitch (funny that I never think of him as Alexei) wasn't there – don't know where he is he's always going somewhere either abroad to buy pictures or into junk shops I suppose junk shops as he is so often in the slum areas where junk shops abound and where these agitators as I read in the papers are tub-thumping like that man at Marble Arch. So in they went and I followed them and saw they were opening the drawers of his desk and rummaging among his papers and they then started on his file cabinet and sorted out the names of the people who had left pictures with him to sell. I told them 'You can't search the prince's private files. What do you want with those? Or anything here?' They said 'We are here to investigate any suspicious characters who may be inciting communism in this country.'

I really saw red then – (seeing red is rather an apposite choice of word!) I then went upstairs calling for Serge. He wasn't in so I had to deal with them myself. I said 'You are on the wrong track here. Prince Riabovitch is a Russian exile, a White Russian and a gentleman of the utmost integrity and to whom I am –' I stopped there because I was just about to say engaged but I wasn't going to tell them that. Instead I substituted 'with whom I am closely acquainted as so is my father Lord Rodborough, and I consider it a breach of your authority to intrude upon the prince's private premises and to accuse him of being involved with these Communists.'

They then tried to conciliate me by saying they had no evidence that the prince was involved with any Communists, but they were merely obeying orders to search all houses or offices that might be on their list of suspects.

I got hotter than ever then and told them, 'I don't know under whose orders you are authorized to search the prince's art gallery and I greatly resent that you are doing so. I am acting as his assistant and my father will take up this disgraceful intrusion in the House of Lords.'

Of course he would do nothing of the sort being still *hors de combat* in the drawing-room and not yet allowed upstairs but thank God so much better that he will soon be able to resume normal life but only very limited golf. What I said had no effect. They went on rummaging through his files but the one who had first spoken to me said quite politely that he was extremely sorry to have caused me any inconvenience and he assured me I was not in any way involved in what they had been ordered to perform in the execution of their duties. He spoke in rather a cockney accent and I wondered if they were really what they said they were and that they might be burglars who any minute would lay me out with a cosh or whatever it is they use and steal the pictures. I ran upstairs again and went to the telephone and asked the operator for the police but they came after me and the same man caught hold of the phone and said 'Pardon me your ladyship but we are the police so it is useless your telephoning for any more of us.'

I didn't believe it and told him 'Let go of this telephone or I will go into the street and call the nearest constable.' They took no notice of me and began ransacking the flat opening drawers and cupboards. They then went into the room where Serge slept and did the same there. I made a bolt for the door to go out and call a policeman when I heard the door of the gallery open – it has a bell that rings when it is opened and who should rush up the stairs but Russton!

He asked, 'What's going on here?' Before they could answer I said 'Get these men away. They have been ransacking the gallery and the prince's flat and going over his private papers and files. They say they are policemen. I am sure they are thieves and I was just about to call the police when they stopped me and laid hold of the phone.'

He said something to them in a low voice much to my surprise for surely he would have turned them out. But instead he too produced a card or whatever it was. They both said something in their turn again so low that I couldn't hear and then the one who seemed to be the spokesman apologized a second time for having caused me any trouble and they were quite satisfied that they had done what they were ordered to do and went away. I don't know if they took anything with them certainly no pictures.

I asked Russton what these police officers had to do with him if they *were* police officers.

'Nothing more' he told me 'than that I also am under orders which they and I have to obey.' He then asked me – before I could take him up on that – to go with him and have a drink or something as I looked as if I needed it. I told him *No* and that I was as suspicious of him as of those two barging in here and passing themselves off as the police.

They probably knew that Serge the prince's man was out and didn't expect to see me here. Anyhow I wished to know how he had happened to come here just at this moment. 'You see,' I said, 'always on the spot when –'

'When,' he interrupted with that really charming boyish grin of his – perhaps cultivated as part of his confidence tricks – 'when you are *in* a spot.'

We had come to the door of the gallery and I told him I was going through the files and things to see what they had pinched. And if he were under orders he had better go before I called Scotland Yard to put them on the track of those two. 'And of you too!' I told him. For I began to think he was in with them. And I quoted or misquoted that saying of President Lincoln 'you can fool me some of the time but you can't fool me *all* of the time!'

He said again with that grin which I did not now think so charming. 'Yes,' I said, 'you can smile – or grin – but it's the smile on the face of the tiger you spoke of in connection with the Communists!'

And not one whit abashed he answered, the grin developing into a laugh, 'You've got me properly taped! So long.' And with that he left me thoroughly mystified and undecided whether or not to ring for the police but I thought better not until I had found if anything of importance was missing.

I went through his desk and his files. They were all correct, just the names of purchasers and of artists who had brought their pictures to sell but I saw under P that the card of Poppycockski – the only way I can spell his name – was missing. But perhaps it hadn't been there at all or finished with. I then went up to the flat. There again nothing missing as far as I could see but of course I didn't know what his private papers were if locked away. All his drawers were locked, though if they had skeleton keys they could have got at them but I was in the room while they did their rummaging and I didn't notice if they had skeleton keys or not I was in such a state. Then I saw that the framed banner on the Sheraton stand with the embroidered crest of the dragon's head was just a bit askew. Of course it may have been askew before when Serge dusted it. However I examined it and went behind it and saw that the bottom of the frame was a bit loose. I gave it a pull and it came out disclosing a kind of secret drawer. I remembered how Poppycockski some time ago brought a picture with a backing that opened and Riabovitch showed it to me with some writing in red ink on the back of it. That picture was painted on wood but it had like this one a sort of narrow aperture quite wide enough to hide something small in it either papers or perhaps jewellery. I had it open when I heard the gallery door bell and then Serge came up. I told him what had happened and showed him the banner-backing empty. I asked him if the prince kept any articles of value there. I know he did sometimes have antique snuff boxes brought to him and eighteenth century miniatures and some jewellery. He had acquired in Florence a Benvenuto Cellini ring which he had bought to give me as an engagement ring when he said we would be officially announced as engaged. He showed it to me a lovely thing with a ruby (but it might have been a garnet!) set in silver elaborately carved. Serge said in his broken English that His Excellency did keep articles of value there and that he would at once call the police.

After that I don't know what happened. I was so upset that I left the gallery and went home. It was no longer my affair but I was really in a bit of a fright lest the police would come asking me questions. They didn't which greatly relieved me for had they questioned me I would have had to bring Russton into it and con man or not or crook (or – what?) – I wasn't going to get him into any more trouble than he was probably in already . . . I had no sleep more than two hours and rang for coffee and rolls in bed was so exhausted with it all.

Annie brought the Daily Mail on my breakfast tray. Headlines glared at me.

TWELVE COMMUNIST LEADERS ARRESTED

There was a whole page about it. I couldn't wade through it all but I read enough to see that the police had laid hands on anything that might be of use in making out a case against the Communists . . . But why come to the gallery? Surely they were not suspicious of a White Russian prince?

H

217

Anyway he wasn't there. I had a postcard from him only this morning brought with my breakfast posted from Portsmouth saying he had gone to a sale at Southsea and was told of a Constable at Ventnor in the Isle of Wight and would be going to see it . . . A Constable! I thought to myself that's rather coincidental. He couldn't know we had constables of another sort searching his gallery! Thank goodness he wasn't there. But what of Russton? . . .

NINE

Well might Felicity wonder 'what of Russton?' And again she might ask herself what of that other, more than ever elusive since the invasion of his gallery by police officers.

The account in the national and provincial press that leading Communists had been arrested had caused the utmost consternation throughout the country, yet it left her still in doubt as to the authenticity of those two self-designated 'policemen', who could well have taken advantage of the general investigation of suspected persons and their property to invade the prince's premises as plain clothes police officers with intent to rob him of his art treasures. But they had seemed to have taken nothing of value, unless any jewellery or objets d'art had been concealed behind the framed banner of the dragon's head.

As for Russton, she did not care to allow her suspicions to run riot concerning his part in what the more sensational of the daily papers described as 'Incitement to Mutiny under the Act of 1797', under which the twelve arrested had been charged.

'But why bring in an act that must be obsolete now after more than a hundred years?' she asked her father.

'Never obsolete where incitement to mutiny or revolution is involved,' he told her. 'Let us hope they have pulled in the worst of them to be tried at the Old Bailey.' And looking up from *The Times* – they were at breakfast – Lord Rodborough remarked:

'They are probably after Riabovitch also as suspect of Red or Left Wing sympathies, especially since Zinoviev's Red Letter that resulted in the "Red spy scare".'

She had never let him know that she had been at the gallery during the raid upon it; he was already prejudiced against her choice of a prospective alliance with a Russian, but at this remark of his she flared up in defence of Alexei, since her father had voiced what she had hardly dared to think, much less to say.

'You have no right to suspect Riabovitch of being mixed up with these Communists just because he is Russian. He is intelligent and tolerant enough to see both sides of the disaster that plunged his country into revolution.'

'Yes, and murdered his Czar,' said her father acidly.

'And didn't we murder our King in our revolution or civil war, which is the same thing? Really, Dad, you and all of you in the Lords and Commons should cultivate some sense of proportion.'

'Our sense of proportion does not agree with you young moderns' socialistic clap-trap. Oh, I know', he raised a hand to avert interruption, 'that you have frequented the 1917 Club in Soho where the youth of this post-war generation like to hobnob with MacDonald and his satellites, the Cripps and Webbs and Shavian fraternity who see themselves as pioneers in a community of a nation's welfare state which could prove to be nothing but an *ill*-fare state should it ever materialize. But they'll grow out of it when they've cut their wisdom teeth. We all go through our teething troubles. Even I did once.'

'You, too, Dad? Did you try to set the world to rights – or would it be Left?'

'A smart Alec – or Alex – aren't you? We at Magdalen, when I was a freshman more than thirty years ago, had similar enthusiasms for joining an army of campaigners, a body of mistakenly valiant St Georges out to fight the dragon of bureaucracy.'

'The dragon!' She echoed it. 'Did you consider that your tutors or dons or whoever was the Government, which would have been either Conservative or Liberal in your day, were dragons and that the youth of our day to which I do *not* belong, being past my teething troubles, are all out, as were you, to fight against the old order of things, which was a jolly sight better than the new order of things, that wants to destroy whatever may be left of decency and loyalty?' And again she thoughtfully repeated: 'The Dragon – whose head is to be feared.'

But her father, once more immersed in *The Times*, did not hear or pay any attention to that.

During the next few days Felicity was at the gallery about twice a week. With Serge in charge she had nothing much to do but attend to the few infrequent customers or those who only came to look and not to buy. She had heard nothing from Alexei since the postcard she had received on the morning after the raid, but on the Saturday of the following week he was back again.

She greeted him with:

'Do you know what went on here while you were away?'

'I have seen the papers,' he said with his thin smile. 'I understand that over-zealous police have invaded my premises because, I presume, I happen to be Russian and all my compatriots, whether White or Red, seem to be suspect of Communism. I am taking up this unwarrantable intrusion with the Home Office and with the Member of Parliament for the Westminster constituency.'

'I hope you will.' She was somewhat relieved. 'I can't think why they should dare to come here if they *were* police officers, which I doubt. They took nothing of value as far as I could tell, but they must have opened this.' She pulled out the hidden drawer at the base of the banner that was in the flat. 'There seems to be a secret hiding place here in which Serge said you kept pieces of objets d'art and such like. And it was empty. Do you think they took anything from it?'

'Of course it is empty.' He slid an arm around her shoulders and kissed her forehead where a lock of the gilded copper-coloured hair had strayed. 'Before I went away I sold a charming little miniature supposed to be of Madame de Maintenon that I kept there with your Benvenuto ring which is locked in my safe.'

'I didn't know you had a hiding place in this, nor that you sold these little pieces, nor' – doubt again possessed her, she removed herself from his arm – 'that you had a safe in the flat.'

'It is behind the panelling. No one could know of it, not even the police or those two who passed for the police nor,' his eyes narrowed as they searched her face, 'any others who came with, or after them, and with whom you are, as Serge reported, acquainted.'

'What can you mean?' she cried. 'How could Serge know that the man who came while they were there is an acquaintance of mine? Serge didn't come back until after all three had left.'

'He saw a certain person leave the gallery just as he returned. He has seen him with you before, he tells me, at the Savoy and other places. You should be more selective in your choice of your – associates.'

'Do you employ Serge to spy on me,' she demanded, her temper rising. 'The man you speak of and whom Serge may have seen leave the gallery is an acquaintance of mine, one whom I nursed when I was a V.A.D. in the war at my father's house in Grosvenor Square which was turned into a hospital and is no longer ours. It was sold with all the rest of my father's property. I have every right to dine or to go anywhere I choose to go – ' indignation got the better of her '– with any man whom I wish to – to meet, for I am not to be dictated to by you or anyone as to the choice of my friends. If that is to be your attitude to me when or *if* we marry then there is no more to be said of an engagement whether private or public.'

He made an attempt to take her in his arms. She held herself aloof. She saw that he was white about the lips, and his nostrils, above the streak of moustache so like an eyebrow, were pinched.

He spoke huskily.

'I realize that you have never been sure of me or of yourself. I have been patient. I have conceded to you all that you have asked, a time of waiting which has been an anxious and irksome time for me. Félise, I want you – I love you – '

'This,' she broke in, 'is the first time I have ever heard you say it.'

'What need of words?' And now she let herself be taken.

His mouth sought and found hers; against her will she responded and returned his passion with a fervour that dissolved her doubt of him. Yet, when he released her she turned away, feeling that she could not meet his eyes, and said:

'Why do you want to marry me? What can I give you that you do not already have? You have taught me much about art of which I knew so little. You can have nothing – nothing at all from me of material worth. We shall both be as hard up as we are now if we marry. The only recompense for that would be if we were sure of each other, to live and to – ' she faltered – 'to love to the end of our days.'

'Yes,' he said eagerly, 'that is what I want and will have from you. I, an outcast, exiled, suspect as are most of us who have escaped the Terror, living on the hospitality of your country who have received us out of pity for our plight. But,' his voice rang out strongly, 'I, Riabovitch, do not want pity. I want recognition that I may hold up my head and be as one with all of you. To take as wife an English woman of my choice – you!'

To her dismay he knelt to her and buried his head between her knees. She felt the tremble of his body. 'You', his words were muffled, 'have always been so – so sympathetic – unlike the many I have known, men and women who look upon me as an encumbrance with all my other exiled compatriots. Oh, my beloved! Do not refuse me – anchorage!'

A constriction of her throat as she listened to this outpouring from one whom she had always thought to be so self-controlled and self-possessed deprived her momentarily of speech. She stroked his dark sleek hair in which she discerned some threads of grey.

'Please,' she found voice to beg him, 'don't! Don't kneel to me. Tell me what troubles you – you can tell me anything if you will, but do let me know how and why you should become involved – if you are involved – in all these Communist arrests.'

'I am not involved!' He struggled to his feet striving for composure. 'I have told you that I and all of us here in Britain are suspect unless married to an Englishwoman or can give some other proof of our loyalty to the Royalists in Russia, of whom only a few are left who would save their skins in alliance with the Soviet Union. They are our traitors!'

'So', collectedly she made herself say, 'you want to marry me for my nationality that you may be a naturalized Briton. But you can be naturalized without marrying me.'

'No!' He denied it loudly, then contradictorily, 'Yes! But that is not why I want you as my wife – my British wife, born of noble forbears to match my own who descend from the ancient line of the Riabovitch.'

She said: 'If you marry me you aren't marrying my forbears. Or would you have wished to marry me had I been the daughter of a – Thistlewaite, for instance?'

'Ah!' he stepped back from her; his face had paled and until that moment she saw what she had never seen nor cared to see before; a hint of cruelty in his thin-lipped smile. 'You and all of you misconstrue us.' His accent had become more foreign as his words slipped from him. 'Thistlewaite? Pah! Product of the many who have inherited their millions from the sweat of those who labour for them at a wage not enough to feed a dog, let alone a wife and family. It was the same in my country only worse. The wealthy and not so wealthy bourgeoisie here in Britain and other countries which I have visited of late in search of beauty and to give you, my *dushka*,' he made again as if to take her to him, and again she eluded him, 'you whom I treasure more than the priceless offerings of the Uffizi, to give you all that once I had and no longer have, until such time as I can claim you for my own that you may live according to your rank and mine.'

Impatiently she shook her head.

'I have no rank. I care nothing for titles and ancestry. I care only for what people are, whether of the common herd or kings. If that is Communism then I am one! But,' as he exhibited shock, or feigned it, 'I don't hold with blackmail as in this threatened strike, to bleed their employers for more wages and bring about a national disaster. We have awful unemployment – that is our cross and theirs, but you forget we have had a European war – a war against the overwhelming tyranny of an Emperor who tried to subjugate the world. And doing so he lost countless thousands – no, millions of young lives. We are still paying for that war. We shall always be paying for it, and if another war should come what hope is there for Britain or your Russia or Europe or America whom we look to for financial aid? And you talk about rank!'

He passed a hand across his forehead where beads of sweat had moistened it.

'What', he asked her, 'do you want of me? Your husband or your – hanger-on, as others may have hoped for just that much condescension from the Lady Felicity Ross-Sutton?'

Stifling a hot retort she told him quietly: 'You may ask me that in – shall we say six months' time? I gave you a year and it is not yet a year since we both agreed to wait.

225

But these latest events have rather changed our or my decision. If you love me, as now for the first time you have said it, you will go on waiting for me until I and both of us are sure.' She held out her hand to him. He took it in his dry warm clasp. His eyes, pleadingly on hers she saw, with a startled tremor, were wet. 'I must be sure,' she said firmly, determined not to give way to pity which, she thought wryly is, in this case, *not* akin to love – 'sure of you and of myself. I am not sure yet.'

She left him with that half promise and walked all the way home deep in self-communing. . . . These incessant indecisions of hers, not his, were a continuous tug of war between her own two selves. This lurking, half-confessed mistrust of him and, yes, of Russton who, against her better judgement, engaged too much of her interest. . . . Why, she wondered, could she not be as other girls, and not so much of a girl either at twenty-seven, almost – she was ruefully reminded. And at her age when to be un-married was a disparagement, a slur upon her female attraction that the Younger Brighter Things, call 'It', and of which she decided she had none. She wouldn't want to be hunted and caught by the predatory male and decked out in bridal white to kneel at the altar and promise to love honour and – *not* to obey. That should be cut out of the marriage service. And he to promise with his body to worship her. Who would want to be worshipped? Only a down-trodden little Thistlewaite would promise to worship with his body – his poor little – No! Rich little body – and with all his worldly goods to endow his Ethel. But for me, she asked, what did she want from life? Marriage? Not yet. Not until she could find the one whom she knew was the one and only man she would love with all her body and, yes, her soul if she had a soul which she doubted, and if in this ugly material world of greed and strikes and threatened revolutions all other souls were lost. And how was it possible that Riabovitch were that

one of all men she could love and honour? . . . Never!
She would have to tell him so. Yet, remembering his tear-
wet eyes as she parted from him in his flat not half an
hour ago, she shrank from hurting him more than he
already has been hurt, he's lost all he ever had, his
country, his relatives, his wife. Yes, he had a wife once.
She too was dead. . . . But you can't marry a man because
he has suffered as all these exiled Russians have suffered.
He would do far better, she thought, if he went to live in
Florence where he could have all the art and beauty his
soul, if he had a soul, could crave, and find a rich American wife who would love and marry him for his title. . . .
Suppose she told him that?

She didn't tell him that for, although she knew it not,
fate, chance, destiny, or what you will, had shaped their
ends.

It was a raw November day when, having made an
appointment with her hairdresser, she took a taxi to Bond
Street, and after a shampoo and set, was seated under a
dryer with that week's *Tatler* in her hands. Idly turning
the pages her indifferent attention was diverted by a voice
in the curtained cubicle next to her own. A foreign lilting
voice speaking to the man who coiffed her.

'Yes, I am here in London from Paris where I have
been zese t'ree monss.'

'*Oui, madame?*'

Rudolph, as he named himself, was not French but had
been born of the house of Moses in Whitechapel. Having
apprenticed himself to a famous Parisian coiffeur in Paris
he had now reached the pinnacle of his career as one of the
most fashionable ladies' and gentlemen's hairdressers in
London. He had also acquired a tolerably good French-
English accent.

'*Madame* is from Paris, *mon* Paris?'

'*Mais oui.* Your Paris, is it?'

'*Oui, madame, mais* – it is a many year since I was zere.

227

Madame will permit that I make the smallest *soupçon* of a *frisette*?'

'If you wish.' The voice was bored but livened to the question: 'I am told that Prince Riabovitch' – at which Felicity pricked her ears to strain and hear – 'has a picture gallery in Duke Street in San' James. Do you know if it iss open to ze public every day?'

'*Ah, oui, madame*, I t'ink. I can inquire if *madame* would wish, as m'sieur le prince is honneured client of *le département pour les messieurs*.'

'*Ça ne me fait rien*,' was the reply again in the same bored tone. 'I can visit the gallery if I wish to see his pictures. But I can buy what I want at any od'er of the picture shops here in London.'

Parfaitement, madame. Is *madame intéressée* in ze art?'

'*Çela dépend . . .*'

There followed a silence. Felicity was now occupied by her own smallest *soupçon* of a *frisette* supplied by one Antoine, he a genuine Frenchman. And then:

'*Merci, madame*,' from Rudolph to the lady in the adjoining cubicle. 'Zank you, *madame*. *Enchanté, madame*. If *madame* will make ze appointment wiz ze secretary . . .'

Felicity, having passed a tip to the fawning Antoine, she and her neighbour, both simultaneously about to leave their respective cubicles, met and all but collided in the narrow passage way between the starry-blossomed chintz curtains.

Politely murmured apologies were exchanged, and both met again at the *caisse* where they made their respective appointments with the secretary.

'And the name, *madame*?' to Felicity's neighbour who had preceded her.

'Madame Lubovoska,' it sounded like.

'Thank you, *madame*, at ten-thirty today week. Shampoo and set.'

228

A card was handed to her, 'Should madam care to cancel, giving twenty-four hours' notice.'

'*Merci.*'

While this was going on Felicity took note of the lady. She had discarded her hat not to disarray her coiffure; her hair, dark and centre parted, was held in a plaited coil at the back of the well-shaped head. Two 'smallest *soupçons* of *frisettes*' were plastered against the cheeks under the lobes of the ears. Obviously Russian, Felicity decided, perhaps one of the Ballet, come from Moscow en route for London via Paris; or maybe of the Moscow Art Theatre, which is advertised to appear – where is it – at the Palace Theatre or somewhere?

She too paid her bill, went her way, and dismissed the lady from her mind.

Little did she guess how and under what unlikely circumstance she would meet with that lady again.

*   *   *

Of the twelve Communists sentenced at the Old Bailey, seven had been released a few weeks before what the Communists described as the most disastrous calamity in the history of British Labour, the General Strike.

During the six months which elapsed before that fatal third of May. Felicity had more personal matters to occupy her mind than the problems of a nation. Riabovitch had gone again upon his travels, having left London to seek works of art, and sent her word briefly of his whereabouts on postcards until a letter came from Paris. Couched in more amorous terms than he had ever spoken, it may not have produced quite the same response as was intended.

Félise, your eyes, the greenest of things blue, the bluest of things grey as your Swinburne has it, haunt my dreams. I wake from the ecstasy of holding you in my arms in toto.

(In toto? She wrinkled her nose as she read that. What next?)

This came next.

I have spent hours in the Louvre, have seen a Cimabue to whom I kiss my fingers, and have bought from what you would call a junk shop a not yet so elect of English masters of the early nineteenth century, an Etty. He specializes in the nude, exquisitely. I have also seen an appartement, and I wait with what trepidation your approval at such times as you may terminate my agonized suspense while you come to a final decision as to whether you will or will not make me the happiest of mortals —

If he thinks this sort of blah is going to make him the happiest of mortals, was her instantaneous reaction, then he looks to be the *un*happiest of mortals . . . She read on.

Yes, I have seen an appartement on the Left Bank here in a charming *cul de sac* where you and I could live in peace and happiness. In London where however much I am tolerated as are others of my compatriots, I realize I am looked upon with suspicion as *per* that outrageous invasion of my gallery by the police. I did receive apology for it from the Foreign Office due to my friend Rakovsky's intervention. He is, as you probably know, the Soviet Union's *Chargé d'Affaires*. But if you, my best beloved, would marry me and live with me in Paris, that I feel would be my Mecca and all I ask of life which has treated me so cruelly. Meanwhile Serge holds the fort at the gallery where he tells me you are gone so seldom there. In any case it is making a dead loss to me and I hope soon to negotiate for a gallery in Paris. And so, my dearest, adieu. I kiss your lovely mouth in my dreams and send you all my love.

Ever yours
Alexei

She read it through a second time; this, the first love letter she had ever received from him or any man. . . . If, she told herself, it could be called a 'love letter'. Far from enhancing his hope of a termination to his 'agonized suspense', he had prolonged it indefinitely, if not to a complete annihilation of his hopes. As for living in Paris, how could he think she would leave her father? No! She would not; nor would she answer this appeal. Let it rest. Time enough to let him know when he came back from Paris. . . .

The weeks fled into months with intermittent postcards from him. No more letters, but his messages on brightly coloured photographs of la Côte d'Azur gave her to understand he was touring the South of France. On one of these communications, written in French, he informed her he had been viewing a villa at Menton with a prospect of buying it. How, he added, would she care for that? Which suggestion again was left unanswered.

She had seen Russton only once since the raid on the gallery; he too, if out of London, had not told her where, nor did she hear from him until one morning in the spring of that year, 1926, he telephoned her at her home.

'Have you been wondering if I had vanished off the face of the earth?' was his greeting over the wire.

To which, resenting his inference that she had missed him, she replied with ice:

'I have not given a thought as to where you have been, whether lost, stolen', she said pointedly, 'or strayed.'

There was laughter in his voice as he answered that with:

'If you mean have I been one of the twelve stolen – or arrested – by the police on the day when we last met, or am I one of the seven released from quod, or have I strayed from Brixton Gaol, I can tell you that I have been in very close quarters to certain of my fellows in Brixton and the Old Bailey. But as for lost – well, yes, I have been lost for a sight of you after all this time. So can we meet and ride or dine or walk and – talk again?'

To which, slightly disconcerted, and in doubt as to the implication of his words that would lead her to believe he was on the verge of a confession that he too had been one of the Communist suspects held for trial, she was silent; and he breaking in on that lengthy pause inquired, 'Are you still there?'

'Yes, I'm here.'

'Well?'

'Well what?'

'Can we meet? Tomorrow? It is May Day tomorrow and Richmond is in the height of spring's glorification.' And he crooned into her ear: "In the spring time, the merry ring time, in the spring time the poets sing, girls come out to show their dimples and young men come out in pimples in the spring time, the merry — "'

'You sound very pleased with yourself,' she interrupted distantly, but her mouth quirked at the corners, 'and as for meeting you tomorrow, I am engaged tomorrow.'

'I am sure you are not engaged tomorrow or any other day, if by engaged you mean that a betrothal of marriage has been announced between the Lady Felicity Ross-Sutton and Prince Riabovitch, so will you engage yourself to me?'

At that she banged down the receiver and stood looking at the instrument, her cheeks hot and her heart in a flurry. She put her hand to the telephone as if to call him back, but remembered that she had not his number. And for goodness' sake why do you want to have any more to do with him. He was obviously an impostor whether or not he had been pulling her leg when he implied he had been arrested, in league with those two who said they were the police when they raided the gallery, and he had arrived just at the precise moment. . . . Then the telephone rang. She let it ring until Wilson came in.

'The telephone, my lady. Will you answer it or shall I?'

'Yes, you answer it. Ask who it is and if a Mr Russton I am not available.'

232

'Very good, m'lady.'. . . 'What name?' asked Wilson into the receiver. . . . 'No, sir, her ladyship is not available.'

'And if he rings again you can tell him the same thing.' She went to her room.

Neither he nor the telephone rang again and she who was due at the gallery left to find Russton in his car outside the entrance to the flat.

He got out of the car and approached her, baring his head.

'Am I in disgrace?'

'You should know.'

'Can I give you a lift to wherever you are going?'

'No.'

A prowling taxi passed. She hailed it, gave the address of the gallery and left him standing there.

Arriving at the gallery she saw that Riabovitch was in conversation with the woman whom she recognized as having been at Rudolph's and at the Savoy with Serge some months ago; yet her hair, she recollected, had then been pageboy-bobbed and was now grown long enough to coil at the back of her head. Yet she was confident it was the same woman.

They were speaking Russian; but at Felicity's entrance the bell that in the absence of the prince had rung to admit visitors was now silenced so they did not at once perceive her.

She passed in quietly and would have gone on into the office so as not to interrupt a possible sale when Riabovitch, on seeing her, came forward.

She thought he looked harassed, was paler than usual.

'Ah, my dear, this lady is a – is from Russia, recently arrived in England. Allow me to present Madame Lubovoska, Lady Felicity Ross – '

'No!' came the harsh intervention. 'Zat is no my name – not since I was marry to zis man!' Who at those words bowed his head and stayed there silent.

'Your . . . wife?' Felicity heard herself say in stunned incomprehension. And again, 'Your *wife?* I thought' – she turned to him – 'I understood your wife was dead.'

'I am not dead.' The woman, as pale as he, her hand feverishly searching in a crocodile bag she carried, answered for him. 'He left Russia in ze Revolution wiz others who escaped.' She broke now into voluble French saying, 'Pardon mademoiselle, zat I speak not so good ze English. I speak better French. . . . Always I had the intention to find Alexei Alexandrovitch, my husband, who left me to the Bolsheviks. But my God! How I suffer to know that he, a Riabovitch, one of the great families of our country as am I, and him I married in the good faith and I hear he came to your country in support of Lenin, Trotsky, and the villains who destroyed my Czar and my adored Czarina! I was for her – what you in English call – dame in attendance. Her favourite lady. I loved her. . . .' She struggled for composure through the tears that choked her voice. She pointed a trembling finger at Riabovitch who still stood head bowed and mute. 'I loved my Czarina and all of the Family Royal. None remain. All dead – murdered. And he – he came to your country in support of the Bolsheviks, a false traitor to us all. He thinks – I believe he thinks – he is what is an idealist, a crusader against tyranny and oppression but he is paid – ' her voice rose to a shriek – '*paid* for his information that he gives to his deserted country in the power of the usurpers that they may have the secrets guarded by your people and the people of other countries to make war on Europe for world domination of the devil that is called Communism here and in America, and so I come to *kill* him!'

Her whole body in a tremble now, she took something from the bag she carried, a shining toy-like thing and levelled it. A shot rang out and, missing Riabovitch by several inches, shattered the glass of a picture frame behind where he stood as if in a trance. But at that shot and the tinkle of glass he sprang forward and caught the

234

woman in his arms as she swayed sideways and would have fallen.

With a hand to her mouth suppressing a cry, Felicity joined him as he lifted the inert body of his wife.

He said between taut lips: 'She is mad. Do you believe her?'

Recovering herself with the iron control that her hospital training had taught her, Felicity took command of this horrific situation to answer him:

'I believe some but not all she has been saying. It would account for much I did not understand.'

He was helplessly looking round for somewhere to place her he held as there was no settee in the gallery. Felicity felt her pulse.

'It is only a faint. Take her upstairs and lay her on a sofa or a bed. I will attend to her.'

He obeyed, still as if in a trance. Felicity followed and sat beside the sofa where he had laid his wife with a cushion behind her head.

'Bring brandy,' commanded Felicity.

He brought a bottle, a spoon and a wine glass. She measured a dose and held it to the pallid lips of the Princess Riabovitch. She swallowed a few sips; her eyelids fluttered open. 'I did not kill him,' she said in French, and in a breathless voice. 'I would have killed him happily,' her voice gained strength as some colour returned to her face with another larger dose of brandy. 'Yes, I would kill him for conspiring against my Czar and my Czarina. You are veree kind,' she told Felicity in English. 'I am 'appy to save you from a marriage wiz zis bad man – zis traitor.'

'I am no traitor,' he spoke not to his wife, but to Felicity. 'It is true I conveyed information to Russia for I hold to my beliefs that the capitalist world is doomed unless an entire reformation can be achieved. Many of your and my generation here and in the countries I have visited in these last few months think the same. I have sounded their principles and there is too small a minority as yet to agree with my beliefs. But a traitor –' he emphasized that word with outspread hands '– a traitor I am not! Before God I swear I am no traitor to the Russia that once was mine, nor to your country, nor am I in the pay of the Bolsheviks for my sympathies. No! I am not in sympathy with their principles. There is much I would attempt to abolish and have sought to find a saner approach and more feasible solution by which the Communists in this and other countries do seek to solve their grievances. Believe me I speak the truth.'

'He has no truth!' His wife attempted to raise herself from the couch. 'He is a liar – ' she spoke in French. 'He deceived you as he has deceived me.'

He paid no heed to this and went on in an even calculated tone which carried conviction that he held by what he said.

'The Kaiser's Imperialist war which strove with nation against nation caused in Russia a civil war fighting class against class. I, too, fought with my class – the royalists against the revolutionaries, and that is why I believed my wife Anna to have died with the Imperial Court of Russia when the Emperor and Empress were murdered. I was at Kiev with my regiment when the murders took place and we – our cavalry of the White Army – were defeated in the war against the Reds. Those who were not of the slaughtered made our escape. I have told you when I came back to Moscow that I went disguised until I managed to get away and came here to England. I believed Anna, my wife, was dead until this very day –' there were beads of sweat on his forehead; he wiped them off with the back of his hand. 'How can I convince you of this?'

'He speak lies,' cried Anna. 'He know I am not dead. His man Serge, he know I am here – I was here last year and then in Paris, and I am back from Paris now.'

Felicity said: 'I remember that I saw her – your wife –

with Serge at the Savoy some months ago. How, then,'
accusingly she asked him, in as steady a voice as his while
he gave what amounted as evidence in his defence, 'How
if she, your wife, were here and with your servant Serge,
could you not have known she was alive?'

'I did not know, but what I have discovered is that the
man Serge is an agent for the Bolsheviks and what is called
a double agent, that is to say he operates for your country
and with the Communists for payment. Anna, poor soul,
it is she who is deceived. Not by me, by the man whom she
paid to have me watched until she could find sufficient
proof against me of espionage in the pay of the Bolsheviks.'

'As he is! He is *espion*!' hysterically came from Anna
as she dashed aside the glass held to her lips. It spilled
upon her sleeve. Felicity wiped off the drops with her
handkerchief.

'She believes that,' said Riabovitch again with a gesture
of his hands, 'but I swear before God I have never received
any payment for what I have striven to accomplish.
Class war against class is wrong. Class hatred is wrong –
is venomous, a poison that is at the root of all evil, as
money, or the want of it, is at the root of all evil. If my
endeavours have been on the side of the oppressed it is as
the word of Christ has taught – to love your neighbour as
yourself.'

'So!' An embittered laugh escaped her who listened,
only half comprehending what he said in English. 'He bring
in the Lord Christ *pour s'excuser*. Would he have you,
pauvre innocente, and me also *illusionée* to be – how you
say – *trahir* – into seeing him as he would see *soi-même*,
sauveur des misérables?'

'*Soyez tranquille*.' Felicity laid a soothing hand to
Anna's forehead. 'She has a temperature. Have you a spare
room here?' she asked the prince.

'No, only the room for Serge. He is not here today. It is
his day off. I have no doubt that he arranged for Anna to

come here knowing he would absent himself and leave me to be confronted with this – this *débâcle*.'

'I could take her home with me,' Felicity continued calmly, 'so that she may rest. She is ill.'

'Yes,' he spoke still in that same even almost expressionless tone. 'She has an *idée fixe*, amounting to mania, that I and others who fled to Western Europe are Bolsheviks, and in part responsible for the extermination of Russian Imperialism. But on my life – for what it is worth – I swear I am no Bolshevik and I repeat that I have never received one rouble in payment from the Reds against whom I, with the White Army, fought until wiped out. I have, I admit it, gained information that may be of use in the reconstruction of the world from its present chaos to more tolerant, more sane, more peaceable conditions which the European war, that is supposed to have ended all wars, may bring about. But not unless a communal unity of the Allies – forget the League of Nations – will lead us to that Utopia in which we all work towards one sole aim and purpose – equality, fraternity and tolerance.'

She said, and she too was pale with the shock of it all, 'You have told me this before – that you hoped for a permanent world peace, but not through Communism as I understood you. And I do not think you are a traitor working for the Bolsheviks. When the police raided the gallery – and now I know they were the police – '

'They found nothing,' he broke in, 'with which they could have arrested me under the charge of which the Communists here were convicted.'

'Yes,' she reminded him, 'but they opened the banner of the dragon's head – your crest.'

'And found it empty. I told you I had taken the miniature it contained and your ring – ' a spasm crossed his face '– the Benvenuto ring that would have been your engagement ring, and I placed them in my safe. And again I swear upon my solemn oath that what I have done or attempted to do was and is for the cause to which I am

238

dedicated, and not for monetary gain. This gallery which I opened and sold some of the works of art I managed to save from the wreckage of my home, is my sole means of livelihood.'

And again the woman cried out: 'He lies. He tell you lies – lies! *Mensonges!*'

As if unaware of interruption he went on: 'I may be an idealist who has failed as others before me have failed in a crusade that can only lead to a dead end. My dead end is that I have lost you . . . Excuse me.'

He sank down on to a chair and buried his head in his hands. His shoulders heaved with the silent sobs that shook his whole body.

Felicity went to him and, with a hand on his bowed shoulder, she said: 'I do believe you are honest in your convictions as are some of those who have been arrested. But there is too much I cannot understand. Why did they search behind the banner that framed the dragon's head that holds a secret drawer?'

He looked up at her; a faint smile twisted his tightened lips.

'It is an old device often used by your own secret service. Why do you suppose I was so anxious to secure the Gerard Dows that were in the possession of Mr Thistlewaite?'

'Good heavens! Did those Gerard Dows also have a hiding place behind their frames?'

'One of them had, as that gentle gentleman,' another twisted smile came upon his lips, 'Mr Thistlewaite, did substitute a second pair copied by an expert in the Hague. I know him and I know how he secured world fame with his copies of the masters. But Mr Thistlewaite, himself no mean judge of art, realizing I might well recognize a copy, he let me have the originals in which he had carefully inserted a plan of a certain bomber and also of the R Y Z under construction at Fordington research station. But it was a ruse to – as you would say in English – fob me off.

And I knew it was a ruse. No use to me. Would it be likely that the Air Ministry would allow any possible access to secret plans of air defence aircraft of any kind? Airships, even if an improvement on the German Zeppelin, would be of no use in air warfare ten or twenty years hence. We who hope to prevent a world war greater and more disastrous than the great war of 1914 – what if we should fail in our endeavours? As we will,' he said brokenly, 'as we will.'

She was scarcely listening.... 'Mr Thistlewaite? Did you say ... Oh, no!' Incredulity struggled with amazement. 'How does Mr Thistlewaite come to know anything about – or have anything to do with air defence plans hidden behind those Gerard Dows?'

'Because,' he was speaking more naturally now, and in his eyes dawned a faint gleam of amusement, 'your Mr Thistlewaite is one of the most active members of the British Secret Intelligence for which he volunteered during the war and has been in it ever since to give his service free to his country as I do for my cause, however mistaken it may be. And perhaps, as a secondary consideration on the part of the excellent Thistlewaite', and there was no doubt now as to a hint of whispered laughter as he spoke, 'that he might have an interest beyond the autocratic government of his good lady.'

'Ber ... but he stutters.' She too found herself stuttering, 'he seems to be so – so absolutely meek and mild as if butter wouldn't melt – '

'Much rationed butter, to say nothing of guns, would have melted in his vicinity during the war if the good Mr Thistlewaite had not been so zealous an agent in the service of which he was and still is employed gratis at Whitehall and elsewhere. And as for his stutter, that is genuine and an admirable façade for his purpose when it suits him to use it. But he has not managed by his, as you say, meek and mild demeanour to hoodwink me. No, not from the first day, if you remember, when you accused me of gate-crashing on his wife's *thé dansant* where I met my fate – you.' He got to his feet saying: 'I realize I am under suspicion, not only from you whom I think I can never convince of my – my honest purpose. But,' as she made attempt to speak, 'of those who are on the trail of the Communists, guilty as they undoubtedly are, of implementing the General Strike which is imminent. Nothing I nor any of us, including the present government who would avert it, can stop the tidal wave that might sweep this country into revolution.'

'That is what the Zinoviev letter threatened. You', she said pointedly, 'know all about that.'

'Yes, I know. And this I can tell you, what your ostrich-headed government will also know soon – or perhaps late – perhaps too late – that the Red Letter, as they called it, is a fake. A trumped-up fake to bring down the Labour Government – which it succeeded in doing. But Baldwin and his Tories still believe it.' He looked at her; she saw that his eyes, usually so dark and smouldering, were wet; something slid from both of them on to his whitened cheek.

His lips quivered to the words:

'You suspect me as all will suspect me until I can prove myself *not* guilty, more than on my solemn oath that I am no secret agent in the pay of the Bolsheviks. Do you believe that?'

'Yes,' she spoke uncertainly, bewildered, stunned, 'I do believe that but . . . I don't know what else to believe.'

'This you can believe', he took her hand in his, 'that those of your Britons who will rise against your country tomorrow or this week, or any day in a General Strike, have not my sympathies. World peace can never be attained by blackmail of the workers against the employers, only by unity between men of all classes and all creeds. If all of us believed in and followed the word of God, there would be no wars, no strife, nor revolt of man against man and master. And that is what I, in my small but sincere way, have striven to do and – '

'*Mensonges!*' the woman struggling up from the couch gave out a harsh discordant laugh. 'He speak of God! But he has no God, *seulement le diable*! You t'ink he speak tru't. I tell you he speak only lies, he and ze revolutionaires. Zey leave me and my Czarina – zey kill my Czarina – and he go wiz ze Bolshevik. *Enfin!*' Again that hysterical laughter and she burst into tears. 'He speak of God!'

Felicity beckoned Riabovitch.

'Get her to bed, if she will go. She is not fit to be left alone and I think she would do better here with you if she will stay. Or else you must leave and go to an hotel and I will bring a doctor to her and remain with her here rather than take her to my home.'

'I quite understand there would be some explaining to your father if you took her to your home,' said Riabovitch with that ghost of a smile; and he knelt beside the sobbing Anna. To her he spoke in Russian, low voiced and at some length. . . . At last she gave a deep sigh and held out her arms, drawing him into them.

Said Felicity below breath:

'Either she, he, or I – are mad!'

And unobserved by the husband and wife, she stole from the room.

TEN

Extract from Felicity's 'Book'

. . . Am only just coming to after that appalling scene. These Russians! None would have believed it if they had not seen or heard. It would need a Strindberg to have written one of his satirical short stories or dialogues how that Anna after hurling abuse at him and accusing him of all sorts of awful things – treachery, espionage, working for the Bolshies against Czarist Russia or what remains of it and incidentally against us in Britain and worst of all of murdering her Czarina, she then falls into his arms both of them in tears and reunited! I can't help but think that in tracking him down she was biding her time to recapture him in which she has triumphantly succeeded. I do really believe he thought she had been killed with the Czar and the Czarina when they and all the Court were assassinated. Yet why did she wait so long before she found him again? Perhaps she had taken a lover meanwhile and was either abandoned by him or he by her. . . . But why speculate? All I can know is in this letter I received today from R. in which he says 'Forgive and forget me, I am not that of which she in her agitation did accuse me nor did I know, I swear it, that she is still alive. It is a resurrection for us both. I did once love her and I have loved her memory as I have loved her and as God is my witness, I love her still as I have loved and wanted you. . . .'

What a relief this is to me! I shall not have to break with and hurt him if he can be hurt of his pride or his 'want' of me, which never was love. I think he can love nobody and nothing but his hot Gospel idealism which as I understand from what he has told me is a sense of superiority that he and the friends of his age in St Petersburg shared in their

243

social and political acceptance of life as they saw it through their own distorted vision.

I told Daddy it is all over between R and me and he said he was glad I had come to my senses at last and that is all he did say and all I told him. He is full of the General Strike just on today (May 3rd) and he didn't seem particularly interested in anything else. I drove him to the Lords. They will be discussing and debating it all day. I was out with the car giving transport to any one who needed it. Wonder how long the strike will go on and now that it is over with R I shall be at a loose end and am thinking but haven't mentioned it to Daddy yet what has been in my mind for some time knowing I was not going to be tied up in Holy – or unholy – wedlock that I would like to train as an S.R.N. nurse at one of the large London teaching Hospitals Guys for choice because that is where Lord Halstead was a student donkey's years ago and he could perhaps put in a word for me there as he is a friend of Daddy's. But not until the strike is over if it ever is over without a revolution. Have heard nothing from Russton lately. I wonder what *he* is doing in the strike . . .

From its fortuitous onstart through an inconsequential course to its finale it affected every man, woman and child in the kingdom. If tens of thousands of British citizens had their work, their homes, their livelihood disrupted, to others it was a jamboree, in particular to the younger generation. Students and eighteen-year-old schoolboys were allowed to 'do their bit', such as collecting tickets on railway stations or to work the escalators on the Tubes. Girls and women of all classes gave their services as waitresses in canteens at the London termini or wherever they would be required to dispense hot drinks, soup, sandwiches, to the volunteers.

There was one man of the Labour Party who, when the strike began, created order out of preliminary chaos: one Ernest Bevin, whose name was to resound throughout the Coalition Government of more than a decade later, when all disputes and disagreements were resolved in the struggle for Britain's existence in the second and greatest world war. He was no revolutionary nor an opportunist to seize upon a political crisis to further the cause of Labour's destiny. He fought with his back to the wall, not to make the strike victorious over the Government but to negotiate with the then Government, irrespective of what the result of such negotiation might be. Baldwin and his party put up a determined challenge to the trade unions, insisting (and rightly) that the strike was a threat to the Constitution and to Parliament.

This challenge was met by Labour with a call for an immediate general election as the only possible solution to the crisis. Had this come about they might have won with a majority of panic-stricken electors who thought they were in danger of a revolution or civil war.

Lord Rodborough, probed by Felicity who found the whole thing 'frightfully exciting', told her:

'The leaders of the general Trades Union Congress have cold feet. They insist, not very convincingly, that they are not challenging the Constitution but only partaking in an industrial dispute. It is almost certain they will capitulate and leave the miners to fend for themselves. Baldwin shows up very well in this. He has scared the life out of the leaders – has treated them with the contempt they deserve. He'll come out on top, you'll see.'

'I think', she said, 'that the public are being splendidly co-operative. Everyone to whom I've given lifts is entirely for the Government and ready to face whatever may come, just as we were in the war and not to jib against what can't be helped but to do all they can to fight these Communist swine who are out to smash us and the British Constitution.'

'It was bound to come,' said her father. 'It's a necessary purge to irrigate a redundancy of Socialistic waste matter that has been accumulating over the last few years, although MacDonald to save his face says that he and his Labour crowd never intended or wanted to bring about the strike. It was never meant, he tells us, to be a political issue.'

'Well, whatever it was meant to be it gives us all a chance to rally round and show these Communists – for I am sure it is the Communists who have worked for this – that they can never overthrow government as we know it and will have it now and for ever, as it was in the beginning and as it will be to the end.'

'Let us hope,' Lord Rodborough gloomily commented. 'But there is more than you or any of us can foresee should, as one of the Labour leaders, J. H. Thomas, stated and will say it again in the Commons, that if the strike gets out of hand, every sane man would know what he was in for.'

'That', she said, 'doesn't tell us anything we didn't know already.'

'More than the rumblings of distant thunder before the storm breaks. It's a fifty-fifty chance that it *will* break, but Baldwin,' her father chuckled, 'who has made Churchill editor of the *British Gazette* – you'll see the first issue tomorrow – says it is the cleverest thing he, the P.M., has done, otherwise Winston would shoot the whole damn lot of them.'

Yet there was no shooting of anyone of the 'damn lot', nor any serious disturbances in London, although in various districts and the provinces there were local riots and spontaneous outbursts of violence summarily dealt with by the police and special constables. Convoys of supplies were brought up by the Army and Navy while Hyde Park became a military camp. Armoured cars rumbled through the streets bringing food from the docks and manned, not only by volunteers of the civil population, but blackleg dockers who risked being lynched for their pains.

Through all these nine critical days Felicity saw and heard nothing of Russton, but she received a postcard

246

from Riabovitch in Paris when the strike was under way, telling her:

'I am here with Anna. We have taken a small apartment on the Left Bank and are opening a gallery here shortly. Have sold the Duke Street lease. Will let you know our address when we are settled in. Anna joins me in the hope that you will visit us in the not far distant future. Love from us both. Hope all well with you in this awful Strike. Yours ever, A.R.'

Will wonders never cease? was Felicity's reaction to this. Turgenev, she thought amusedly, would have revelled in it. He was so good at caricaturing the young Russian movement and what one might call their imbecilities of which Riabovitch is a living, but not so young, example. Through knowing him, I am beginning to understand the Russian writers more than I ever could but I still think Strindberg, the Swede, could have done that scene with Anna better than many of the Russians. . . .

It was when the strike had gained impetus and as yet no sign of a settlement, that Felicity, having fetched her father from the House of Lords, dropped him one evening at the flat in Ashley Gardens, and said:

'I shan't be in to dinner. Am going out again. I can give lifts to people who live in the suburbs and are working day and half the night on volunteer duty. I can get a sandwich and coffee at a canteen.'

'I forbid you,' enjoined Lord Rodborough, his face an exasperated red, 'I forbid you – do you hear me? – to go giving lifts to any Tom, Dick or Harry at any time of the day or night. You were out until one o'clock this morning. Heaven knows what risks you run being picked up by all and sundry. You might find yourself robbed or murdered, God forbid, with these ruffians running riot – these damned Communists. You look worn out. You will come in to dinner and go to bed early.'

'Don't fuss, darling. I bet Nannie has put you up to this. She still thinks I'm in my pram. It's a thousand to one I'll not be robbed unless they take the car and they would have to chuck me out of it first – or be murdered or raped if that's what you mean. I promise to come back *virgo intacta*.' She waved her hand and left him visibly appalled.

Driving leisurely along Victoria Street she was hailed by a girl with rather too much make-up on, a pretty vapid little face and a profusion of peroxide hair under her hat.

Felicity halted.

'Want a lift?'

'Well, thanks, yes. I 'ave to be on in an hour. We're openin' early 'cos of the power cuts. 'Lectricity.'

'Right. Hop in.'

She hopped in and: 'Where do you have to be on in an hour?' she was asked.

'The Metropolitan in Edgware Road if it's not too far out of your way. D'you know it?'

'I believe so. What do you do when you're on?'

'Well, me an' 'im – we're the Just So's – sort of acrobats. 'E does most of it – jugglin' and throwin' up what look like great balls o' lead – on'y car'board reely an' catchin' them an' swingin' on ropes an' that, an' I'm 'is stooge. I on'y 'as to turn somersaults an' do the splits an' 'and 'im the props but I can't do much now, 'cos – ' the cockney monotonous one-toned voice stopped abruptly. Glancing sideways Felicity saw that the girl had a trembling underlip and covered her mouth with a hand.

'Why can't you do much now? Have you strained a muscle or something?'

'No, not reely, but,' she removed her hand to say with a sob in her voice, ''e won't let me orf not at such short notice an' we're doin' the number ones next week if the trains'll run but – ' with a rather tinny metallic show of indignation as if a clockwork doll had suddenly come to life, ''e can chuck me out now if 'e likes – much I care, the dirty sod – 'scuse me French, Miss, an' 'e never tol' me 'e's gotta wife. Said 'e was divorced. 'E isn't. She turned up after the show one night an' let 'im 'ave it *an'* me. As

248

if I'd known an' me four munss gone. 'E won't believe it's
'im.' She gave another sniff. 'But it is. There's never bin
anyone else not since I run away from 'ome and me step-
father – if you can call it 'ome. Couldn't stay there the
way 'e uster beat me black an' blue – me mum died yer
see an' 'e 'ated the sight o' me – me step-dad did, so I went
into pictures as an extra an' that's 'ow I met 'im. 'E was
an extra same as me and out of a job but 'e sees me doin'
me acrobatics for fun like an' that's 'ow it began . . . Why
am I tellin' you all this?'

The girl's eyes, blackened with mascara, slewed round
at her with a furtive hunted look. 'I shouldn' be tellin'
you.'

'Tell on, I'm listening.'

'There's not much more to tell . . . 'Ere we are, Miss, if
you'll drop me just 'ere an' thanks everso. You're everser
kind.'

Felicity opened the door for her and she got out. In the
waning light the face of the girl showed her as an over-
grown child.

'How old are you, if you don't mind my asking?'
Felicity said gently.

'Well,' a pause, then defiantly, 'I'm twenty-one.'

'I don't think you are. You're well under age, aren't
you?'

She nodded. Her eyes, very blue and round, and so doll-
like. Felicity expected her answer to be a squeak.

'Well, I'm – well, I'm seventeen almost come July but I
told 'im I was nineteen when 'e took me on an' if I'd a
told 'im I was only sixteen I'd never 'ave got the job. 'Is
wife used ter do it before they packed up an' she can do
it agyne, now.'

'Seventeen almost. A great age!' smiled Felicity. 'May
I call for you after the show and take you home? Where
do you live?'

'No, Miss, thanks, I don't live nowhere not since that
old bag, 'is wife, turned up and took on so about me, 'e

won't 'ave me in digs with 'im so I'm in a 'ostel just round the corner from the Met. I didn't know what it was until I went there an' she don't want me 'cos I'm no use to 'er with the fellers what comes for the girls me bein' – you know. She soon spotted that so I've gotta go. Anyways we're on the North number ones next week if we can get there with this strike an' if I'm not chucked out by 'im so I'll say goo'bye, Miss, an' thanks for the lift.'

She turned away and Felicity jumped from the car and went after her. 'Look here, you are not going back to that house and you are not going on number one tours if it means you have to tour the music halls turning somer-saults in your condition. If you will let me find you some-where to live I'll see that he doesn't bother you. You mustn't go back to him.'

'Oh, Miss, no! I must! 'E'd 'ave me up for what he calls breeks o' contract. I'd 'ave to pay 'im somethink awful if I broke me contract an' I gets nothink from 'im now I've left 'im only what I've saved from me salary an' I'm payin' ten bob a week for me room with 'er an' nothink much left over for me food. I'm 'ungry arf the time an' I owe 'er two weeks' rent.'

Another sob tore at her throat. She rubbed her mas-caraed eyes with a rather dirty finger.

'You are under age so there is no question of breach of contract and in any case I'll take care of that – and you. We must get you out of that house at once and you'll be looked after now and when the baby comes. What is your name?'

'Susie, Miss, but I'm billed with 'im as the Just So's.'

'So – Just So Susie, go along now and do your turn for the last time and I'll be waiting for you here. When do you finish?'

'We're on second, not top o' the billers and never shall be . . . Oh, no, Miss, I can't tyke it, reelly I can't,' as Felicity pressed three one-pound notes into her hand.

'Yes, you can take it, and you must pay your rent or

whatever you owe to that woman where you lodge, and get yourself a decent meal. After the show you must go back and pay her and I will pick you up here. It is better I don't go with you as she might be objectionable if she thinks you have been telling tales about her.'

'Oh, Miss, you are kind, but – 'Ere!' sudden suspicion dawned with alarm. 'You ain't one o' them white slavers, are you? It 'ud be worse for me than with 'im if I was nabbed by one o' them! It's just what them white slavers does to get 'old of girls down on their luck. They don't mind if we've got ourselves caught. They gets rid of it an' then ships us off to Bewness Airs or somewhere. No, Miss, not me! An' if you think you're goin' to ship me off to Bewness Airs I'll call a pleeceman!'

'No need to call a policeman, Susie, there's one here.'

The girl gave a scream, and Felicity, swinging round, saw him who had parked his Aston Martin at the kerb and had Susie by the arm.

'Yes, Susie, you haven't brought it off this time! We've had a tail on you and your Just So of a husband – he is her husband,' to Felicity, who stood aghast, dumbfounded, 'he has never been on the halls with you, Susie, or with anyone else although you may both have done your turn on Hampstead Heath on Bank holidays and elsewhere – you to pick a pocket and he to stir up trouble tub-thumping wherever there are crowds to hear his Revolutionary Worker's campaign . . . Yes, you've got away with it this time once too often, put up to it by him who's primed you well. Now then, don't try that on – ' for she was struggling and spitting at him with a volley of obscene language. He held her fast. 'Yes, you've done yourself proud as have others of your kind since this devil-sent strike, getting lifts from gullible young ladies and benevolent old men. What about the good old gentleman in the Rolls last night who picked you up on the Embankment and gave you a fiver for your hard luck story – a different yarn each time – how you had nothing to eat for three days and had run away from your drunk of a father and had been sleeping rough on the Embankment and starving when he found you. But you gave the slip to the police officer on duty there before he could catch you. As for you – ' to Felicity who could scarcely believe her ears or him, and was in two minds whether to whisk the girl away in her car or leave Russton to deal with this incredible situation, 'as for you,' he repeated, 'it's a good thing our Susie happened upon you because we've had our eye on her husband these six months, ever since he was released from Wandsworth after his trial when he and seven other Communists of the twelve who were arrested for incitement to mutiny last October, were let out before the other five had done their time at Brixton. But he'll do *his* time again now to be finished off at the King's Pleasure ... Steady on, Susie!' who was twisting in his grip and kicking at his shins, 'the game's up. You've had a good run for your money but I'll take this – ' he grabbed her fisted hand that held the notes Felicity had given her and received another volley of execrable language.

'You dirty buggerin' cop! It's a lot o' bloody lies, Miss. Don't you listen to 'im. We *are* the Just So's an' if we ain't on at the Met tonight it's because 'e was a bit pissed larss night and the manager chucked us out and he owes us a week's pay, the sod!'

'Come off it, Susie.' Russton tightened his grip. 'That's a new one, isn't it? Although I guess him more than a bit on wherever he was last night, which wasn't here at the Met, because it's closed owing to the strike. A convenient place for the young lady to drop you, with his lair just round the corner where we've tracked him.' He nodded over his shoulder, and as if risen from the ground a police constable appeared. "Take her, Thompson. You've got the man?'

'Yes, sir. P.C. Phipps and I hauled him in an hour ago.'

'Right!...Oh no, you don't!' as Susie, ducking her head, dug her teeth into the back of his hand. 'Here's a

252

pretty token you give me as memento, but I don't want to have rabies as a gift from you. Go along with the nice policeman, Susie, and he'll give you a nice hot cup of tea at the station.'

The girl, still spluttering epithetical abuse, was dragged away by the stalwart, poker-faced P.C.

'Pity her teeth aren't as false as her tale,' said Russton, wiping a trickle of blood from his hand. 'Don't look so – what shall I say? – disappointed, that your do-gooding hasn't done her any good. We had to take her in. There's a hell of a racket going on since the strike when you and other sympathetic innocents are giving lifts indiscriminately to everyone who hopes to get a rise out of you. But she and her lot are part of a gang and she's quite something of an actress, isn't she? And well over twenty-one. But it's hard luck on the perfectly respectable "Just So's" whose name she has taken from this evening's little game, having seen them billed on the list of performers outside here. She and a good many others are making hay while the sun shines on the strike.'

'It's too awful!' exclaimed Felicity. 'What a fool I am. I'm always being taken in by the wrong people on trust.'

'Including me?' he eyed her quizzically. 'You don't trust me either, do you? Which is not surprising since I've unfolded a packet of tales to tell you, but all of them are, in their own sense, true.'

She turned on him, her face aflame.

'No, I don't trust you! I can't believe a word you say except that you are, as that poor little beast called you, a cop!'

She made a dash for her car. He came after her as she got in.

'It's a night off for me now. Would you honour me by dining somewhere?'

'No!' she slammed the car door on him; he stayed her through the window as she put in the clutch:

'Listen. I told you once, some time ago, that I would give you chapter and verse of what I am and what I do when the time should come. It has come, so shall we? Please. I owe you an apology and an explanation and am prepared to give it. So may I take you to dinner somewhere high up above the city and the Susies and the Coms? Hampstead Heath, for instance? The Spaniards Inn can offer us a decent meal. Please. I do so want to talk to you – there's so much I have to say. '

She found it difficult to refuse him. His eyes so bright, his mouth so comically pursed in that endearing schoolboy look of his as if half expecting a wigging from his master . . . But I don't want to be his master, she told herself, and furiously flushed as the thought flew at her, I would rather be his. . . .

She choked back a spurt of laughter, saying:

'Very well. Hampstead Heath. I used to ride there in the good old days and I know the Spaniards – Dick Turpin's highway. But what about your car?'

'I can leave her. She'll be quite safe. There's a special constable on duty here. He'll keep an eye on her – they all know she's mine. Will you drive or shall I?'

'You had better drive. I might not yet have learned to discriminate, and if some poor little "Susie" wanted a lift – '

'She wouldn't get it from me. I'd know her for a wrong 'un at sight.'

As he started the engine: 'How,' she asked, 'could you know if she were a right or a wrong 'un at sight?'

'It's my job to know it.'

'Did you know about Riabovitch?'

'Aha! I thought we would be coming to him. Yes, I – we – knew, but he's such a silly enthusiastic ass seeking the Holy Grail in the hope to elevate the downtrodden, finding excuses for the revolution that destroyed his world and looking to build another, a near Utopia on the ruins of it, that he gave himself away all along the line. But we

254

thought it best to keep him under observation since he was prowling around the Fordington research station trying to nose out what he believed would be of use to his Pinks, not Reds, in the event of a second world war. He and a few other fanatics are hoping to avert another catastrophic Armageddon which would mean that aerial warfare and not the massacre of the trenches would bring about wholesale destruction and the use of poison gas. We know all that too. We don't need Riabovitch or any of his pacifists to tell us what a second world war would be. But he is, I can honestly believe this, no traitor to Britain nor to any country. He is following his own idealism, to give to humanity a brave new world based on Fraternity, the Brotherhood of Man, and all the rest of it. That is what the French revolution, or the idealistic promoters of it, were determined to do and where did it lead them and France? Half of the nobility to the guillotine including their King and Queen, and the rest of them into the Terrorist jungle. His man Serge is one of our operatives but we have reason to think he's a double.'

'What's a double?'

'Double, or one might say treble, agent working for both Red and White Russia, *and* for us. He gets well paid by all sides. We can't afford to lose him. Thanks to him he dug up the wife of Riabovitch. He may have guessed it would bring about a reunion between the pair of them and so rid us of a perpetual itch. We could never tell where Riabovitch's dream of reorganizing the world into one co-operative whole for the common weal of "Brotherhood and Freedom" would lead him, with the Reds pumping him as a benefactor to humanity in the cause of Right and Justice, and picking up any stray crumbs that would fall from the table of the Ministry of Defence.'

'He knew all about those Gerard Dows,' said she reflectively. 'How did he know?'

'He knew enough for us to mislead him when he was ferreting at Fordington for a new type of bomber that he thought to find and hand over to his associates with which to confront the Allies and persuade them not to use it, neither for the destruction of a civilian population, nor in any warfare. But he was on to a wrong wicket there because Fordington specializes in airships which would prove useless in aerial warfare. We had a bogus set of plans hidden where he could get hold of them and he has a bagful of sand in his eyes if he but knew.'

She let out a deep breath.

'I'm hopelessly lost. . . . He told me that Mr Thistlewaite was a nit-wit, not in so many words, but he led me to agree that the little "Waites" – my father is on the board of his directors – is a harmless simpleton entirely under the thumb of his wife. As all that Daddy has to do with the board is to give it his name and sit on it occasionally, he wouldn't know much about Thistlewaite either. And when Anna descended on Riabovitch and made that ghastly scene – a sort of tragi-comedy as it turned out to be – in the very midst of it he told me that Thistlewaite is an active member of the British Intelligence. Is he?'

'One might say . . .' Russton adroitly avoided an oncoming volunteer on a motor bike that was doing about fifty. 'I was saying he might be described as an inactive member of the service but nothing of a nit-wit. Like our Susie, he is as consummate an actor as she is an actress.'

'But why,' she was still pursuing the Riabovitch-Anna motif, 'why did Anna try to shoot him? Did she want to kill him?'

'Of course not. The shot was deliberately fired wide to hit the picture behind his head. She's a good shot. She practised shooting when she escaped the Revolution. She has been hoping to find and bring him back to her ever since. She's an ardent royalist.'

'But I still can't understand what he is supposed to be. According to you and him, he is no Bolshevik. Are his sympathies equally divided? You know – I suppose you know as you know so much – that he fought against the Reds in Russia. He was a White cavalry officer and he made his escape and went about in disguise in Moscow until he could come to Britain, and now – *is* he a pacifist?'

'As are so many of our young and older fighters, or those who didn't come back maimed, blinded, crippled for life and determined never to fight for King and country in the world they have saved, should a second world war come down on us. But they or their sons would fight to the last drop of their blood if called upon to do it. That is why Riabovitch and his kind have made it their business to snoop around and gain whatever information they can find as to the type of armament to be used in this and other countries, and so to assemble sufficient material to counteract a hypothetical enemy. While Serge and a good many other secret agents, whether doubles or not, do it for money, Riabovitch does it for love. And if he has any ordered ideological vision of a brave new world, it is similar to that of Churchill who has denounced as "bestial the passions and appetites of Leninism".'

'So Riabovitch *isn't* an enemy agent as I thought he was or must be.'

He took his hand from the wheel to lay it on hers. 'You thought that of me too, didn't you?'

'I don't know what I thought of *you*. I'm past thinking of anyone. Everyone seems to be what they are not, or not what they appear to be, including Mr Thistlewaite. I'm the world's worst dupe That's all I am.'

'The world's loveliest and most lovable dupe.'

With a heightened colour in her cheeks she regained her hand that she had allowed to stay in his, when, having come through Maida Vale and into St John's Wood, they were now passing Lord's and he swerved to avoid a motor bus, manned by a young driver in plus fours.

'He is doing his damnedest for his King and country,' grinned Russton, 'but he has a flat tyre, bless him!' And he called to him:

'Hi! you've got a flat!'

'I know,' was shouted back to him. 'I'm just taking her to the depot and dropping the fares at Baker Street.'

There was a girl conductress whom Felicity recognized in her makeshift uniform as one of last year's debs, and who, in mutual recognition, called to her:

'Hullo, Felicity! Isn't this a rag?'

'Friend of yours?' asked Russton.

'Sort of. She's a second or third cousin, once or twice removed on my mother's side. I don't know her really. She is years younger than I and I never know what is meant exactly by first or seconds or thirds – removed.'

'I have a cousin once or twice or three times removed knocking about somewhere,' said he, changing gear as they mounted the hilly Fitzjohn's Avenue to the Heath.

'In England or in Canada?'

'In England. I've no relatives in Canada.'

There was a silence between them as they drove on to the Heath. At the crest of the hill some shrill-voiced urchins were gathered, sailing toy boats or paddling in the muddy water churned up by a dog or two swimming after sticks and clambering on to the path beside which a few cars were parked, their occupants who, like themselves, had come to breathe in the pure clean air of London's most beautiful heath.

A bridge of dusk was spread between evening and the dying day, and far below the heights of Hampstead the city lay bathed in the last of the sun while through a fringe of trees in the west a ball of fire sank. The voices of the children were hushed by distance as they returned in the quiet of the evening.

'So', Felicity exhaled a long sigh, 'the Dragon has turned out to be St George.'

He looked askance at her, his eyebrows raised.

'I don't get you – or do I? The Riabovitch crest is a dragon's head, I believe.'

'You ought to know. You have probably done some

ferreting on your own account behind that banner screen in his gallery.'

'You still hanker after your dragonish St George, don't you?'

'I do not.' She said it with a finality that, to him, was rather overdone.

'I have often wondered – ' his eyes travelled from her tip-tilted nose that had collected some sun-sprayed freckles.

'Wondered what?' she took him up quickly on his pause.

'What could have been the attraction.'

'You mean why I was fool enough to be attracted to the point of a promise – or rather half promise of marriage – to one of Dostoevsky's idiots?'

'Or,' he was smiling down at her now, 'to tales told by an idiot?'

She made a negative gesture, her forehead – she had removed her hat – furrowed in a frown.

'I don't know,' and in a kind of desperate earnestness she repeated, 'I just don't *know*. I liked and more than liked – '

'Him? You more than liked him?'

'No, not him – his knowledge of things that mattered to me more than persons. His appreciation of the great Florentine masters, his love of the Renaissance and all the beauty and art of life in the past that we, of this internal combustion age, have lost. Not that I despise the internal combustion engine which gives us speed as in this little car of mine and every car and aeroplane, but it also loses us the leisure which gave us, in England, Shakespeare. Could there ever be a Shakespeare in our mechanized age of speed?'

'Yet Shakespeare had not much leisure as a strolling actor, that is if Shakespeare wrote what his name has given us.'

'Are you a Baconite?' she asked him indifferently, her

mind still dwelling on her first glimpse of Florence under moonlight. 'But' (continuing her thought aloud) 'it was Marconi, not Riabovitch, who gave me Florence for the first time.'

'Marconi? I've not heard of him from you before.'

'There is much you haven't heard from me of anyone.'

'That's true. I have seen and heard you too seldom to know you and hear you more than in my dreams. . . . But let us return to *nos moutons* which is more delicately put in French than to our muttons, and descending from the sublime to the ridiculous – without offence – of your attraction to the dragon's head, or whatever it was about him that did attract you, and being thoroughly material, shall we say that attraction could have been merely biological?'

The cheek nearest him showed a dimple with her answer, not looking at him but at the young crescent moon risen above a fringe of distant trees in the reddening sky.

'Perhaps all attraction between male and female, which happened to those two in a Garden, millions of years ago, is biological.'

'Yes, and it may be a crude but none the less imperative description of what I feel for you and have felt ever since I first saw you through a fog of fever and you – a ministering angel leaning over me so that I thought I was already dead and gone to a heaven which I had no right to deserve until' – he pulled a lock of her hair – 'this, escaping from under your nurse's cap, told me that angels don't have red hair however glorious, if they have any hair at all. But if *this* is biological, then I love you biologically and with all of me – ' he told her, out of breath. 'I want to marry you, although I know I haven't a dog's chance in hell. Have I? . . . So,' he started the engine, 'let's to dinner.'

Not another word was passed between them while she,

in a turmoil, considered this singular announcement that left her as breathless as he.

Then, drawing up at the Spaniards Inn he parked the car in the drive, got out, opened the door for her, saying, unnecessarily: 'Here we are,' and with cool politeness: 'Allow me to lead the way.'

She followed him, still feeling a trifle dazed, where he was met by a welcoming landlord.

'Dinner for two, sir? Certainly.'

A table in an almost empty dining-room was offered with a menu copy-typed in mauve, presenting a choice of point steak or roast lamb.

'The steak,' said Russton, 'grilled while you wait, and broccoli with new potatoes is indicated. Or would you prefer lamb?'

'Anything you like. I'm not hungry.'

'I am. Point steak then for two.'

Conversation, of the most impersonal kind, flagged while they ate. When Stilton and coffee had been served, the bill paid, the waiter generously tipped, Russton said:

'The night is young. Shall we take a walk? The time has come to give you, as I promised, chapter and verse of myself. The verse is given in that I love you – terribly, and I want to marry you. The chapter . . . here's a seat.'

They had come to a copse of young birch trees, their stems silvery under the blossoming star-strewn sky.

'Like little virgins,' murmured Russton. 'Shall we sit?'

They sat. His face, with that blond hair (he had removed his hat), was averted from her, but the articulation of a clear-cut jaw line was dimly silhouetted against the gathering dark so that it looked less like the face of a man than the ghost of one. 'Although', she whispered on a laughing breath, 'a very tangible ghost.'

He heard nothing of that, or if he did his thoughts were not of anything more than what he had to tell.

The scent of Harris tweed mingled with the dew-fallen,

earthy smell of moss and leaves, just full; no wind, no sound other than the distant bark of a dog and the near hoot of an owl.

He handed her his cigarette case.

'Will you smoke?'

She took one; he held a lighter to it, lit his own,. The birch tree copse was misty and mysterious, impermanent, as if it were a mirage.

'Wonderful to think,' he said, 'that we are only about four or five miles from Oxford Circus.' And turning to her suddenly: 'Much of the chapter – of my chapter, you have already known, or guessed, that I'm a cop, as Susie not incorrectly called me.'

'I knew that. A sort of policeman?'

'Yes, and I do serve – and wait.'

'I guess you to be a secret agent. Are you?'

'I am employed as such. When I left the army I was paid for my services by the Intelligence Department. Not now. Not since my mother left me sufficiently well provided to serve my country gratis to the best of my ability.'

'As Mr Thistlewaite does. I see. But that doesn't explain why you take jobs as a waiter and a footman – ' she examined the glowing tip of her cigarette '– or what use to the Intelligence Department you can be spying in night clubs.'

'Spying is an ugly word, but I suppose it is applicable to all operatives who take their orders from headquarters, and it has to be done in peace as in war.' He threw down his cigarette and put his foot on it. 'You saw me at the Thistlewaites' house-warming.'

She nodded. 'Yes, you were doing a footman's stunt there.'

'Exactly. I had to keep an eye on Riabovitch, who might have got hold of some valuable specifications at Fordington, not only to do with the building of airships, which are costing the earth and would not be of much use in aerial warfare; but there are certain plans of bombers at Fordington issued by the War Ministry, and if any foreign power could have a look at them we had to issue alterations which would render them useless.'

'Was Riabovitch being used as a spy by a foreign power, or by the Reds?'

'Yes, but he was not aware of it. He thought he was saving the world from a convulsive revolution – world communism. He is no Communist. He's just a – bloody fool.'

She knitted her forehead in puzzlement.

'That could explain away an idealistic – Pygmalion fool, but it doesn't explain how you turn up so opportunely wherever I am involved, as in that scrum at Hyde Park.'

'Ah, yes. Apart from that I and others of us are rounding up the Communists. Wherever possible I have kept a look-out on you for my own satisfaction in case you got yourself good-heartedly involved in some awkward situation.'

'As with Susie. For which I ought to thank you. Is this the whole of the chapter?'

'There's one page more.' He took another cigarette, offered his case again, she shook her head.

'No. What is this one page more?'

He blew smoke through his nostrils before replying; and now in the failing light his face was a blur.

'I told you as we drove along up here, that I had a cousin. It would be a second or third cousin removed, I reckon, here in England.'

'Well?'

'Well,' he sought and found her hand, 'You are my cousin, distant, and – I am a Ross-Sutton, too.'

She snatched her hand away.

'How much do you think you can kid me? How can you be a Ross-Sutton if your name is Russton?'

'It isn't. My father assumed the name of Russton, not

by deed poll but for other reasons when he went to Canada after his father, your grandfather's cousin – a second cousin I believe – was found to be a wrong 'un and a disgrace to his name. He was cashiered from his regiment for cheating at cards, did time for forgery and was your grandfather's sole heir until your father was born.'

She sat very still; then as seconds passed:

'My brother was my father's heir,' she said, 'and there is no heir now.'

'No heir unless,' he lowered his head; one of his hands tightened on his knee cap, 'unless your father marries again.'

'I hope he will because if – I don't say I will – but if I should ever marry, he would be very lonely.'

He looked up and round at her. Then:

'You have quite decided that I'm – that I'm a wash-out?'

'No, not quite. What I have half decided is to take up nursing seriously when the strike is over.'

'And I – if I don't marry, that is if I don't have you I shall never marry, I have half decided to – in fact I've bought a house near Newbury where I can have a racing stable and make that my life's compensation for the loss of you. But if – I say with little hope – if you don't go in seriously for nursing and decide that you would like to marry even one so unworthy as myself you wouldn't have to live in or near Newbury although it is a good old house with twenty acres. You could live in Florence if you like. I've had my eye on a villa in Florence. I made inquiries about it when I met you there. You remember?'

'You have it all mapped out, haven't you? Are you so sure?'

'God!' He flung away his cigarette. 'I wish I were!' And he got to his feet. 'Let's go. I don't want to behave like a biological beast but if I stay here any longer I shall. I'm not made of stone.'

264

She sat looking up at him. Her eyes in the darkness seemed to shine.

'I,' she said with a catch in her voice, 'I'm not made of stone either.' She held out her hands, and he pulled her up to him, searching her face, unbelieving.

'That doesn't tell me anything, does it? Do you – would you,' he asked huskily, 'will you marry me?'

'Cousins', she murmured, 'ought not to marry. My Great-Aunt Harriet says,' and there was laughter in her voice, 'they could have idiot children.'

'We aren't near enough cousins to count.' He tightened his hold of her hands; his mouth hovered above hers.

'Please.' She loosened her hands and moved away. 'If I were the marrying kind I might think about you, although I know nothing of you except what you give me in chapter and verse which all sounds very unlikely. But I don't want to marry – anyone. Not yet. I want to do something with my life because,' she faltered, 'suppose I should lose my father – I mean he is all I have in the world, I would want to lead my own life and not be tied to you or any other man.'

'I see.' He stood very still. She sensed rather than saw the hurt she had dealt him and made an impulsive movement as if to take his hand again while words shaped upon her lips.

'I would if I could only – '

But he missed his chance, abruptly to tell her:

'It's time we went. It grows chilly here. I've drawn a blank. It's a closed book now, so I'll turn down the last page of the last chapter. Would you mind walking back to the car or shall I fetch it and pick you up along the Spaniards?'

'You go. I'll meet you on the way.'

They drove back in a silence . . . 'so heavy,' she wrote in her record of that evening, 'it felt like a blanket of lead. What have I done? Have I lost him? Do I want to lose him? If we are cousins twice or whatever removed – I wonder? How can I trust him? Is he what he says he is or pretends to be or am I a — Pygmalion fool to have let him down on the last page?'

*   *   *

The General Strike was called off on 12 May, but the miners' strike went on for another six months. Many who had taken part in it were victimized. The plight of the miners, who had lost sixty million in wages, was appalling. Few of the leaders on either side emerged unscathed any more than the ordinary citizens or the soldiers, the students, the volunteers who had willingly endured unprecedented hardships in this harsh test of democracy.

Yet the outcome of it all, which would not bear fruit for another two decades, was the embryo of a Welfare State.

Calling on Lady Caversham when all was over – 'Bar the shouting,' said Aunt Harriet – Felicity was treated to a diatribe, or as much of it as she could follow from the old lady's ramblings.

'Let us hope Baldwin and a Tory Government will stamp them out. Blacklegs. Blackbeetles. Bolshies. Yours is one or is he done with? You haven't married him after all, or have you? Nobody tells me anything. Think I'm deaf but I can hear what I want to hear. We've lost four hundred millions. Bates read it out to me. We'll pay for it in taxes. Another sixpence, shouldn't wonder. When I was your age – Darling,' to the Peke, 'don't snore. Adenoids. Short noses. Yes when I was your age there were two classes. What Disraeli called – that's a man for you. Jew. Salt of the earth. Said there were two nations, the rich and the poor. But he was all things to all men – and women. I knew his wife. Not to know only to see from the stairs when she came to dinner. I was in the schoolroom. My father knew her. She was a character.

266

The Queen made her a peeress. He said she deserved it more than he. Not until she died, then he did. Beaconsfield. Your Uncle Jeremy knew him too before I ever saw him. Wearing rings and things on his white kid gloves. Hair in curls. That was before we went to India. Not Dizzy as they called him. He was never in India although he made her Empress of India. Those were the days. That's where we first came across Dick Harrington. *He* was a lad. Red-haired. I've often wondered. Halstead knows something. What are you doing with yourself now you aren't driving all and anyone to have your throat cut?'

Having managed to unravel a solitary thread from this entanglement, 'I think,' said Felicity, 'that I would like to take up nursing.'

'Eh? Nursing? Did you say *nursing*?'

'Yes, Auntie. It's all I'm fit for.'

'Nonsense. Nursing. Sister Agnes. I knew her too. The King. Not this one. His father. Edward. He knew her. I had one of her footmen. Said the King used to dine with her once a week in Grosvenor Place with Mrs Keppel and the Langtry. All three of them together at the table. No other women. Yes, those were the days. No strikes to speak of. No Communists. No Bolshies. And what's come of it? Four hundred million for Churchill to fork out – from us. Why did Baldwin want to make him Chancellor? Firebrand. But he's what we need if we want to get rid of all these Bolshies and Reds and – Yes, what is it?' To the butler at the door.

'A telephone message for Lady Felicity, m'lady.'

She rose.

'Who from?'

'Lord Halstead, m'lady.'

'Who wants you?' inquired Lady Caversham, her ear trumpet raised.

'Lord Halstead, Aunt,' Felicity told her.

'What does he want you for?'

'I – ' her mouth dried. 'I don't know. Daddy is at the Lords. I drove him there this morning.'

'Halstead doesn't often go to the Lords,' said Lady Caversham. 'I expect he is wanting to discuss something with your father.'

'He wants to speak to *me*!'

She ran from the room and was conducted to the telephone in the hall.

'Yes, who . . . '

'Is that you, Felicity?'

The voice of Lord Halstead spoke into her ear.

'Yes – I – what is it, Lord Halstead? Is Daddy with you?'

'Yes, my dear. I am sending my car to fetch you from Lady Caversham's house. I was told at your flat you were there.'

'But why – is anything wrong?' Fear, sickening, whitening, seized her. 'Daddy . . . is he ill?'

'He is ill, my dear. He has had a – second attack. The car will bring you to him.'

'Where is he? Why have you rung me here? Is he at home?'

'I thought it better he should be brought to hospital. I am with your father in a private room at Guy's. All is being done for him here, far better than could be done at your home. The car is on its way. It should be there by now.'

She went back to Aunt Harriet. Her knees shook under her as she climbed the stairs . . . A second attack . . . at the Lords . . . Was Lord Halstead there when it . . .

'Well?' asked Lady Caversham as she entered the room. 'What did he want?'

'Daddy – he's been taken ill. Another heart attack.' She surprised herself that she could speak so calmly when it felt as if every drop of blood in her veins had ceased to flow. 'Lord Halstead is with him. His car is fetching me. Daddy is at Guy's Hospital.'

The old lady put out a shaking hand.

'My dear child! Always the way...Suddenly. Your Uncle Jeremy. Just the same. Press the bell. Take Bates with you. Have tea first. You're white as a sheet.'

'No thank you, Aunt, I...'

'Bates,' as Miss Bates appeared, looking more than ever like a plucked and worried hen. 'Take Lady Felicity to the hospital.'

'The hospital, my lady?'

'Guy's. Sent for. Car on its way. Lord Rodborough... Last of the Ross-Suttons. Not the last. If Halstead knows something. Don't fret yourself, my dear. They can go on for ever. Your Uncle Jeremy. Lived to be as old as – older than I am now and I'm – and he had two and a third. Years older than Rodborough. The Ross-Suttons are long lived.'

'The car, m'lady,' said the butler at the door.

Lady Caversham held up her face for Felicity's kiss which was not given for she had rushed from the room followed by an agitated Miss Bates.

'Go with her, Bates. Not fit to be left.'

But Felicity was in the car before Bates had the time to put on her hat, her coat, her gloves, while Felicity, having left her gloves, handbag and her hat on the sofa beside Lady Caversham, was on her way to the hospital in an agony of suspense.

The drive seemed to be endless, although the chauffeur expertly manipulated the Rolls through the traffic that had considerably increased since its nine days' suspension during the strike.

Arriving at the hospital she was met in the entrance hall by the matron, blue gowned, white capped, imposing and bosomy.

'Lady Felicity Ross-Sutton? Your father, Lord Rodborough, has asked to see you.'

'Is he...' her tongue stuck to her palate and tasted suddenly of lemons, 'is he...very ill?'

269

'He has had a heart attack. Lord Halstead is with him.'
Then officialdom shed, she became a woman. A kindly
hand took hers. 'My dear, he is very ill, but conscious, and
– while there is life, there's hope.'

The platitude fell on numbed ears.

She was led to a private room on the ground floor. Lord
Halstead met her at the door.

'My father,' her voice froze, 'How . . . is he?'

The old doctor put an arm around her shoulders.

'He still lives.'

'O God! Is he . . . dying?'

'Come.'

His arm supporting her she was brought to the bedside
where her father lay. As she approached, his eyelids lifted,
and she saw a dawning light in his eyes. His lips, blue
tinged, moved in a whisper as, from some far-off vacancy,
she heard:

'My . . . darling . . . all's well . . . You shall not be . . .
alone . . . Luke will . . . '

Then on those last words with his last breath his eyelids
sank.

ELEVEN

What can be said of so sudden a loss to the grief-burdened girl? While the old woman who had nursed both the father and daughter mourned him with copious tears, Felicity had no such refuge. With cold, unnatural calm she attended the last rites when he was laid to rest at Rodborough in the family vaults of the Ross-Suttons. When the Abbey had become a health centre the tombs of the Rodboroughs were walled off from the rest of the estate that had been sold.

Lord Halstead, who made all arrangements for the funeral, had been in debate at the House of Lords at the time of the fatal heart attack. He had sent for an ambulance from his own hospital, Guy's. Although the Westminster Hospital was nearer, he could be more certain of securing a private room on demand for the patient at Guy's where he was an honorary consultant.

During the ensuing days he gave himself up entirely to Felicity. His secretary attended to the numerous letters of condolence following the obituary notices in the national Press.

So passed the first desolate week.

Lady Caversham invited, or rather commanded, that Felicity should stay with her at Green Street. The message was brought to her by Miss Bates. Mournfully arrayed in black, she presented herself to Felicity, who, somewhat disconcertingly, appeared in a summery cotton dress.

Fancy! no mourning, inwardly commented Miss Bates. These young people have no hearts.

After offering suitable condolence 'on your irreparable loss, dear Lady Felicity', she proceeded to repeat the message she had been ordered to convey.

'Lady Caversham has sent me to tell you that she does not wish you to stay alone in this flat with only the servants, and she asks that you will come with me to Green Street. The nurse will pack your necessary things for the present and then later – ' she was evidently repeating verbatim that which she had been told to say – 'when you feel more settled you can return here. Her ladyship understands that Lord Halstead – a real friend in *such* sore need,' an obvious impromptu of Miss Bates accompanied by suitable woe, 'and so good and old a friend – ' this a reversion to the words of Lady Caversham – 'of his late lordship and so – '

'And so,' Felicity cut in, 'you may thank Lady Caversham for her kind invitation but I cannot leave here until I have sold the lease of this flat. I intend to place it in the hands of a house agent at once and then find somewhere else to live.'

'Oh, but – ' Miss Bates was greatly put about ' – I – we – can't bear to think of you here without your fa . . . his lordship, dear Lady Felicity. I know only too well,' a wisp of embroidered handkerchief was produced, and the tip of her nose, always a trifle dyspeptically pink, showed rather more pink than its wont with the application of lace-edged lawn, 'excuse me if I allude to my own never absent sorrow at such a time but – it brings it all back to me. I have lost my own dear father and many years ago – forgive me, dear Lady Felicity, for speaking of myself – in the Boer War when I was young – younger even than you, dear Lady Felicity, he, my fiancé – he was an army chaplain, a curate, and he joined u-up with the C.I.V's, the City Imperial Volunteers as an army chaplain and he was k-k-killed. So I can offer you my heartfelt sympathy. But please, my dear Lady Felicity – ' (If she calls me that

272

again I shall scream, said her dear Lady Felicity; but this she did not say aloud.) What she did say was:

'I am sorry, Miss Bates, that I can't accept my aunt's offer, and sorrier for you to have to give her my refusal. I hope you won't get into a row for it, and I do understand what your own losses – ' she hunted for the right words and achieved a quotation from one of the many letters of condolence she had received . . . 'But time is a great healer, Miss Bates, and I hope you will have found it so. (As if time could ever heal, she inwardly parenthesized, losing first Ronnie and now . . .)

'Yes, indeed, dear Lady Felicity,' Miss Bates tearfully concurred. 'Time and courage to face whatever cross or sorrow we are called upon to meet, are the great healers. As my dear – late – fiancé used to say when I lost my father, and my mother only two years before, God never gives us a burden greater than our spirit's strength can bear, and let us be thankful for . . . '

'Mr Thistlewaite, my lady,' was thankfully announced by Wilson at the door, 'is on the telephone. He asks to speak to you if you are not engaged.'

'Excuse me, Miss Bates. If you will kindly tell Lady Caversham . . . '

Reluctantly Miss Bates accepted her dismissal as Felicity took up the receiver of the extension on the writing desk.

As Miss Bates followed Wilson from the room:

'Mr Thistlewaite?' said Felicity into the mouthpiece. And what does *he* want, she asked herself.

'My dear Lady Felicity,' she closed her eyes. Not *again*! 'If I am not intruding may I call and see you on behalf of myself and my Board of Directors to offer you a suggestion that has been unanimously put before the Board and agreed upon, subject to your approval?'

No hesitancy in the speech of Mr Thistlewaite as he propounded this proposition.

'Board of Directors?' she repeated, her thoughts afloat.

'It is a suggestion, my dear Lady Fel . . . '

'You wanted to see me, Mr Thistlewaite?'

'At your convenience, of course. I am in my house at St John's Wood just now, and if I could call upon you perhaps this afternoon?'

'Yes, please do.'

Nannie came in as she hung up.

'I couldn't help hearing what you were saying to Miss Bates about leaving here – '

'Eavesdropping, Nannie?'

'Where anything is to do with you, lovey, yes. I want to tell you that if – or when – you sell the flat I will be with you wherever you are, and Wilson too. We're both agreed about that and no wages. We've enough put by to be comfortable with our board and keep, and his lordship has left us pensioned, the solicitor told us so. And do you think we're going to leave you ever – unless you marry, as you will, and even then, my darling – '

She held out her arms and Felicity went to her.

'You are still and will always be my baby,' murmured the old nurse. Then, for the first time, and at last, came the blessed relief of tears.

When she had wept herself empty of the flood that overswept her, and after she had managed to eat a luncheon of Dover sole, prescribed by Nannie and, when duly rested, her swollen eyes bathed in wych hazel, she was ready to receive Mr Thistlewaite.

An entry in her 'Book', the first since the fatal day when all she had known and loved was taken from her, tells us:

He was nothing like so stammery as usual. And very kind. Much too good for that – I was going to say bitch of a wife but bitch is too nice a word. Why is it supposed to be a term of opprobrium when a dog is more of a friend and much more loving and loyal than are most humans? . . . Mr Thistlewaite came to tell me that the Board of 'Waites' and he as Chairman wanted to make me a director 'In the honoured place' he said with his funny little old fashioned bow 'of your late lamented and revered father. There would be the same director's fee, of course, if you would bring yourself to accept the offer in your goodself's good time.'

Goodself's good time! That's how the Bank wrote to me your 'goodself' . . . I told him I was greatly honoured at being asked to be a director but I didn't think I would be any use as I know nothing about business and I couldn't accept a director's fee (a thousand a year Daddy had. It would be a help) because it wouldn't be fair I told him.

He said my name as 'your good father's before you' – he is quite Victorian the funny old thing – 'is worth more than the director's fee offered, and he was sure any suggestion I would make when certain minutes and data were under discussion would be invaluable. So would I oblige him and the co-directors who would welcome me as one of them by thinking it over. . . . (I have thought it over and as I want to be a nurse how could I go sitting on boards? We had little enough free time as V.A.D.'s). Before he left he told me that if I had thought of selling the flat – and how did he know that? – he had a would-be purchaser in mind who was ready to offer a substantial price for the lease – (have just remembered. Mr Pickering of Pickering Smythe and Pickering Daddy's lawyer is the firm of solicitors who deal with Waites. Yes, Daddy told me that ages ago when Pickering was seeing to the sale of the Abbey). Mr T. also said he owned a small Regency house in St John's Wood and he would be willing to lease it to me for as long a period as I wished and that it had a pretty little garden of about a quarter of an acre and the gardener would be included in the rent which was he said a peppercorn rent whatever that may mean as he did not wish the house to remain untenanted since the present tenancy was ended and he could not be sure these days of finding a reliable and desirable tenant. I have a strong suspicion he was offering me this lease at next to nothing because he must have known how hard up Daddy was selling the Abbey and everything – he could have found that out from Mr Pickering or one of the firm and how hard up I am now with Daddy's director's fee gone which is why he has offered it to me. He is the dearest kindest man and the Intelligence Dept is lucky to have him working for them if he is and if Russton is to be believed which I doubt for I can't help thinking Russton is a consummate liar and as I first thought him – a crook. Except that he did come in on the Susie episode and seemed to be in with the police. Perhaps a C.I.D. man. He could have been pulling my leg with all that rot about ten thousand a year and the same name as mine – a sort of cousin or he may be a bit mental. Wouldn't be surprised. The war did that to them sometimes. I must say I think it rather much that he hasn't even written a word about Daddy. He must have seen it in the papers. Total strangers have written and Sister who was in charge of me at Grosvenor House – that's seven years ago – and I've never seen her since and the house was sold and even *she* wrote. Not that it matters if he didn't write because it is as he said a closed book . . . Must remind me to talk to Lord H about how to start training for Guy's or at some other hospital he could get me into. . . .

The opportunity of asking Lord Halstead as to how and where she could start her hospital training was presented the next day when he rang her up to inquire after her health, having prescribed a sedative; she had been suffering from insomnia due to shock. She asked him, tentatively, if he could advise her regarding her entry as a probationer at Guy's, to which he replied he would call and see her one evening after consulting hours and would discuss that and other matters with her.

Accordingly two or three evenings later after dinner he was announced.

'We are looking more ourselves,' remarked the old doctor taking her hand and with a finger on her pulse at the same time. 'Sleeping better?'

'Yes, thank you. Since I've made up my mind to be a nurse.'

'An admirable vocation, but,' he lowered himself into an armchair, 'I can think of a vocation to which you would be even more admirably suited.'

She nodded, smiling. 'That goes without saying. I ought to be a wife and mother before it is too late for me to marry – I am getting on to the too-lates – at least from the point of view of your generation who can't yet accept – or can you? – that we who now have the vote (and I shall have it when I'm thirty, in three years' time), don't particularly want to be wives although most of us want to be mothers. I do. Only we don't have to marry for that, do we?'

She offered him a box of cigars with a mischievous smile that lightened the shadows limned about her eyes.

He took a cigar and lighted it with the lighter she held to him.

'I don't think you are as modern,' he said, twinkling, 'as you would wish an old fogey of my generation to believe. As to your nursing, if you are really determined about that, I can help you there. The matron of Guy's is an old friend of mine, but I do not recommend you for such exacting work as your training would demand. I would have to put you through a thorough medical examination before I would care to pass you as fit for the arduous training of a State Registered nurse. Then again, as the trustee of your father's estate, for there is, as Pickering may have told you – '

'He has told me nothing yet. I didn't want to hear about the Will,' she said, her lips in a tremble.

'I was about to say', he examined the glowing tip of the cigar, 'that I understand you have had the offer of a house in St John's Wood at a very reasonable rent. You must have somewhere to live while in training – that is on your off time – for you would have to live in the nurses' quarters, you know.'

'I know all about that. I was a V.A.D. in the war and I am half trained already. But how did you know about the St John's Wood house? Did Mr Thistlewaite tell you? I suppose you know him?'

'I know him – as an acquaintance,' was the evasive answer.

'And do you know that he offers me this house for a peppercorn rent, whatever that means?'

'He did mention it to me. He would be grateful for a reliable tenant at a reasonable rent. As you are probably aware, money is no object to Mr Thistlewaite; his chief concern is to lease this house to someone whom he knows will care for it. In these days of snatch and grab and strikes that have cost the country millions, even millionaires are anxious to see their properties in the right hands.'

'What', she asked, '*is* a peppercorn rent? I have always associated peppercorns with pepper-pots or cooking.'

'It means merely a low rent, as much for the convenience of the lessor as for the lessee.'

She nodded.

'I see. I suppose you and Mr Thistlewaite are in league together to see that I am not completely broke. It is very kind of Mr Thistlewaite but I don't want charity even from a millionaire.'

'My dear child!' he held up a protesting hand. 'As your trustee I can assure you that you will have ample subsistence for your requirements while you remain single. And if you marry, as a young lady of your peculiar attractions is bound to – '

'Never mind my peculiar attractions by which you may mean my hideous red hair and – '

'Your beautiful hair!' he interrupted.

'If you think so. But putting aside my hair and the rest of my peculiar attractions plus my freckles – let us forget about marriage as far as I am concerned. Some are born spinsters – of course we are all *born* spinsters unless, as in olden times, a marriage was arranged between families at the birth of a girl – and some achieve spinsterhood and some have spinsterhood thrust upon them. I am in the second category.'

After a moment's silence while he asked himself what the deuce to do with her, he said:

'As your trustee I am bound to think of the possibility of your marriage, for I have to remind you that you are a life tenant only of your father's estate unless you marry and have children when, after your death, it goes to your child or children of your marriage and if childless to your next of kin.'

'So whether I remain an old spinster or not I can only have the income, whatever that may be?'

'Plus your director's fee which is at least a thousand a year.'

'But if I am not a director how much income will I have, doctor – I mean Lord Halstead?'

'Doctor, which I prefer to be called. As far as Pickering and I have reckoned, you will have left from your father's inconsiderable estate – about five hundred a year. But if you accept your father's directorship – '

'We'll cut that out, please. I'll be able to earn something once I'm trained, either as a private nurse or attached to a nursing home. Quite a few of the girls I trained with as a V.A.D. are now State Registered nurses.'

'You are well of age so I cannot interfere with your decision, but. . . .' Watching her closely he thought: Any amount of spirit and Dick Harrington's will of her own – and his. Then, laying aside his half-smoked cigar, to smoulder in an ash tray, he got up, saying:

'There is one thing more I have to tell you. It has been presumed that your father's earldom became extinct at his death. This is not so. There *is* an heir, as Pickering, I and the College of Heralds have discovered. I knew your – er – your grandfather when we were both young men, and I have known your father these many years almost before he was . . . ' he stopped abruptly, hemmed, caressed his chin.

'Were you going to say before he was born?' she

279

prompted laughingly, thinking, he's getting a bit gaga; he must be nearly eighty.

'So', he continued, 'this heir, though not directly in the line of succession as with father and son, being of a cadet branch, yet is indubitably the one and only rightful heir to the earldom.'

'Did my father know of this?' she asked, turning a trifle pale as the incredible thought struck her. Never Russton?

'I think – no, I am sure not. None of us knew. It is only since the loss of your father and through information we have ascertained, that the heir, reluctantly it seems, answered to inquiries and is, without doubt, the present earl. But I understand he is unwilling to assume his title for he may wish to stand for Parliament and he could not, as a peer, offer himself as a candidate.'

'For Parliament?'... No, it couldn't be Russton. He has never said or hinted that he wanted to stand for Parliament. 'Is he married?'

'Not as far as we know, but it is possible he will marry.'

Seating himself he resumed his cigar and sat gazing at her through the smoke of it. 'He is still in his early thirties and may wish for an heir.'

She let out a sighing breath.

'I am glad the peerage is not extinct. It would be a pity if it died out. We go back to a greater great-great who was created Viscount Ronulshere under James the First. He was probably one of the James's boys – 'Lord Halstead batted an eyelid – 'and then Charles the Second made him Rodborough for services rendered in restoring him to the Throne. He was a member of the Sealed Knot, the secret intelligence of the Royalist party.'

'History', he murmured, 'repeats itself.'

'How?' she asked quickly. 'How does history repeat itself in this case?'

'It could be a question of heredity which can crop up after many generations. I breed bulldogs, and I have traced certain characteristics as well as similar points that indicate regeneration as from a remote forebear. My present champion throws back to Rodney Stone, as like him in points as in temperament. I knew Rodney Stone in the early part of the century and *he* was one of my boy's greater great-greats. Well,' he held out his hand, 'I must be leaving you. I have much to do on the report of a case sent to me today.'

'And I haven't offered you a drink? How awful of me. Won't you stay and have one now?'

'No, my dear, I will have my night cap later, which is a glass of hot milk and', his keen professional glance scanned her face, noting the dark circles round those eyes and a slight hollowness of the too pale cheeks, 'I prescribe for you the same,' he said, 'it will help you to sleep better than a sedative, which should not be required at your age.'

As he moved to the door, she stayed him. 'Please, Lord – doctor, about this heir. Who is he? Where is he?'

There was a ring at the front door bell.

'I think, if I am not mistaken, he is here . . . now.'

And with surprising mobility for a near octogenarian he went or rather bolted from the room, colliding in the hall with the newcomer, announced by Wilson:

'Mr Ross-Sutton, my lady.'

He stood, his back to the door, and on his face that same well-remembered engaging schoolboy look, almost but not quite a grin, for he was obviously not sure of her greeting or his welcome. Nor was he left long in doubt.

Springing to her feet, her face that had whitened was suffused with a rush of colour.

'I should have known!' Words in torrential incoherence poured from her. 'You've been fooling me all along. You knew it all the time – in hospital when you were dithering with fever – same name as mine ... Russton you called yourself. Secret Intelligence. Sort of Scarlet Pimpernel playing me up. Serving to *wait*! But you've had your innings and you can get out! *Take* your peerage or don't take it. Sit in the Commons where you'll have one thing in your favour with all the rest of them and never mind which party, Tory, Liberal, Labour – all the same, all good liars or there'd *be* no House of Commons! So go! Get *out*. I've done with you!' She dashed for the bell, but he held her back.

'If you've done with me I've not done with you. Yet we had both done with each other – you remember, along Dick Turpin's way on Hampstead Heath?'

'A fitting way for you to take – the way of a highway-man!'

He took a step forward, seizing her by the arms, searching her face.

'Do you hate me so much?'

'I don't care enough about you to hate you. What I do hate – ' her lips quivered; her eyes were suddenly too bright '– is – being made a fool of.'

'You told me once that you couldn't be made a fool of *all* of the time.'

'I was mistaken. I am and have been the world's worst fool *all* of the time and – here! What do you think you're doing? Let me go!'

He had caught her in his arms; she struggled to free herself and was held close and closer. Her charming face upraised to his was wonder-charged and lighted as from some inner source. And in that moment, unforeseen and just conceived, her eyes, widely open meeting his, had that in them to set his pulses racing.

'I've waited,' he said unsteadily, 'too long for this, and I'll ... never let you go!'

*   *   *

'No reception, no church wedding?' said Lady Caversham stroking the satiny head of Chin-Chu nursed on her lap. 'First time a Rodborough hasn't been married at Calloden.'

'We neither of us wanted a lot of publicity, Auntie,' Felicity told her. 'He hates it as much as I do.'

'You'll get no presents with no invitations. A Registry Office of all things! It's where the divorcees get tied up so they can get untied again without offending the Church. Especially the Catholics. But they don't. The Pope won't have it. Quite right.'

'We shan't get untied,' said Felicity, her eyes aglow.

'His mother did. Went off with an American. Blood will out. Hope not with this one. Skipped a generation. His grandfather did time. Prison. But his father – your young man's father. Ashamed of it. Took himself, wife and son off to Canada. He'd have been Rodborough had he lived. What's this I hear about him dropping it?'

'Dropping what, Aunt?'

'The title.'

'We are going to wait and see if – ' the glow in her eyes deepened ' – if we have a son. If not then, maybe, he will stand for Parliament.'

'In any case you'll both be Ross-Suttons. Change the name and not the letter, marry for worse and not for better. Yours seems to be for better according to Halstead. His mother left him enough. More than I could ever leave you. I hear that Waites W.C.s has given you a house. Where is it?'

'In St John's Wood, Auntie ... No, not St James's, St John's ... I said Wood – St John's *Wood*.'

'Don't shout. Split my eardrums. Where that actress lived. One of King Edward's. Langtry. All the R.A.s too. Thought he has a place at Newmarket or New something.'

'So he has – for the horses. This will be a *pied à terre*,

and Nannie and Wilson will live there to look after it because Russton — '

'Who?' Lady Caversham inclined an ear.

'Russton. It's the name I call him. But his Christian name is Ronald.'

'Newmarket. Racing. Halstead told me. Take care he don't lose the lot. You'll have a cheque from me. Not that you will need it if he has what Halstead says he has and is settling on you. Fifty thousand . . . Want to go out?' To Chin-Chu who had got down from her lap and was moving to the door, tail unfurled, and bored with all this. 'Press the bell.' Felicity pressed it. The butler appeared.

'Tell Miss Bates,' her ladyship pointed, 'Chin-Chu. Doodies.'

Chin-Chu disposed of, Lady Caversham resumed:

'Thought him a nice enough young feller. Manners, too, which few of them have these days. Wonder he wasn't snapped up. Would have been if it had got around who he is and how much he has. Girls in the vast majority since the war. Take another twenty-five years to get level. *He's* not red. Of course not. I mean colour not politics. We hope.' The old lady nodded. 'Luke Halstead knows a thing or two. So do I. Mine's guess-work. His isn't. But he would never let on. We both knew Dick Harrington.'

'You have mentioned Dick Harrington to me before, Aunt. Who is he?'

'Eh?'

Lady Caversham put the trumpet to an ear.

'Dick Harrington,' Felicity repeated loudly. 'Who is he?'

'Don't *shout* at me. He isn't. He's dead. Halstead and I and your Uncle Jeremy knew him years ago. In India. Before your father was born.' The old lady pursed her lips. Then, after a pause, 'Got your wedding dress?'

'Yes. It's not a dress, it's a suit. Grey gabardine for

284

travelling. We are going to fly to Milan and then on to Florence.'

'Fly?' A straightening of her back, a sliding of her wig as she jerked up her head. 'Did you say – fly? Don't like the idea of you flying. There's no heir yet, He's the last of them.'

'It's as safe to fly today, Auntie, as to go by train and so much quicker.'

'Paper bags to be sick in. Disgusting. Is none of us to be invited to see you fly off?'

'Of course you'll be there to see us fly off – or rather tied up. Just you and Lord Halstead and Mr Thistlewaite.'

'Waites W.C.s?' Aunt Harriet chuckled. 'Wonder he don't give you one along with the house.'

'He has given us three, one in each of the bathrooms. He's a darling old thing and a friend of Russton's. They both met at the Ministry.'

Up went the ear trumpet.

'At the where?'

'The Ministry, dear.'

'Is this young man of yours a minister?'

'Not in the clergy, dear; but he's been lots of things including a waiter.'

'A what?'

'I said a . . . never mind.' She stooped to kiss the rouged old cheek. 'Goodbye.'

Extract from the Commonplace Book of Lady Felicity Ross-Sutton

This is the last entry I shall make in my Book and my last night of spinsterhood which I have *not* achieved! For tomorrow and tomorrow and all our tomorrows I shall not be one but two persons in one. I remember Russton saying to me that ever since the first surgical operation performed on Adam's fifth rib that gave woman to man for man's undoing he said with that adorable grin of his that you have been trying to get back to us again to make us one as in Hermaphroditus. He said a good deal more about that which I can't write down here because I am keeping this book to show our son and we must have a son because I do so want a Rodborough to go on and if we don't have a son there won't *be* a Rodborough. . . . 'Call back yesterday, bid time return'. I don't want time to return I want it to be now and for ever with him and me as it will if we are to believe there is no death. I told him I was afraid of loving him because all those I have loved die on me. He said he wouldn't die on me for we'll be together for always and afterwards. . . . If only Daddy could have known of him and me together for always and afterwards. Perhaps he does. . . . Had a most surprising and rather touching present sent me by registered post today following a telegram from Riabovitch in Paris saying, To wish you both all happiness tomorrow. . . . How does he know about tomorrow? We deliberately avoided announcements but there was a paragraph in the gossip column of the Daily Mail. Some nosy reporter must have got hold of it from here. Wilson would never split on us. Perhaps from Russton's flat in Whitehall Court which he used to tell me was in Pimlico (not quite but within walking distance). They must have got hold of it somehow and I suppose Riabovitch saw it in the Paris editions. When the parcel was undone there were the two Gerard Dows! The originals which Mr Thistlewaite had let him have instead of those two copies. Russton told me this because of a secret backing in one of them with plans of something that might have been of use to an enemy country – not intentionally that is. R's sole aim and purpose as he honestly believed was to save humanity from another devastating war and to make all mankind equal having seen what happened to Russia before the Revolution where equality was not. And as Russton says – how I keep on about Russton. Hope I am not turning into a Mrs Micawber! But as he says Riabovitch was all out to fulfil his Messianic cause in a brave new world on which he thought to build a house of rock that has dissolved in a house of sand. . . . I'm thinking of those miners, poor devils, fighting for their cause lost in a house of sand or . . . coal dust.

286

And when these two small pictures emerged from the wrappings I found a gold-edged card with the coat of arms and crest of Riabovitch in its heraldic colours and the words in his thin spidery writing

May every happiness be yours
is the true wish
of
The Dragon's Head.

The Uniform Edition of
Doris Leslie's works

ANOTHER CYNTHIA
AS THE TREE FALLS
CONCORD IN JEOPARDY
FAIR COMPANY
FOLLY'S END
FULL FLAVOUR
THE GREAT CORINTHIAN
HOUSE IN THE DUST
I RETURN
THE PERFECT WIFE
PERIDOT FLIGHT
THE PEVERILLS
POLONAISE
ROYAL WILLIAM
THAT ENCHANTRESS
THIS FOR CAROLINE
A TOAST TO LADY MARY
WREATH FOR ARABELLA